BLOOD and SIN

LAURA THALASSA
DAN RIX

BURNING EMBER PRESS

This is a work of fiction. References to real people, events, establishments, organizations, or locales are intended only to provide authenticity, and are used fictitiously. All other characters, and all incidents and dialogue, are drawn from the author's imagination and are not to be construed as real.

A Burning Ember Book
Published in the United States by Burning Ember Press, an imprint of Lavabrook Publishing Group.

CHAPTER 1

Lana

The clothes I wore felt strange. Strange and coarse.

Foreign.

I forced myself to avoid fidgeting in them as I crossed the parking lot to the small, fairly nondescript building labeled American Blood Bank.

A native wouldn't fidget in their clothes, I reminded myself. They all looked so sure of themselves. Even the ones who you could tell wanted to be someone else. They still moved with surety.

I stopped myself from grimacing as I passed the trash bins tucked away behind the building. Everything about this place grated. The smells, the sounds, but most of all, the sights.

I tightened my grip on the satchel I carried.

This place was foreign to me, but I was also foreign to this place. The natives sensed that the longer their attention focused on me. These clever humans missed nothing.

I cast my own gaze above me. It was still very early, the sky a deep blue. Too early for work. I checked the clock I wore on my wrist, just to be sure.

5:32 a.m.

The first employee didn't get in until 6:30, which gave me roughly an hour, for whatever good that knowledge was worth. Counting time was still a relatively new concept to me, but humans did it, so I had to as well.

The rear door of the building was lit, I noticed with disappointment. Last time I'd been here I'd knocked the light out. People had such absurd fears of the dark. Then again, things like me lived in it, and I was something to fear.

I tried the back door of the building.

Locked. Not surprising.

There was a simple enough way to enter. Simple and forbidden because it was inexplicable to the natives. That's what had gotten others like me killed in the past. The inexplicability of our ways. They were breadcrumbs for hungry humans to follow. I wasn't dying today, so the simple way was out.

I slid my hand into my pocket and pulled out the lock picks I carried with me whenever I came here. I fitted them through the slot in the door knob, angling and twisting them like I learned to do long ago. I heard the lock tumble. Pocketing the picks, I entered.

Ignoring the light switch next to me, I headed up the dark hallway to the main room at the back of the building, where a large "L" shaped desk took up most of the space. I moved behind it, eyeing the computer that faced me.

Opening a shallow drawer, I reached inside and drew out the metal key I was looking for. Crossing to the other side of the room, I used this key to unlock another drawer. The inanity of it all.

Rolling the drawer open, I peered inside. A handful of plastic, rectangular cards waited for me. All served the same purpose—unlocking yet another room I needed access into. So many keys when only one was necessary. The only difference between them were the names printed on each.

The natives were careful, crafty, I'd always been told. They thought in ways I didn't and likely never would. But this felt less careful and crafty than it did redundant and impractical.

Their world, their rules.

Picking one at random, I pocketed the metal key and the plastic one, then headed down the hall, my shoes squeaking against the floor.

This place always raised the hair on my arms. It smelled unnatural—a place where life came to rot.

I tugged at my pants. Seams and zippers and buttons. Odd, all of it.

Stop fidgeting, I reminded myself.

I had to be cautious, take no chances.

In and out.

I stopped in front of a thick metal door and held the

plastic card to a box next to it. A light blinked green, and the door unlatched, venting chilled air that made me shiver. I slipped inside and stared.

From wall to wall, nearly floor to ceiling were rows upon rows of blood. My fingers twitched at the sight of it all.

I set my satchel down on the ground. And then, one by one, I began to remove the bags of blood.

Asher

I DESPISED CAVES.

Try wedging your body down half a mile of the blackest, putridest, most kinked-up asshole of a crawlspace you can imagine.

Of course the anomaly had to be down here.

Of course.

It couldn't have been in a meadow or on a beach or on *top* of a mountain.

No. It had to be half a mile under it.

Arms pinned beneath me, I crawled deeper into the cave, toiling under the weight of my gear. The tiny space amplified the clinking of my clips, my raspy breath, the scuff of my gear on rock. Deep breath. Focus on the breath. *In . . . out . . . in . . .*

Silty mud splashed into my mouth and I coughed at the acrid tang. As I did so, my helmet banged the ceiling, reminding me I had zero wiggle room.

"Fuck you, cave." I muscled another foot, teeth gritted

against a wave of sickening claustrophobia.

Caving alone.

Not a good idea. But I trusted *no one* with what I was about to uncover.

The cave walls shrank around me until they cut into my shoulders, halting my progress.

Wedged in like a cork.

The light from my headlamp illuminated a small, jagged opening to pitch blackness, out of which whistled cold, dank air. Breathing heavily, I computed just what inhuman contortion I would need to adopt to fit, and I didn't like it.

At least I liked the cold.

Topside, the West Virginia backcountry around White Sulfur Springs would be dripping with the muggy late-summer heat.

I unclipped my pack, so I could pull it through after me, and angled my shoulders sideways to squeeze through the chokepoint. It smelled different on the other side. Colder, more cavernous, a hint of ash lurking under the wet tang of corroded minerals. Instinctively, my nose wrinkled.

The echo of my breath changed too, perking my inner ear. The sound of wide open space.

Getting closer.

I couldn't crane my neck far enough for my headlamp to illuminate the other side, so I squeezed my flashlight through and panned it forward.

A glassy pool of water gaped below me, its banks overgrown with lumpy stalagmites. They glittered in the light, their ghostly shadows dancing around the walls of a large cavern.

This was the spot.

I could feel it. The way the hairs stood up on my fore-arms.

Sliding the rest of the way through, I lowered myself down among the stalagmites, now careful to stay quiet. Drips echoed in the darkness, but nothing else sounded, save for the quiet moan of air rising from deep in the earth, like the cave itself was breathing.

Place gave me the creeps.

With the flashlight off, I flipped the thermal imaging scope down over one eye, and my palm went to the Glock at my hip.

I surveyed the cavern through the lens, my surroundings cast in dim shades of blue.

Nothing else living down here.

Thank God.

If there was, its body heat would have stood out as bright white.

The tension in my shoulders relaxed. Slowly, my hand inched away from the holster. Could never be too careful.

Time to get to work.

I dragged my pack through the hole. Weighed down with shovels, pickaxes, and dynamite, it landed with a crunch at my feet, probably crushing millennia-old limestone formations which would never grow back.

Bummer. But I didn't give a rat's ass about the minerals.

I was here for something else entirely.

From the pack, I slid out a thin metal equipment case

and opened it on a nearby stalagmite. Inside, set into a foam pad, thirty nickel-sized, quartz oscillators all displayed 00:00 on their faces. They were essentially nothing more than fancy stopwatches.

The only difference was these cost several grand.

They were wired to each other, so they could all be started and stopped at the same exact time. This would matter.

I made my way around the cave, planting each one in a rough grid pattern. I even tossed a couple into the pool for good measure—they were waterproof, so they'd be fine. For this first measurement, I just wanted to get a general idea of the anomaly's location.

I could zero in on it later.

As I moved around the pool's milky, crystallized banks, shadows grew and shrank behind me, like figures ducking out of view. Freaked me the hell out. My hackles stayed up the whole time.

Behind me, the sound of a stone skittering down into the cave broke the silence. The chamber's echo made it sound like an avalanche.

I spun around and leveled my gun at the cave's exit, my normally cool pulse now quickening.

Nothing there.

Keeping one eye on my exit, I went back to placing oscillators.

Once I'd placed them all, I began the experiment.

The experiment.

Back at the case, I clicked on the master switch that started all the timers simultaneously. A green indicator light told me they were perfectly synchronized at the time of starting.

Then I waited.

A minute and a half.

While thirty tiny clocks did my work for me.

After exactly ninety seconds, the master timer in my hands automatically sent a signal to each of the thirty others spread about the cavern, telling them all to stop at the same time.

Start. Stop.

Nothing but a fancy stopwatch.

I began reeling in my net of oscillators. As expected, the first one displayed ninety seconds exactly—90:00.

No surprises there.

I checked the second one.

Also 90:00.

I checked the third one, which had recorded at the edge of the pool. Ninety seconds exactly.

I moved on to the fourth, drawing it out of the center of the pool. The readout was identical to the three before it.

So far, time was being well behaved.

I circled to the far bank and checked the fifth in line, which had come to rest upside-down at the foot of a bulbous stalagmite. Flipping it over, I leveled the tiny screen under my flashlight.

My nostrils flared.

"Nuh-uh-uh, *that's* not allowed," I muttered.

Here, time was being very naughty.

CHAPTER 2

Lana

I WALKED INTO my apartment, dropping my satchel onto the couch. It made a sloshing noise as the bagged blood inside it bounced.

Rolling my shoulders, I moved to my room and began to change, first untying the laces of the men's work boots I wore. Then the scratchy socks, followed by the large, coarse jeans. As I undressed, I felt my hair thicken and grow, prickling my scalp and tickling the skin of my back as it lengthened, several dark locks draping themselves over my shoulders. My limbs shrank and narrowed, becoming rounder, more feminine.

My true form.

Even in my natural skin, I was nearly indistinguishable

from the natives. All but the eyes. They were just a smidge too violet to pass for human.

Carefully I placed the clothes in my bedroom closet and slipped the men's work boots next to a pair of child's sneakers. I exchanged the native's clothes for my own, sighing as I dragged my formfitting, full-body suit over my hips, then my breasts, wiggling a little as I pulled it up. I felt the stretchy material cinch around my waist like a second skin as I threaded my arms through the long sleeves. I slid on my boots and grabbed my sheathed daggers, attaching the weapons to my pants. The familiar weight felt comfortable against my outer thighs.

Now that I was back in my own skin and clothes, I felt better, but not much. I needed to get back home. My people were counting on me.

Returning to the living room, I opened my satchel.

One by one I lifted the blood bags out of it and spread them across the couch, counting the number I had taken. Twenty-six. Not enough for my people. Not nearly. But still enough to go noticed by the blood bank.

The natives would ask questions.

So many, many questions. They used inquiry the way my people used magic. And they got results.

Those cold, calculating creatures would somehow find me if I lingered long enough.

I swallowed. I'd have to find a different blood bank after this. Hopefully I wouldn't have to move my outpost from this city. It was hard enough to set up the first time. I couldn't imagine doing what others of my kind had—hopping from place to place, living as ex-patriots in this world.

Trying to get by as a human.

We weren't, and we never would be. Thank goodness.

I made my way over to the map of the United States that hung on the far wall. I searched the eastern side of it, looking for the city I was currently in.

There.

Roanoke, Virginia.

Home to nearly 100,000 humans. In this single city alone there were a hundred times more natives than there were of my entire race.

My dying race.

I packed up the blood. From the front closet of my apartment I grabbed a human hoodie and tried not to shudder as I slipped it on. Then, hauling the satchel over my shoulder, I glanced at the map once more.

With my finger, I followed the crooked highway that led from this city a deceptively short distance to the tiny human town.

White Sulfur Springs.

My destination.

Asher

I STARED AT the digits on the timer, my scalp bristling.

87:01.

At the foot of this stalagmite, only eighty-seven seconds had elapsed—*three seconds less* than had elapsed everywhere else in the cave.

Three seconds less. Which meant that, in this particular location, time moved *slower*.

Definitely not allowed.

This was the spot. The location of the anomaly.

Slowly, my gaze gravitated up the stalagmite, up the hideous, lumpy growth to where it fused with a glistening stalactite hanging from the ceiling, forming a natural pillar. I was no geologist, but the thing looked ancient.

Whatever lay entombed in the limestone, it had been here for hundreds of thousands of years.

Now how to unearth it . . .

I reached for one of my explosives, then paused. Thinking it through, the dynamite tactic seemed suicidal. If I knocked out the pillar, it would destabilize the entire cavern, probably cause the whole thing to collapse on my idiot face.

Bright idea, Asher . . . detonating explosives in a confined space under eight trillion tons of precariously balanced rock.

Pickaxe and shovel then.

But first, I read the times off the rest of my oscillators.

Out of the thirty, four more registered time anomalies, also near prominent stalagmites. Pockets of space where time passed a little slower. Without synchronized clocks, you wouldn't notice.

I took one step out between the columns, and a wave of vertigo nearly made me upchuck.

My ass you wouldn't notice.

Feeling seasick, I had to brace myself on one of the spires. Up close, they reeked of ash, that smell I had grown to despise. I recoiled with a grimace.

There were five anomalous stalagmites in total.

Five of the oldest, baddest, foulest looking stalagmites in the cave.

With a tape measure, I took the distance between them. Equal.

They formed the corners of a perfect pentagon.

Or, more precisely, the five corners of a star. A pentagram.

Truth was, I didn't give much of a fuck what shape they made. For all I cared, they could make Mickey Mouse ears.

I didn't come here to play connect-the-dots.

I fetched my pickaxe and took a good, hard swing at the base of the first stalagmite. Rock shards splintered off, ricocheting between the other spires.

I pried out a chunk of limestone with the flat end of the axe, then let it fly again. More fragments sprayed off into the darkness.

Pausing to wipe my damp forehead, I slid out of my breast pocket the dog-eared photo of my dead wife, age twenty-six, blonde and blue-eyed and fucking gorgeous, and kissed it. "This is for you, Nikki."

It was all for her, really.

I swung again, yelling this time, and kept swinging until mineral dust stung my nostrils, until icy sweat dripped off my nose, until my lungs heaved from exertion, until the pillar of limestone at last crumbled open at my feet, exposing something that had absolutely no earthly business being inside a stalagmite in a cave that no human had ever set foot in before today.

I knelt and peered at it, taking heavy gulps of air.

Gaping out at me from a jagged wall of crystal, where

it had been entombed for millennia, were the empty eye sockets of a hominid skull.

Human.

But not.

Anthropologists would have a hissy fit at what I was about to do. Oh, but they'd thank me later.

I stood and raised pickaxe, then let it fly one more time. The spike punctured the forehead, and the skull shattered like porcelain. A deep thump reverberated through the cave. The air around me seemed to vibrate.

One down, four to go.

I staggered to the second stalagmite, the second corner-stone. Then proceeded to beat the crap out of it, too.

Buried in the rock, another hominid skull crumbled to pieces around the spike of my pickaxe. The cave rumbled, and I staggered sideways as dust sprinkled down from the ceiling. Behind me, ripples spread out across the pool's glassy surface.

Two down.

Panting now, I slogged to the third one, raised my axe, and buried the steel up to the hilt. The spire broke open around it, cracking like glass.

Another skull.

I bashed it in, pulverizing the embedded fragments into the cave floor.

Another seismic tremor rocked the cave. A sliver of limestone cleaved off an overhanging stalactite, hurtling down like a spear. It exploded on the floor inches from where I stood.

Going to have to do better than that.

Three down.

I bashed in the fourth stalagmite, busted the skull inside. Like nothing.

Its base destroyed, the pillar of limestone fissured and tipped sideways, crashing through more mineral spires before it shattered against the ground.

Around me, an unearthly moan rose through the cavern, the wind screaming through the tiny exit hole as it evacuated the cave. My ears popped as the pressure dropped, before the wind all came howling back with a chest-crushing thump.

Four down.

I paused at the fifth, the final pillar, wiped my mouth with the back of my hand, wheezing in the limestone dust. Last one.

I drove the spike down with everything I had. The steel sparked on the rock, chipped off whole chunks, crushed them. The fifth hominid skull cracked down the middle and exploded into dust.

The anomaly ruptured.

In front of me, the space inside the pillars seemed to cave in to nothing, creating a whirlpool in midair. The space contorted, spinning and tightening until it cinched shut.

And then it exploded.

A shockwave slammed me in the chest. I was lifted off my feet and jettisoned across the cave and into the pool. Limestone dust swept over me, and across the cave, dozens and dozens of stalactites broke off from the ceiling, shattering against the ground. The sound of it all was deafening. I covered my head.

Yeah, destroying their portals always caused a kickback.

But it was done.

I coughed, gasping for breath as I dragged myself out of the pool and rested against my pack. I grinned into the darkness.

One less doorway to hell.

Lana

SOMETIMES I FOUND it hypnotizing to watch time like a human might. And sometimes, like right now, it was agony.

My body swayed inside the bus as trees and houses blurred by. One hour and fifty-seven minutes had passed since I got inside this hellacious *machine*.

My hands squeezed my thighs, my fingernails digging into the leather. The smell of all these tightly packed bodies, the walls that seemed to close in on all sides, the unnatural speed of this thing—it was all the most acute kind of torture.

Buses could rot in the flames of Abyssos.

Slowly the town of White Sulfur Springs rolled into view. One sad building followed the next. The whole place looked as though it had just given up. I wondered how much of it was my people's fault. Magic always came at a price.

These people had more than likely paid their fair share.

The bus shuddered to a stop in front of a boarded up store. As soon as the vehicle's doors hissed open, I fought the urge to jump out of my seat and claw my way past the bus's other occupants just to get through first. Instead I stood and took my time shuffling into the aisle, pretending I was bored rather than barely keeping my anxiety and the contents of my stomach down. And I tried not to gasp in my first breaths of fresh air once I left the bus.

I made my way between the buildings. Beyond them, the wilderness stretched on. As soon as I hit the tree line, I tightened my satchel, and then I ran.

The wind of this world felt the same as mine, the ground felt the same. If it weren't for the absence of magic that my homeland was steeped in, I could almost believe the two worlds were the same.

But this one wasn't war-torn. Not like mine.

So many humans. And they were thriving. So few of us. And we were dying.

I passed a tree shaped like a trident, which marked the end of my run. The portal was just up ahead.

The smell of exhaust pulled me up short.

Wrong.

That smell didn't belong here.

I continued forward slower this time, sheltering my form behind tree trunks, just to be safe. I was nearly to the caves. So close to home I could almost taste it.

I scented the air again, and again I smelled the exhaust right before I saw the car.

A big heifer of a vehicle. It'd been parked alongside the overgrown dirt road I thought was abandoned.

Apparently it wasn't.

Infernari didn't travel by car. Which meant . . .

Humans.

I HID BEHIND a tree, pressing my chest against the rough bark.

As a human might say, *fuck me.*

Crossing worlds was hard enough on its own. Now I had a human to deal with.

I'd never encountered this particular issue before.

I could always resolve the situation with magic, but there were those that looked for such disturbances. They'd follow the residual magic left behind like carrion to a kill. And this close to a doorway . . .

No, no magic.

I could simply chance it; I could assume that whoever had found themselves here would not be near the caves. That they would not see a strange girl disappear below-ground without any sort of human tools to accompany her. Or if they did, that they would not ask those questions they were so infamous for.

Assuming was just another sort of risk I was unwilling to take.

I fixated on the car as I moved about the trees, keeping my footsteps silent like I'd learned to as a child. And then—

The car rocked.

I must've imagined it. But, even as I tried to reassure myself, I saw it shake again, like something was inside it.

The owner? Please, Great Mother above, let that be the owner. Then, after they were done with whatever nonsense had brought them out here, so far from their beloved cities, they'd drive away and I would not have to waste any additional time waiting or investigating.

The car shook harder, and then a sound from within it rose.

Something that sounded a lot like a pained cry.

What in all the worlds?

My eyes searched the car over again, noticing all the details that I didn't see at first blush. This wasn't just any vehicle. Normally the natives made cars from fairly rickety materials. Not this one. It was armored. And then came that horrible cry again, like the sound of a wounded creature, and it came from *inside* the vehicle.

Reflexively, my hand went to one of my weapons.

Sometimes humans ventured out to wild areas like this one, seeking adventure. But this wasn't an adventurous human.

This was something else entirely.

Use caution, they're crafty.

I waited.

More noises came from the car. The healer in me found them hard to ignore, even if it was a human that made them.

Perhaps the owner of the vehicle was hurt and could not drive away. I would be waiting quite a long time if that were the case. Making a quick decision, I dropped my satchel behind the tree. I would see what I could do.

Still, I pulled my daggers out.

Injured or not, this was a conniving human. I wouldn't put it past them to harm me even as I helped them.

Twigs and underbrush snapped in the distance, and my head jerked toward its source. Humans had culled most of their fellow creatures, but things still lived in the wild areas, things I might need to use magic against.

Now on guard, I twirled my weapons between my fingers as I crept to the car, a nervous habit of mine masked as an intimidation tactic.

Believe you are dangerous and, more importantly, make sure your enemy believes it.

My father's words echoed in my head as I circled the vehicle.

He'd made sure everyone knew just how dangerous he was.

More foliage crunched close by. Again I peered toward its source, my senses heightened by fear, for now I could make out the distinct sound of footsteps—

I felt it then, that nervous tingling at the base of my spine.

Not one of us.

Human.

It was coming straight toward me.

In a rush I slid the daggers back into their sheaths and sprinted for the tree line, my footsteps silent, unlike the blundering human heading this way.

Whoever it was, they were still far enough from the vehicle that I managed to slip back to my original lookout unseen.

Hidden once more behind the tree, I peered at the car. I could still hear the tormented cries of the native inside the vehicle. Perhaps the person heading this way was a friend. Perhaps they were bringing help with them. Perhaps I would not need to intervene, and I could go home soon.

The injured human made more noise, all of it indistinct.

Muffled, I realized.

I hadn't heard them sooner because their cries had been muffled.

A friend wouldn't muffle his injured comrade. He'd want people to hear so that help could come sooner.

Foe.

I didn't have time to think of the implications before a great beast of a man cleared the forest to my right.

I was wrong to think the person tromping through the woods was a blundering human. I stared at the man as he headed to the vehicle, utterly captivated. He was human, yes, but *fearsome*. Someone like that wouldn't have to mask their presence. He was surely the most dangerous thing out here.

Other than me, that was.

I watched him cross to his car, my heart in my throat. I couldn't say why exactly I was so terrified. Besides the fact that physically he was bigger than me, he couldn't possibly wield the kind of magic I could.

But he had that look about him, the same look mercenaries and assassins of my world had. Fierce. Stoic. Frightening. Only on a human face it looked particularly cruel and emotionless.

Shame he was handsome. Those features were wasted on someone who would slit your throat before he'd make small talk.

He moved to the rear of the car, which directly faced me. I took in the broad expanse of his corded back as he removed his helmet, setting it on the roof of his car before he unlocked the doors. It was odd, seeing a human that strong, that toned. Most of them looked soft, *domesticated.*

Not this one.

He swung the rear doors open.

Finally I caught sight of the person inside.

I shoved my fist into my mouth to silence my cry.

That wasn't an injured human.

It was an Infernarus.

CHAPTER 3

Asher

INSIDE MY HUMMER, trussed up like a turkey, my prisoner winced against the light, his eyes still bruised from the beating I'd given him earlier to get the location of the portal.

In a bucket by the wheel well, his severed hands sloshed in an inch of blood.

Could never be too careful.

I fanned my nose against the stench of ash and blood. "Since you led me to the right spot," I said, "I'll make your death as quick and painless as possible."

My prisoner thrashed against his bindings, jerking like a bull, rocking the truck back and forth. His duct-taped mouth screamed garbled obscenities.

"What was that?" I said, cupping my hand over my ear. "Buddy, you got to speak up."

He screamed louder, his cries muffled by the tape.

"Nope, still can't hear you—"

He managed to spit off the tape, which flapped under his hot breath. "You gave me your word, you filthy, cold-blooded, traitorous rat!"

"I'm not particularly insulted by that, actually," I said, sliding out my hunting knife, tilting the blade up to the light.

In my periphery, a figure shrank behind a tree. My skin prickled.

No, just the shadows deepening.

"Have you no honor?" he spat. "Have you no *pride?*"

I leveled my eyes at him over the blade, no longer smiling. "Exterminating a creature that has no right to be on my planet—no right to *exist*—has nothing to do with honor or pride. There's an infestation, and I'm dealing with it. End of story. I don't have to think too hard on that."

He glared at me. "You gave me your word."

"Yeah, you said that. Starting to sound like a broken record." I vaulted into the back of the car and advanced toward him.

He recoiled. "You and your doublespeak. It sickens me. Release me, *human.*"

"Logic. Let's try it." I held the knife to his throat, calculating the best angle to cut. "Two reasons I can't let you go. One, you make portals. Kind of counterproductive, if you think about it."

He jerked his head to the bucket. "I can't make portals

without my hands. Right now, I'm powerless."

"Two, first thing you're going to do is run home and tell all your aunties and sissies and cousies who I am. And I *know* you know who I am."

The creature's lips curled. "Jame Asher," he spat. "Hunter of Infernari. Of course I know who you are. You're supposed to be dead."

"And I'd like to keep it that way." I sank the blade into his throat, and his last words died in a gurgle.

Lana

I PRESSED MY palm to my mouth, forcing my scream back down my throat. This was some horrible nightmare. Jame Asher, the infamous Infernari hunter back from the grave. Back, and butchering Fidel, the portal master.

Asher sawed away at his neck. As if the hands weren't enough

He'd taken Fidel's power with his hands, and now he was taking his life.

A silent tear trickled down my cheek, then another.

I was surprised humans even had a word for honor if they were capable of this.

Save him while there's still time.

A native might be beyond resurrection, but not us. The soul didn't leave the vessel immediately. And while it lingered, a body could be repaired and life restored.

Dropping my hand from my mouth, I turned to my satchel, my resolve overriding my terror. I hurriedly unpacked all twenty-six blood bags, careful to keep my movements silent.

This blood was supposed to help dozens, if not hundreds, of lives.

Today, if I was lucky, it would save just one.

I began murmuring the old language under my breath, moving my trembling hands over the blood bags again and again, calling it to me. A wisp of smoke rose along with it. Immediately I felt the magic respond, drawing towards my fingertips and palms. I breathed deeply as I culled it.

Inside the bags, the blood began to bubble. Tiny, ethereal flames bloomed along the surface of the blood, blackening the plastic bags from the inside as I converted the liquid from its crude from to something more refined.

My major affinity was healing, and now I used that affinity to reach out to Fidel as I continued to cull, the magic building up in my veins.

He was dying; I'd seen it, but now I could feel it. Like a fire starved of oxygen, his essence grew dimmer, dimmer . . .

I spared a brief glance over my shoulder. Asher had walked around to the driver side of the car, leaving Fidel unattended.

Perfect.

Turning back around, I forced the magic out of me, shoving it down the affinity-based connection I shared with Fidel.

I knew the moment my power found him. I felt his body jolt as though I shocked him. His essence still lingered beneath his flesh, just as I believed it would. It brushed against my magic, and even though I was petrified, and even though he was still in great danger, I smiled a little. Souls felt like sun on skin. Beautiful things.

I flooded his system with power, enough to jumpstart a stilled heart. Enough to bring the dead back to life. All the while I continued to draw out magic from the blood, funneling the chaotic power into a form I could use.

It took an obscene amount of magic to bring an Infernarus back to life, and this would take even more than usual. I had to waste some of it disguising the sight and smell of the blood as it combusted. It was what the natives called a parlor trick, an illusion that would lift as soon as I stopped pouring magic into it. But for now, it kept the human hunter's focus off me.

I could sense, dimly, that Fidel's head had found his body. The magic stitched the mutilated bits of flesh back together seamlessly. I felt him blink his eyes open, felt some base emotion that might've been wonder—or thanks. He knew help was here.

Now that he was sentient, it only took him seconds to collect his hands, and with my guidance, we merged them to his wrists. I assisted sealing the last of his wounds, and then I let him take full control of the magic I fed him.

I smiled a little. Jame Asher had picked the wrong day to hunt.

We'd see just how much the hunter enjoyed being hunted.

Asher

I REACHED INTO the front of my truck to get the rest of my supplies. On the passenger seat sat a canister of gasoline connected to a hose and a foot pump—best way to dispose of demons.

Turn them back to the ash from whence they came.

Grunting, I hoisted the canister and slammed it down on the ground.

A faint bump sounded behind the truck, and the vehicle's suspension squeaked a little. I jerked my head up, ears prone.

No other sounds.

Just the body slumping to the side, right?

I dropped the hose and ran back to check.

The armored, bloodstained enclosure came into view.

One look, and all the breath whooshed out of my lungs.

Empty.

The body was gone.

The head, too.

"Fuck," I muttered, spinning around three hundred sixty degrees, the skin all down my back bristling with pins and needles. No one in sight.

The figure I'd seen . . . could it be?

Groping behind me, I caught the rim of the bucket and yanked it out, overturned it on the dirt.

Blood trickled out.

Blood . . . and nothing else.

He'd taken his hands with him.

"FUCK!" I yelled.

Demons were notoriously difficult to kill. Like cockroaches.

Cut off their heads, cut off their hands, eviscerate them, drown them, it didn't matter.

A scuffle of footsteps reached my ears. From the other side of my Hummer . . . no doubt circling back around to ambush me.

Now it was hunting me.

I drew my Glock and flattened myself against the passenger side, panic afire in my lungs. It shouldn't have healed like that.

The western sky dimmed to teal, the shadowy woods darkened and encroached on my truck.

Night.

In darkness, there was only one smart way to fight a demon—or *demons*, if what I suspected was true.

Run.

Run your ass off.

Demons were natural born predators. They had superior night vision, more acute senses, quicker reflexes, better hand-eye coordination.

I had shit.

Shit *and* a big ass problem. No other demon knew I was still alive. If I let this one escape, I'd have three hundred demons' dicks trying to crawl up my asshole in about twelve seconds. Which meant I better stay and fight.

The thermal scope. Had that too.

My hand slapped the top of my Hummer, where I'd set my helmet. Scanning the forest, I dragged it over my head and flipped down the scope over my left eye. The world came alive in shades of green and yellow trees, still warm from sunset.

But demons' blood ran hot—104° Fahrenheit—thing would be glowing like neon.

Explained their vicious hot tempers, too.

Like the fact that this fucker had stuck around to take on Jame Asher when the smart thing to do would be to escape and call in reinforcements.

Still didn't mean I liked it.

Crouching on all fours, a glowing white figure crept into my periphery, slinking behind the tree line. A tiger creeping in for the kill.

I tensed, my knuckles tightening on the grip, but didn't let on I'd seen him.

My scope used a fisheye lens, meaning it compressed a hundred and eighty degrees of infrared vision into a nice little bubble. With my truck protecting my backside, the scope let me literally see in all directions at once.

Demons think we have lousy peripheral vision. We do.

But not tonight.

The figure burst from the trees and closed in with lightning speed, appearing as a blurry white streak to my left eye through the scope.

I spun, dropped to a knee, and fired three shots before it reached me. To my left eye, the bullets made white-hot welts in its torso, their entry points glowing even hotter than the demon's scalding flesh.

But if cutting off the beast's head and hands—both re-attached, to my horror—didn't kill it, then three bullets stood no chance.

The demon kicked the gun out of my hand, pried off my helmet, and flung it aside, plunging me into sudden blackness. Only the whistle of air alerted me to the kick aimed at my head.

I ducked, but not fast enough. The blow slammed my face into the dirt. My lip cracked, and blood mixed with the chalky taste of silt in my mouth.

I blinked away stars. The next impact, I knew, would pack enough punch to break my neck.

I threw myself to the side, and the kick grazed my ear, leaving my eardrum ringing.

With a lunge, I caught the creature's ankle and gave it a hard twist, wrenching it around with all my might. He rolled into it with ease, somersaulting over me, and landing on his feet. He came at me again.

Well, shit.

Not a chance of besting him in hand-to-hand combat, not at night.

His heel blotted out the sky. I could picture it then—my skull crushed in, dead in an instant.

I whipped myself into a roll, and the demon's heel slammed the ground where I'd been, lashing me with dirt.

I kept rolling, all the way under my truck, and popped out on the other side.

His footsteps sprinted around to meet me. I lunged for the driver-side door. The demon vaulted over the hood of the car, metal groaning under his weight. A race.

My fingers jammed under the handle and yanked the door open, slamming it into his face as he swooped in from the side. For a split-second, it stunned him, and I used the distraction to sink my hunting knife into his side, twisting it in up to the hilt.

He staggered backward to yank it out, giving me a chance to get inside my Hummer.

No sooner had I slammed the door shut behind me than the demon's face thumped against the glass. Rocked the whole truck.

Thought that was a regular window, asshole?

He'd just gotten a faceful of bulletproof glass. Demon proof.

His black eyes narrowed to slits, glaring at me while his hot breath misted on the window.

"Going to wish you didn't hang around, bud," I muttered, cranking the ignition.

The engine roared to life, coming alive like a monster under the hood.

He seemed to realize his mistake.

Should've escaped when you had the chance.

He backed away, shifty-eyed, then turned tail and ran, his loping silhouette receding into the trees.

I peeled out after him, flicking on my headlights, the high beams, the side-mounted floodlights, and the overhead light rack, bathing the forest in dazzling blue-white light.

Not night anymore, is it?

The reflectors on his tennis shoes bobbed in and out of the glare. I floored the car, and the Hummer lurched over a boulder and blasted through a rotted out log, keeping right on his heels. His palm flashed as he shoved off a tree.

Again, *how?* His head and hands had been severed . . .

Unlike humans, demon cells continued to live and multiply despite massive organ failure. Deprived of a beating heart, oxygenated blood, a central nervous system, their flesh merely entered a state of suspended animation, which could last for days, for weeks . . . indefinitely, given the right conditions.

I'd learned the hard way.

The demon wasn't dead until he was a smoking pile of ash.

Their limbs re-sprouted, their organs grew back. Their heads . . .

Apparently those could be reattached.

Biologically, they were tough-as-hell little shits, honed over millennia of evolution. They were spirits of darkness inhabiting bodies of flesh. They were held together by evil. By the death and misfortune they harvested from us.

But still.

They were animals.

Once you cut off the head, even if the flesh still lived, the organism would cease to function in any real capacity. That was simple anatomy. A decapitated demon you could safely treat as dead until you got the chance to burn the body.

Only this one didn't play by the rules.

Suddenly, my quarry feinted left, veering toward the thickest part of the woods. Cursing, I gave the wheel a desperate yank, fishtailing in the mud before the off-road tires gripped, and the vehicle plowed into a nest of undergrowth. Bushes whacked the front grill, clawed at it like skeletal hands before they were dragged under. Visibility down to zero.

"C'mon, c'monnn," I muttered, white-knuckling the wheel.

I burst clear onto an overgrown trail, wrestling the Hummer back up behind him, riding his ass hard.

My eyes narrowed on the speedometer. *The hell . . . ?*

The needle crossed twenty . . . then twenty-five . . . then thirty . . .

This guy was freaking Seabiscuit.

His legs pumped faster and faster, whipping back with inhuman speed, driving him straight toward a thicket at the end of the trail.

He topped out at 45 mph—the speed of a thoroughbred racehorse. No, even demons couldn't run that fast.

He was being helped.

And demons didn't run in straight lines.

Normally, they zigzagged, ping-ponged all over the place, skittered back and forth like spiders, never straight lines. They knew better.

I sensed it then.

Trap.

I slammed on the brakes just as the demon vanished into the thicket.

The Hummer blasted into it and careened through a tunnel of vegetation. Once the vegetation fell away, I got a good look at what lay ahead of me.

Open air.

Fifty feet away, land ended. Now thirty. The Hummer

was eating up the distance far too quickly. Twenty feet remained. I gritted my teeth as my foot held steady on the brakes.

Ten feet.

At last, the vehicle shuddered to an agonizing stop, the front wheels crunching over the edge of a cliff. I could only stare as the demon soared off the sixty-foot drop, arms and legs spread-eagled before it landed on a slab of bedrock at the bottom of a ravine, bounced into a roll, and hit the ground running, utterly unharmed.

Bitch had been leading me toward a cliff.

Clever animal.

I had one more shot at this. Seconds left before he slipped out of range.

I punched the roof hatch open and from behind the seats dragged out my *coup de grâce*—the six-barrel machine-gun I'd paid a fortune for—and locked it in place on the roof mount, my ammo belt clanging against the metal.

Then I lit up the ravine.

The weapon blazed like a torch, firing off a constant stream of bullets. Down below, the bedrock erupted in a shower of sparks. Screaming my lungs horse, I fired the shots across the demon, then back again, cleaving him in two, in four, ripping him to shreds.

He fell to the ground, his flesh flayed under the on-slaught. His clothes caught fire, yet what remained of him continued to writhe.

Still, my finger crushed the trigger, still I sprayed bul-lets. After a minute of continuous fire, the gun fell silent, its smoking barrels glowing a dull red as they finally spun to a stop.

Out of ammo.

But the creature was dead at last. There could be no regenerating from this.

I panted from the exertion, ears ringing. I'd probably go deaf by age thirty.

But to be sure, I should go down and burn the body—

The impossible happened.

Out of the shredded body parts, the demon rose again. His spilled blood and guts withdrew back into his body, his torn skin resealed, and his broken, dislocated limbs straightened with a series of sharp cracks. He stood slowly, now stark naked, and threw a final look back before he loped away, spry as a gazelle.

My jaw tightened.

No. Fucking. Way.

Glaring after his receding form, I bellowed at the top of my lungs, "Go on, tell them! Tell them Asher's back!" I wheezed, then yelled again. "Tell them I'm coming . . . and tell them I'm going to burn every last one of you!"

My voice echoed back to me. The demon dropped into a crevice and vanished.

I wiped off my mouth with the back of my hand.

I was so fucked.

That shouldn't have happened—him healing like that. Demons heads didn't fuse back onto their bodies in five seconds flat. They didn't get pulverized only to reform before your eyes.

It didn't work like that.

As far as I knew, this particular demon didn't have

an affinity for accelerated healing. Sure, he would have healed eventually, but only marginally faster than a human.

He'd been helped.

My gaze went back to the dark forest, now creaking with night sounds.

Instinctively, my nose wrinkled.

There was another demon in these woods. Operating behind the scenes.

I should have known.

But to have healed one of its kind from a distance . . .

I'd never encountered that kind of power before.

I needed to capture it. Tonight.

Come tomorrow, I would have the entire race of demons hot on my scent and I would be a dead man for sure.

If this one was smart—and it must be smart, since it hadn't shown its face—then it would probably head straight for the portal.

Lana

WE CALL IT misfortunate magic.

Just as an animal must give its life to feed you, so too must creatures pay a tithe for the magic that sustains us. It's all part of the circle of life. Why the victims must pay that debt is the mystery of the ages, but that is the way it's always been.

And now, somewhere in the world, twenty-six blood

donors would be having a very bad day. I murmured my thanks for their sacrifice, unwilling though it might be.

I rose silently to my feet, listening to the sounds of the night.

I knew Fidel escaped—that much I could sense through our connection. Which meant that somewhere out there, the most formidable human known to Infernari just lost a kill.

He would be angry.

He would ask questions.

He would figure out Fidel had help.

He would hunt me.

He would kill me.

I whispered a prayer to the Great Mother, and then I sprinted for dear life toward the cave entrance.

If I died, my kind would be doomed. That was how tenuous our existence was.

I paused just inside the cave's mouth, where the ground fell away and plunged deep into the darkness below. Salvation lay somewhere down there.

I threw a glance over my shoulder. My ears twitched.

Utter silence.

I faced forward again, took a deep breath, and jumped.

The trip down wasn't particularly smooth or pleasant this time. I was too fraught with panic for much finesse, and I hadn't thought to save much power for myself to make up for it with magic. Foresight was a skill better suited to humans than Infernari. And still, despite my hurried movements, the descent felt like it took ages.

The cave narrowed abruptly, and my hands slapped the

wet, gummy walls as I lowered myself. The cave opened once more, and I knew I was getting close to the bottom. So close.

Even in the deep darkness, I saw the cave floor far beneath me. A mass of stalagmites covered it, several thicker at their base than the tree I'd hid behind.

Abruptly, I released my hold of the wall, dropping down. I landed in a crouch between two large spires, my excitement mounting.

I'd be home in less than a minute.

I stood, casting a glance far above me. No sign of Asher.

Jame Asher.

No wonder I had been so intimidated by him even before I learned his identity. On some level I knew, I *knew*, how formidable the man I stared at was. And then, to see him in action . . . He managed to turn the portal master into nothing more than raw meat. Twice.

I had to tell the others that Asher was alive. That he was just as powerful and ruthless as the stories made him out to be. No human should have been able to capture, let alone kill, a portal master.

But he had.

I headed towards the lapping water, towards the portal.

That's when I felt it—or rather, when I didn't feel what I should've.

The alluring pull of the gateway was absent; the cave lacked its usual breath of magic.

My heart pounded faster, forming a melody of sorts with the dripping water. I moved through the cavern, the chill of the place seeping into my bones. So achingly cold down here.

My gaze roved over my surroundings. If my magic couldn't find the portal, my eyes would.

There.

Next to the shallow pool, I recognized the familiar cluster of columns from some of my earlier trips. I had thought at the time that they looked like the most ancient, abandoned castles of my homeland, their walls rounded and smoothed by thousands of years of wind and rain.

Only now, now these pillars lay scattered in fragmented heaps.

I strode over to them, not daring to breathe, not daring to *believe*.

Something crunched beneath my boot. I lifted the heel of my shoe. Several sharp, porous shards had embedded themselves into my shoe sole. I picked one between my fingers, brought it to my nose.

Bone.

Only the most residual magic still clung to it. But I could tell the difference between a human bone and an Infernarus. This was the latter. And I knew from my studies that portal masters often used our ancestors in the creation of these gateways. To find the bones smashed to pieces . . .

I walked over the area where the portal should've been. My surroundings did not melt away, and the fusion of magic that came with crossing never washed over me.

Cold dread coiled low in my gut.

The portal had collapsed, doorway irreparably smashed.

I was marooned.

Panicking, I spun back toward the cave exit, just as a blinding light blazed out of the darkness, forcing me to squint and shield my eyes.

"You creatures never learn," said Jame Asher, his shadowy face hidden behind the glare.

CHAPTER 4

Asher

THE DEMON DARTED behind the stalagmite, where I caught only the faintest flicker of red in its feral eyes before it shrank into the shadows. Gave me the willies. I'd tracked this one—a female—back down the throat of the cave to the portal chamber, where her gateway now lay in ruin.

The creature had been understandably traumatized to find herself cornered.

"I've never seen a demon heal like that." I pushed myself off the wall, keeping my flashlight trained on her hiding spot. "You're doing, I assume?"

The echo of my voice faded into silence.

I flared my nostrils to take a slow breath. She'd covered up her ashy scent with cheap bubblegum perfume—probably bought at a toy store; they never knew how to fit in—but her smell was still there. The cave reeked of it.

"Demon, I'm talking to you," I called. "Show yourself."

Again, no reply.

I panned the light around the cave, making sure she was alone.

Good.

The other demon had busted my thermal scope, leaving me no way to see them in the dark.

"These yours?" I cast the empty blood sacks I'd found topside into the pool. They floated on the ripples, clouding the milky water red. "From a blood blank, huh? I liked it better when you bled us yourselves . . . gave us the dignity of knowing why our lives ended up cursed, at least." Before I came after her, I'd scrubbed all Fidel's blood off me so she couldn't use it against me.

Still no answer.

"Demon, I know you're hoping and praying and crossing your fingers I didn't see you, but I saw you. I smell you. I *sense* you. I'm not just shining my light at that limestone dick you're hiding behind because I like the way it looks. So why don't you come out so we can chat about that little healing power of yours."

Another flicker of those red eyes. Just a peek. Then she flinched back.

"I don't have time for games," I said. "Demon, you listening to me? Demon, I'm talking to you—"

"It's *Infernarus*," she said, breaking her silence. "We are *Infernari*."

Her voice surprised me. Higher pitched than I'd expected. Younger. Softer. Even when hardened with fury.

"Very good," I said. "Now step out where I can see you."

"We call your species by its chosen name, *human*," she spat. "Call us by ours."

"Why should I?" I sat down on a low mound of minerals and laid my gun on my lap, instead removing the Taser I'd taken from my glove compartment. Whether she could heal herself with a bullet in her brain remained to be seen, but I wasn't taking any chances. Electricity scrambled nerve impulses just as well in demons.

Had I known my earlier pursuit would end in failure, I would have reached for it first.

My mistakes tonight were costing me.

She chose silence again, so I continued, "I've never seen a demon heal like that. You tell me how you did it, I let you live. You don't . . ." I let the threat hang in the air, taking the moment to pick dirt out of the grooves under the slide of my gun.

"You filthy liar. You swore that exact oath to Fidel, and you broke it." She stepped out from behind the stalagmite, chin held high. "There. So you can look me in the eye when you lie to me, Jame Asher."

Like humans, demons came in all shapes and sizes. Fidel—the demon I'd tried to kill earlier—had had an ugly mug.

This one happened to be quite the opposite.

Tall, lean, distractingly pretty. Her long dark hair seemed to fluoresce as I panned the flashlight over her, emitting a rainbow of greens and blues.

Just a trick of the light.

"I get it, you guys are sensitive about the lying," I said.

"You have no honor, Jame Asher."

"Yeah, that's what your boy out there said too. Let's try to move past it." I stood up, holstering my gun. "So, you some kind of healer?"

"I can kill, too," she said. "And I don't need your pathetic *machines* to do it."

I shined the flashlight in her eyes, which reflected a cat-like gleam. Like other nocturnal hunters, bright lights unnerved them.

Her eyes, I noticed, weren't actually red. More like violet. If I hadn't known what to look for, she might have passed for human . . . save for the stench of evil rolling off her in waves.

Often the prettiest things were most poisonous.

"You healed him without touching him," I pressed. "How? How'd you do it? How far can you go? Can you do it between our realms?"

"How does that human gesture go?" She tilted her hand, raising each finger in turn until she got to the middle one, which she extended my way. "For you, Asher, I like this gesture."

Trying to bait me into anger. I ignored it. "You're powerful; how come I haven't heard of you?"

Her gaze flicked to the cave's exit behind me, mind on one thing only—escape.

But seriously, what idiot puts a portal in a cave with only one exit?

"Answer me, demon."

Her glare snapped back to me with a vengeance. "If you

think I'm *ever* going to betray my people, then you're stupider than you are wretched. And my name is Lana."

"Don't give a fuck what your name is, demon." I angled the light right in her eyes, relishing how she shrank back. "We're going to play a game now. I call this game, 'Tell Asher what he wants to hear.' The rules are simple: you have exactly five seconds to tell me how you healed your boy out there, or I start hurting you."

Her jaw clamped. "How about you put away that weapon," she said, "I'll put away mine, and we can fight hand-to-hand, like the gods intended."

I chuckled. "It's called a flashlight, demon. It's not a weapon."

"Oh yeah? Then see how you fight without it," she taunted.

I opened my mouth to respond—

She dropped into a crouch and in a single fluid motion, swiped a stone off the floor and whipped it toward me.

Her aim was perfect.

The projectile knocked the flashlight from my hand, and it cracked against the wall. The bulb popped, plunging the cave in sudden, terrifying blackness.

Shit.

A flurry of her footsteps echoed in the darkness, impossible to trace.

I scrambled for the spare pen light on my belt and went for my Glock out of reflex, leveling the gun over my flashlight hand.

Once clicked on, the feeblest little crap beam illuminated the stalagmite where she'd stood a split-second earlier . . . and of course, she was gone.

Skin crawling, I backed against the wall, jerking the pen light around.

Shadows swooped behind every stalagmite, movement everywhere. And I'd just given away my location.

Tonight was an off night for sure.

In my periphery, a figure darted between two mineral spires.

I spun and squeezed off two shots. The flashes lit the cave like a strobe light, and the echo stung my ears as an avalanche of brittle limestone crumbled into the pool, dislodged by the bullets. But she'd vanished again.

I ducked and edged around the pool in the opposite direction, moving in jerks so she couldn't aim another rock. Hunting a demon by flashlight in a cave half a mile underground . . . *not* how I'd planned this evening to end.

Right now, I was supposed to be toasting a Scotch to bringing the number of demon portals down to single digits.

I'd underestimated her. She'd looked too young to be dangerous. Early twenties, maybe.

A juvenile.

Should have known she'd be unpredictable, reckless.

Another scuffle sounded across the cave. I yanked the light to its source, where a rock fragment skittered to rest at the base of a lumpy spire. No sign of her.

Then a splash yanked my gaze to the pool, still rippling from all the disturbance. Then another splash, closer.

As in . . . chunks falling from the ceiling.

The ceiling?

Slowly, I lifted my gaze.

Moving in a blur, the demon was moving along the roof of the cave, weaving between the hanging stalactites like a chimpanzee.

Oh, come on!

I jerked the gun up.

Her leg swung down and kicked it out of my hand, along with my second flashlight. Crap. I went for the Taser next. Swinging again, she landed a kick square on my chest, knocking me onto my back. Jagged rock crunched underneath me, making me wince.

Freaking gymnast, this one.

The pen light, made with a sturdier LED, had mercifully stayed lit. In its weak glow, I just made out her silhouette as she dropped from the ceiling, body unfurling in midair as she drew a blade from a thigh holster.

I pointed the Taser straight up and squeezed the trigger.

The bolts of electricity hit her square in the chest, and her convulsing body landed on me, her blade clattering harmlessly off to the side.

Wasting no time, I looped my arm around her neck and, while the Taser continued to immobilize her, I squeezed her windpipe until she stopped breathing, until her heart stopped beating, until by all human standards she would be clinically dead.

But I knew better.

I should finish it this time. I should.

Burn her to ashes.

But I still didn't understand her power. And what I didn't understand, I wanted to study.

This one, I was going to keep.

Asher

Back on the highway, I jammed my fingers through my hair and dragged my palm down the back of my neck, exhaling slowly through flared nostrils. Then I cursed and punched the steering wheel.

I had been hunting demons for two years, and I had survived purely because no demon had ever seen me alive . . . and lived to tell the tale.

Because every demon believed Jame Asher had died alongside his wife and two-year-old daughter on Friday, October 13, twenty-two months ago.

Not anymore.

My gaze slid to the photo of them taped to the dashboard.

Nicole and Joy Asher.

I should have died with them. I should have been in that fire with them. I should have suffocated and choked on ash and screamed right along with them.

But I hadn't.

I had been cursed to live on, burdened instead with this task of eradicating the demon scourge from the earth.

For twenty-two months, I had picked them off one by one as a ghost, lived as a ghost, survived as a ghost.

Demons couldn't attack what didn't exist.

But now, thanks to the juvenile female chained up in the back of my Hummer, they would be coming for me with a vengeance.

Again.

My fingers turned white on the steering wheel. I pried them off and squeezed my jaw, then tugged at my shirt, fanning out the collar of heat rising around my throat. I was in such deep shit.

A white minivan emerged out of the grayish dawn and crept up behind me. I tensed, and my hand slid toward my holster.

But then the minivan flashed a turn signal and veered around me.

I let out my breath.

This paranoia was only going to get worse.

I needed to get to my safe house, ASAP. Lay low for a while. Study the female. Regroup. Then track down the next portal. Destroy it. Keep going. This didn't change a damn thing.

Plugged into its car charger, my smartphone lay in the center tray. I kept glancing at it. Rather than grabbing it—rather than giving in—I tightened my hold on the steering wheel.

The female.

Her healing power. It unnerved me, I didn't like surprises. I liked knowing exactly who and what I was fighting at all times. But the connection she'd formed with the other demon . . . it had been invisible, and distance didn't seem to affect it.

Whoever she was, she was powerful. Probably some warlord's daughter, knowing my luck, and by noon I'd have fifty of her brothers coming for my blood. Could I use her as leverage?

I glanced at my phone again.

No, Asher.

Two dark objects swooped overhead. I jerked forward, craned my neck, my heart palpitating at the base of my throat—

Just crows.

Demons couldn't track me down this fast.

My gaze flicked to my phone.

Fuck it. I picked it up and navigated to his number. I stared at his name a moment, then chucked it into the passenger seat, fuming.

There were about a thousand demons left in existence, less than twenty on earth itself. If I had succeeded in destroying all the portals before they caught on, I would have trapped their kind in their own world, ending their predation on humans once and for all. Then I would have had only twenty unsuspecting, lesser demons to kill.

Without their beloved portals, it would be like shooting fish in a barrel. Hell, they'd probably die on their own of some human borne disease before I got the chance to do the job.

But now, thanks to my sloppiness, and thanks to *her*, it would be Jame Asher versus all of demonkind.

They would come pouring up through the portals, flooding out from the gates of hell, sniffing me out like bloodhounds and feeding off human misfortune like a pestilence.

One man against a thousand demons.

I didn't stand one dick of a chance.

Finally making up my mind, I grabbed my phone and dialed his number.

Linking with the dashboard via Bluetooth, it rang over my Hummer's speakers.

He answered.

"Jame fucking Asher . . . you better have a damn good reason for calling me after two years, you son of a bitch."

Brad Hawkins, former best friend, best man at my wedding, my daughter's godfather . . . the closest thing I had to a brother and the only family I had left.

"What, you sitting by the phone waiting for me to call?" I said. "Get a life, dickhead."

"What'd you do this time, Asher?"

I dragged my hand down my face, thinking how to phrase this right. "One slipped through my fingers. I don't know, this stupid portal master. He knows who I am . . . he recognized me."

Silence.

"Listen, there's an opening at my firm," Brad said finally. "It's entry-level, but it'd be something to get you on your feet . . ."

"Did you hear me?" I said.

"Pay's shit, I know, but the commission structure's gravy. Give it a few years, you'll be raking it in—"

"Does it sound like I give a rat's ass about your commission structure?" I spat. "Did you hear me?"

"Yeah, I heard you. You fucked up. What do you want me to say?"

"I don't know . . . *help me!*"

"I don't do that anymore."

"Look, I captured a female, too. Some kind of healer. You'd probably know more about her . . . I need your expertise on this one, bro."

"I have a *life*, Asher."

"Bullshit. You and me, we know these animals. We practically grew up with them. This is what we do, Brad . . . this is what *you* do."

"I don't hear from you for two years, and when I finally do, this is what you have to say to me? Next time, do me a favor and don't call me with this crap. I'll read about your mutilated corpse in the paper."

I sucked in an impatient breath and let it out a hiss. "After they kill me, what do you think they're going to do? They're going to start asking why I was still alive, they're going to wonder who betrayed them . . . and that's going to lead back to you. Way I see it, we're in this together, whether you like it or not."

He cursed quietly. "You stupid fucking idiot."

"Yeah, now you understand. Look, I'm sorry. I never meant to drag you back into this."

"Yet, you did. Where are you?"

"My safe house. In three hours. Like I told you, you should have let me die." I hung up the phone.

Lana

I WOKE TO nausea and a pounding headache.

"Uggggh," I groaned as I blinked my eyes open. I lay on my side, my body swaying with the rocking of the ground.

My cheek pressed against the cold metal floor.

So disoriented.

I tried to reach out to rub my forehead, when I realized my hands were bound behind my back.

That's not right. I should be back home by now.

Fidel. Asher. I'd been marooned.

Not just marooned. *Captured.*

Captured by that filthy oathbreaker.

The floor continued to rock back and forth. Beneath my ear I heard the familiar roar of the metal machine Asher drove.

Son of a traitor. I was in another blasted car.

If only that were the worst of my problems.

I was bound, my daggers gone, and a slow, painful death surely awaited me. Asher would enjoy killing me too—I saw it plainly on his face when he threatened me.

Can't die.

I pinched my eyes shut. My nostrils flared as I breathed in that horrible scent the female natives loved wearing, the scent I now wore to blend in. Beneath it, I smelled something even more cloying.

Blood.

I bit back a cry. Fidel had lain right here, caged in this unnatural machine, his hands removed. Asher had left them close to him.

Left them close to torment him.

The car bounced, and I couldn't hold my rising sickness down. I retched, feeling a hundred different sorts of miserable.

My fate would be the same as Fidel's unless I escaped.

I rolled my forehead against the metal floor. I wasn't going to beat this bastard at his own game.

This was amounting to be a gods-awful day.

Can't die.

That thought alone was enough to drive me to action.

I bit down on my lower lip until the skin split and I tasted the sweet tang of my blood. I felt the brush of heat and the lick of flame as I culled it. Whatever misfortune I'd have to pay as tithe, it couldn't be much worse than what I already faced.

I breathed in the magic that laced my blood, feeling it slide into my veins; there was precious little of it.

Focusing on the chains that dug into my wrists. I rubbed my arms against them, putting a little of my magic into it. Under my ministrations, the metal began to bend and weaken. Slowly it gave in to the magic until, eventually, one of the links broke apart. Bringing my hands around, I stretched the pliant metal of the cuffs until I was able to squeeze my hands through each. The shackles clattered to the ground.

I pushed myself up, and more chains clinked against my ankles.

For the love of—

I had only vapors of my magic left. I reached for my ankle cuffs, and I began to rub my thumb and index finger against one of the metal links, massaging the last bit of my magic into it. Under my fingers, the metal thinned then finally snapped, allowing me to separate my legs.

Biting my lip again, I culled more blood, using it to free my ankles from the last of the chains. The bruises they left would just have to heal without the aid of magic.

I picked up one of the discarded chains, playing with it as I glanced around. I was free from the bindings, but not free from the metal box I was imprisoned in.

No windows. Two doors. I tried the handle for both. Neither gave.

No windows and two *locked* doors, I amended.

I twisted around, looking at the wall my back rested against. A small, closed slot was embedded into it. I pried at the edges until I managed to slide it back.

I caught a glimpse of the interior of Asher's car, the section not meant for prisoners. Impeccably clean, save for the weaponry. None of it, unfortunately, was within arm's reach.

Cruel, wily human.

I still clutched the chains, and as my anger got the better of me, I silently gathered them into my fist then threaded my arm through the slot.

Asher heard the clank of metal.

"What the—?"

Too late.

I threw my chains at him. The metal links whipped against his face, not enough to hurt him, unfortunately. But the bastard was surprised.

The car swerved, and I heard someone honk their horn.

"Clever girl . . . you're going to regret doing that," Asher said.

"I regret *nothing*."

The vehicle slowed, pulling off the road.

He killed the engine, and the silence that followed felt

ominous.

Asher sat there for a second. Then casually he reached across to the seat next to him and grabbed his gun.

Fear threaded its way through me.

"I'm awfully curious about your healing ability, demon. The scope of it, the *limitations*," he said, unbuckling his seatbelt.

This was where it would begin.

Asher got out of the car only to slide into the back row of seats. He was so close I could almost grab him.

He studied me through the slot, and behind the stoic calculation in his eyes I swear I caught a flicker of anger. Endless, bottomless anger. He shored it up inside him like I did magic.

"We could test the limitations now, or you could settle the fuck down and let me drive."

"Damn you to a thousand deaths, Asher." I don't know if I ever met a more depraved being in all the worlds.

He looked bored. "Will you behave?"

I sank away from the opening.

"I'm taking that as a yes, demon, only because I'm not interested in cleaning blood off my car twice in one day."

I worked my jaw. "My name is *Lana*."

Asher leaned forward. "Because you creatures are so dense, I will tell you again: I don't give a shi—"

I lunged forward, my hand darting through the opening to swipe him.

He jerked back just in time, his face a mere breath away.

When he recovered, the corner of his mouth curved up. "Careful now, demon . . . that temper's going to get you into trouble."

CHAPTER 5

Asher

As I TURNED into the Tudor-style estate house an hour west of DC, I surveyed the steep gabled roof and half-timbered walls for signs of a break-in. But if demons had beat me here, they were exercising uncharacteristic restraint. Place looked untouched.

My safe house.

Nicole had inherited it from her parents when they died in a car crash, and over the years I'd fortified it into a fortress.

I pushed the remote clipped to the sunvisor and took the Hummer down the cobblestone driveway into a bunker-like garage, where a blast door sealed shut behind me. From outside, it looked like a normal garage door.

Nothing here was normal.

The entire subterranean level had been built to withstand a siege—reinforced concrete walls, diesel generator and battery backup, water and rations to last six months. The contractors had been led to believe they were building a bomb shelter.

I called it my safe house, but really, this was my only house—not counting my one-bedroom apartment in LA.

I parked and sat for a moment, breathing heavily.

What a clusterfuck I'd gotten myself into.

I reached back and opened the slot to the cage.

"Demon, talk to me." I watched the rectangular opening, hand on my gun in case she tried anything again. "How you doing back there?"

"Die in hell," she grumbled. By the sounds of it, she'd gotten sick.

"You have two choices," I said. "I can leave you in the truck, and in the morning I'll see how well you fared . . . *or* you can behave yourself, and I'll take you inside, and I'll feed you, and I'll give you a bed. Your choice."

She glared at me through the slit. For some reason, of all things, I fixated on her long eyelashes.

"Why do you ask a question when the answer is obvious?" she said.

"It only *seems* obvious," I climbed out, jingling my keys, "because I gave you two options. Trust me, if I hadn't spelled it out for you, you would have tried to stab me in the eye."

Don't give her any ideas.

But still.

Even though she was a simple healer, even though her blood magic had run dry, even though she was half my weight and I could easily overpower her, even though she was unarmed and *very* aware of the consequences of misbehaving, she was still a demon.

And demons were hot-blooded, reckless creatures who loved to die for their pride.

Opening the rear doors, I stood back and aimed my Taser at her torso, waving her out of the back of the truck. "You so much as look at me wrong," I threatened. "You're going right back in there, understood?"

Earlier, I'd taken off her hoodie to search for weapons. I would have strip-searched her, except her skin-tight leather jumpsuit had no seams to speak of. It was molded to her long legs and slender torso like a second skin.

Which, it might actually be, considering the fucked-up way demons accessorized.

She glowered at me, her gaze not even a hint less nasty. "What is the *wrong* way to look at you?" Her words dripped poison. "Are you presuming to tell me what expression I should wear in your presence?"

"How about a smile, kid?"

She plastered on a fake grin, baring two razor-sharp canines. More like a snarl.

"Good girl." I let the matter drop.

Chewing my lip bitterly, I gave her another once-over—now starting to really not like how pretty she was—then wrenched my gaze off her formfitting jumpsuit and beckoned she follow me toward a second blast door, which led to my dungeon.

Infernarus, my ass.

I'd captured myself a freaking succubus.

From the garage, a narrow, dingy hallway led past my armory into my underground pad. It looked like your typical man cave—black leather couches, big screen TV, fully stocked bar—except for one detail.

Sunk back in the shadows, steel bars cordoned off a holding cell. Inside it rested a thin mattress on a rickety cot and a stainless steel latrine.

Not my proudest moment, building that thing.

Grabbing the demon's arm, I shoved her inside and bolted the locks. On the other side, she threaded her fingers through the bars and watched me silently. I could sense a deep, soulful despair sinking in behind her blue-violet eyes.

I paused.

It didn't seem right. I'd built this cell for hardened killers, demons that would crawl out of the dirt in the night and bleed you dry.

Instead, I felt like I was caging an exotic bird of paradise, a creature that shouldn't be caged.

She was a *healer*. The equivalent of a medic.

She had a name.

Lana.

I pushed the thought from my mind. She was still a demon, still unnatural, still evil incarnate.

They *all* needed to die.

They preyed on human misfortune. Those blood bags I'd found earlier—whomever that blood belonged to would soon find their life fraught with catastrophe. A car accident, a heart attack, a debilitating work injury. What was borrowed had to be repaid . . . always by humans.

So long as even one demon haunted our world, none of us would be safe.

The demon wrinkled her nose. "I can smell your car's *fumes*."

"And I can smell your evil." I backed away from the cage, perturbed by my lapse of conviction, and opened the nearby fridge to peer inside. "So what do you eat? Raw horse meat? Blood? Carrion? Little children?"

She inhaled sharply. "You keep little children in that box?"

"Yeah, I cut them up and put them in my stew." Seeing her aghast expression, I added, "It's a joke, demon. Sarcasm."

"Every lie you tell carves out a piece of your soul," she said.

"What I got is frozen dinners." Ignoring her, I picked one out—meatloaf and potatoes and corn—and popped it in the microwave. "You don't like it, you starve."

"That would be the happiest thing that could happen to me in here." Running her finger between perpendicular bars, she inspected her cage.

"Those bars are an inch thick and welded together with tungsten," I said. "Go ahead and bleed yourself dry trying to escape . . . it's going to take a lot more magic than you got to get through those."

She flashed me a glare.

"So how'd you heal that other demon?" I folded my arms and leaned on the couch. "You still haven't told me."

"Ah, so that's why you haven't killed me."

I held her gaze. "Let me explain how this works, demon. I'm going to kill you *unless* you tell me. Then, if you tell me where the next portal is, I'll let you go."

"Liar," she hissed. "That's exactly what you told Fidel."

"Yeah, well, I didn't like the way he looked at me."

Her eyes narrowed.

The microwave dinged, and I kicked the steaming tray toward her cage. "Eat."

She poked at it, frowning. "This isn't food."

"Well, it's not a dick."

She peeled up the plastic and sniffed the grayish slab of cardboardy meatloaf. I couldn't read her expression, but I doubted it appealed to her.

Why the fuck do you care what she thinks of your food, Asher? She's your prisoner.

She looked at me. "Aren't you going to eat?"

Her long, dark hair fell to her hips in loose waves. Like everything demon, it seemed to flow around her like smoke. These animals were more spirit than flesh.

"Lana," I said, testing her name on my tongue for the first time. It had a nice lilt to it.

She chewed the inside of her lip, and I got the feeling she seriously regretted giving me her name. It gave me power over her.

"Jame," she said, staring right back at me.

There.

There it was, for a split-second.

That glint in her eyes.

I'd seen it before, too. When I could have sworn she

was playing my mind games right back at me.

Learning from me.

Demons didn't communicate on that level. They *shouldn't*, at least. They talked straight. Deception and calculated psychological manipulation was a human thing; it boiled their blood.

Then again, she was no ordinary demon.

Clearly, much, much more went on behind that young, pretty face than I'd given her credit for. The spark of scary intelligence in her eyes worried me most. This demon would try to get under my skin.

She already had.

I had to remind her who had power here, or else I'd have a petulant *and* spiteful demon on my hands.

"Eat," I ordered, "or I will shove that meatloaf down your throat."

"Ugh, just fucking kill me." She flung the tray aside, splattering the wall with gravy, and began to pace like a caged panther, her mane of hair sailing out behind her.

"Fine. That's the last food you get. Ever." I continued to watch her, my fascination getting the better of my anger.

Who was this demon and how come I'd never heard of her?

I was still watching her when Brad rang the buzzer to be let downstairs, yanking me out of my trance.

After I unlocked the blast door, his heavy footsteps clomped down the stairs into the basement.

He halted in the doorway, his face two years wearier than I'd last seen it.

We regarded each other, unsmiling.

"You look like shit," he said. "As usual."

"Ditto. How much weight you gain since I last saw you?" I asked. "You getting fat on me?"

"It's all muscle."

"Bullshit."

We stared each other down for another moment, then broke into a grin at the same time and collided in a great backslapping bear hug. Like no time at all had passed.

Like nothing had ever come between us.

"Alright, let's take a look," he said, steering clear of the subject altogether. "You said you'd captured one?"

"You fucking blind? Right there." I jabbed a finger at the cage. "Juvenile female, healer, early to mid-twenties, my guess . . . she gives me the willies, bro. Been freaking me out all morning."

Her captivated eyes, I noticed, flicked back and forth between us . . . missing nothing.

Lana

I PACED BEHIND the bars.

Trapped.

Trapped in this world, this house, this room. Inside all this *welded* metal, as Asher had been so eager to inform me.

Once I got my hands on some blood, he wouldn't be so impressed with his welded metal then.

The other human—the one he called Brad—startled at the sight of me. "Asher, you have a fucking cell down here?

How many of them have you brought here?"

"A lot less than the number I've killed."

"To your *house?*" Brad said. "Bro, you sleep here."

"That's never stopped them from coming in before," he said darkly. "Now, at least, they have proper accommodations."

Brad took a tentative step forward. He was nothing like Asher, save for the mercenary build. He was light to Asher's darkness, his hair the color of dry grass, his eyes the clear, cerulean blue of sky, skin the color of dry sand.

This one made me nervous. For one thing, he looked at me the way Infernari did when they wanted to court you. For another, he seemed to be Asher's opposite, and I wanted to like him simply because of it. But humans were all the same when it came to us.

Brad walked over to me, and the way he stared . . . I felt like I was on exhibit. The man was transfixed. I stared back. He could be on exhibit too.

He dipped his head, not quite managing to look away. "You've probably noticed, Jame here, he's kind of a dick—"

"She's lucky I haven't done worse," Asher growled.

Fidel's severed hands, his decapitated head, all that blood that pumped out of his neck . . . I could see it like it was happening all over again.

Asher glared at me, as if the fact that I was still breathing personally upset him. Knowing what a psycho he was, it probably did.

Brad turned back to him. "This is wrong, imprisoning her down here."

"She should be used to it. The fucker's love those

shithole caves."

A growl began low in my throat.

Asher's friend stepped in front of my line of sight. "Ignore him."

I forced my attention to drift to Brad. "You humans think we don't understand your ways, but in our world, we also question prisoners this way—one man good, the other bad. So save your lies for someone who can't see through them."

He placed his hand over his heart. "I'm on your side, sweetheart. Swear to God." Leaning closer, he jerked his thumb over his shoulder and whispered, "I don't even *like* this asshole."

"Then why aren't you trying to get me out of this cage?"

"Because he doesn't want to get shanked," Asher called over. "He may be soft as baby shit, but he's not an idiot."

I hissed at him in response.

"Whoa, everybody chill," Brad said, motioning his hands, palms down, toward the floor. "And fuck you, Asher."

I exhaled, glaring at Asher, then resumed pacing.

Brad tapped his chest. "I'm Brad, let's start with that, alright?"

"I already know your name."

Brad watched me, his eyes twinkling. This one, he didn't seem so hateful or irreverent. "And yet I still don't know yours."

My eyes flicked to Asher, who had been very adamant about not learning my name.

"Don't look at him," Brad said. "Look at me."

I breathed in and out through my nose, and forced my gaze back to Brad. He had kind eyes for a human. And unlike the other natives I had met, he knew what I was.

"Lana," I said. "My name is Lana Malesuis."

Asher stood, and the way the couch sighed as he rose, the way his clothes creaked—everything about him sounded *big*. Predatory. It made me want my daggers all over again just to feel a little less intimidated.

He came over, his footfalls sounding heavy against the cement floor. The closer he got, the angrier I became. Because on one level he scared the shit out of me, but on another, I enjoyed looking at him. He was all coiled muscle. And the harsh set of his features, they were worn on a handsome face. His nose was a little crooked—no doubt a result of violence—and tiny white scars speckled his face and neck. All of it attractive in a very rugged way.

He stopped right at the bars, leaning his forearms against them as he stared inside.

The movement was supposed to seem casual, but those eyes of his had a vendetta in them. And this close . . . We believe the soul sits in the eyes. And his dark ones were burning.

"Why'd you come topside?" Brad asked.

"She had blood bags on her when I found her," Asher said. "She was trafficking them back to Abyssos."

I fixated on Asher's forearms as he spoke. They were thick, corded things, and he pressed them right against the bars. Close enough to cull from.

I lunged.

He moved away before I even came close.

I slammed my palms into the metal bars, jarring them ever so slightly. "You filthy carcass! Let me out!"

"Do that again, and I'll snap your wrist."

"I'd like to see you try," I said.

Brad sighed in exasperation and faced his friend. "You want to let me work, or you want to fuck it all up? Now, you mentioned earlier there was a gatekeeper . . . Fidel, right? How'd you end up with her?"

"She stumbled across us and healed the bastard while I was trying to kill it . . . from half a mile away."

Brad stared at him. "She *healed* him?"

Asher grunted in affirmation.

Brad gave a low whistle. "That ain't good. I thought you were in balls deep before, but shit. This time you might be beyond saving."

That didn't seem to scare Asher. Or if it did, he didn't wear his fear. Not like most natives.

"Why?" The notorious hunter readjusted his stance to grip the cell's iron crossbeam high above my head. My gaze drifted down his corded arms to where his abs peeked out from beneath the edge of his shirt.

I forced my gaze away from him, but not before I caught a glimpse of his narrowed eyes.

Brad ran a hand over his face. "Last I heard, there were two healers left. One is the primus dominus—he was one of the warring demon lords during their civil war. He now rules over all demonkind."

My pacing got more agitated.

Asher's eyes flicked to me before returning to Brad. "The other?" he asks lazily.

"His beloved daughter, the princess of Abyssos. My guess is, we're looking at her."

Asher studied me with more interest.

"He doesn't have any daughters," Asher said.

"Infernari—"

"*Demons*," Asher corrected.

"—think of family in more ways than we do," Brad said. "Those that share affinities consider themselves connected through their powers."

"Is this true?" Asher asked me.

My upper lip curled. "Like I would tell you."

He and Brad shared a look, one I couldn't begin to understand.

"Yo, take five," said Brad, nodding toward the hallway. "Let me talk to her alone."

Asher hesitated, and for just an instant, I saw more than just a burning soul in those eyes of his. And in that instant he looked at me like Brad had, like I was something beautiful and captivating. Then the look was gone, swallowed up by his hate.

He scowled at me, but gave his friend a jerky nod. "I'll be in my room." He backed away from the cage.

"Bye Asher," I said, lifting my hand and flashing him that finger these humans found so offensive.

"You haven't seen the last of me, demon," he said. And then he was gone.

Now it was just me and Brad.

"The bad interrogator left. The good one remains. And

I'm still not going to talk."

"Listen, I get it, you want to help your people out. I know what that's like," Brad said.

I actually laughed at that. "I doubt it, Brad."

His eyes fixated on my lips.

Lustful human.

"You know, you fit in pretty well. How long you been coming here?"

I pressed my lips together and peered at my nails.

"Lana, I'm going to get you out of here, I promise . . . but I need your help, alright?"

For one brief moment, hope bubbled up. If I could get out, I could find another portal . . .

Don't trust them.

Hadn't I been told that a thousand times?

"You should let me go because it's the right thing to do," I said. "I can't help Asher. Once my people learn of his existence, and they will, he will die."

Brad folded his arms and leaned back on his heels, regarding me with raised eyebrows. "I think you can do better than that, Lana. See, that man is the closest thing I have to a brother—"

"I'm sorry for your choice of family," I said.

The corner of his mouth lifted. "Is that a joke?"

"No."

Brad ruffled his hair. "My point is, him dying . . . not an option. So right now, you and I need to work together to keep him alive. You give me your word you can talk to some people, you can make that happen, *then* you can go free. Simple as that."

"I will *never* make that oath," I spat, revolted at the mere idea of arguing for Asher's mercy.

Brad went back to studying me. "Are things still bad there? In Abyssos?"

I nodded before I realized I was doing so.

"And you still want to help your people?"

I gave him a scathing look. I wouldn't risk this very situation if I didn't need to.

"Just asking, just asking," he said, holding his hands up, his palms flashing at me.

I bristled at the aggressive gesture before I remembered—*human*. He couldn't attack me with magic. Brad seemed to notice the faux pas then, because he quickly dropped his hands.

Then he went back to staring at me.

"Ask your questions, Brad."

"What kind of name is Malesuis?"

I walked up to the bars and pressed my body against them, wrapping my hands around the poles.

His eyes flitted up and down my torso, and I saw his subtle swallow.

"It means *badlands*. I am Lana of the Badlands." The red, craggy earth, the dozens of sand-worn castles long since abandoned. These were the first sights I took in when I entered the world.

"Aren't the Badlands abandoned?"

He shouldn't know all this. The primus dominus had made sure to exterminate the humans that knew too much.

It would be a shame to end one war only to begin another,

he'd said.

"My parents were on military tour at the time."

"And you're named for the land you were born in," he finished, a smile blooming along his face as he put it together.

"I have many names. Malesuis is just one."

I was also Lana Skinwalker and Lana Lifebreather.

Brad's grin still hadn't disappeared, and it reminded me of slippery things.

I needed to stop talking. I also needed to release this hope I was clinging desperately to. I wouldn't be making it out of here alive; it was foolish to believe otherwise.

"Where's your family now?" he asked.

"Some are in the ground, and some still breathe," I said, shifting my weight. "But all of them are on the other side of the portal your friend destroyed."

I could tell that wasn't the answer he wanted.

I was getting better at reading the natives.

"How many blood bags did you take?"

"Ask Asher," I said.

"Dozens?" he guessed.

I didn't bother answering. Wisps of smoke curled off my hair as I paced.

"That's a lot of blood magic," he said. "That, and the fact that you're fairly well adapted to human culture . . . You're not just saving a few people, are you?"

I didn't respond.

"Could you save a human?"

I huffed out a laugh. "As if I would save a human."

"But if you wanted to?"

My gaze pulled to Brad. "No."

"Can you heal multiple Infernari at the same time?"

Despair was beginning to set in. It didn't matter whether I could or couldn't, so long as I was stuck in this cage. I turned my back to the human and lowered myself to the floor.

Wrapping my arms around my legs, I leaned my head against the wall. "It doesn't matter anymore."

I wouldn't escape this place.

Asher

WHILE BRAD INTERROGATED her, I sank onto the squeaky mattress in the bedroom up the corridor, furnished not much better than Lana's cell—moldy concrete walls, dim light bulb in a wire cage, horrible stench of gasoline.

The house had plenty of bedrooms, but none of the rooms upstairs were safe.

If demons came—and they *would* come—they would burn it to the ground.

Hopefully, they would presume it empty. Even if they did learn of the bomb shelter, it would take them days to dig us out. For now, we were safe.

Hopefully.

Brad's and Lana's relaxed voices drifted up the hall, too muted to hear, and it ticked me off. The jerk was shooting the shit with her, not interrogating her.

Making small talk. With a *demon*.

He was more of a carrot guy. I liked the stick.

This bedroom also served as my war room. Pinned to the wall over a stainless steel desk, a map of the world bore dozens of crisscrossing lines and arrows—my notes on where the portals were located.

I had shit.

They hid their gateways well, and no demon knew the location of more than two portals at a time. So assholes like me couldn't get gullible demons like Lana to squeal and blow their whole operation—and I *would* get her to squeal.

If, for whatever reason, they needed access to another portal, they would use magic to erase their memory of the first two, thus covering their tracks.

Clever bastards.

But so far, their strategy had worked against them. Without complete knowledge of the portals, they hadn't caught wind I was destroying them.

I'd picked off three so far, in addition to the one I'd busted up yesterday—mostly out-of-the-way back entrances into our world, the ones they rarely used and wouldn't miss. But now I was getting to the more heavily trafficked portals, the demon thoroughfares, the ones they would be guarding. Especially now that I'd blown my cover.

Nine left.

Two more, I believed, in the Americas. Four in Europe, two in Asia, and one in Africa.

Apparently, they didn't give a fuck about Australia.

But with demonkind weakened by civil war, no new portals had been built in a thousand years.

Portals took time and many generations to create. A

portal master would pass on the task of weaving a new portal to his kin. But to do so, he needed access to both sides. Earth, and that ashy shithole from which they spawned.

It came down to a simple truth, a realization I'd had years ago.

If I killed all the demons on Earth and destroyed all their portals, the connection between Earth and Hell would literally be severed. Cut off from human misfortune, demons would gradually wither away and die.

Never before had the complete annihilation of demons been feasible. Throughout most of human history, they had numbered in the millions. Their magic made them all but invincible. To the Egyptians, they were gods. To medieval Europeans, they were witches and warlocks. They were always our superiors.

Then two things happened.

A brutal, centuries-long civil war had cut their numbers to just over a thousand. That, and the ultimate triumph of human ingenuity—technology.

Technology leveled the playing field, made us equals. Humans and demons.

They had their magic, I had my machines.

Now, for the first time ever, they could be driven from our world.

I was going to go for it. A Hail Mary.

But I couldn't fight a thousand demons at once. Twenty, yes. A thousand, no.

Which meant I had to close those portals ASAP, before I had every demon and his grandma riding my ass. But first I had to find them.

I paused to listen again, and caught another snippet of Lana's doll-like voice—*the succubus*—interspersed with Brad's murmurs of understanding.

Really? How long were they going to chat?

When I wanted info, it took ten seconds.

Ask the question . . . cut off a body part . . . threaten to cut off another . . .

It wasn't freaking rocket science.

Ten seconds, tops.

Did I have to go back out there?

Focus, Asher.

Brad was a pro at this, he tricked them into trusting him . . . and Lana wasn't my usual captive. Probably better to get her to talk willingly.

Still bristling, I shut their voices out and turned my attention back to my map.

Two more portals in the Americas. Where would a demon put them?

Well, they hated the cold. *Despised* it.

Leaning over my desk, I crossed off Canada.

That left the United States, Central America, and South America.

Okay, getting warmer . . .

I hesitated at Florida. Nah, not their style.

Louisiana, though . . .

I rubbed my jaw, considering it. Plenty of ghost stories and haunted houses in New Orleans . . . could be attributed to a nearby demon portal.

I drew a question mark over New Orleans and moved on to Mexico and Central and South America.

The Aztecs, the Incans, the Mayans, blood sacrifices, ancient ruins, vast unexplored cave systems . . . it had demon written all over it.

"Bingo," I whispered, circling the whole region.

I'd bet my left nut there was a portal there.

Brad stepped into the war room. "So . . . we got a problem."

I checked the time on my phone. "The hell took you so long? You were supposed to be interrogating her . . . not boning her."

"I'm going to ignore that," he said, taking a seat on the bed. "You want to know what she said? Or you just going to be a dick?"

"Go. Let's hear it." I leaned against the wall and ushered impatiently for him to continue.

"So she is the daughter of Primus Dominus, like I thought."

"So I'm fucked."

"Asher, you're fucked in so many ways I can't even keep count . . . and now I'm fucked too, because I put my life on the line for you."

I nodded grimly. "What else?"

"So Dominus is going to be coming after you. Hard. Because you're hunting his species, you tried to kill his portal master, and now you kidnapped his beloved daughter. Real smart, Asher. Real smart."

"How was I supposed to know it was his daughter? What's he doing sending his daughter up here, anyway?"

"They're desperate, they need blood. Not a lot left who can navigate Earth . . . especially now that there are *rumors* humans have been destroying portals."

"Nine left," I said. "I'm close."

Brad peered at me. "You need to stop."

"I can't. You know that."

"You're committing a genocide. Let her go, she's innocent."

"*No* demon is innocent," I said. "What happens when they build back up? Ten thousand demons . . . a million demons . . . a hundred million demons. We'd be right back in the Dark Ages. It'll be ten thousand years before we get another shot like this, and by then maybe *we'll* be extinct."

"It's supposed to be balanced," Brad said, "our world and theirs. It's been that way for centuries . . . for as long as there's been civilization."

"She tell you that? Them using us like cattle, you think that's balanced?"

Brad sighed. "This isn't about balance. This is about Nicole and Joy."

My jaw tightened at the mention of my wife and daughter. "They *hunt* us."

"You hunt them."

"Forget it. I'm not talking about this with you. What about her healing ability? You get anything on that?"

"She's a healer."

"And?"

"Like we thought."

I stared at him. "The hell is this? Am I interrogating *you?* Fucking give me something, Hawkins. I saw her regenerate the portal master out of a pool of blood from over half a mile away. How'd she do it? What's her minor affinity? Besides giving you bedroom eyes and making you forget how to move your mouth."

"You know what, I don't need this crap right now." Brad stood and ambled toward the door. "Call me when you're ready to be an adult."

"Sit down," I barked. "You leave, and you're a dead man. They'll be coming after you, too."

He shook his head at me. "Man, how do you sleep at night?"

"I don't." I raised my palms. "Truce, alright? No more name-calling. What else did she say?"

He peered longingly at the door, then exhaled loudly and paced back across the room. "She talked about a connection to other demons," he said. "Might have been figurative, I don't know. She's healing a lot of demons with that blood."

"Yeah . . . fuck." I squeezed my jaw. "She has to die. She's too dangerous. With that kind of healing ability, every demon could be as strong as an army. A thousand of them . . . they could overrun Earth. They'd be invincible."

"Primus Dominus pretty much *is*."

I drew my hunting knife. "You want to do it? Or should I?"

He flinched. "Jesus, Asher. Just . . . just chill out for ten seconds, alright? Do that human thing. *Think*. Bargaining chip, dude. You're in a tight spot, you got Dominus coming at you hard, he's about to rip your head off—but wait, wait, you have his daughter . . . do I smell a trade?"

I conceded his point with a grim nod. "No, that's smart.

I agree. But I don't trust her."

"*Her?* She's a kid. Look at her, man. She's a lamb among wolves."

"I trust the ugly ones." I thrust a finger in the vague direction of her cell. "Not *that* . . . whatever that is."

"What's she going to do to you? You're Jame Asher."

"She's *distracting*."

"Ah, not so easy to villainize anymore."

"Shut up. A demon's a demon." I slipped the knife back into its sheath and tossed it onto my desk. "I'll sleep on it."

"Thought you said you didn't sleep."

"Central America," I announced, ignoring his quip. "That's where the next portal is."

Brad drew back. "She . . . she told you that?"

"No, but she's about to . . . ." I strode to my map, squeezing my jaw again. "If I can shut down their access to this continent, I can buy us some time. Somewhere near ruins, I'm guessing. A Mayan temple or something like that. See if I can get her to narrow it down."

"Bro, you can't do this. Those portals have been there for thousands of years, longer . . . freaking geological timescales. They're part of their mythology. They're *sacred* to them."

I kicked the desk leg and faced him. "My wife and my baby girl were sacred to me . . . and those creatures slaughtered them, used them up like tanks of gas . . . and for what? Some parlor tricks? Every human life is sacred, and they burn through us like kindling to fuel their magic . . . one cursed family member at a time. So don't you talk to me about sacred."

He held my gaze. "This is wrong, Asher."

A faint scratching reached my ears. I tensed, scanning the room for its source, and my gaze slid to the air vent behind the desk, which pinged and began to hiss air. My hand inched toward my gun.

"It's your AC, dude. You're a fucking spaz."

"I heard something else."

He rubbed his shoulders. "Why do you keep it so cold, anyway? I feel like I'm in a meat locker."

Though my heart continued to pound, my muscles began to relax. "The cold throws them off."

"You're sick."

I planted my palms on the desk and took a slow, agonized breath. "You're sleeping in the armory," I said. "I'll get you an air mattress."

"Nah, I'll just take a guest room upstairs. You've got like a billion—"

"Lock the door. If anything comes at you, shoot it. Then burn it. We check on the creature every hour. I take first rounds at midnight, you take one. Do not interact with it, do not listen to it, do not give it anything it wants . . . or she'll fucking bewitch you."

"Oh, this is just giving me warm fuzzies."

I straightened up. "Did you forget what these animals are? Two years is a long time to be out of the business."

"No, actually, I was hoping for a lifetime, you douchebag—"

A chittering sound cut him off.

We shared an *uh-oh* look, and then our gazes swiveled as

one to the air vent, where it had come from.

"Knife," I said, holding out my hand. Brad whacked the hilt into my palm.

Ducking under the desk, I tossed the weapon and caught it with a better grip, then stabbed it behind the air vent, prying it loose.

Inside, something skittered away.

I plunged my arm in, caught a fistful of claws and leathery wings before it could get away, and yanked the creature out.

It was the size of a rat, its mottled skin the exact gray of my concrete floors, blending in perfectly. As it writhed in my hand, squealing and sinking its claws into my wrist, I made out a hideous, horned face, a sinewy humanoid torso, a scaly serpentine tail.

A gargoyle.

Grimacing, I pinned it under my boot and cut off its head, leaving a smear of black blood.

While I sucked on my own cuts, I motioned for Brad to hand me the acetylene blowtorch at the foot of my bed. The body continued to wiggle under my boot.

I ignited the torch and lit the creature up, sweeping the blue-white flame across its carcass until it bubbled and turned to a puff of white ash.

I cut the flame and sat on my haunches for a moment, breathing heavily. "Trackling," I muttered. "Let's pray this was the only one . . . or we're in for a rough night."

Brad eyed the pile of ashes. "They knew to look here? I thought this was your safe house?"

"They know. They always know." With my heel, I

ground the ash into the concrete and swept it under the desk. "Don't tell Lana."

CHAPTER 6

Lana

I SHIVERED ON the cot, my body curled into a tight ball.

The thin mattress was devoid of even a blanket, and here the air was bone-chillingly cold.

Made to make an Infernarus suffer.

Heavy footfalls sounded down the hall. I'd listened to them for several hours, pacing as I had paced. It had been a long time since Brad had talked to me. I knew he told Asher everything I said.

I wondered if they got the answers they needed.

Once they did, I was expendable. That's how these fickle humans worked.

The footsteps stilled, and that was all I heard before my eyes fluttered closed and I drifted off.

The creak of a door woke me.

I sat up, pulling my legs close to my chest.

A light flicked on down the hall that branched off this common area, and the footsteps came closer, thumping against the cement floor, footsteps that could only belong to one human.

"Could you be any louder?" I said.

"Hate to break it to you, demon, but your precious beauty sleep is not my number one concern right now."

I narrowed my eyes just as Asher stepped out of the hall and into the main room. He flipped on the lights.

I shielded my eyes with my forearm, squinting against the glare to get a good look at my captor.

His gaze fell heavy on me as he grabbed a chair, dragging it forward and stopping only a couple feet short of the bars. Just outside of my reach. He sat backwards in it, resting his forearms on the top of the seatback.

I dropped my arm to wrap it back around my body. I tried to control my shivering, but it was impossible.

"You're going to kill me?" I said.

He nodded. "Eventually."

I rested my chin on my legs. "I will fight you," I said.

"I know. Every demon I've killed has."

And unlike other Infernari, I wasn't one of the true warriors.

"Get on with it then," I said.

"Why did you save the portal master? Could have saved a hundred demons back at home with the amount of blood you wasted."

I rubbed my arms. Asher's eyes dipped to the action.

"If you saw an Infernarus killing a human, you would do the same," I said. "It's instinct."

His jaw clenched, and the way his body straightened gave off the impression that he was being slowly suffocated from the inside out. Something about what I said . . . like striking a blow.

"You *have* seen it happen," I said. "And did you save the human?"

"If you want to survive the night," he said, "drop the subject."

I cocked my head. "How depraved you must think we are," I said, studying him through the bars.

"Your kind *are* depraved." He said it with such conviction. I wasn't going to change his mind. Not that I was intending to, but it bothered me how very adamantly he believed his own words.

I studied him a little more. His hair was mussed, as though he'd been running his fingers through it over and over again. And I found I enjoyed his eyes on me, regardless of—or maybe because of—how dangerous he was.

An intense shiver racked my body. My arms tightened their hold around my legs. I was bleeding heat.

Asher's eyes fell on my shaking form. Almost angrily he stood, the chair scraping as he did so. He stalked to the couch, where a blanket lay haphazardly over the back of it.

Snatching it up, he said, "Get to the corner of the cell."

For once, I decided not to bait him. I was cold, he had a blanket.

I stretched out my stiffened legs and made my way to the back of the cell, near that abominable metal toilet. I wanted to cry out; exposing this much of my flesh to the subterranean air worsened the shakes running through my body.

Asher strode back to the cell. "Stay put, demon—"

"*Lana.*"

"—You so much as twitch," he continued, "this thing's going back on the couch."

I gave him an aghast look. My entire body was trembling. Even my teeth were clicking. He'd primed me for disappointment.

"I didn't mean that literally," he said, and I swear I saw the corner of his mouth twitch. "You'll know when I'm trying to torment you."

He lifted his brows in an unspoken warning for me to stay put, and slowly threaded his hand through the bars, stuffing the blanket through. It crossed my mind to grab him and scour his arms with my nails until blood freely flowed. I locked that particular fantasy away and held my ground. Only once Asher had dropped the blanket and sat back down did I come forward and pick it up.

"Thank you," I said softly. The words tasted bitter. Thanking this man who so gleefully killed my comrades.

His mouth thinned and one of his legs began to bounce. He wasn't dealing with it any better. I bet he already regretted the small kindness.

I wrapped the small blanket around my body.

It carried a distinctive scent, something foreign yet familiar. It smelled like Asher, I realized.

It didn't stop me from pulling it close. I untucked my hair, letting it drift around me.

Asher's eyes moved to it.

I touched it self-consciously, a tendril of smoke sliding through my fingers.

He blinked a few times, then I saw him grimace.

The expression had my hands tightening on the blanket. It was one thing to hate the heart, and I hated his heart, but it was another to hate the shell. That was always uncalled for.

I sat down on the cot and crossed my legs. "You still haven't killed me, and now you've given me a blanket." Back to taunting.

"Don't let it get to your head," he said.

I was getting impatient to fight him—impatient and cold.

I dropped my blanket and stood in one smooth motion. "Why don't you come inside and we end this now, little man?"

"Little?" He raised an eyebrow. "Does *anything* about me strike you as particularly little?"

My eyes dropped his midsection. "Nothing that I can *see*."

Now both eyebrows go up. "You've been topside more often than you let on."

It was frightening that a native could tell that easily.

Without the blanket, I began shivering again.

"Why does the primus dominus like you so much?" he asked.

"Why does your mother like you so much?" I replied.

He narrowed his eyes.

I narrowed mine.

"Come kill me, little man," I said. I was tired of cells and questions and staring and that gods-awful smell of car fumes that lingered in this place.

He leaned forward in his seat, a lock of his hair falling into his eye. "I bet you'd like that wouldn't you? Dying honorably while trying to kill Asher, the last great threat to your people? It's not going to go down like that, demon." He rose from his chair and swiveled to go. But then he paused. "Enjoy the room," he said over his shoulder. "We'll see tomorrow if the chill has killed you."

I glared at Asher's back, fresh out of curses.

Halfway across the room Asher added, "Oh, and you remember how I said you'd know if I was tormenting you?

"Now you know."

BRAD WAS BACK.

I heard him long before I saw him, his bare feet padding against the cement floor. Not loud like Asher's footfalls, which were sure and determined.

These were quiet. Sneaky.

I stiffened on the cot, where I lay with my back to him, still languishing. Infernari were hardy creatures, but we weren't meant to be caged.

"Lana," Brad whispered, "you awake?"

I didn't answer him.

He flipped on the light.

Great Mother, that burned my eyes. I blinked several times, allowing my gaze to get used to it.

Moving slowly, I flipped over to face him. Even with

the blanket Asher gave me, my joints hurt from the chill.

Brad stood on the other side of the bars, clad in nothing except a flimsy pair of boxers. I shivered on his behalf. My eyes trailed over his exposed skin.

A very human plan was forming.

I took my time perusing him over before my eyes found his. "Did you come to keep me company?" I asked, my voice lower, huskier this time around.

He swallowed. Brad was looking at me that way again. Like he wanted to be my lover.

How very foreign these natives' customs were when it came to mates. How very dissimilar they were to ours.

"Why are you here?" I asked. "Did Asher send you to kill me?" The coward.

Brad rubbed his palms against his eyes and nodded, then shook his head. "No—no. I just . . . I don't know. Fuck."

He began to leave.

"Wait."

He paused.

I sat up and wrapped the blanket around me. "Don't go."

He swallowed.

I leaned my head back against the wall, eyeing Brad. I let my gaze drift over him once more. "Not all humans look like you," I said. "You look like a warrior."

Male egos seem to be the same both in my world and in this one because Brad rubbed the back of his neck and said with false modesty, "Yeah, well, it used to be my job to stay in shape . . ." He flexed as he spoke.

"I've always wanted to touch a human male," I mused. "I've wondered just how similar our two species really are . . ." I let my gaze drift where it may.

Too overdone.

I knew it immediately when Brad's hands came up.

"Whoa," he said while I stifled a flinch at the sight of his raised palms. "Look, you're really pretty, and I'm sure you're a nice girl and all, and it's nothing personal, but you hit the sack with an Infernarus chick once and the next thing you know, she wants to be mates, wants you to move worlds when it was just supposed to be a good lay, and when you politely decline, she sics her hundred brothers on you—"

Halfway through his words I began to frown, and when he kept speaking, my annoyance only deepened.

"—and then people die, and the whole thing's messy—"

I stood, which seemed to cut off his words, and I let the blanket fall from me. Ignoring the cold, I paced to the bars. "I'm going to die, then Asher's going to die and you're going to die," I said. "We're all going to die, and until then we're just killing time."

I let him consider that.

"So you can come in here and keep me warm for a few hours, or you can enjoy your cold, lonely bed. Alone."

"Jesus, woman," he said, backing away.

I'd overdone it again. Not surprising; I knew nothing of human flirtation and their casual sexual encounters.

But Brad hadn't left.

I sighed like he was a great fool and returned to the cot, laying down and turning my back to him. "If you change your mind," I said, "the offer will still be there."

My words and my actions seemed to deflate whatever fear he had. He had stopped backing away. I could hear him breathing, fighting with himself I'm sure.

Finally, I heard him mutter, "Fuck it."

I smiled to the wall as I heard the jingle of keys and then the bars slide open.

I sat up. "I'm glad you changed your mind." I didn't have to pretend to look eager as I pushed off the cot and approached him.

"Lana," Brad said, "Asher can't know about this. Please don't make me regret—"

My hand snapped out, my palm shoving up against his nose with all the force I could manage. He cursed and stumbled back as something crunched. I almost sighed as his blood began to flow. I converted it while it was still on his face. Wispy, iridescent flames burned it up. I took my first deep breath in a long time when I felt the magic hit my bloodstream. I made use of it immediately.

My body thickened and lengthened, my clothes stretching with it, until I was the largest, scariest Infernarus I'd ever come across.

Brad took one look at me, and, "Aw, fu—"

My fist slammed into his temple before he could finish. Brad's eyes rolled up into his head and then his body collapsed on itself. Blood still poured from his nose, enough that I didn't have to give him a fresh wound to cull the amount I needed.

Quickly I shrugged out of my clothes. Great Mother above and sprites below, it was *fucking* cold.

I turned to Brad.

He wouldn't like it when he woke.

I stripped him of his boxers, studying his naked body. It *was* lovely, but that's not why I was looking. I needed to make sure I got every detail right.

I stepped into his boxers as my magic pulsed through me, shortening my hair and contorting my body until I was a mirror image of the man sprawled at my feet. It took only several more seconds to pull the magic from what was left of his blood.

Then I was ready.

I muttered a quick prayer to the Great Mother on Brad's behalf, then spared him one last glance. His nose was horribly crooked. As a parting gift, I knelt near his face and reset it.

Then I left the cell and headed to the other side of the building. Right where I knew Asher would be.

Asher

MY EYELIDS SPRANG open. A hulking figure loomed over me, silhouetted against the near pitch black of the underground bedroom, lit only by the glowing LEDs on my laptop.

Wide awake, I lunged for the cord dangling from my desk lamp and flicked it on, kicking up a flurry of blankets.

My eyes adjusted to the glare, and I almost laughed out loud.

Wearing only boxers, Brad shielded his eyes from the light, one leg raised like he'd been about to climb onto my bed . . . onto *me*. He froze like a deer caught in headlights.

"Uh . . . what the hell, dude?" I raised an eyebrow.

"I, mmh . . . hello, Asher." His voice sounded strained.

With both of us in only boxers, he had some explaining to do. "Leg *off* my bed, please."

He seemed to finally realize, and he lowered his leg to the floor, shuffling awkwardly. *Yeah, you better feel awkward.*

My eyes narrowed. "You sleepwalking? What? What is this? What do you want?"

He stared down at his empty palms. "I, well . . . I wanted to . . . check on you and see how you were doing?" His gaze lifted to my torso, and then—very conspicuously—traveled down my abs and paused on my tight boxer briefs. He bit his lower lip.

Okay, I did *not* just see that.

His eyes snapped back to mine, and I could have sworn I saw him blush. "You seem to be doing just fine," he said, his voice oddly stilted. "I'll just go . . . you go back to sleep . . . please."

"What do you want, Brad? You coming out of the closet? What is this?"

"I didn't come out of the closet," he said, putting his hands on his hips. "I came in through the door . . . *obviously*."

I sat up and woke my smartphone, rubbing my eyes to focus. "The hell's wrong with you? Are you high?"

1:09 a.m.

In my periphery, he edged closer. Ah, he was up making his rounds. "So you checked on the demon?"

"It's Infernar—" Brad clamped his mouth shut.

I peered sideways at him, my eyebrow notching up even higher.

"Demon," he agreed, nodding too enthusiastically. "Yep, she's definitely a demon . . . a terrible, wretched demon." He avoided my gaze.

Now I started worrying. "Is this about her? She hex you?"

"She doesn't *hex* people," he said hotly. "She's a healer, and she's completely innocent, and she's actually a really caring, loyal creature, and you should go back to sleep . . . you monster." Seeing my disbelieving look, he quickly added, "She didn't hex me. You're not a monster."

"Then snap the fuck out of it." I seized my water cup and chucked it at him, dousing him in liquid.

He flinched and covered his torso, breaking into a fit of shivering. Glaring at me, he resembled a dripping wet cat. Not my tough-as-nails best friend.

Something was wrong with him.

All down the back of my neck, the hairs were standing on end.

I leapt to my feet, my heart thudding at the base of my throat. "Talk to me, Bradley. What'd she do to you?" I swiped a flashlight off the desk and aimed it in his eyes.

For an instant, they flashed red . . . before he shrank back like a cornered animal.

It could have been a trick of the light.

"Shh, go back to sleep, Jame Asher." He backed toward the door, gaze shifting from side to side. "I'm just going to go."

"Don't you move a fucking inch," I barked, shoving past him. The cage holding Lana came into view at the end of the corridor. "Whatever she did to you, she's going to pay—"

The words died in my throat.

Inside the cell lay Brad's naked, unconscious body, next to her discarded jumpsuit . . . shed like a snake skin.

No Lana.

"Shit," I muttered.

I felt the creature's hot breath on the back of my neck. Before I could turn around, something heavy and blunt slammed into my head.

Searing pain shot through my skull, then blackness.

CHAPTER 7

ASHER'S BODY DROPPED to the ground with a dull thunk. I stood there for several seconds, shifting my weight.

Now was when I killed him.

A sick feeling curdled my stomach at the thought.

Daggers. I needed my daggers. Forged from steel mined from the deepest of our caverns and crafted by a weapons master specifically for my grip, the knives were my weapon of choice. I scoured Asher's room, pushing aside the scattered papers he had lying about.

I didn't see them anywhere.

I did, however, find a gun. I turned the human weapon over and over in my hands, then looked uncertainly at Asher. Already, I could see him starting to stir.

The gun felt foreign in my hand. Heavy. Dirty. *Wrong.*

Do it.

I hesitated. I didn't even know how to use the weapon I held.

Asher groaned.

Do it now. Before he wakes.

He spared my life once.

It was the honorable thing, to reciprocate.

Stop lying to yourself. This has nothing to do with honor and everything to do with your weak, weak heart.

Still holding the gun, I rubbed my forehead.

It was rare for an Infernarus to be reluctant to kill. Rare but not unheard of, and when it came to the art of death, I always choked. It made me weak. It had also saved my life.

So many others like me had been put to the blade. I'd been spared.

Spare the weak, kill the strong.

I lowered myself until I straddled Asher's back. I threaded my fingers through his hair. Everything about this was intimate. And Asher couldn't fight back. There was no honor in that. It wouldn't be a victory in the heat of battle, it would be a cold-blooded execution.

I pressed the barrel of the gun against his temple and breathed in and out of my nose.

Pull the trigger, I ordered myself. *He's not an Infernarus. He wants you and all others like you dead.*

Still, I hesitated.

He *hadn't* yet killed me. This man I was about to execute, someone somewhere at some point in time cared for him. Even the coldhearted humans loved.

I hung my head.

Gods above, I *couldn't*.

I wanted to scream. I was weak, weak and cowardly.

I pulled my arm back and slammed the butt of the gun against his temple. Then I threw the weapon far away.

He wouldn't know how close he came to death.

I grimaced and released Asher's head. It banged against the floor. I stood, still in Brad's skin and his boxers.

Another will kill him.

I backed away from Asher. And then I ran.

BRAD'S BODY WAS heavy.

I discovered this as I sprinted away from the house Asher kept me in, my bare feet digging into the wet grass. Most men's bodies were. All that upper body strength bore down on his legs as I ran. Still, the guy was fast. Faster than me, and that was saying something.

I could feel the night in my bones. The cold wind bit against my skin and threaded through my short hair.

Night was not kind here.

But it didn't bother me nearly as much as it should have. A heady mixture of excitement and fear coursed through my veins. I wasn't yet free, thanks to the fact that I didn't kill the one man I needed to, and there were so many steps I had to take to get home, now that one of the two gateways I knew of had been destroyed. The other was located a continent away. That meant folding myself into more human machines. Ones that *flew*.

My stomach dropped.

Coward. Coward. Coward.

My feet hit the pavement, and I pushed this body harder, faster.

I heard the roar of an engine in the distance.

No.

I showed Asher mercy. Surely he realized that.

My stride became frantic, jerky.

I hadn't yet seen another house, but if I followed this road for long enough, surely I would. And when I did, I could break in just like I broke out of Asher's. Inside there would be phones. I'd painstakingly memorized the numbers of several Infernari who spent much of their time topside. I could place a few calls. Expedite my return. Or at least leave them some information about where I was, who I was with, and the threat looming over all of our heads.

Jame Asher.

He wasn't just hunting Infernari. He was also destroying portals.

That was very, very bad. It took dozens of generations of portal masters to construct a single one, and then they had to be maintained. If we lost our gateways, we might never get them back.

All the more reason why Asher needed to die, why I felt so wretched for being unable to do this simple thing.

I heard the engine accelerate in the distance. It was coming for me.

I pushed my legs faster.

These humans loved their buildings, and yet I saw

none. Naturally I was cursed to be held hostage with the one human who lived away from his people.

And now that infernal metal beast he drove was quickly gaining on me. I could hear it as the tires squealed and the engine roared. Abominable thing.

Far ahead I finally caught a glimpse of a house. There was no chance I'd make there before Asher caught up to me.

I threw a glance over my shoulder.

A mistake.

Asher's vehicle was eating up distance at a frightening rate.

Jerking my head forward, I laid on the speed and sprinted with everything I had.

I still never made it.

Roaring, the vehicle swerved around me and squealed to a stop.

I didn't slow. Rounding the car, I continued forward, my legs pumping. Sweat dripped down my brow from the exertion. I was no longer cold. Quite the opposite. I had one goal, and that was to reach the dimly lit house I made out in the distance.

Behind me, the car door opened, then slammed shut. I heard those heavy footfalls at my back.

Asher's body would be even denser than Brad's. All that muscle packed on his upper body should slow him down. And yet, the bastard was gaining on me. Fast.

I began to zigzag when I heard his heavy breathing no more than a few arm lengths behind me. Even this was futile.

He barreled into me, his arms wrapping around my torso, tackling me to the ground. I hit the road hard, my breath wheezing out as Asher fell on top of my body. I jerked my head back, cracking it into his skull.

"Fuck!" he roared, "Stop hitting me in the goddamn head!"

His hold didn't loosen like I'd hoped it would. If anything, he tightened his grip.

I rolled us, trying to knock him off my back. He released one of his arms and clamped it around my neck. I wheezed, the strangled sound coming out of Brad's voicebox.

He pulled me in close. "Thought you'd cut and run?" he whispered in my ear, and I felt the odd intimacy that comes with violence.

I jabbed my elbow up between our bodies, slamming it into his diaphragm. Asher's breath left him in a whoosh. I flipped over him and drove my fist right into his temple. He grunted and gritted his teeth.

Perhaps I'd get another chance to kill him. I'd be able to live with his death if it was in self-defense.

But just as soon as I began laying into him, he flipped us once more, his legs straddling my hips. Asher's fist slammed into my face, and it felt like an anvil. My vision instantly darkened, and my hold on Brad's form dissolved. I tasted blood in my mouth, followed by the smoky taste of magic as it burned away.

"Doesn't feel very fucking good, now does it?" he said.

My shoulders shrank, my waist narrowed, and my hips widened.

Suddenly I wasn't a mostly naked Brad pinned under Asher, but a topless Lana.

The hunter hadn't been prepared for that. Nor, for that matter, had I. There were two of us and a whole lot of skin, considering that Asher was still in just his boxer briefs. I felt my cheeks flush, pressed together as we were.

Asher reared back, getting an eyeful.

I growled and thrust my palm up against the cartilage of his nose. He cursed, reflexively releasing me.

I scrambled away from him, my skin scraping against the rocky pavement. Behind me I could hear him recovering.

A hand wrapped around my ankle. "Not so fast, demon." I pulled my other foot back and kicked at his face. It glanced off of his cheekbone.

Ignoring my efforts, he began dragging me backwards. I clawed at the road, grappling for purchase. I felt one fingernail rip away. Then another. I suppressed my magic even as I cried out. No use healing something that would just reinjure.

"You should've killed me when you had the chance," Asher gritted out.

He dragged me like that all the way back to his vehicle, scratching up the delicate skin of my stomach and chest. More fingernails ripped away. Still I fought him.

Utterly useless. He was at least two heads taller than me and twice my weight.

When we reached his vehicle, Asher pulled me roughly to my feet, and opened the car's back doors. Once I saw where he intended to put me, I struggled anew.

I couldn't go back into that cage. There weren't even windows to look out of.

"Asher, please—"

He tossed me into the back of the car and slammed the doors in my face.

I cried out, less from the physical pain than from the distress of being back in this cage. I could smell my earlier sickness, and it made my nausea rise.

For once I wished I could be hardened like the warrior class of Infernari. Or cold and crafty, like a human. If either were the case, Asher would be dead and I'd be on my way back home.

But I was somehow the worst of both worlds. My spirit too soft. My intentions too transparent.

And I was back in the monster's clutches.

When Asher swung open the doors, I huddled in the corner of the cage, my knees pulled up against my breasts.

He folded his arms over his bare chest, and his dark eyes assessed me for several seconds. I glared back at him.

A muscle in Asher's jaw ticked when he caught sight of my bloodied fingers.

"Why haven't you healed yourself?" he demanded. I swore I caught the barest hint of concern in his voice.

"What do you care?" I continued to glare at him.

Finally, he broke the staring contest and reached in, wrapping a hand around my wrist.

"Don't touch me!" I said, trying to jerk my wrist out of his grasp.

He ignored my protests and dragged me out, forcing my hands behind my back.

"I spared your life," I cried.

"Your point?" he said, pushing me through his house.

I bit back a retort. Of course a human wouldn't get it. Especially not the one at my back. Asher guided me back down into the subterranean floor of his house, and I was helpless to do anything but let him lead me on.

Brad glared at me from one of the couches. A moment later, he seemed to realize I was topless, his face transforming from annoyance to surprise. My lips thinned. He, I noticed, had found some clothes.

I passed Brad, and then I was led back into the cell. Back to the metal toilet and the rickety bed. Back to being trapped in a cage below the earth, deep in the enemy's den.

Asher released my wrists. I swiveled around just as he stepped out of the cell and slammed the door shut.

Gods above, I was living a nightmare.

Asher

"DID YOU FORGET she was a *demon?*" Pacing in front of Brad's miserable self on the couch, I jammed my fingers through my hair. "Are you *insane?* No, seriously, are you literally insane?"

"Oh, shut up." He zipped up his fly and reached for his shirt. "I thought she was being serious. They're supposed to be crappy liars."

"Have you *seen* her try to lie?" I gestured toward Lana's cage. "She's got like a billion tells. She's a freaking open book. But no, you weren't thinking with your brain, you were thinking with your dick."

Reinstated in her cage, Lana shielded her chest as she stretched on her skintight jumpsuit, her lower lip quivering as she tried not to cry.

For a split-second I felt bad for her, and it made me bristle.

I jabbed my finger at her, averting my gaze with a clenched jaw. "Lana, put your goddamn clothes back on and quit trying to make us feel sorry for you . . . I know your tricks."

"I'm *not* . . . I'm not doing anything," she whimpered.

Brad frowned. "What's your problem, man? She's a freaking healer. She had no problem with humans until you went and made a problem. Now she hates us. All of us. You know, it's people like you, you and your stupid hate . . . and you wonder why demons despise us."

"Brad, even if, by some fluke, you did score a quick lay," I said, doing my best to ignore the shame and sadness wafting off her, "demons mate for life. She would have been bonded to you. You think Dominus hates us now, imagine how he'd feel after you boned his daughter. I mean, shit, compared to you, I'd seem like a saint."

"You would have fallen for it too, you ass."

"No, I wouldn't, because she's a demon and she terrifies me, and I'd rather be stuck in a cage with a giant Anaconda."

"Look, my bad, alright? At least we figured out her minor affinity is seduction."

"*Seduction?*" I shook my head in disbelief. "No, you oaf, her minor affinity is taking on other people's bodies. Major affinity—healing. Minor affinity—taking on different bodies." I counted them off on my fingers. "Two affinities accounted for. No seduction. That's not even a thing. Why? What'd she say to you, anyway? What got you all hot and bothered?"

"Uh . . ." he scratched behind his ear, "to be honest, she was spitting some pretty mad game there, she might have thrown in some hypnosis, kind of lost track . . ."

I peered at the demon, who was slumped forlornly against the bars like a wilted flower. I could hardly fault Brad for falling for it, for her. *Just look at her.* Unlike other demons, she hardly seemed capable of evil. Watching her fall apart, I had to fight the sudden urge to comfort her, to protect her, like I would a human girl.

My nostrils flared. *Careful, Asher.*

Like a siren, it was her very nature that was seductive, tempting, poisonous.

I opened my mouth, but never got the chance to respond.

The ceiling creaked.

I stilled and pressed my finger to my lips, my senses on high alert.

Slowly, footsteps crossed overhead, loosening thin streams of dust.

"What's up there?" Brad whispered, easing himself to his feet.

"We're right under my bedroom," I replied, licking my

dry lips.

The footsteps halted, and after a moment of silence, trudged on.

There was someone—some*thing*—in my house.

"No one make a sound," I hissed. "It doesn't know we're down here."

"It will," Brad said. "It's sniffing us out."

I glanced at Lana, who gaped up at the ceiling with just as much wide-eyed fright as I did. It was her fear, more than anything, that terrified me.

"Brad, stay with Lana." I ejected the ammo clip from my Glock and slotted in a new one. "I'm going up."

"The hell you are," he said. "We're in a bomb shelter. What's it going to do?"

"I don't know." I holstered the weapon on my hip as I charged into the armory, walls lined with racks of guns and ammo. "That's what I'm going to find out."

He followed me. "Then I'm coming with you."

"Stay with Lana," I ordered. "*Guard* her. We need her alive."

I yanked an M4 carbine assault rifle off its rack and pulled on an ammo vest, icy adrenaline buzzing in my fingertips.

Fighting demons, I could already tell, would be very, very different when they were hunting you.

"You need backup—"

"I've been doing this solo for two years," I said. "Now *move*." I barged past him and strode into the garage, where a trapdoor exited into the backyard behind a hedge.

What I didn't say was he had already risked his life coming to help me, so if he died, his death would be on me.

God knew I had enough guilt in my life already.

I never should have called him.

At the top of the ladder, I unlocked the trapdoor and heaved it up, uprooting the carpet of dead vines that had grown over it, then crawled out into the garden, lungs heaving.

Every window in the house was dark.

Crouching below them, I slunk toward the back door, the dry husks of dead bushes scraping my cheeks. I'd fired the gardener after Nikki died.

I tried the handle. Locked.

Opening any door or window in my house should have tripped the alarm.

The demon—if it was, in fact, a demon—had either magicked its way past the alarm or slithered in through a chimney or something.

I unlocked the back door with the key under the third flowerpot, now full of yellow weeds and rotting leaves, and inched the door open into the shadowy kitchen, creaking on its rickety hinges. Then I slipped inside and switched off the M4's safety.

Mounted on the wall, the alarm control panel lit up and flashed a warning.

I keyed in J-O-Y, my daughter's name. The LED turned green.

Joy Asher, scarcely two when demon magic cut her life short. She would have been four, now. I could barely remember what her smile looked like.

My face tightened. I needed to focus.

Cleavers and knives glinted in the dark kitchen. Backing into the shadows, I listened.

No more sounds. No more footsteps.

Yet I could *feel* its presence, tugging at the hairs behind my neck. Something evil here.

I took a deep breath and tiptoed up the hall, flattening myself against the wall outside the master bedroom suite. Directly below me, Brad and Lana would be hearing my footsteps right now—where the demon had passed minutes earlier.

From inside the doorway, a faint scuffle pricked my ears.

My hands tightened on the assault rifle's grip.

It's just inside . . .

Lana didn't realize she needed only to scream to give away the presence of my underground hideout.

She had been in position to kill me—and Brad—yet she hadn't, and it bothered me. Demons might not be conniving, but they were vengeful. Always. Surely, she hated my kind as much as I hated hers.

So why hadn't she?

She had every reason to slit my throat. I had sworn to exterminate her species.

She had chickened out. I knew then. I'd been able to sense the shame in her body language—she'd chickened out, and in so doing had doomed her entire race, and now she felt worthless, guilty, dejected. She'd given up.

I chewed on my lip, more bothered by that than I cared

to admit. Every hour she seemed more and more human, and it messed with my head.

A scratching sound came from inside the bedroom, jerking me back to attention.

Later, Asher.

Right now, I was about to pump a demon full of lead. The scratching continued, moving around the room's perimeter. I recalled the suite's layout, trying to picture it. Like Brad said, the creature was sniffing out the entrance to the shelter, which it would find at the back of the closet.

But not if I killed it first.

Then, ever so faintly, came the telltale scrape of the sliding closet doors retracting. *Gotcha.*

I spun into the bedroom doorway and leveled the assault rifle at the closet, my finger ready to squeeze the trigger.

But the room was empty.

The closet, now open a crack, appeared abandoned. *The fuck?*

Heart pulsing like crazy, I strode inside it, sweeping the weapon to each of the corners. Nothing, nothing, nothing.

I crossed the room and pushed into the bathroom, and my reflection in the mirror nearly gave me a heart attack.

Empty.

Oh man, if there was a demon that could make itself invisible, I was going to shit myself.

A shadow flittered in my periphery.

I whipped around, just as a figure stepped into the doorway of the bedroom.

A man.

But no man.

His eyes glowed a dull crimson in the darkness, smoldering from within. He wore a black suit and tie which, like him, seemed to dissolve and reform around him like a swarm of insects.

Blocking the doorway, he'd cornered me in the master suite. A trap.

He'd laid a trap.

Before I could squeeze off a shot, the demon gripped the doorway, his fingers splintering the wood frame, and his mouth opened wider than any human jaw—*aiming* at me.

Crap. I dove behind the bed.

Fire roared from his mouth in a white-hot jet. In an instant, the room blazed in an inferno. Rippling heat rolled up the walls, the blankets caught fire and combusted, flames singed my hair. Making an ungodly screaming noise, the demon swept the stream of fire around the room, incinerating everything on contact.

Major affinity: fire breathing.

They wanted to burn me, like I burned them. As retribution.

The bed made a tiny bubble of shelter, but already flames licked around the edges, nipping at my extremities. I laid low, eyes watering from the heat, and I choked on a lungful of blistering ash.

Through tears, I risked a peek at the top of the bed, where the fire parted around me like a river of lava.

I had to reach up into that to shoot.

Nuh-uh, I'd lose my hand and the gun.

But I couldn't do nothing. The whole room had turned into a furnace. I'd get roasted alive.

Already, the edges of the steel bed frame were beginning to glow. My skin tightened and began to prickle, then sting.

He had to run out of breath eventually. *I just need one shot . . .*

Yet his flamethrower mouth continued to spew fire.

This was magic. With seven billion humans on Earth, and five liters of blood apiece to cull from, demons had a near infinite supply. And this demon, he appeared to have stocked up before he paid a visit.

My gaze darted to the window behind me, my only escape. To get to it I'd have to walk through fire.

Cornered like a rat.

No, I refused to die in my own house.

Lightheaded from the smoke, I locked my fingers under the bed frame—hot to the touch—and gave a mighty heave. The bed lifted, deflecting the fire over my head. Grunting, I drove my shoulder against the underside and tipped the massive bed on end. I muscled it toward the demon. With a wrench of metal, it toppled against the doorway, blocking the creature's attack.

Blue flames slithered around its edges. As I stared, the center of the mattress caught fire and began crumbling to ashes.

He was burning right through it.

Fanning away the scalding fumes, I flung myself to the window and gripped the sill through the fireproof fabric of my ammo vest, then yanked it upward. Clean, cool air swirled up my nostrils. Behind me, the mattress went up in flames. I kicked out the screen and threw myself clear of the structure just as the demon stepped through the cinders and the room once again filled with fire.

I landed in a thorny rosebush, and winced. Crawling free, I staggered to my feet and took aim at the demon through the windows.

"Suck on this, fucker!" The M4 lit up in my hands.

The demon receded into the flames.

I circled the suite, tracking him and firing on full automatic. The stream of bullets blasted out shards of plaster and wood, and it blew out glass until the gun fell silent. I reloaded and emptied a second clip, my finger numb from squeezing so hard.

As I fired, the inferno spread to the rest of the house. Either the demon was burning to death inside or getting mowed down outside. One way or another, this bitch was toast.

Except it wasn't.

My bullets could have been BBs. Ignoring the gunfire, ignoring the flames blazing around it, ignoring everything, the demon strolled through the burning bedroom and crouched in front of the closet, then blew out another blue-white jet of fire, focusing it like a laser beam at the floor.

I let go of the trigger, and the gun sputtered and died in my hands.

Of course. The demon breathed fire. Part of its major affinity must be immunity to heat—it *couldn't* be burned.

Fuck.

They'd sent a demon after me that couldn't be burned.

Or shot at.

No sign of a hit whatsoever. I doubted I had enough bullets in my armory to bring this beast down.

If Lana was healing this thing, she'd have hell to pay—no, she didn't have nearly enough blood. And of course she would try to heal any demon in sight. That was simple survival instinct. In her position, I would do the same.

But she wasn't healing it.

Which left only one possibility.

Major affinity: breathing fire.

Minor affinity: some sort of immunity to bullets.

Still wheezing to catch my breath, I planted my palms on my knees and watched my house go up in flames around the creature.

Only one way to kill a demon like this. Don a fire proximity suit, rip off its head to deprive its lungs of potency, then do the next best thing to burning a demon—dissolve its flesh in acid.

None of which was happening tonight.

I'd gotten my ass kicked.

I squeezed off a few more halfhearted shots, which the demon ignored. Crouching on all fours, it continued to blast the floor.

The floor.

With a twist in my gut, I realized. It was going through the floor.

Below the floor lay my safe house, all my weapons, my machine shop, my Hummer, and Lana—possibly the most valuable prisoner I'd ever captured.

That kind of fire, its bluish color . . . it would be hot enough to melt the rebar in the concrete slab.

My insides turned to ice.

I'd once thought it would take weeks to dig me out of my cave. With a major affinity like that, it would take minutes.

And I could do nothing but watch.

Brad. He was still down there.

Once that slab broke, he'd get fried.

Shit. I sprinted back around to the trap door, where I dropped back into the basement.

"Brad," I called, charging up the corridor. "Brad, get your crap, we're gone! Let's go, go, go!"

The room was empty.

Huddled in the corner of her cell, shivering, Lana watched me from behind a curtain of her long, iridescent hair, which seemed to be weeping greens and blues under the fluorescent light. Her eyes glistened.

I felt a pang of sympathy. It was a reflex, not an actual emotion. Seeing another creature in distress, no matter if they're your mortal enemy, it affects you.

I shook it off. "Where's Brad?"

"He went up to help you," she whispered, "after we heard shooting. By now, he's surely dead. That Infernarus up there—"

The ceiling shuddered, yanking both our gazes.

"No, Brad's tough," I said, fighting the growing weight in my chest. "Which door? Trapdoor or stairs?"

"No, you don't understand—"

"Which door, Lana?" I shouted.

She pointed to the stairs.

I bolted up them and wrenched open the metal blast door.

Waves of heat rolled over me, singeing my eyes. Angry white flames clawed at my face, forced me back, coughing. Shielding my face, I stumbled back down the stairs as smoke billowed down from above. *Brad, no . . .*

He'd walked right into a burning house, right into a blast furnace . . . he must not have realized we were facing a fire-breathing demon.

I pictured him passed out from the fumes, skin bubbling and melting off his face, frozen mid-scream. Dead.

My brother was dead.

Before it could sink in, a crack formed in the concrete above me, the sound hitting my ears like a whip. Pebbles broke loose from the ceiling and pelted the floor.

As I stared, too numb to react, the crack widened, exposing glowing rods of rebar deforming in the blackened concrete. A red-hot fragment landed on the couch and sizzled a hole in the leather, sputtering up wisps of smoke.

If I didn't leave now, I would end up dead too.

Lana seemed to realize this. Her gaze fell to the bars of her cage, and a deep sadness welled in her eyes. She assumed I was going to leave her to burn to death.

By now, wisps of smoke hissed through cracks in the ceiling, burning my lungs. The ceiling groaned and lurched an inch downward, blasting out more dust and debris. Inside the cage, the ceiling caved in over Lana in an avalanche of sizzling shards, which rained down around her. She shrieked and swatted the cinders out of her hair, scrambling back into the corner, where she let out a pathetic cough.

It was now or never.

She was too valuable a prisoner to leave behind.

I threw down the M4 and dangled the keys in front of the bars. "I let you out, swear to me you'll cooperate."

"I'm not afraid to die," she said defiantly.

"Yes, you are," I growled. "Every living organism fears death. Swear to me you'll cooperate . . . and I'll let you out."

She shook her head, an ashy tear rolling down her cheek. "I can't, you know I can't . . . I'm an Infernarus."

"Good enough." I fumbled with the key and jabbed it at the lock—

With a hideous moan, the ceiling began to collapse.

Still intact, a huge slab swung down and crushed her cage, forming a lean-to against the floor above. My breath escaped in defeat. Fire poured into the basement, driving me back and tripping me onto my ass. The keys slid into the rubble.

Too late.

The concrete had just sealed her in her tomb. She was trapped behind that slab. If she wasn't already dead, the inpouring smoke would asphyxiate her, and her body would slowly smolder away as the rubble around her became superheated.

My heart felt heavy, for no reason I could think of other than her death seemed like a loss.

Fucking demons. That was what happened when you

sent your biggest, baddest warrior to do a valuable hostage extraction—you lost the hostage.

Crouching above me, the demon peered down at me over the wreckage he had caused and smirked. "Look me in the eyes, Jame Asher," his voice slithered like a snake, "so you can know the face of the Infernarus that ended you."

Still lying on my back, I drew my Glock and fired at his head. The gun bucked in my hands.

Red welts appeared in his cheek, and instantly healed over.

The demon leaned out, his jaw opening wider and wider as he gripped the edge of the crumbling slab for support—

Knowing I was about to get torched, I lowered my arms a notch and fired at the slab under his palms. Already brittle from the heat, it blew out from underneath him, and he lost his balance and pitched forward. He somersaulted and landed on his feet.

But I was already sprinting toward the garage, toward my Hummer. I slammed into the passenger side of the vehicle, scrambled over the hood, and tumbled into the driver's seat. As I cranked the ignition with feverish adrenaline, I jabbed my finger at the garage door opener. The demon prowled after me.

The garage door retracted in the rearview, and beyond it I glimpsed a sliver of freedom.

I jammed the gearshift into reverse and slid my foot to the gas.

But hesitated.

Lana.

Helpless, abandoned, trapped in a pile of rubble that would become her grave.

This demon didn't give a shit about her, it only cared about killing me.

Her death . . . it seemed like such a waste.

But she's a demon. All demons must die . . .

The fire breather burst into the garage, galloping toward my car.

Ah, fuck it.

I was going to die today anyway. Might as well die doing something selfless.

I shoved it into drive instead and floored it, and the Hummer barreled toward the interior wall. The wrong direction if I wanted to escape. The right direction if I wanted to save Lana.

"The fuck you doing, Asher?" I muttered, gripping the wheel as the wall rushed up. *This chick's going to be the death of you.*

Sidestepping the vehicle, the demon braced itself and unleashed a river of fire. Gritting my teeth, I steered through the flames and rammed the partition that separated my garage from my basement. Made of wood and drywall, it splintered over the hood.

Engine roaring, the Hummer burst into my bedroom in the bunker. Then, lurching over rubble, it slammed into the next wall. The engine lugged.

"C'mon, c'monnn . . ."

At last, the vehicle exploded into the open area, now a raging inferno, and bounced over crushed furniture.

Like a battering ram, the front bumper bashed into the concrete slab that had pinned Lana in. The Hummer managed to crack a corner of it. I reversed and hit the slab again, finally breaking loose a chunk wide enough to crawl through.

I leapt from the car—into an oven—and scrambled through the hole I'd made, ignoring how the burning concrete scorched my hands. Every breath felt like inhaling pure lava. A minute in these fumes would kill me.

Behind the mangled bars lay Lana, unconscious.

But not crushed, thankfully.

I found a gap where the bars had bent and, scooting her sideways, managed to extract her slender body. Then she was free. Heaving her onto my shoulders, I staggered back to the truck and dumped her into the passenger seat.

Behind us, the fire-breathing demon clawed its way through the rubble, blocking the car's only way out. But my four-wheeled baby was *born* for off-roading.

The slab that had fallen on Lana's cell made a convenient ramp up to the ground floor. Stomping on the gas, I felt the tires grip the edge and haul the vehicle upward. With a sickening lurch, the Hummer climbed out of the basement and barreled through the burning house, crashing through the blazing walls like they were tissue paper before it burst into the clear night.

The last thing I saw in the rearview mirror, before I skidded onto the street, was the demon stepping onto the front porch, straightening his immaculate suit despite the house burning to the ground behind him.

Lana coughed and stirred next to me, still unconscious.

First order of business: get her into the back, where she couldn't tear my throat out.

Second order: figure out what the hell I was going to do now that I'd lost everything—my shelter, my machine shop, all my weapons . . . and my best friend.

CHAPTER 8

Lana

MY KNEES WERE pulled up to my chest, my arms wrapped tightly around them.

Azazel.

I stifled a shiver. I had met the man several times, and I love all my people, I do, but Azazel's ways were unsettling—and he terrified me.

He'd come for Asher like he had so many Infernari during the war.

Had Azazel known I was in that house? Had the primus dominus? After all my sacrifices, it felt like a betrayal.

I still felt the scratch of soot deep in my lungs, the eye-watering urge to cough, the whistle in my throat that stung every time I tried to breathe, forcing me to take tiny sips, right at the edge of breathlessness.

But there was another ache in my body, this one deep down, paralyzing . . . humiliating.

I wished I had died.

I wished the hunter had left me to burn.

I gently tapped my head against the vehicle's metal wall, sinking into despair.

Jame Asher had saved my life.

Not just spared my life this time, but actually *saved* it. To Infernari, those details mattered a great deal.

Azazel would have killed me, but Asher had risked his life to rescue me. A human had saved me from an Infernarus.

No, no, no.

I closed my eyes and swallowed.

It couldn't have been just any human either.

It was the sworn enemy of my race.

I should have killed him when I had the chance.

The whole situation left me hollow. My body shook listlessly with the car as it drove into the night. I laid my cheek on my knees, my heart and soul hurting for what I would now have to do.

I don't know how long we drove for. It was probably hours, but crammed in that cage, with the smell of sickness and blood and death, it felt like a miserable eternity.

I felt ill. Not just carsick, but a bone-deep chill that was spreading. I'd stopped shivering a long time ago. Whatever this was, it felt ominous.

Wounds weren't the only thing that could kill Infernari. We could die from a broken heart. It happened to widowed mates all the time. Outside of that, it was less common.

But lifebreathers—healers—were prone to this sort of death as well.

I closed my eyes and centered myself. And then I tapped into my major affinity.

There was an entire world inside of me. A web of lives that stretched on and on, each interconnected with each other. Azazel was one of them, as was Fidel, as was the primus dominus.

This was the great secret that all healers held within them—we were physically bound to each and every Infernarus. This was why I couldn't kill easily, why I could heal at a distance, why I had a reputation amongst my people for being too forgiving.

Me and every other Infernarus were all connected. That knowledge, it made the divisions we created amongst one another meaningless. Because we weren't different, we were all the same blood.

They were why I was fighting.

And now I would be forced to betray them, because the human had saved my life.

I let the connection close, not wanting them to sense my sadness through it. My brethren didn't know yet.

In fact . . . Asher didn't know yet, either.

I opened my eyes, sensing the tiniest flutter of hope.

He must never know.

If he didn't know, then nothing had to change. I could still be a nasty thorn in his side, I could still fight him every step of the way, I could still force him to answer for his crimes. I could try, at least.

My body, which had begun to wither away and die, sensed I still had a purpose and began to fill with life again. I started to breathe again.

And since I wasn't dying—yet—I still had to tend to my physical needs.

I healed the worst of my wounds, then, ignoring my nausea, I sat up and slid open the metal slot. "I'm hungry. And I need to use a bathroom."

Asher didn't answer.

"Did you hear me, Asher?"

Again he didn't answer, but not too long after we pulled off the road.

I would have to be very careful from now on to disguise my intentions, to be hateful and scathing toward him, when every fiber of my being wanted just the opposite.

Because from this day forward, the most ancient and sacred of Infernari oaths dictated my behavior. When he risked his life to save mine, he had created a debt that all Infernari must honor, a debt that I was required to repay.

From this day forward, no matter how much it plagued me, I was sworn to protect him.

CHAPTER 9

Asher

A POTTY BREAK.

The demon needed a goddamn potty break. As if this whole situation wasn't absurd enough.

I exited Interstate 81 and pulled into the nearest gas station, but didn't let her out right away. Instead I sat there, clutching the steering wheel and breathing hard through my nose in an attempt to calm down, my brain and body still feverish from what had just happened.

Brad. Dead.

"Damn you, Brad," I muttered. "Always got to be the fucking hero."

I'd told him to stay put, told him to guard Lana. But no. First chance he got, he charged out like a cowboy, guns blazing.

Even if he had somehow stumbled clear of the fire, the demon would have tracked him down and roasted him.

Harbingers of death, demons were.

They brought catastrophe and misfortune to all whom you loved, descended on them like a sickness, like a plague.

You idiot, Brad.

I gritted my teeth, preferring anger to the much worse pain of grief.

This was the second time he'd risked his life to save mine, and the second time he'd shackled me with a burden instead.

The first time, he'd burdened me with the deaths of my wife and daughter, when the humane thing to do would have been to let me perish at their sides. Now, he'd burdened me with his own death.

The three people I loved most in this world . . . all dead.

All dead because of me.

My nostrils flared, and a fresh tear welled in my eye, which I smeared away with the base of my palm.

Didn't want the demon to see this. Better if she viewed me as a stone-cold killer, not a broken man barely keeping it together.

But it didn't matter.

Nikki and Joy . . . Brad . . . none of that mattered anymore.

I had sworn to exterminate these vile creatures or die trying, and it was starting to look like I would die trying.

Gladly.

I would *gladly* die and take my place beside my family

in the dirt.

Only a matter of time, now. Hell, I probably wouldn't live through the day. Lately, I'd majorly sucked at killing demons. Zero for two with the last two demons I'd encountered, zero for three if you counted Lana, who'd outfoxed me with her little Bambi eyes when I should have burnt her to ash ages ago.

Losing my touch. Getting soft.

Yeah, I was a dead man for sure.

That thought took the edge off the pain.

Brad, ol' buddy, I'll be seeing you real soon . . .

For the last hour, I'd been driving aimlessly southwest, heading vaguely in the direction of Mexico or Louisiana, didn't much care anymore. But I had no other place to go. Didn't have a plan, didn't have weapons, didn't have jack.

No, that wasn't true.

I still had Lana, the daughter of Primus Dominus—lord of all demons.

She could turn out to be more valuable than all my weapons and all my gadgets combined.

And I still had a job to do. Destroy demons, destroy their portals, eradicate them from Earth.

Louisiana was a crapshoot; I had no idea if there was a portal there.

But Central America, I would bet money on. There was definitely a portal there. A *big* one.

And right about now I felt like shoving a big fat dick up it and fucking demonville raw.

Okay, new plan. Get my ass to Mexico and find that portal.

I would need Lana to locate it precisely. At the very least, I could use her as collateral when the next demon came after me.

More excuses not to kill her. It was becoming a habit.

I let out a weary sigh and circled around back to let her out, vowing to kill her the moment she stopped being useful.

Lana

WHEN THE DOORS to my cage opened, and I caught sight of Asher, my breath caught.

He looked like all that was holding him together was pounds and pounds of muscle and raw determination. I marveled again at how handsome he was—his strong jaw, his gleaming eyes, the wicked curve of his lips. Even when he was frowning, as he was now, my gaze didn't want to leave him.

His frown deepened when he caught me staring.

"Out," he barked, like I was disobeying him by lingering in this dreadful prison.

I slunk out of the vehicle, nervous about pretending I wanted him dead. Infernari didn't pretend well. As I passed Asher, I caught a whiff of his scent. He smelled like smoke and ash.

Above us, the streetlamps flickered in the night, and I could hear them buzzing with the effort of staying on.

Tentatively, I looked around us, poorly disguising my curiosity. We had pulled into a lone gas station, which sat on an otherwise empty road. Flat fields spread out from us in all directions, as far as the eye could see. Rows and rows of tall stalks swished gently in the moonlight.

Could I still run?

Would that violate my oath?

If I ran, Asher wouldn't have a hope of tracking me through that—

He grabbed my wrist roughly. "Lana, the shitter's this way."

"Shitter?" I asked.

He sighed. "Bathroom."

I raised my eyebrows. "*Oh.*"

We headed toward the building, Asher's grip on me ironclad. Through the convenience store's bright windows, I made out an overweight man with a stained T-shirt standing behind the counter. So far as I could see, we were the only customers at this hour.

Instead of entering the store, we walked around back, where two weary-looking his and her restrooms sat.

I flared my nostrils before we even entered. It smelled about as foul as some of the war zones I'd been in.

I hesitated.

"This is all you're going to get for the next several hours, so you better make use of it, demon."

I sighed. Back to demon.

"I might as well go out in the bushes," I muttered. "It would lessen my chances of death by asphyxiation."

"Stop stalling," Asher said. "You have sixty seconds."

I glared at him. He knew full well that it was hard for Infernari to judge the passage of time. Yanking open the door, I stepped into the bathroom, wincing at the smell of the place.

I could still hear Asher outside, his boots crunching against the gravel. And then I heard it.

Intervention.

Another car rumbled as it pulled into the gas station.

If I ever hoped to escape Asher's clutches, now would be the time.

I might be sworn to protect him, but that didn't mean I had to stay and babysit him, did it? And should some other Infernari come along later and slaughter him, well, that wasn't my problem . . . could I really be held accountable for violating my oath?

Infernari honor codes were fuzzy on this point.

I still had a tiny bit of magic coursing through my veins from Brad's blood, which I'd been saving. Just enough to change my appearance, my outfit shrinking with me.

I closed my eyes and shrank smaller and smaller, until I was half my normal size and my skin was many shades darker. A toddler, as the natives called their young. One that looked nothing like Asher.

Asher began to bang on the door. "Lana, time's up."

I chose then to open the door.

He didn't see me at first; he was looking for a woman, not a child.

When he did eventually see me, his face hardened. "Lana—" He grabbed my wrist roughly.

I started screaming for all I was worth. "I want my *dad!*" I sobbed through my screams.

Asher crouched in front of me. "Lana, fucking *listen* to

me. You stop this right now—"

I stopped wailing long enough to say, "I'm not getting back in that cage of yours." My words sounded ridiculous through the child's vocal cords.

Then I began screaming again.

His lips thinned. He spoke quickly, his voice a harsh whisper. "I won't put you back in the cage if you behave—"

"There a problem here?" A deep voice said from behind Asher. A man stepped up to us. He looked like what the natives called a cowboy. He had friendly eyes, but right now they were boring holes into Asher.

Asher gave me a hard look, his upper lip twitching in anger. "My daughter's just throwing a tantrum. Ignore her." He didn't bother turning to face the man.

"She don't look like your daughter," he said, spitting to the side, keeping his eyes trained on the hunter.

"Stepdaughter. You got a problem?" Asher said. And now he did partially turn, loose rocks skittering beneath his boots.

"Where's her mother?"

"In the bathroom, asshole. Is this an interrogation?" Asher stood. "I'm so sick of you racist fucks thinking I'm some sort of pervert when I'm trying to take care of my own daughter."

The man puffed his chest out, taking a step closer. "Now who you calling a racist?"

"Do you see anyone else out here?" Asher asked, opening his arms and making a point of looking around.

The man focused his attention on me. "Is this your stepdaddy?" he asked me.

I hesitated, weighing my options.

"You can tell me the truth," he encouraged.

Asher stared down at me, his face unreadable. I was being offered two ways out. I could leave Asher's side and make my way back on my own. Or I could stay with him and try to bring him back with me to Abyssos for justice, Infernari-style, which would consist of him being tortured to within a hair's breadth of death.

But not death.

If I couldn't kill him, then my duty was to bring him back to Primus Dominus alive. If I ran, I might avoid having to betray my people by saving him *from* them.

But abandoning him was as good as a death sentence. Azazel or another Infernarus would corner him and kill him.

No Infernarus would ever be that cavalier about repaying a life debt, and I was disgusted with myself for even considering it. I had spent too much time on Earth; their treacherous ways were rubbing off on me.

I had to stay and protect him.

That was the only thing my conscience would allow.

While I was repaying my debt, I would do everything in my power to stop Asher from killing Infernari and destroying our portals. I was *not* going to let my people die for this.

Asher edged behind the cowboy and, imperceptibly, his hand crept toward his holster. The threat in his eyes was perfectly clear: if I accepted this man's help, Asher would kill him on the spot.

The man was still waiting for me to speak.

Finally, I nodded.

It was barely perceptible, but I saw Asher exhale. His hand moved away from his hip.

The man stared at me for a little longer. "You sure about that?"

In response, I walked into Asher's arms, wrapping my little ones the best I could around his broad torso. The infamous hunter's arms came around me, pulling me into him. I would've assumed Asher would be awkward when it came to giving a small child affection, but there wasn't any hesitation on his part. He was a natural at it.

He stood, picking me up with him.

Wrapped up in the arms of an Infernari killer.

My decision suddenly seem like a poor one. I pressed my forehead into Asher's collarbone, wondering if I made the wrong choice.

I'd find out soon enough.

The man reluctantly left us, his shoes crunching against the gravel as he walked away.

As soon as he was far enough away, Asher dropped me.

A human child would've tumbled into the ground, hurting themselves along the way. I landed in a crouch.

The ass.

Asher's upper lip curled at the sight. "Don't pull shit like that again on me," he threatened.

"You need to be nice to me," I said. "I can still scream."

He folded his arms and looked down his nose at me. "You'll get whatever I give you."

I mirrored his stance, folding my arms. I knew full well how absurd I must look. "Then this is what it will be like at every—single—stop."

We stared each other down, Asher working his jaw as though he tasted something bad in his mouth.

My stomach chose that moment, of all times, to growl, somewhat diminishing the ferocity of my threat.

Food, right.

That was the whole point of this stop. I was *starving*. I couldn't even remember the last time I'd eaten. Now fixating on my hunger, I gazed longingly past him at the convenience store, then looked to him for permission.

His eyes took on a calculating glint.

"How would you like one of those?" He pointed to a large picture mounted in the windows that showed some kind of charred meat, glistening with oil, nestled inside a puffy, flaky bun, covered with red, yellow, and green sauces—a *hotdog*, if my memory served me correctly.

My stomach rumbled again, and I nodded, trying not to look too excited.

Humans *did* have a way with food.

"Yeah? You want one? Just makes your mouth water looking at it, doesn't it?"

"Not if you're going to dangle it in front of me like that," I snapped.

"Tell you what, I'll buy you one of those, and whatever else you want in that store . . . *if* you agree to cooperate from now on."

My eyes narrowed. He was tricking me, of course.

Never make deals with humans.

"That means no more throwing tantrums," he began listing off on his fingers, "no more changing into little

138

girls, no more trying to kill me, and no more trying to escape, you understand?"

"Why in the world would I agree to that? Those are all my favorite things."

"There's another portal in Central America. That's where I'm going. You need to get there, too, because you need to go home. We'll get there faster if we cooperate, and . . ." his throat worked through a swallow, ". . . I'll let you sit up front."

Up front? With *him?*

The thought was both exciting and terrifying.

I had no knowledge of this portal he spoke of—the one I knew of was across the sea—and I knew the hunter would get to the portal whether I cooperated or not. The question was whether I could slow him down.

"Swear to me you won't destroy it," I demanded, chiding myself a moment later. A human's word meant nothing.

"Or," he said, pointing over my shoulder, "I could dump your ashes in that field."

"So all this really is, is a death threat disguised as some kind of a good deal, which it is not."

His eyebrows pinched together. "You've been here too long."

But I had formed my own plan. "I accept. You have my word I won't kill you or try to escape . . . or *misbehave*," I added with a curled lip, "provided you take me to the portal."

Since my debt already forbid me from killing or abandoning him, I wasn't giving anything up. We'd go to the gateway together, and rather than letting Asher destroy the portal, I would simply force him to cross over with me. I almost smiled at the thought of out-tricking the trickster. Once we were back in Abyssos, I'd strike a deal with the primus dominus that would allow him to live . . . albeit in the Dungeons of Furor.

I could keep my oath *and* save my species.

My pride didn't last a heartbeat. The way I'd tricked him felt upsettingly duplicitous. Upsettingly *human*.

Without another word, Asher turned and strode toward the convenience store.

"Five minutes, Lana," he called over his shoulder. "I'm grabbing a hotdog, get what you want."

He just . . . left me.

I glanced around, wondering if this was another ploy. Likely.

It didn't matter anyway. I'd made my decision.

As quick as I could, I returned to my original skin, running my hands through my hair and over my clothing, before heading toward the convenience store. I glanced at Asher's car as I walked. I had to get back in the thing after this. And not just for a couple of hours, which was bad enough. Central America was a far distance from here. It would take days.

My stomach clenched just at the thought.

I pushed open the door and slipped inside the store, where Asher already was picking up supplies. As soon as he caught me staring, he gave me another one of his stern warning looks, daring me to put one toe out of line and suffer the repercussions.

I didn't bother glaring back at him.

A human food store. It captivated me completely.

Slowly I walked down the first aisle, taking it all in. It wasn't that I was unfamiliar with convenience stores. I traveled topside too many times for that. It was just that they never ceased to amaze me. I stretched my arms out, letting my fingers brush against all the pretty packages. This was how humans ate. They walked into a store, headed down a certain aisle, and grabbed exactly what they wanted.

The food was even *wrapped.*

And the flavors!

I began grabbing things, largely based on how striking the wrapper was, or how strange the item inside looked, or how brightly colored the food was. Soon I couldn't hold everything I wanted. I dropped it on the ground, gaining the attention of the cashier, who watched me with narrowed eyes, and Asher, who just looked heavenward, shaking his head.

Ignoring them both, I went back to the front of the store and grabbed a plastic basket before returning to the aisle and dumping all my booty into it.

Moving onto the next aisle, I hesitated, catching sight of a large metal machine. My first instinct was to edge away, but I was too curious. Warily, I crept in closer and peered at it. A small window had been fitted to the metal front, and through it I could see some bright red liquid churning. Too bright to be blood. I read the label.

Slurpee.

A picture showed a woman drinking this Slurpee.

I'd only grabbed things to eat. This would be my drink.

I took one of the cups stocked next to the machine. It took me a moment to figure out exactly how the metal device worked. Eventually I tried pulling down the lever in front of me. Instantly, bright red liquid dripped out of the machine, and I hurried to put my cup underneath it. My drink overflowed before I could figure out how to turn it off, and I spent several moments wiping the excess Slurpee off on a nearby rack of shirts.

"*Miss!*"

I licked the sticky red substance off my fingers.

It was *good*.

I capped the drink, grabbing one of the little red tubes—*straws*, I remembered the name an instant later—and stuck it in my drink. Then wiped the rest of the sticky substance coating my hands off on the shirt rack.

"*Miss, you can't do that!*"

I turned, lifting the Slurpee to my lips and drawing a deep pull of it.

I eyed the man behind the counter, who looked a bit peeved, though his annoyance seemed to be evaporating as I watched.

My gaze moved to his bare arms. I could really use some more magic right about now. It would take an instant to hop over the barrier that separated us. My nails were sharp enough. I could drag them down his arms and get some blood flowing.

And then I would cull it.

I took a single step forward.

A heavy hand fell to the back of my neck. "Don't even

think about it," Asher growled into my ear.

I started at his presence so close to me, and the fact that he knew my exact thoughts.

"You're not a mindreader," I said.

"It doesn't take a mindreader to figure you demons out."

He released me roughly, and I staggered back.

"Your five minutes are up." His gaze landed on the Slurpee in my hand, then slid to the items in the basket at my feet.

"Jesus, Lana," he said, scowling down at it, "do you want to buy the rest of the store while we're at it?" He lifted the basket and began pawing through my items.

"Don't touch them," I said, pushing his hands away. He squashed something called a Snowball, much to my dismay.

"Can you even eat this?" he said, still poking through the items.

I began to frown. "You're being mean again."

He glanced up, his eyes catching on my lips. "I'm trying to fuc—I'm trying to help," he said.

"I don't need your help. And I want all of this."

He gave a long-suffering sigh, then took the basket from me and headed to the front of the store, muttering under his breath.

I sipped my Slurpee some more, watching his backside as he walked away from me. He had a very nice backside.

"Stop eye-fucking me, Lana," Asher said, not turning around.

Great Mother, what a waste of perfectly good flesh.

My excitement over human food waned once we approached Asher's car. I lowered the Slurpee from my lips and stopped short, remembering I had to get back in that metal deathtrap.

Asher didn't seem to notice, circling around the driver's side and throwing in the plastic bag he carried.

He slammed the door shut. Only then did he catch sight of me.

He nodded to the front seat. "Get in."

I swallowed, the sweet drink souring in my mouth. Traveling in a car for days with the most infamous Infernari hunter in this world. Asher didn't need to cage me to make me suffer. My situation was tormenting enough.

Just as Asher's eyes got hard, I crept toward the door and reluctantly opened it, my throat tightening as I slid in. No other Infernarus could have possibly gotten themselves into this situation. It required a level of stupidity that I solely seemed to possess.

A moment later, Asher hoisted himself into the car, the vehicle rocking under his weight. He glanced over at me, then closed his eyes and shook his head, pressing his lips tightly together. I imagined that he was thinking similar thoughts.

I tapped my fingers anxiously on the surface in front of me. I searched for the name the natives called it.

Da-something-board. *Dartboard?*

Hmmm, no.

The engine roared to life, startling me out of my musings.

My Slurpee slipped from my hands as I clutched a handle near the door, splattering against the floor.

Asher cursed. "Tell me you did not just spill a goddamn Slurpee all over my upholstery."

His words were lost on me. My chest rose and fell quickly as I braced myself. "Just get it over with," I said.

He opened a compartment in front of me. Removing a gun, he grabbed the stack of napkins underneath and dropped them onto my lap. "Clean it," he said.

I ignored him, my eyes peeled to the dark horizon as the car began to move.

Breathe in and out.

Asher took one look at me and cursed again. His hand fished around behind him, delving into one of the plastic bags. He looked over his shoulder at what he was doing. All the while the car rolled forward and I continued to practice inhaling and exhaling slowly.

Finally, Asher faced forward, dropping a small plastic container into my lap that held round pellets. "Eat one of those," he said.

Watermelon Splash Gum, the label read.

My first instinct was to toss the item out the window. It was Asher after all who gave it to me. But I picked out the item myself, and if the hunter wanted to hurt me, he had far more gruesome ways than forcing me to eat Watermelon Splash Gum.

I pried my hands away from the car's frame long enough to pick away the plastic wrapper and open the container. Tentatively I took one of the small pellets and put it in my mouth. More sugar, and a flavor that tasted entirely foreign.

I chewed and chewed as Asher turned his attention back to driving. He turned back onto the long, lonely stretch of open road, and the car began to accelerate faster and faster. I closed the container and resumed gripping whatever I could.

"Your medicine's not working," I said, still chewing, and starting to panic. The Watermelon Splash Gum refused to break apart between my teeth. I finally gave up on it and swallowed it whole, getting a very uncomfortable sensation as the lump traveled down my throat.

"It's gum, not medicine," he said, not taking his eyes off the road. "The chewing helps with the nausea. And make sure you don't swallow it."

I gulped. "What . . . what happens if you swallow it?"

"And . . . she swallowed it," he muttered, shaking his head.

"You didn't tell me!" I cried, bolting upright. "Am I going to die?"

"Mmm . . ." his lips twitched, and I swear I heard him chuckle a little, "that's doubtful."

I wrapped a hand around my throat and stared at the gum container in horror, not getting the joke. "What's the point of a food you don't actually *eat*? Of all human inventions, this has to be the most useless."

Asher pressed one of his fist to his mouth. "Can we just . . . can you just shut up? No more talking, demon. I prefer silence."

Not talking was fine with me. I spent the next several minutes keeping my eyes trained on the horizon and evening my breathing. I also tried out another piece of gum, which wasn't so bad once you got used to it.

The carsickness I was used to never came. Perhaps it was the gum. Perhaps it was not being trapped in a windowless cage like some animal, or perhaps I was just getting used to these metal beasts.

Now that my panic had subsided and my car sickness hadn't set in, I was actually beginning to enjoy myself. My hair began to float up and around me, glowing blue, then violet. I pulled my feet onto the seat, only belatedly realizing my boots smeared the Slurpee onto the upholstery.

Eventually, I allowed my gaze to venture away from the horizon to a photo taped near the car's digital clock. It was of a woman with blonde hair, blue eyes. She had a glorious smile—the kind that made you want to join in—and she held a small child with ruddy cheeks and equally bright blue eyes. My eyes slid to Asher. His mate?

Whatever I'd been thinking, whatever interest I found in the photo, vanished immediately at the sight of the hunter.

His eyes were glued to the road, the edges of them red.

Only now did I notice he'd been crying earlier.

Brad. Asher's comrade and friend. His brother. He hadn't made it out of the fire.

It was hard to see any mercenary, human or demon, undone by sorrow.

Asher had lost a friend and saved an enemy's life all at once. Hadn't I seen the same thing as a medic on the battlefield before? The Infernari, with all their complicated oaths, often ran into this very situation.

"The gods have welcomed the great warrior Brad

home," I said quietly. "He is at peace."

"Don't feed me that bullshit," Asher said.

I watched him for several seconds, my hair beginning to resettle with his somber mood, before I decided to let it go.

The road ahead of us was long. No need making it longer.

But it was Asher who broke the silence.

"Do you know why Brad died?"

"He died trying to save you, trying to save his brother, which is the most honorable way—"

"That's not what I'm asking. I'm asking why?"

"Because of the fire, because Azazel—"

"Yes, I agree, that's *how* he died—no, tell me *why*, Lana."

I hesitated, his icy calm scaring me. "Because of you, then? I don't know. Because you got him involved when he was perfectly fine living his own life . . ." Seeing Asher's lips begin to pucker, I trailed off. Best not to provoke him when he was like this. If he needed to express his grief as anger, fine.

"Brad died . . ." the words came out in a menacing whisper, ". . . because you culled his blood, and when you culled his blood, you cursed him. That's why he died, Lana. That's the *only* reason he died."

At his accusation, my chest seemed to tighten into a knot.

"Do you understand that?" he asked.

I fidgeted in my seat, picking at my skin. "You imprisoned me," I murmured. "You left me no choice. I didn't curse him on purpose."

"No, you didn't . . . you never do it on purpose, do you?" He fixed me with a hateful stare now, and he bit out his next words. "When they culled my wife's blood, you think they did it on purpose? . . . Nah, they just needed their fix, needed their next hit, just a couple of junkies out for a good time, little shits probably had no idea what became of her . . . See, it doesn't matter, doesn't matter how cute and innocent you pretend to be, doesn't matter if you use it to heal, or get yourself off, or whatever the hell else you want, because at the end the day, that's what you are, and that's what you always will be . . . a *demon*."

CHAPTER 10

Asher

I WAS USUALLY good for long stretches of driving. I could get in an almost Zen-like state, and the miles would just fly by.

But not today. Not with Lana spilling food everywhere and chatting my ear off and having to pee every five seconds. Damn Slurpee.

The miles *inched* by.

I tapped my speedometer. Could have sworn it was broken and we were really crawling around fifteen miles per hour rather than the seventy it read out.

"I feel sick," Lana moaned from next to me, clutching her stomach in the passenger seat.

I glanced over at her, at the pigsty that was her side

of the car—food wrappers everywhere, half-eaten Hostess cupcakes discarded in the cupholders, crumbs mashed into the seats. My nose wrinkled.

"How old are you?" I asked, beginning to doubt my earlier assessment of early twenties. *Please tell me she's not a teenager.*

"Twenty-three. Did you poison me? I think I'm going to puke."

"Swallow it. What is that in human years? Twelve? Thirteen?"

"*Twenty-three,*" she corrected, sitting up. "Humans and Infernari age at the same rate. Do I look like a twelve-year-old?"

"No, but you're acting like one."

"How old are *you,* Asher?"

"Clean up your mess, and I'll talk to you."

She opened the glove compartment to get to the napkins, and her gaze froze on the Glock. I didn't have to be worried. She wouldn't know how to operate a firearm. Even if she did, she wouldn't try to kill with it.

She reached around the weapon, careful not to touch it.

"Pick it up," I said.

Her eyes flicked to mine, fearful.

"The gun. Pick it up," I ordered.

Because that's the smart thing to do, eh, Asher? Make the moody demon girl handle your gun.

"I'm not going to touch that vile thing," she said.

I took my focus off the road long enough to look her straight in the eye. "And that's why humans will always kill demons. You fear what you don't understand. Pick it up."

With a defiant look, she lifted the gun out, holding it like a dirty sock.

But just to be sure, I swiped the weapon out of her hands, ejected the magazine, and racked the slide to empty the bullet out of the chamber, swerving a little. The metallic click made her flinch. "There. No bullets." I plopped the one that had been in the chamber in the ashtray. "You know how a gun works? Every time you pull the trigger, there's an explosion that propels the bullet—"

She took the gun back from me and, closing one eye, peered down the barrel.

"Jesus . . ." I yanked her hand away from her face, swerving again. "*Never* look down the barrel of a gun."

"But you took out the bullets. Is that bad luck?" Those big doe eyes again.

I sighed and rubbed my jaw. So many things wrong with this girl's survival instincts. "First of all, I'm a *human*. You're a demon. I want to kill you. That means you should never trust anything I say. Second of all, I could have made a mistake. If there was still a bullet in the chamber and the weapon fired . . ." I trailed off, seeing her blank look. "Never mind."

"You're Jame Asher. I thought you never made mistakes."

"Yeah, well, I do. I've made about a hundred mistakes since I captured you."

"Like showing me your gun?" She climbed onto her knees and pressed the barrel to my temple. "It must be so soulless to kill with the press of a button."

I grabbed the gun and wrenched it away from her. "Arl-right, you're done. Sit back down and clean up your god-damned mess . . . and put your seatbelt on." When she didn't budge, I grabbed a wad of napkins and dumped them on her lap. "Here. Clean."

She didn't clean.

Instead, she pulled a crumpled packet out of the glove compartment—my application for a concealed weapons permit in West Virginia, which I still hadn't submitted.

"Put that back."

"So you're twenty-eight," she said, reading my birthday from the front page.

"A demon that can subtract." I stuffed the packet back in the glove box and slammed it shut, now wishing it locked. "Whoop-de-doo."

"I learned arithmetic before I came here, I'm not stu-pid. You take away the year you were born from the year it is now. It's hard, but I learned how," she said proudly.

"Kids learn that in second grade here. That means you have a second grade education."

"Second grade, huh?" She seemed impressed with this and sat up straighter. "Is that a high grade? What grade are you at, Jame Asher?" She challenged me with an eyebrow raise.

Had to think about this one. "Sixteen," I said finally, unable to mask my smirk.

"Grade *sixteen?*" Her her voice betrayed hurt. "How did you get to grade sixteen?"

"Six years of elementary school, two years of middle school, four years of high school, four years of college," I listed off. "You think arithmetic is hard? Try multivariable calculus. You learn that in grade thirteen."

Her violet eyes flashed crimson for a moment. "And I suppose you think you're some kind of wise man? Because you got to grade sixteen?"

I flashed her a warning look.

"Your education is useless," she said.

"I don't disagree—"

"Do you know how to train a gargoyle? Do you know how to craft a bone shiv? Do you know how to weave a portal? Do you know how to cull blood and coax out magic? Do you know how to resurrect the dead? Do you know how to control your mind and body so your heart beats only once per day?" She folded her arms. "I didn't *think* so."

"And yet," I said, "you're the one eating Snowballs and drinking Slurpees and stuffing your face with candy like it's Halloween . . . you second-grader."

We made it four hundred miles—a measly six hour drive—before I couldn't take being in the car with her anymore.

By then we'd left Virginia and crossed into Tennessee. Thirty minutes shy of Knoxville, I took an exit for the nearest town and pulled into an Econo Inn.

It wasn't that I didn't have money, I did—being a mercenary for demons for half a decade paid well, and I was still living off that. Yeah, funding my war against them with dirty money. I didn't lose sleep over it.

But I wanted to keep a low profile.

So Econo Inn it would be.

154

I checked us in and unlocked a room reeking of mildew with a single queen bed and a pullout couch. Bruised and moldy from water damage, the ceiling peeled and sagged under its own weight. Long as it didn't fall on me, I wasn't complaining.

But it might fall on me.

Lana crinkled her nose at the smell of the place, her gaze also warily taking in the scenery.

"Ooh, this is nice." Lana, ever the fucking optimist, ran her fingers along the moth-eaten bedspread.

"It's not," I said, sinking onto the mattress to unlace my shoes. "I thought you were some kind of princess? You guys don't have linens?"

"Of course we have linens," she said. "And skins and furs and rich tapestries, but the craftsman who wove this must have been an artist . . . and the design, accurate down to the individual thread . . . it must have taken years to accomplish."

"It was woven by a machine," I said, "in a factory, where they're mass-produced as cheaply as possible and dozens are rolled out every minute."

"Oh." She frowned. It struck me how impressionable she was.

"This place is a dump," I said, "but it's got a bed, and it's got a bathroom . . . so now you don't have to ask me every time you have to piss." I kicked off my shoes.

She saw what I was doing and took that as permission to step into the bathroom and lift one foot into the sink. Thinking that's what we were doing now, she turned on the faucet and started scrubbing down her own boots, clotting the basin with mud and grime and remnants of her Slurpee while humming a strangely haunting tune. For a moment, I couldn't help but stare at her, transfixed by the graceful, unselfconscious surety of her movements, the way her long, dark mane shimmered down her back, the ends of it fading out in smoky wisps. She was such a wild, savage creature. An exotic creature.

A beautiful creature.

It unnerved the heck out of me.

She peeked my way, and our eyes met—for once, not in hate—before she let her hair fall between us and went back to cleaning her boots, her scrubbing extra vigorous.

My jaw tightened.

Keep it together, Asher. She's a demon.

Kneading my forehead, I swiped a flyer off the bedside table and ordered in some pizza and buffalo wings from a nearby place.

I'd encountered attractive female demons before, sure. Admittedly, none quite as distracting as Lana, but demons had a certain feline allure going for them. I wasn't above noticing that. I'm human. But I never minded killing females before because they all stank of evil. Every last one of them.

It was Lana's innocence that got to me.

It was her innocence I feared.

She's a healer. Yeah, that's what Brad would have said. Healers rarely killed, so they never got that crazed glint in their eyes, they never lost their humanity.

Their *humanity.*

Bad word choice. It was slip-ups like that that were going to cost me.

A demon has no humanity, it has no conscience, it has no soul. It is death and ash wrapped up in flesh. It isn't truly *alive* in any real sense.

Lana. I didn't like what she was doing to me. I needed to focus.

While I unfolded the map I'd bought from the convenience store to check our progress, she shut the door and—after some frantic clicking—managed to lock it. Then I heard her strip down, and it sounded for all the world like she was washing her jumpsuit in the sink.

I didn't bother telling her about the laundromat next door.

But I was curious what she intended to change into while her stuff dried. She had no change of clothes and no underwear—at least, none that I had seen—just boots and one skintight leather jumpsuit. I should probably get her something else so she blended in better.

Nah.

A moment later, the hairdryer came on, answering my question. She continued to hum, just audible above the sound of her wet suit flopping on the counter as she fanned it with the hairdryer.

Poor girl. She really thought she had human living mastered.

"Where do I sleep?" she asked, emerging an hour later in a dry jumpsuit. Impressive.

I lounged on the bed with a piece of pizza and the map. Not looking up, I held out the cardboard pizza box. "Eat."

She took a piece and sat crosslegged on the floor like a

kid. "You didn't answer my question."

"There's another bed." I got up and wrestled open the pullout, unfolding it into a double bed.

Her mouth fell open, and her pizza slice dropped onto the carpet, cheese side down. "How did . . . how did you do that?"

"Does it matter?" I said.

She stared at it, rapt. "Do all couches do that?"

"Just the special ones," I said. "This is where you'll be sleeping. You happy?"

She swallowed. "What if it folds back into a couch while I'm on it?"

Huh.

It was a legitimate fear.

"Just don't piss it off," I said.

She eyed it nervously, then she peeled the pizza slice up from the rug, plucked off the lint, and raised it to her mouth.

"Lana, don't eat—"

She took the bite.

"—that. Noo," I groaned, cringing.

As she chewed, she gave me a weird look—like *I* was the crazy one.

Where she came from, they didn't have herpes or HIV or cholera.

Food that fell on the ground was still food.

Maybe I was the crazy one.

"So how much longer until we get to America?" she asked, between bites.

"*Central* America." I dropped down next to her and unfolded the map so she could see. "We're already in America."

Her eyebrows pinched together. "I thought we were in the United States."

"Of *America*. Look, it's right here—" I pointed out the US on the map. "We're in Tennessee now, which means we're about eighteen hours away from the Mexican border. That's two days of driving."

"And where's the portal so we can go—so *I* can go home?" She leaned closer to see, and I felt her hair brush my shoulders.

My nostrils flared. "Not so close, okay? Please."

She edged away, and I swear hurt flashed in her eyes.

"My guess is near some ruins or in a cave somewhere." I peered sideways at her. "Where do you think it is, Lana?"

"I don't know, Jame." Her voice carried a hint of attitude, which I ignored.

"You know where it is. You've *known* where it is. You just need to get past the spell blocking your memory." The spell that only allowed her to remember two of the portals at any one time.

"I don't know how to. I don't control that. The primus dominus does."

"There must be some residue. When you delete a computer file, you're just erasing the pointer to the data so the computer can't find it anymore, but the data's all still there. I'm guessing it's the same with your memories."

"My brain is not a machine."

"No, your brain is far too irrational to be machine," I bit back. I was being mean to her for no reason. A defense mechanism. Because I wanted to push her away. Prove to myself I still hated her.

"Ugh, it's *your* heart that's the machine." Her violet eyes took on a predatory glint. "When I cut it open, Jame Asher, will I find gears and cogs and oil inside?"

She was seeing how far she could push me. There are few things I hate more than people testing my boundaries.

I moved too fast for her to react. My hand wrapped around her throat, pinning her to the bed. "Threaten me again," I said slowly, moving my face inches from hers, "and I will burn you, and burn your portal, and burn your world, and burn every demon I find—man, woman, or child—until there is nothing of your species left but the ash stuck to the bottom of my boots."

Her upper lip curled, and I half expected her to hiss. Instead, she stared mutinously back at me.

Several seconds passed, the two of us glaring at each other, before I released her. Warily she moved away from me, rubbing her neck.

It was my fault. I'd let her get too close, I'd lashed out.

"Go to sleep," I growled, getting up to turn out the lights.

But the last thing I saw before the light winked out was the hurt in her wounded violet eyes.

And the last thing I felt before I fell asleep was a pang of guilt.

I WOKE SOMETIME later, my gaze fixed upon the water-stained ceiling. Even in the dark I could see the discoloration, and the way it sagged. The whole place smelled like stale smoke, and in the bathroom I could hear the constant drip of a leaky faucet.

Abyssos didn't have places like this. We had the time-worn bones of abandoned cities, and out in the wild and war-torn places, we had temporary huts and yurts. And then there was the capitol, our single surviving city state. But our buildings, none of them had this malaise that seemed to touch many human structures. I could smell the rot that was decaying this structure from the inside out.

I turned onto my side, gathering the threadbare blankets tightly around me, suppressing a shiver.

I tried to fall back asleep, I really did. I just . . . couldn't. There were too many odd anxieties that came rushing in— my precarious situation, the hunter's plans, another day spent trapped in a prison on wheels. My worries wouldn't let me sleep.

Quietly, I pushed myself up.

Across from me, no longer separated by bars, Asher tossed about in bed.

He was a restless soul.

Beyond him, the first rays of dawn glowed beneath the curtain covering our window.

Careful not to wake Asher, I slipped out of bed, my

movements utterly silent. I changed quietly in the bathroom, donning my gear, and then I slipped out of the room.

I took my first easy breath once I exited the building. I stretched, a yawn shaking my entire frame.

I got my first good look at the human city since we arrived. What I saw didn't impress me. Weathered, faded signs, cracked asphalt, boarded up buildings.

I frowned. What was the point of creating a structure that you couldn't move and wouldn't last? It seemed a waste. But most of what these people did was a waste.

I rounded the hotel, heading to the back. The only other person out this early was a woman pushing a cart of linens.

A compulsion overtook me then, an uncomfortable craving. I could go up to this human female and force her to the ground. It wouldn't be difficult; the natives didn't teach most of their own to fight. I would cut her delicate skin and take all the blood I needed. Even a single human held so much of that precious liquid. There would be plenty for me and all the Infernari I'd funnel it to.

She headed inside the building, and the urge passed, evaporating away as though it had never existed to begin with.

I sagged a little. I was unused to going so long without blood.

This world was getting to my head.

I placed a hand against the motel's dirty wall, then the other. I began crawling up, my hands seeking out what divots I could find. I climbed higher and higher until eventually my palms met the edge of the roof.

I hoisted myself up and over the lip of it. Foul, tainted puddles of water gathered in several places. No wonder our rooms had issues. The roof was rotting.

Humans and their rickety, eroding structures. I was glad all over again that I wasn't one of them, even as I ate their food and slept in their beds and culled their blood.

I turned in a circle, surveying the land around me. The town we were in was nothing more than a strip of stores and establishments. Beyond that, the world was flat, spread out on all sides like some great sea of vegetation.

I sank down to a patch of roof that was dry and stretched out on my back, tucking my hands under my head.

High above me, great plumes of clouds rolled across the sky, the dawn casting them in shades of pinks and oranges.

Not so different from my world, I thought to myself. A pang of nostalgia hit me. I wanted to get back. I wanted to see the red, rising sun, and feel the sizzle of summer heat.

I would go back with Asher.

He would hate that. Infernari would hate that. Most of all, the primus dominus would hate that.

But the moment the hunter saved me from death, he had bound me by an unspoken oath to save him as well. That was the way of Infernari.

I owed him my life.

Taking him back to answer for his crimes was the only way. I would argue for his lifelong imprisonment, not his execution. Only then could I be forgiven as well.

Slowly, the color bled away from the clouds and the sky

brightened to a faded blue. I didn't know how long I lay there, hypnotized by the sight of the sky and the shift of the air as this strange world awoke.

And then, at some point, a noise drifted in that shouldn't be there.

The sound of buzzing filled my ears.

I rose to my feet, my eyes trained on the horizon as my stomach tightened with unease.

My eyes widened.

No.

Impossible.

This was a horror that should have stayed in my world.

In the distance, the blue of the sky was smothered by a dark haze. A *moving* haze.

I DASHED INTO the hotel room, where I found Asher pacing.

He paused when he saw me. "Where did you—?"

"We need to go, Asher. *Now.*"

He must've believed the very real panic on my face and in my voice because immediately he started grabbing our things.

"What did you see?" he asked, pulling his gun from his holster and checking the chamber.

"The bringer of blight."

Clades Solem.

"In English" he said, re-strapping the weapon to his side.

"An Infernarus, a very powerful one. He can control

the lesser creatures." I thought it was impossible for our magic to influence the animals of this world. I couldn't heal humans or any other earthly creature. Just the beings of my world.

It appeared Clades' magic worked differently. That, or he brought Abyssos's swarms with him.

I couldn't think about that possibility.

"This is bad because . . . ?"

"A swarm is coming our way."

We both burst out of our room, directly into the parking lot. The buzzing noise was already loud, and it had yet to reach us.

Asher squinted at the horizon. "A swarm of what?" he asked.

Slowly, slowly, the horde moved across the sun. The light above us dimmed. He wanted to know what great monstrosity rode the wind.

"I don't know." I had to raise my voice to be heard.

It didn't really matter what the swarm was made up of. When there were that many of them, even a feather fly could be lethal.

I began backing up, all my instincts telling me to flee. You couldn't fight something like this.

Asher, meanwhile, hadn't moved, and he stared fearlessly at what was certain death.

Savage man.

Grimly, he rotated away from the storm, his jaw hard, his eyes harder. He strode toward his car, jerking his head for me to follow.

That was all the cue I needed. I ran to the metal beast I

so detested a day ago.

I slid inside, slamming the door behind me.

I swiveled to Asher just as he cranked on the engine. "Drive as fast as you can."

THE VEHICLE'S WHEELS shrieked as we skidded out of the parking lot.

I was beginning to panic. Another Infernarus was coming for Asher, this one just as lethal as Azazel.

Asher, meanwhile, was as calm as the Mead Sea.

I glanced at the side mirror. Behind us, the horizon was darkening, and the buzzing was getting louder.

One of my legs began to jiggle. "You need to go faster," I said.

"I'm flooring it, Lana. The truck's geared for off-roading. It's not a freaking racecar."

I took my eyes off the mirror to look at him. "Then we're doomed."

Asher shook his head grimly. "Looks like your king really wants you back."

Through the side mirror, the sky was nearly black, and the swarm now stretched across the landscape, higher than any human building I'd seen. "The primus dominus really wants *you* dead," I corrected, then added, quietly, "I'm no longer important."

Asher's eyes flicked to me. "I thought you Infernari were loyal." His tone was insulting.

"We *are* loyal." I didn't bother mentioning that that loyalty was partially responsible for the countless deaths that had cut down our numbers. Infernari liked to avenge violence with more violence.

"You destroyed one of our portals," I continued. "You're a risk to our people."

"So your father would sacrifice you just to kill me? That doesn't sound very fatherly."

"I didn't say that he was willing to kill me." But gods help me, it appeared he was.

The hum of the horde flooded my ears.

I closed my eyes, inhaling deeply. "Back in Abyssos, I've seen swarms strip Infernari's flesh from the bone. It is not a good way to die." The images from the war were replaying over and over behind my closed eyelids. "All that's left afterward are their mangled bodies, nothing more than grizzled cartilage and bone."

"Lana, this might come as a shock to you, but I don't want to know." Asher had to raise his voice to be heard clearly.

The first creature thunked into the car.

I flinched, my eyes snapping open. "It's happening," I said, my voice ominous.

Another *thing* pinged against the car. Again I jumped.

I made the mistake of checking the mirror again.

A wall of black rose up behind us, the sound of so many creatures thundering in my ears.

"How did your 'bringer of death' know where to find us?"

"We're not completely incompetent," I snapped.

Asher grunted, like he disagreed.

Two more thunks sounded over the noise. Then another.

It was quiet for a few seconds.

Then I heard three separate thumps in quick succession. Another pause, then a handful more.

I didn't have to look at the rearview mirror anymore to catch sight of the swarm. The edge of it was overwhelming the car. And now I got my first good look at what this storm was made up of.

Insects.

Earthly beasts that could sting, and bite, and poison their victims. Creatures that could strip whole fields of their harvest.

In front of us, uninterrupted highway stretched out as far as the eye could see. There were no other human settlements in sight, with the exception of the occasional farmhouse off in the distance.

Nowhere to hide.

"Gods above," I said, "we're doomed."

"Where's your sense of adventure, Lana?"

I looked over at Asher like he was mad. "Infernari don't have this sense you speak of."

"We don't—never mind."

The thumps came more frequently. They were beginning to sound like terrible drumbeats, their momentum picking up.

A bug hit the front window, its body splattering. They'd completely overtaken the car, which meant the vortex of this living storm was getting closer.

Clades would be at the center of it.

More bugs followed, killing themselves on impact, their

bodies exploding and obscuring what little view there was now that the swarm had enveloped us.

The ride became rockier as the vehicle drove over dozens of them. Asher flicked on the windshield wipers, and I cringed as blood and guts smeared across the glass.

The buzzing became a sound that didn't simply surround us, it felt like it was inside my bones. Worse, the insects now pelted the outside of the car, and I could hear their wings and legs scratching along the cars innards.

And then the first one crawled its way in from gods knew where. All I know is that it flapped its way onto my lap. I brushed it off with disgust, then crushed it beneath my boot heel.

Another soon followed, buzzing inside the car, repeatedly banging into one of the windows until it flopped onto the dartboard, its wing broken, giving me the chance to get a good look at it.

I leaned forward and studied it.

Infernal had bigger insects—much bigger ones—but the biggest creatures were not necessarily the deadliest.

And these ones—

"They look lethal," I said.

Asher began to laugh next to me.

"What?" I said, glaring at him.

"Cicadas!" he yelled, like somehow that made any sense to me.

When he saw my confused look, he elaborated. "Big, dumb bugs. They die real quick."

It was at that precise moment when the car gave an odd lurch.

"Motherfucker!" he cursed. "I can't see jack."

The car began to slow.

"What are you doing?" I shouted.

"I can't see!"

Shit. Shit, shit, *shit*.

He pulled the vehicle off to the side of the road—at least that's where I think he angled the car. I could no longer see anything out the windows. The roar of the swarm was defeaning. It was all around us, and now it was breaching the car.

We were going to die unless I did something.

I bit the inside of my cheek until it bled.

Clades was an Infernarus. One of my own.

I would either stop him, or I would meet my end straight on.

The car shuddered to a stop. Before Asher could tell me otherwise, I opened the car door.

"*Lana—*"

I slammed the door shut behind me, cutting off his words and surely trapping dozens of insects inside with him. For his sake, I hoped he was right about them being harmless.

For his sake and for mine.

Because almost immediately, insects pelted me, the force of the impact bruising. They were a living, breathing gale. The noise of all those wing strokes was deafening out here. The abyss was screaming in my ear.

The sheer force of them knocked me back. I felt their wings against my skin, their bodies tangled in my hair.

I began moving away from the car, cringing against the

feel of so many bugs battering against me.

Somewhere out here, Clades walked. I was going to find him, and I was going to convince him to end this madness.

Asher was under my protection and the Infernarus would not intercede on it.

I had to cover my mouth to speak, the insects were so dense.

"Clades!" I shouted. My own hand muffled my words.

"Clades!" I yelled louder. "*Clades!*"

It was no use. He'd never hear.

I was getting close to the vortex, though. The denseness of all the insects was the most obvious sign. Walking was like trying to move through a wall. I made little headway.

I stopped, knowing that fighting against the swarm would be fruitless this close to its epicenter. Dropping to my knees, I closed my eyes. I had essentially no magic left. But it didn't matter. I carried an entire universe within me, something I did not need any magic to access because it was magic itself. Now I focused on it.

Down that magical web I moved, seeking out Clades Solem. Every Infernarus had their own unique essence, and I knew exactly what each was made of. I moved past legions of other Infernari, catching bits and pieces of who they were. One that reminded me of the smell of the earth and rain, another whose soul felt like the tide rushing over you. I passed Azazel's—his was like the breath of scorching, desert air—until finally, finally I found Clades.

I was so far in myself, I could no longer feel the pelt of hundreds of insects, nor hear the roar of their wings.

This deep within myself, nothing terrible could touch me.

I spent a moment immersing myself in the cyclone of this Infernarus's essence. Beneath his stormy exterior, Clades' spirit was warm sand and flapping hides and snapping hearth fire. Comforting. Familiar.

Clades, I spoke to his spirit, *brother, stop this.*

This was no direct connection, and I was no mind whisperer. I couldn't be sure he had heard, as my words would resonate within the deepest, most unconscious part of him. But we Infernari were intuitive creatures. I could only hope.

I spent a moment longer with that essence of his, and then I withdrew, moving back up the connection. Up and outwards until I released the world inside myself.

I inhaled and exhaled, then opened my eyes.

The swarm still surrounded me completely, but now they parted like a stream around my body.

As I watched, the air cleared.

From it, Clades stepped forward.

NOT ALL INFERNARI appeared like humans did. Clades was one such example.

When he stepped into the clearing, I saw his hooves first. Coarse fur covered his calves. His legs tapered from animal to man above the knee, though the tan skin of his thighs were mostly covered by the loincloth he wore. He'd come from the tribes of the far south and kept the customs of his lost people.

His chest and arms were all human, but his blood-red eyes had horizontal pupils, and his nose was more stag than man—and the bull's horns that spread out from his head . . . well, those were all beast.

Necklaces of bones jangled against his chest as he stepped forward. More bones decorated his wrists and ankles, as well as the leather throng that tied his loincloth around his waist. Strapped around his body were two holstered sabers. I'd seen firsthand just how quickly he could draw those two blades. How ruthless he was to his enemies, how loyal he was to his comrades.

You see, Clades and I were friends.

"Lana Malesuis," he said, his voice pitched deeper than most Infernari, "you dishonor me with your plea, you who have been marked for death."

I swallowed delicately. Deathmarked.

I stared up at him from where I knelt.

"I don't understand," I said. "Please, as my friend, tell me why the primus has ordered me to die."

Clades came closer. Around us, the swarm still buzzed, enclosing us in our own room of sorts. "You've failed to kill Jame Asher, the one who seeks to destroy our kind, and now you *help* him?"

I felt my nostrils flare. "I was his *prisoner*. And I—I tried to kill him, but . . ." I swallowed. "I couldn't do it." I looked up at Clades, letting him see my shame. "I've never been able to," I whispered.

Clades knew this, that being a healer made killing nearly impossible for me.

The Infernarus stared back at me unflinchingly, and I

couldn't read his expression.

"When Azazel came for Asher," I continued, "I got caught in the crossfire. He saved my life. Now I'm oath-bound to protect him."

Clades came forward, kneeling before me. He placed a warm palm on the side of my face. "He cannot live, Lana. So long as he does, and so long as you protect him, you both will be deathmarked." His gaze was sad. Because he knew the lengths I would go to—the lengths I must go to—to save Asher's life.

I felt my eyes well. "I know," I whispered.

I couldn't kill Clades to defend Asher either. I had already sworn an oath to protect my race. I now found myself in the same situation countless other Infernari had found themselves in. Bound by contradicting oaths. Forced to die with honor. I thought I had avoided this fate entirely by healing rather than fighting.

"What must I do, brother?" I asked.

"You must surrender and step aside. Return to Abyssos on your own. We will spare you then."

"I *can't*," I pleaded. "If I step aside, you'll kill him, Azazel will kill him . . . I'm supposed to protect him."

"Then *he* must surrender," Clades said. "He must kneel before us and pledge his loyalty to our kind. That's the only way he lives. He's a predator. One way or another, he has to be defanged."

I nodded, my throat dry. I had pieced together as much myself. "I'll get him to surrender," I said firmly, my voice much surer than I felt. "Just give me some time . . . time to convince him."

Clades studied me, his eyes grieving like he had already lost me. "He cannot be changed, Lana. If we give him time, he will only kill more Infernari, he will destroy more portals, he will destroy *you*." Hand still resting on my cheek, the bringer of blight lowered his voice. "But you are dear to me. I won't let this hunter be the death of you. There *are* ways."

The back of my neck prickled. Ways that involved side-stepping oaths and a formal plea for mercy.

What he was proposing, if I understood him correctly, was dishonorable. It was so very *human*.

I eyed him suspiciously. "Clades . . ."

The Infernarus dropped his palm and stood. He grabbed the hilts of his two sabers and unsheathed them, his expression grim. "I will make this as painless as possible. When you wake, we will be back."

I *had* understood him correctly. He was going to incapacitate me. And while I was unconscious, he would execute Asher.

I rose to my feet, my hair beginning to snap around me. "Brother, *no*."

"The primus dominus will spare you when he hears your story." Clades began stalking toward me then.

"Don't make me fight you," I said softly. "I won't let you kill him."

Clades raised his sabers.

The gun blast took me by surprise.

The sound shattered the silence, and I screamed as the tan skin of Clades' torso exploded open like overripe fruit.

Asher stepped through the rapidly thinning swarm of

bugs, his gun smoking. "Like I said before, demons are going to keep dying unless they learn."

I could only spare a moment to stare at Asher in horror before I lunged for my friend, falling to my knees. I pulled his upper body onto me and cradled his head in my arms.

I could hear his wheezy breaths.

"Take the blood, Lana," Clades breathed, his body twitching in pain.

Blood for magic.

I needed it. Desperately so. I could use it to heal him.

"It'll curse you," I argued weakly.

"Take it," he repeated.

I could sense Asher approaching, gun still raised, the end of it trained on Clades. I ignored him long enough to move my hand over the Infernarus's stomach. He winced as his blood began to sizzle on his skin, going up into luminous flames that flickered in every shade of the spectrum. My veins filled with the magic. I sighed as I felt it collect within me.

And then, pressing my hand to Clades' stomach and murmuring in the old tongue, I began to heal him.

Asher stepped up to us.

"Move aside, Lana," he commanded.

My spine stiffened. I shook my head, continuing to chant.

"Last time, Lana—move."

I heard a click, the sound of metal rubbing against metal.

"No." I spread my body over Clades. I couldn't let Asher die, but I couldn't let my people die either. "If you're going to kill him," I said, "you'll have to kill us both."

Asher grabbed my upper arm and yanked me up enough to aim. I made a desperate attempt to dive back down, but the hunter had been prepared for that. The second deafening shot hit Clades in the heart.

And now I fought like a mad woman.

Squaring his jaw, Asher began to drag me back to the car, even as I scratched up his arms and kicked at his ankles, feral in my attempt to get back to Clades.

He tossed me into the driver's seat, then followed me in, trapping my body beneath his.

He cranked the engine on.

Mother above, we were *leaving*.

I made a pained attempt to squeeze my body out from under his.

He laid on the gas and the tires squealed as the car shot forward.

I let out a cry, bucking beneath him. I managed to get part of my leg out.

"Goddamnit, Lana, stop fighting me!"

"I need to save him!"

"He's just going to kill you!" Asher yelled at me.

"He's my friend!" I shouted back at him. I could feel the hot burn of tears in my eyes. I fought the urge to hiss at him.

With a cry, I managed to finally extricate my body from under his.

I crawled over to the front passenger seat, pressing my face to the window. I couldn't see Clades.

Damn these metal machines!

A whine moved up and out of my throat, and the hand of mine that was plastered against the glass now curled into a fist. I fell back into my seat, closing my eyes. I would just have to heal him at a distance.

"If you heal him, he'll only try to kill us again," Asher's annoying voice filtered in.

I was breathing heavy. "I cannot *not* heal him," I snapped.

"Try."

I opened my eyes. "You want me to go against everything that I am. Jame Asher, you are *mad.*"

"Listen to me, Lana," he said slowly, carefully. "I know you can heal from a distance. I am asking you to give us long enough to get away before you do that."

"You're not *asking* me anything, Asher. That is a plea, and pleas are for the weak."

"It's not a fucking plea," he said. "I'm giving you a choice. You can either wait to use your magic, or I can knock you out and we wait for as long as I deem appropriate."

"You savage," I spat.

He had the nerve to smile for a split-second before it evaporated back into the scowl he usually wore. "I don't want to knock you out, Lana."

I glared at him.

"Will you wait?" he asked.

"It depends on how long you want me to wait."

"Three hours."

An eternity.

It bothered me.

Lana had warned me of that cicada swarm . . . *why?*

She was my hostage. It would have been her perfect chance to escape.

No, she had given her word she wouldn't try to escape.

Again, why? Why would she make a deal like that?

Here I was, threatening to end her kind, and still she *helped* me.

Plus I could have sworn that demon back there had drawn his sabers like he'd been about to execute her.

Something wasn't adding up.

As I mulled it over, we drove west on Interstate 40 across Tennessee and into Alabama. My goal was to make it to Texas by tonight. We'd reach the Mexican border tomorrow.

I'd chosen the route that would take us via Interstate 10 right past New Orleans, another potential demon hotspot, in case we came up with any leads along the way. Since we'd gotten dick so far, I wasn't hopeful. Damn me, I should have steered clear of that haunted city. I was probably driving right into an ambush.

We'd get there late this afternoon, and I was starting to get nervous.

Hemmed in by thick trees on either side, the uninterrupted highway stretched out under a blue sky dotted with puffy white clouds. It had that eerie still feeling, like the calm before a storm. It had me on guard.

What wasn't Lana telling me?

We drove in silence for a while before I finally brought it up.

"I think it's time we talked about your . . . *status* among demons," I said. "That's the second time a demon's attacked me without regard for your life . . . and the second time you've chosen to escape with me rather than be rescued. I'm noticing a pattern here."

"First of all," Lana said sullenly, "they didn't come to rescue me—"

"Clearly."

"—they came only to kill you. And I didn't *choose* to escape with you the first time. I was unconscious, and you came back for me."

I peered sideways at her, but she wasn't meeting my gaze. "And?"

"So I didn't have a choice. I'm your prisoner."

"At the gas station yesterday, you chose to stay with me."

"I need to get to the portal so I can go home, and you're the only way I'm going to get there. We made a deal, remember?"

I studied her, a nervous tic in her cheek betraying that she was lying.

"Nuh-uh," I said. "I don't buy it. Smart thing to do would have been to let them kill me, then go back with them. Cut and run. You have no loyalty to me. But you *warned* me of that fucker's attack—that bringer of blight or whatever."

"Clades," she said, her voice barely a whisper. She peeled up one sleeve of her jumpsuit and scratched absently at the inside of her arm.

"If you hadn't," I continued, "I might be dead. Both of us, in fact. Sure looked like he was about to kill you, too."

Her eyes were anguished. "He wouldn't have killed me, but . . . in my world, warriors don't have much regard for life," she said softly. "It's not their fault. And I'm . . . behaving badly as an Infernarus right now."

She continued to scrape her fingernail back and forth along her arm, back and forth.

I raised an eyebrow. "I thought Dominus wanted you back?" I said.

"He does. He did. I don't know." She shook her head. "I mean, he does . . . but you're even more important. Dead."

"Maybe," I mused, rubbing my jaw. My valuable prisoner was starting to seem not quite so valuable. "Or maybe, they never gave a shit about you in the first place."

She stiffened at my words.

"Lana, what is this about?"

Her lower lip trembled, then all at once, her expression crumpled. She buried her face in her hands. "I betrayed them," she moaned. "When I couldn't kill you, I betrayed them. Now they see me as a betrayer."

Ah.

"So make it right. Step aside so they can kill me."

"I can't," she grumbled into her palms. "When you saved my life, you bound our fates . . . I'm now honor-bound to protect you."

I frowned. "So whatever, just break it."

"Break my *oath?*" She stared at me in disbelief. "I'm an

Infernarus. I can't."

"Hmm." I nodded grimly, not liking where this was going.

"And an Infernarus who's honor-bound to protect a human—and *you*, of all humans—I'm already dead to them, and I'm only going to keep betraying them to save you, because I have no choice. That's why they don't care if they kill me along with you. In fact, now they're *trying* to."

"You do realize I'm trying to annihilate your species?" I said.

"Yes, and I hate you for it. And I wish you would die. And you *will* answer for your crimes. But not with death."

"Ah, so you're going to bring me back to Abyssos with you, and there they will torture and imprison me, but as long as I don't die, you've fulfilled your oath and protected your kind."

She pressed her lips together.

I'd just guessed her plan.

"It doesn't matter to you that I would kill you in a heartbeat?"

"Unlike you, Asher, I am honorable. And you wouldn't. You *didn't*."

I would, but I didn't press the point.

Suddenly, I felt bad for her.

She was hated by all humans, and now she was being hunted by demons . . . and here she was, sworn to protect the very man who'd gotten her into this shit in the first place, who *also* wanted to kill her. We made an unlikely team. But a team nonetheless.

Anyone who was universally hated by demons, I would

stand by.

The enemy of my enemy is my friend.

I glanced over to see her still scratching at the veins on her wrist, a motion she had done so much she had left red welts.

A nervous habit of hers.

"Stop that," I said, pulling her hand away.

She flinched, only then realizing what she'd been doing, and tugged her sleeves back down.

"You demons have some twisted notions about honor," I muttered.

She pulled her legs up onto the seat and hugged her knees. "Why do you think we had such a brutal civil war? The delicate web of loyalties and blood oaths became so twisted it finally collapsed under its own weight. Infernari were sworn to protect enemies, they had no choice but to betray their own families, their own mothers and fathers, their children. Brothers slayed brothers to repay debts. Mates were bound by oath to slaughter each other, and many chose instead to die in each other's arms. The war shattered our kind, it broke us, and we've been ghosts ever sense." She pressed her face to the window. "And now I am sworn to protect Jame Asher, the one who will slay my gods and carve out my own heart . . . so my treachery is the most terrible of all."

I gripped the steering wheel tighter, working my jaw back and forth as I sucked in a strained breath through my nostrils. Next to me, Lana radiated sadness. Her body seemed to deflate while her hair wept a melancholy green. Such a pitiful, dejected creature.

Sworn to protect me.

I didn't know how to feel about that. For most of my life, demons had wanted to kill me. But a demon who wanted to *save* me?

I should dump her. Get rid of her. She was everything I *didn't* want to associate with demons—beautiful, helpless, innocent, protective.

I needed to hate her, not pity her. Not feel for her. Not care about her.

Or else I would begin to doubt. I would begin to stumble, when I needed to be surefooted. I would hesitate, when I needed to be focused. I would waver, when I needed to be lethal.

Doubt would only make it harder when I finally did it.

When I finally killed her.

I pushed the thought from my mind.

Absently, Lana rolled up her sleeve again and picked at the vein in the crook of her elbow, right where the skin was softest, where a heroin addict would shoot up. The sight made me oddly dismayed. As I watched her scratching, picking, her movements twitchy and compulsive, a lump settled in my throat. She was itching to draw blood.

I seized her wrist, startling her again.

"Stop it. Stop doing that to yourself."

"I'm just scratching," she muttered, folding her arms tightly across her chest.

"So if I save a demon's life," I said, steering our conversation away from emotional territory, "they're honor-bound to protect me? So what if I just saved a bunch of demons as a strategy? Then they can't kill me, right?"

She gave me an unamused look. "An Infernarus *always* knows when your heart is true. Plus, Infernari's lives are rarely in danger. It's *you* they need saving from. Therefore you're proposing to both kill *and* save them, which is the most two-faced and dishonorable of treacheries . . . you *human.*"

"Fair point." I nodded slowly, chewing on my lip. "So when I saved you—yesterday, I mean—my heart was . . . you're saying my heart was . . . ?"

"Yes," she said miserably, "your heart was true."

CHAPTER 11

Lana

Saving the hunter didn't sit well with me. It made my hair snap irately. It wasn't that I regretted protecting his life from my own kind.

It was that I *didn't.*

And now we were driving Mother knew where, and I could practically feel the other Infernari breathing at my back.

The hunter has become the hunted.

My legs began to jiggle, and again I began to pick at the veins in my wrist, anxiously, before I remembered Asher and caught myself. I dropped my hands in my lap.

His eyes cut to me, his brooding look only deepening.

He missed nothing, that human.

Strange, cold creature. He could be cut from ice, he sat so still.

And now I needed to make a decision. A decision I didn't want to make. It wasn't in my nature to weigh cause and effect carefully. Just one more thing that I'd picked up from the natives.

My eyes fixated on the panel of buttons set into Asher's car. On a whim I began pressing them, just to keep my hands and mind busy.

One made air blast from the vents in front of me, another caused the electronic display to flicker *LOAD*.

"Stop that," he said, swatting my hand away.

I dropped my hand, eyeing the row of buttons as my unease grew.

What to do, what to do.

"You're new here, so I'll let you know: you're never to touch a man's—"

I leaned forward and began pressing the buttons again.

Suddenly, the sound of screaming music began to blare at me from all sides, accompanied by loud clashing sounds. I let out a yelp of surprise and clutched my ears.

Asher gave me an irritated look, but I noticed the corner of his mouth turned up as he pressed another button and clicked the sound off. "You've never heard of a radio?"

"I've heard *of* it. I've just never heard *it*." I looked at the buttons with distaste. "That was human music?" Carnage sounded sweeter than that.

"A type of music. Heavy metal."

"*Heavy . . . metal?*" I repeated, not understanding the

name at all.

Asher drew in a breath, like he was about to explain, then released it. "Never mind."

I returned to picking skin around my nails, my eyes finding that photo he had taped to the dartboard.

I was avoiding the topic I needed to broach.

Just say it already.

I swallowed. I didn't have the kind of magic to snatch back words. Once I spoke them, I was committing to this path.

There are no others left for me.

I drew in a deep breath. "I can find your portal for you."

Asher slammed on the brakes, tires squealing as the car skidded to a halt. Dust kicked up around us, swirling over the car as he maneuvered it to the side of the road.

"How?"

"I will only find your portal for you if you come with me to the other side."

He reared back at that. "I'm not going to let you take me to hell."

"*Abyssos*," I clarified. "You hate us so much, but perhaps you wouldn't if you saw what our world looked like."

Asher looked as though I asked him eat something distasteful. "No way you're dragging me to that shithole."

"You kill us because you don't understand us."

"I kill you because you kill *us*." For the merest of moments his eyes flicked to the photo taped on the dartboard. A sick sensation coiled in the pit of my stomach.

I didn't think I wanted to know this man's tragedies.

But I could leverage them.

"Asher, I've lost just about everyone that's ever mattered to me . . . *everyone*. Surely you can understand." I let my gaze move to the picture.

He gave me a hard, hard look. "Don't. Go. There."

So brutal. And protective. I should be annoyed, but all I could think about was how these were traits Infernari were known for. Traits they wore proudly.

He sighed out a breath. "Look, it's not an option. The moment I cross over, you'd all gut me."

I shook my head. "Infernari would respect our oath."

"Lana," and now Asher looked at me pityingly, "don't be naïve."

"You know nothing of my world," I said heatedly.

"I've met enough demons."

"They are not everyone!"

Asher exhaled, running a hand through his hair. "So they wouldn't kill me. They'd simply torture and imprison me."

"I am the heir apparent. Beloved of the primus dominus. They wouldn't dare go against my wishes." At least, I hoped. Considering they'd seemed just fine with killing me, I wasn't so sure.

"And what would your wishes be?"

"You have done horrible things," I said, looking him dead in the eyes. "But so has every Infernarus I know of, save a few." Most Infernari were killers by the age of twelve. "I don't want more death and pain. I want you to see my world, I want you to *understand* . . . if you could just see my world . . ."

He held my gaze for a long time. Just when I thought he'd laugh the idea off, he said solemnly, "Okay."

"I need you to vow it," I said.

"I vow that in return for locating the portal, I will go through it with you and see what's happened to your world." *Before I destroy it.*

I might not be a clever human, but I heard the hunter's unspoken words clear as day.

"A blood oath," I said. "Before I tell you anything further, I want your blood."

"You're not getting a damn drop my blood, demon."

My lips curled back, and it was all I could do to refrain from hissing at him. I was giving him his precious portal.

"Then you will get no information from me, you human swine."

Asher raised an eyebrow. "'Human swine'? That's the best you got, Lanie?"

"My name is not *Lanie*. It's not *demon* either."

"Pretty hypocritical of you to get angry at the names I call you right after *you* insult *me*."

I stared at him, remembering all over again who this man was. "Your lying human words mean nothing to me, Jame Asher. I want your blood so that if you go back on your word like you have in the past, I can curse you."

Asher grimaced, like I embodied everything he found wrong in the world.

We stared each other down, at an impasse. Time drew out, and still I wouldn't look away.

"Blood oath or nothing," I bit out.

Finally, Asher cursed, breaking eye contact to stare

out the window. His leg began to jiggle. He ran a hand through his hair, ruffling it. My gaze unwillingly drank the sight up.

"And you know where the portal is?" he asked, those stormy eyes of his returning to me.

"Not yet." He had an instant to look incensed before I continued. "But I know someone who can lift the memory spell."

He huffed a laugh. "You know someone who can lift the spell," he repeated. "That's cute, but Lana, whoever this demon is, they won't help you, not after what you did back there." He jerked his head toward the way we came, toward where Clades had fallen.

I swallowed down something thick at the Infernarus I left behind. My friend.

War has made both him and you do worse.

"She is not an Infernarus," I said. "Not *exactly*."

Asher raised his eyebrows. "What's that supposed to mean?"

"She is half Infernarus, half human."

It took the hunter a second to react. His nostrils flared. "That ... can happen?" He looked repulsed by the notion.

"Yes," I said, trying not to be offended. The Infernari I lived with found the idea almost equally disturbing. But other clans believed it natural, especially now that our numbers had been decimated.

"She's not bound by the same oaths that we are," I added. "And she does not carry the same grudges we do."

Asher stewed . . . and stewed.

He eyed me. "If this *friend* of yours doesn't deliver on

her end, I want my blood back."

"Agreed."

He lightly thumped the wheel with his palm as he deliberated, that strong jaw clenching and unclenching. He knew my own word was as good as law.

Eventually, muttering to himself, he turned off the car and threw his door open. I tensed, not knowing what he was doing. A moment later he opened the door behind his driver's seat. Leaning in, he began to rummage through a black canvas bag. I heard a clinking sound, and then he was zipping up the bag and returning to his seat.

Gruffly, he handed me a wicked-looking hunting knife and a small glass vial. "Get it over with before I change my mind."

I stared down at the items in shock. A large part of me hadn't believed he would go for this.

I didn't want to think too hard about why a man like Asher carried around small, empty vials. It seemed to me more malicious than the knife.

And the knife, oh, the knife. I wanted to run my fingers along the sharp edge until I felt the bite of pain and the burn of magic in my veins.

"Your arm," I said, setting the vial aside for the moment.

Grimacing, he laid his forearm over the center console.

I grasped his wrist. He jolted at the touch, then before my eyes the straining muscles of his forearm relaxed.

A forbidden warmth spread through my stomach when I saw our skin pressed together. I hadn't touched a human man like this.

I traced Asher's veins with my fingers. They stood out starkly against his tan skin, the thick, corded bans of muscle in his arms pressing them close to the surface.

"Faster, Lana," he said, impatience lacing his voice.

"The location of the cut is important," I said.

"Important for what?"

Potency. But I didn't dare tell him that. Humans had choice cuts of meat. Infernari had choice cuts of blood. Of course, we rarely got to be picky these days.

My fingers stopped at a location where Asher's veins made a diamond shape.

Here.

My hair was beginning to lift.

I began to murmur, thanking the Mother in the Old Tongue for the lifeblood as I pressed the edge of the hunting knife to Asher's skin, the contact so light it raised his gooseflesh.

My eyes rose to Asher's and there they stayed locked. His deep brown eyes bore down on me, his striking face unhappy. I could've sworn I saw fear at the back of his gaze.

With a swift flick of my wrist, I slashed the knife across his flesh. The vial was in my hand before the first bead of blood trickled down his forearm. Asher's mouth was a hard tight line as I touched the glass to his skin and collected the liquid.

I captured almost all of the blood in the vial, then corked it.

Asher ripped off the sleeve of his shirt and used it to staunch the blood flow. Taking the knife from me, he wiped it too off on the material.

I watched him, the urge to burn off the blood and convert it to magic riding me hard. Instead I focused on the vial of it in my hand. I held the container up to the light streaming in through the window.

"Don't lose that," Asher warned.

When this was the only thing holding Asher to his word? "I won't."

Twenty minutes later the vial dangled from a necklace I'd fashioned from some of Asher's rope. I couldn't stop touching it.

"Can you stop looking so fucking gleeful about having my blood around your neck?" Asher said from next to me.

I shook my head, a small smile tugging at my lips.

He had agreed to cross over.

The deadliest, most wanted native had agreed to cross over. And I, an Infernarus, had *convinced* him. I was so proud of myself.

And of him. I peered over at Asher through the locks of my hair. He'd agreed to see Abyssos, despite his hatred. He let me collect his blood as collateral. Neither of these things came naturally to this hardened human.

"So who's this broad we're meeting with?" he asked.

My hand wrapped around the vial. "Gandmaddox. She lives in . . . Nola?" I wasn't sure if I was saying that right. I rattled off the address I'd long since memorized.

"New Orleans?" Asher huffed a laugh. "Hah, I knew there'd be demons there."

IN THE HEART of the French Quarter—a block from Bourbon Street—Grandmaddox's house sprouted like a weed out of a too-small lot wedged between hotels. Top-heavy with ivy-covered iron balconies, the four-story brick Creole townhouse sagged like a Jenga tower. It had already begun to topple, in fact, leaning precariously against the neighboring hotel.

Painted monkey skeletons hung in the dusty, first-floor windows, alongside jars of pickled eyeballs.

Awesome.

The front door jingled and opened into a smoky tea room advertising psychic readings—the demon moonlighted as a tarot card reader, apparently.

Lana pushed into the empty shop ahead of me, which made up the entire first floor, and I glimpsed the vial of my blood dangling over her sternum. Her collateral.

What the hell had I gotten myself into?

Coming here was a bad idea.

Giving her my blood was a bad idea.

Trusting her was a bad idea.

But why not? A demon's word bound them like a physical law. Lana could no more violate our agreement than she could walk through walls.

Around her neck, my blood was safe.

At least, until *I* violated our agreement. Which I would probably do.

Return with her to Abyssos? Unlikely. I would steal that

vial back before we even had the opportunity to cross. Or maybe I would hop down for a quick peek before I destroyed the portal—I could at least give her that in exchange for its location.

She wanted to show me how the Infernari suffered, she wanted to convince me to spare them.

She could try, but it wouldn't work.

My hatred of demons ran deeper than she could ever imagine.

Behind us, a bleeding orange sun set between the buildings, casting the front of the shop into a fiery glare while leaving the back in shadow. On the wall, a cuckoo clock ticked slower and slower, as if time itself was stretching out. Place gave me the creeps.

"Grandmaddox?" Lana said, venturing deeper. "Grandmother? Are you here?"

All around me, shelves slumped under the weight of bone necklaces, tins of incense, jars of insect carcasses. My nose wrinkled, but as I edged away, my hip bumped a rickety side table, spilling a deck of tarot cards onto the floor and rocking a candelabra. I grabbed it before it fell.

My fingers came away smeared with cobwebs.

"Fuck this place." I muttered, stooping to pick up the deck.

Every card landed facedown, except for one—*The Hanged Man.*

I flipped over another one and got *Death.*

Stupid.

I stood to find Lana had ventured deeper into the shop. "Grandmaddox?" she called.

"She's not here, Lana. Place has been abandoned for years," I said, setting the deck of cards back where I found them.

Between a skull candle and an enormous gecko eyeing me warily, I made out one dusty bottle of Reed's Ginger Beer—the one nod to something a human could consume.

"Grandmother!" Lana called again.

Finally, a figure separated itself from the shadows at the back of the shop, and Grandmaddox shuffled into the light. "My lovely child, come, come . . ." she whispered, "let me touch your skin."

I recoiled.

Lana had filled me in on her details on the drive over, but I still wasn't prepared. Grandmaddox might be half human, half demon, and blind as a bat, but she looked *full* demon to me.

Two cloudy glass eyes stared vacantly from a proud, ancient face. Her long, silver hair was tied back with what looked like a rat's tail. Like a relic from the bygone hippie days, she wore sandals and an airy frock that flowed around her like a waterfall.

Instinctively, my hand went to my gun.

The demon groped around until Lana tackle-hugged her, kissing her on the cheek.

"Grandmaddox, I need a favor," Lana said breathlessly, wasting no time, "I need to find the portal in Central America . . ."

"I know, dear. I know." Grandmaddox patted her cheek. "Why don't we discuss it over some crawfish bisque and jambalaya? And Mr. Asher—" one of her cloudy blue eyes swiveled toward me, "—that won't be necessary."

Slowly, I eased my hand off the holster.

Major affinity: some kind of second sight?

Hmm . . . I'd have to be careful around this one.

At the back of the shop, a rickety wooden staircase led to a cave-like kitchen on the second floor, where several boiling pots had fogged up the windows. Wedged under the staircase leading to the third floor, a tiny dining room table had already been set for three. The house was so narrow, most of each floor was taken up by the crooked staircases.

On the kitchen counter, a tank of live lobsters dripped onto the moldy, peeling linoleum. Not just lobsters. Slithering between their legs was another monster. I peered closer, and felt my lip curl. Some kind of water snake. Poisonous, no doubt.

Then I saw the terrarium next to it.

Giant spiders. Hundreds of them. They crawled over each other, chittering madly. A wolf spider the size of my hand had nudged the lid aside and was squeezing its way out, its legs and feelers probing a saucer of butter that had been left above it.

A smaller tank, half full of murky water, held what looked like wriggling leeches. They, too, had chewed their way through the screen top and were making their escape across a plate of biscuits. Making grandmotherly small talk, Grandmaddox picked them off and brought the biscuits to the table, along with the butter saucer, the wolf spider now clinging to the edge.

Jesus, this woman's house was a liability.

Looking right at home, Lana plopped down at the table and patted the seat next to her for me to sit.

My head bumped the staircase, and three cockroaches fell on the table and promptly skittered under our plates.

The first hint of nausea began to rise in my stomach.

"So . . . why should I restore your memory of the portals?" Grandmaddox said, slopping bisque into our bowls with uncanny accuracy for a blind woman. "That's why you're here, I assume."

I studied the woman, chewing on the inside of my cheek. Add clairvoyance to her list of affinities. As if she sensed me looking, her eyes drifted over me, giving me the willies. Without thinking, I draped my arm across Lana's seatback.

That, too, she noticed.

"My backup portal's in France," said Lana. "But I don't know why they even gave me that one, I've never flown before . . . so I'm stranded."

France, huh?

I made a mental note of it.

The bisque wasn't bad, actually. A bit on the salty side. But when I spooned jambalaya onto my plate, my stomach did another squeeze.

Cooked into the stew alongside andouille sausages were bits and pieces of bugs. Scowling, I freed a shrimp from the clutches of a spiders' legs and bit into it. Except for the funny aftertaste, it tasted okay.

Just needed to wash it down with some wine.

I filled up from the jug on the table and tossed back a mouthful of what tasted like bloody vinegar.

I barely managed to spit it back into the glass without gagging.

"Mmm," I pursed my lips, grimacing as I looked around for something to wash the taste out of my mouth.

"Water's in the pitcher by the sink, dear," said Grandmaddox, reading my mind. "Mind you, the tap's broken."

The pitcher she mentioned contained half a gallon of brownish, foul-smelling swamp bilge, its foamy surface crawling with water bugs.

Fuck that.

I grabbed a cup from a nearby cupboard, dumped out the husks of dead silverfish, and held it under the faucet. The handle thunked and squeaked, but all that came out were flakes of rust.

"Is this a fucking joke?" I said.

"How about you listen next time instead of being a dumbshit," said Grandmaddox. "I told you it was broken."

"Hey, demon," I unholstered my Glock and pointed it at her face, "how many fingers am I holding up?"

Lana jumped between us. "Asher, *no!*"

"He'll be happy to shoot you too, dear," Grandmaddox said calmly.

Lana's eyes pleaded with me. "*Don't,*" she warned. "Just . . . behave. Please."

Reluctantly, I holstered the weapon and returned to my seat, eyeing the woman as I did so.

"Grandmaddox, we need your help finding the portal in Mexico," Lana said, trying to get back on track.

"What makes you think there's a portal in Mexico?"

"Well, Jame thinks—"

"Ah, because *Jame* thinks there's a portal in Mexico," the demon interrupted. "So you're on a first name basis with him, Lana?" The question dripped all kinds of judgment. Those nebulous eyes of hers swung in my direction, judging me too

"So you're half-and-half, huh?" I said. "Who's side you on, then?"

Ignoring me, Grandmaddox stood abruptly. "More bisque, dears?" As she reached for the pot, she bumped the table. One of her glass eyes popped out and splashed into the jambalaya. "Oh, that's embarrassing." She fished it out, hastily wiped it on the tablecloth, and pressed it back into her eye socket.

My fork clanged against my plate. I'd officially lost my appetite.

"So you'll lift my memory spell, right?" Lana said, as if nothing had happened.

"What's wrong with the portal outside White Sulfur Springs?" Grandmaddox asked, her back to us.

"It's, uh . . . well, it's broken."

"Destroyed," the woman said, turning back around, "by the very man sitting at this table, by the *enemy*, whom you have brought into my house. Do you know who he is, Lana? Do you know what he wants?"

"Yes, Grandmaddox," Lana mumbled, poking her jambalaya with her fork. "I'm taking him back to Abyssos to answer for his crimes."

"No, you're taking him back because you're hoping he's changed. Dear, I'm sorry, but he hasn't. He won't."

"He *will*," she said, her eyes heating, "when he sees what's become of our people. He just needs to see that. *Humans* need to see that."

"He needs to die."

Lana glanced sideways at me. "He saved my life," she said, her voice lowering. "I'm honor-bound to protect him."

"I'm not. Want me to do it?" The demon gave me a predatory smile, her stony blue eyes looking right through me.

I tensed up, and my hand went back to my holster.

"No," Lana cried, edging closer as if to protect me. "No one else needs to die. Let me take him back to the primus. We'll . . . we'll let him rot in a dungeon."

The demon chuckled. "Oh, Lana, you were never a good liar. That's not what you want."

"Let me take him back," Lana insisted. "Through the portal in Mexico. Please, Grandmaddox."

Grandmaddox considered this. "Why not let Azazel take him back? Or Clades? They're up for the task, I think . . . unlike you."

"They'd kill him," she said. "Look, at least lift the spell so *I* can get back."

"So he can kill you, and then destroy our portal? You are naïve, child."

That was the second time someone had called her that today.

I noticed Lana's grip tightened on her spoon. "He won't do that," she said. "I swear it."

"*You* swear it? Only he can do that. Mr. Asher, you've

been awfully silent."

"Mmm," I agreed.

"He does. He did." Lana looked at me again. "You *did.*"

As I watched the exchange, saying nothing, I felt itchy in my own skin.

Lana was defending me.

I didn't feel like lying anymore, I didn't feel like betraying her anymore. So I told the truth. "Grandmaddox, I made a deal with Lana to visit Abyssos. She hopes to convince me to have mercy on demonkind. I doubt I will, and I intend to destroy the portal after that. But that's the deal we made."

"See?" Lana said, as if I'd cleared up the matter of my trustworthiness.

"Honey, listen to yourself," Grandmaddox said, shaking her head pityingly. "This man is going to betray you."

"He *won't,*" she said.

"I will," I whispered.

"He saved my life. And his heart was true . . . lift the spell."

"You may stay here for the night," Grandmaddox said, standing. "You're a friend Lana, and I respect your oath. You have my word I will not kill him while he sleeps. But I will not restore your memory so I can watch more Infernari perish."

Down a narrow, creaking hallway on the third floor, our two closet-sized rooms each sported a twin bed. I had to climb over it to open the French doors. We had a connected balcony overlooking Toulouse Street, where glowing bar signs had already begun to draw in patrons like moths.

Seeing Lana leaning out over the wrought iron railings, I went out to join her. Her body looked heavy. Infernari were no good at deception. I'd always believed that it was a weakness, but now, taking in Lana's slumped shoulders, there was something disarming and innocent about it.

"It was a nice try," I said by way of greeting. "But it didn't work. I want my blood back."

"You were no help," she said, her tone biting. Without glancing at me, she lifted the cord from around her neck and held it out.

"What, you didn't think I was charming?" I took the vial from her, wondering how to dispose of it. Safest thing would be to drink it and get it back in my body, make sure no demon could use it against me, but after that dinner, I wasn't interested in tasting any more strange fluids.

I closed my fingers around the container and stuffed it in my pocket. I'd pour it out on the ground somewhere, but nowhere near this house and the hag that dwelled here.

"You refused her hospitality," she said, "you spat out her wine, you wouldn't touch her jambalaya, and you pulled your gun on her. Of course she's not going to help us now. It's your own damn fault."

"Because she's a liar," I said. "If that woman is blind, then I'm Helen Keller."

She groaned into her hands. "You were a *monster*."

"No, the monster was in her fish tank. That thing was *eight feet* long, in case you didn't notice. The hell's she doing with that thing?"

She looked at me funny. "You mean *Genevieve?* Her water snake?"

Drunken laughter drifted up from below.

"Jesus, I'm not even going to ask." I patted my pocket before turning back to my room. "Get some sleep. We're back on the road at dawn."

But Lana didn't budge.

She was watching the steady progression of people below us migrating to Bourbon Street with intense interest. "Is there a festival going on right now?" she said.

"No, it's just New Orleans. This is typical." I pointed down to the intersection lined with bars and clubs, which looked to be in full swing. "Every night, that whole street turns into one giant block party."

She continued to stare wistfully, the flashing neon signs reflected in her violet eyes.

I could see where this was going, and I didn't like it. "No, Lana," I said firmly.

"No what? I haven't even spoken yet." She leaned out over the balcony railing to get a better glimpse of Bourbon Street, and the warm breeze swished her long hair.

Yep, just like I'd thought. Distracted by the pretty lights, like any twenty-three-year-old demon. "No to whatever you're going to suggest. So don't bother."

Her eyes took on a mischievous twinkle. "Darn, I was going to say that we should stay here and be bored all night, but I guess if the answer's no, then we *have* to go out." She gave a fake sigh. "If you say so."

"That's cute," I said. "You ready to act your age?"

She squinted toward the hubbub and slowly read off, "*Bourbon Street* . . . so that's where everyone's going?"

I followed her gaze to a distant street sign, which I couldn't make out. Her keen eyesight put mine to shame. "Trust me, it's really boring. You wouldn't like it."

"Well, I don't like it up here with you, either," she bit out.

Ouch.

"Are you *four?*" I said. "Finished with your tantrum yet?"

"Gods, what is it with you and my age?" She stared imploringly at the sky. "You keep talking about how young I'm acting, like I'm breaking a law or something. How about you act how you want to act—like an old, clucking nursemaid—and I'll act how I want to act. Then everyone's happy."

"Gawk all you want, Lana. From right here. But you're *not* going down there."

Her eyes narrowed. "Why are you so worried about me anyway?"

I laughed. "Oh, you think it's *you* I'm worried about. No, I'm worried about *them.*" I thrust my finger down at the oblivious tourists. "I'm worried about what happens when a bloodthirsty demon is set loose on the streets of New Orleans. *That's* what I'm worried about."

She flashed me a scathing look. "Ugh, I'm not going to *eat* them."

"No, you'll do worse. You'll cut them open and drain their blood, you'll heal as many demons as you can, and you'll curse every living soul in this city . . . starting with me."

She gave me a petulant look. "Then come and babysit me if you're so scared. And if I bite someone, you can burn me to ash like you've sworn to do so many times . . . you deceitful liar."

"Lana . . ." I warned.

She stepped up into my space. "Or will you always break your oaths when it comes to killing me?"

I stared at her, the only sign of my turmoil the air hissing from my nostrils.

Below us, a swaggering group of drunk guys caught sight of Lana and started hollering, "Show us your tits!"

"See, not a good place to be." I turned back to my room. "Me? I'm going to sleep."

Lana, if anything, only looked more fascinated.

The moment I returned to my room, her bedroom door banged open and her footsteps stormed down the hall.

"Damnit." I slumped against the wall, utterly exhausted by her.

She was going out no matter what I said. And why shouldn't we go out? Enjoy ourselves for once? I certainly needed a real meal after that dinner. Hell, maybe I could even get her sloshed and wheedle some more information out of her. Could be fun.

It would beat wiling away the evening in Grandmaddox's house of hell.

Fine, Lana, you win.

"I'm getting too old for this shit," I muttered, pushing into the hallway and charging after her.

I caught up with her on the curb and steered her toward Bourbon Street. "You want to see a human shit show? Let's go see a human shit show."

CHAPTER 12

Lana

Holy Mother of Gods, this *place*.

Asher was right, people swarmed the streets. And there were so many of them! It was so unlike Abyssos. So unlike everything I had known.

And the way people dressed . . . I'd once read that long ago our royal court had harlequins—people with painted faces and ridiculous attire who were brought in to entertain the old rulers and their nobles—but mortal memory of those days had long since been wiped away. But I would imagine that if they still existed, they would look something like these people.

Only, with more clothes.

I glanced over at Asher, wondering what he thought

of the crowd. But, as usual, his face was closed off, his expression grim. The man could stand to have some fun.

Everything seemed to glitter in bright, luminescent colors. The lights, the beads, the clothes and makeup people wore. It was all so reminiscent of my magic. Here, humans seemed to revel in it.

People staggered and wove through the streets, and the air was heavy with the scents of sweat, human sickness, and strong spirits.

It was terrible, terrible and wonderful, all of it so contradictory.

Bright purple and green lights hung over the outdoor seating area of the building ahead of us, a string of skull-shaped lights draped in the doorway. The sound of raucous laughter drifted out from inside.

Without thinking, I grabbed Asher's hand, pulling him behind me as I headed toward the store—*restaurant*, I corrected.

For a moment, the hand beneath my own was stiff, unyielding. And then his fingers curled around mine, his hold tightening.

I expected some resistance or, at the very least, a smart remark. But he was uncharacteristically quiet, and he let me pull him along, into the restaurant.

Here the smell of alcohol was strong, as was the smell of cloistered bodies. It brought back memories of gatherings in war tents. Of sweat-slick, oiled bodies and the hot summers of Abyssos.

A pang of homesickness hit me, but what I missed wasn't Abyssos. It was this. *Life.*

Releasing Asher's hand, I took several steps forward, my gaze trying to be everywhere at once.

Music played in the restaurant, and it sounded nothing like Asher's radio. I looked for the source of it; it seemed to me another strange sort of magic to hear singing and instrumentals coming from a box rather than a group of people.

But the music itself was only background noise. Everywhere people talked and laughed and clinked glasses together. So many happy faces. I'd forgotten what it was like to always be at ease.

A woman approached both of us, and I stood there, blinking at her as she smiled at me and Asher, her eyes lingering on the hunter much longer than necessary. The sight of it stirred something in me, something low and restless.

"Just two?" she said.

Asher nodded.

"Great." The smile she flashed him was incandescent. I felt my fingers curl at the sight of it. "Right this way." She spun on her heel and began weaving through the restaurant, toward the tables outside.

A hand pressed against my lower back. Startled, I looked over and realized it belonged to Asher. The frightening hunter had initiated the touch.

I stared at him for a beat longer as he began to maneuver us after the waitress. My roiling emotions settled back down. All because that hand on my back.

Everything that Grandmaddox said earlier came bubbling back to the surface. That I was too soft, too naïve.

I was just tired. Tired of everyone assuming the worst of each other. Tired of focusing on hate and vendettas and war. I just wanted to enjoy a man's hand on my back and forget for an evening that Asher and I were supposed to be enemies.

I was born with too damn many of them already.

Asher

I ORDERED LANA a rainbow cocktail, which had seven layers of colorful alcohol which glowed under the bar's black light. Predictably, she loved it, and I couldn't help but smile. For myself, whiskey on the rocks.

Wide-eyed, Lana watched the parade of passersby on Bourbon Street. They spilled off the curb and into the street, staggering with drinks in hand. Still no flashers yet.

"You don't have places like this in Abyssos?" I said.

"We don't have this many Infernari in Abyssos," she said in awe. "I've never seen so many humans in one place."

"You should see it during Mardi Gras."

The sound of slurping pulled my attention back to Lana, who had drained the drink and was now sucking at the last drops with her straw.

"That's like four shots, you know." I ordered her another one. "Better than Grandmaddox's wine, huh?"

"My own piss is better than Grandmaddox's wine," she slurred, already tipsy.

I smirked, downing the rest of my own glass. "And here

I thought demons didn't have fine palates."

"*Infernari*," she corrected, her eyes flashing dangerously over the rim of her next glass. "Why don't you ever learn? Do you not know how to pronounce it? Say it. I want to hear you say it."

"I'm curious, what'd you think of her jambalaya?" I asked, waving down the bartender for another whiskey.

"Say it, Jame Asher," she commanded, her hair shifting restlessly about her.

Regarding her coldly, I swirled the glass, clinking the ice. "Getting you drunk was a bad idea. God knows you're frustrating enough *sober*."

"I notice this thing you do," she said, now licking the rim of her second empty glass. "It's very human and despicable. When you don't want to answer a question, you say something completely irrelevant."

I tipped up my glass to her. "Good job, you're learning."

"See! You just did it again."

I frowned. "You made a behavioral observation, and I congratulated you," I said, my eyes following a passerby that stared at Lana, dumbstruck by her beauty. His gaze moved to me, and he startled at whatever he saw. I watched him scurry away. "What else do you want?" I continued, returning my attention to her. "You want me to buy you a drink? Here, I'll buy you a drink." I bought her a third rainbow cocktail. "Happy?"

"Very," she said, starting in on it with lustful eyes. Then she stopped. "No, you dodged it again . . . you still haven't said *Infernari*."

"Infernari," I said. "There. I'm not afraid of a word."

"But you are." She smiled wickedly, her long canines looking particularly sharp under the shine of the outdoor lights. "They say a name has power. Now, when you look at me, you'll see an Infernarus, not a demon."

I drained my whiskey and slammed it down, my lips tightening into a pucker. "When I look at Azazel, I see a demon. When I look at Clades, I see a demon. When I look at Grandmaddox, I see a demon. When I look at you . . ." I inhaled sharply through my nostrils, "I don't see a demon, I see something that I don't want to be seeing."

It was the damn whiskey talking.

We lapsed into silence, and I couldn't meet her eye. *Careful, Asher.*

"When I look at you," she said softly, "I don't see a monster."

I frowned down at my empty cup. "I'm not having this conversation with you. Talk about something else."

"Grandmaddox's jambalaya?" she offered.

"Will give me nightmares," I finished, grateful for the change of subject. "I'm serious. Tonight, all I will be dreaming about is centipedes stewing in red Cajun sauce . . . I think some of them were still alive."

"They're basically the same as shrimp and crawfish," she said, "and I saw you eat a shrimp."

"There were spiders too, Lana . . . and cockroaches." I shuddered. That fucking dinner was just *wrong*."

"So? That's not even unique to Infernari. Humans eat spiders and cockroaches, too."

"I seriously doubt that."

"In Cambodia and China. We're not as different as you think."

My nose wrinkled. "Is that what they teach you demons in your geography classes? Which country you can visit to get a good deep-fried cockroach?"

"*Demon* is a derogatory word, you know." The alcohol was making her tongue sharper, and despite her hooded lids, her eyes were piercing when they met mine.

"That's why I use it." This conversation called for more alcohol. I got another refill from the bartender and slipped her a fifty. "Leave the bottle."

"What if humans had killed your family?" Lana asked. "Would you want to exterminate them, too?"

The question caught me off guard. Somehow she'd figured out my sad story. The family that was taken from me by her kind.

I paused, peering down at the ice melting in my whiskey. The alcohol gave me that warm tingly feeling in my stomach, but right now it could go either of two ways.

No, not tonight. Tonight, I wasn't going to mope. God knew I'd drunk myself to sleep plenty of nights before, sobbing over photo albums.

But I *did* want to talk about it.

I wanted *someone* to ask about it. My reasons. My justifications.

"I'm not a bigoted person." I tried to keep my voice even, taking another slow sip. "It's the *nature* of demon magic." I didn't even feel the burn of the whiskey, not now that we'd moved to this topic. "They were cursed because some demon somewhere used their blood for I don't even know what—for all I know, it could have been a fucking parlor trick—and my wife and daughter had to die for that. For no reason." I looked up at her, nodding grimly as I topped off my glass, spilling some on the bar. "It would be different if you cursed us willingly. If it had been Azazel, or Clades, if they had come in and killed them on purpose, then I would get my revenge and be done with it, like you said. But it wasn't on purpose. Their death was a byproduct, a mistake. They died because of the very nature of demons. *That*, I'm not willing to abide."

Now her eyes seemed to have trouble focusing. While she mulled it over, she grabbed the whiskey bottle and filled her own glass. "You think it's not fair?" she asked.

"I *know* it's not fair."

"Do you know what I think isn't fair?" she said. "That there are scarcely a thousand of us left, while there are billions of humans. *Billions*. They're like those cicadas earlier. There's so many that each creature is worth very little. The Infernari are only culling from humans because there's an imbalance." Seeing my unamused expression, she added, "I have nothing against cicadas. But you don't worry about cicadas, do you? You only worry about the rarest creatures . . . creatures you would call *endangered*."

To compare people to cicadas . . .

I wanted to shout at her, but I held back. She didn't understand.

"Try losing the two people you love most in the world," I said, working my jaw, "try doing that, Lana, and tell me every life isn't precious."

She held my gaze. "You think I haven't lost the people closest to me? My father—dead. My mother—dead. My native clan—wiped from existence.

"But it's more than that," she continued. "Being a healer . . . Every time an Infernarus falls, it hurts . . . right here." She pointed at her heart. "I'm connected to all Infernari through their blood; they are *all* family to me, and no, I can't imagine what losing a mate must be like—I haven't been mated yet—but there were years during the civil war where I thought I would die of grief. To me, Infernari are everything; they are precious, they are my soul and blood, and I would die to save them . . . like you would for Nicole and Joy."

I stilled at their names.

She had never spoken their names before. I hadn't even realized she knew them. *I'd* never told her.

Brad must have.

Strange that she remembered when she didn't even remember what the A stood for in USA . . . she remembered the names of my wife and daughter.

That realization sat strangely in my stomach.

"You know," she continued, "your ancestors used to make blood sacrifices to us; they used to worship us. We were gods to them."

She was talking about the Aztecs, the Incans, the Germanic tribes of Old Europe. "Yeah, and those civilizations got wiped out for a reason."

"We also *cared* for them," she said. "We were like shepherds, you were our flock."

"So you were slaughtering us like sheep," I muttered.

"Infernari die if they don't use magic," she said. "For us, it's like breathing."

We were at an impasse.

She was terrified of losing the last of the people she loved. I had already lost mine. But we were the same, too.

"You said you're connected to Infernari through blood? What do you mean?" I asked.

Her hooded eyes took a moment to focus on me, now showing the alcohol. "Their blood flows in my veins, my blood flows in theirs—so when I heal myself, I'm really healing them."

"So that's how you do it at a distance?"

"Uh-huh." She sucked on the rim of her glass.

"You share blood . . . What, always?"

She eyed me. "Only when I want to," she said enigmatically.

"So you're bound to protect me, you're bound to protect your species . . . to *heal* them . . ." I trailed off, unable to look away from her sad eyes, which flickered under the lights like iridescent abalone shells, matching the faint glimmer of her hair. The background murmur of the bar suddenly fell away—leaving just us, just me and this beautiful creature, alone in our own little bubble of grief.

Bound to each other.

"And you want to kill my species," she finished for me, "which means my only hope—"

"Kind of a Catch-22, huh?"

"—is to convince you to change."

I nodded soberly. "I won't."

"Then one of my brothers will kill you. I can't protect

you forever."

I shook off the unsettling moment we'd just had and wrestled the whiskey back from her to refill my glass. "I'm probably going to die, then. I'm too old to change."

She cocked an eyebrow. "You are so many contradictions, Jame Asher."

"Like?"

"You are so meticulous to avoid death, yet so reckless when it comes to life. You're a violent savage to my people, yet fiercely protective of your own. You hate all Infernari . . ." her eyes flicked between mine, ". . . yet you don't hate me."

Her words unnerved me. "Yes, I do."

"Then why did you save me? Why am I not still tied up in the back of your wheeled machine?"

Because you're innocent.

Because you're kindhearted and brave.

Because I might like who you are more than I hate what you are.

"Because it's easier when you cooperate," I said, bristling at her questions. I drained the rest of my glass and slammed it down on the bar, startling the girl on the other side of me. Working the cash register, the bartender eyed me like she regretted giving me that bottle. "Look, you're a good girl, Lana. You might be the *only* good demon out there. If anyone's got a shot at turning me, it's you. Hell, Dominus probably hand-picked you just for me . . . a little doe-eyed fawn to fuck with Jame Asher's head. Whatever . . . I'm drunk." I grabbed the bottle and staggered off the barstool. "Let's get the fuck out of here."

I threw a wad of bills on the counter and, after snatching up the whiskey bottle, I grabbed Lana's hand. I felt her grip tighten around mine as I pulled her out into the crowded street. She wove a little, too, clearly more tipsy than she let on. She better be, considering how much alcohol I'd fed her.

Thanks to Louisiana's open container law, I could walk right down the center of Bourbon Street swigging my bottle of Jack like a sailor. Half the crowd carried Styrofoam "go cups" from the countless lit-up bars and strip clubs lining the street for blocks. Like Disneyland for adults.

The thought triggered a memory. Disneyland on Joy's second birthday.

Instantly, my mood soured.

I washed it down with another swig from the bottle. No one even gave me a second glance.

But oh, they gave Lana second glances. Plenty of them.

Sashaying next to me in her skintight jumpsuit, her eyes a luminous blue-violet and her long hair breezing unnaturally behind her, she had the attention of every guy on Bourbon Street. A whole crowd of douchebags parted around us, eyeing her up and down and whistling.

Their catcalls grated my nerves. But unlike the guy I glared at earlier, they were too drunk to heed my stare telling them to back the fuck off.

"Let's see some titties!" one of them hollered, dancing in front of her, a dozen necklaces of glittery beads clanking around his neck.

Lana had halted, momentarily mesmerized by the rainbow colors.

"I'll give you my best beads . . ." he continued, "this one right here if you show us your tits . . ." He fumbled to get one off.

Nuh-uh. I was *not* in the mood for this crap.

All night, I'd kept it on lockdown. But seeing this little twerp, seeing his crap plastic beads jingling over his fraternity hoodie, seeing him yelling and shaking his beads in Lana's face, I cracked.

I tried to keep my cool, but I couldn't.

Rage flared under my skin, and my fingers clamped into fists.

I tossed the bottle aside, grabbed the guy by the collar, and shoved him up against a nearby arch. "Mardi Gras's in February," I growled. "So take your beads and get the fuck out of my way."

He shoved me back. "It's *always* Mardi Gras where I go." His breath reeked of beer. "That your girl? 'Cause she was eyeing my beads like she wanted some."

My eyes fell to his clinking jewelry. I lifted up the strands of his cheap plastic beads. "You think a girl like *that*—" I jerked my head toward Lana, "is going to show her tits to a little shit like you for crap beads like this?" I flung them in his face. "You know what, give them to me. All of them. You're done." I pried them over his head and stumbled away with a fistful of plastic necklaces.

Smirking, I turned around, and one of his frat brothers punched me in the face and laid me out on the curb. The blow rang in my ears.

The other douchebags danced away, shouting, "Dude, you beaned him!"

Yep, had to get drunk and pick a fight with six frat boys, huh, Asher?

Not my proudest moment.

Rubbing my jaw, I rose slowly, seeing red. "You shouldn't have done that."

I tackled the guy into a nearby oyster shack, bowling over a table and scattering the screaming patrons. Already cocked back, my fist slammed into his face. His nose sprayed blood. Nice.

I was going to go to jail for this.

For defending Lana.

Fuck.

I landed one more punch before his friend dragged me off, arm clamped around my neck.

Tonight was just not my night.

I got my feet under me and thrust us backward. Through sheer dumb luck, I managed to ram him into the archway, earning a grunt. Bits of plaster flaked off above us. Grabbing his arm, I heaved him over my shoulder and slammed him onto his back, knocking the wind out of him. Wheezing, he raised his palms at my cocked fist, and I backed off.

Breathing heavily, I turned back to the other four and wiped my bloody lip. "Anyone else think it's Mardi Gras?"

They looked drunk enough to attack me, too. Probably thought they could take me six versus one.

"Bro, bro, he's got a gun!" Catching sight of my holster, the guys grabbed their buddies and stumbled backward, tripping on their heels.

I called after them, "Come at me, *bros*! I want some

more beads!"

But they were gone.

Idiots. I wasn't even carrying concealed, and it took them that long to notice.

I looked around at the rest of the onlookers—half the street had paused to watch—and they ducked their heads and continued on their way, like I was going to shoot them or something.

"Humans are weird." Lana frowned, clearly still trying to figure out what had happened. "What was that even about?"

I picked up the beads, and led her away by the elbow. "Told you you'd get into trouble."

"That was *you* who got into trouble," she said. "He was just being nice and trying to give me some beads . . . and can I at least *have* one? Or do I have to beat you up and steal them from you now? Is that how the bead game works?"

Her naivety made me smile. "Stop. Look at me."

We paused on a street corner out of the way, those strangely beautiful eyes of hers fixed on me. God, she was innocent. Something protective reared up in me.

I draped all the beads around her neck. "There. Now they're yours."

The way her eyes lit up, you'd think she'd just learned Santa Claus was real. She ran her fingers reverently over the molded plastic balls, her expression wondrous.

I stared at her, unable to look away, suddenly bewitched by her. Like a moth being pulled toward a flame. Her allure was toxic. And I needed to get away from her before I did something I would regret.

But I didn't edge away. Neither did she.

"Wait," she said, "you won them, you should get some too." She lifted off half the necklaces and stepped in close as she reached up to put them over my own head, so close I could smell her ashy scent, a scent I'd come to hate. A scent I was now reconsidering.

Her fingers brushed my chest, and my pulse spiked before her hand flinched back.

She'd felt it too, whatever that was.

Whatever *this* was.

I felt a tickle on my lip, still bleeding, and her eyes darted to it. I licked it away.

She wanted that blood.

Her gaze lifted shyly to mine. "Was that fight about me, Jame Asher?"

She was calling me out, and I had no answer. I shook my head, my heart thumping at the base of my throat.

"About how he was talking to me?"

And looking at you.

"Nah," I said, running a hand through my hair, "I just didn't like his punk attitude. Wasn't about you."

She knew I was lying, she could read it on my face.

I knew I should break the moment, snap out of it, ignore her and keep walking like I didn't want to be here, but I couldn't budge. In that instant, everything else faded away—the drunks swimming around us like fish, the chaos of Bourbon Street, the rhythm and blues thumping from nearby clubs. Maybe it was the adrenaline still pumping through my veins, maybe it was the odor of sex and desire in the air, maybe it was the way her eyes seemed to glow like blue-violet flames, but all I saw right then was her.

And for the barest of moments, it didn't matter that I'd sworn to kill her kind, or that they were hunting me. All that mattered was that for the first time in a very long time, I felt something beyond grief and anger. Something light and good. And even though a part of me knew it was reckless, knew that I was that idiot moth about to get burned, for once I didn't fucking care.

I cupped the side of Lana's neck and I kissed her.

CHAPTER 13

Lana

ASHER'S LIPS WERE magic. Human magic, but magic nonetheless. They glided over mine, so much softer than I would have imagined. Each stroke of them felt like lightning, like gathering power in my veins.

Jame Asher is kissing me.

Jame Asher is kissing me.

And it feels amazing.

My lips moved against his, my arms draping themselves around his neck. Thank the gods for the alcohol that dulled my mind. Sober, I would've wondered about a whole slew of things, but right now all I could concentrate on was Asher's touch and his taste and the odd things they were doing to me.

My fingers stroked the ends of his hair. I was playing with a man's *hair*! How I'd imagined what this would feel like. How I imagined what being enveloped by a man would feel like.

It felt exquisite.

I savored the blood that still lingered on Asher's lower lip. He bled defending me. Heat roared through my veins at the thought, and it was all I could do not to moan against his mouth.

His hand gripped my neck tighter as he held me close, his other arm going around my waist. Had his arm not anchored me to earth, I would've floated up and away.

This was too much. And yet . . . I leaned deeper into Asher, wanting *more*.

Instead, the kiss came to an end.

Asher pulled away slowly, his eyes lingering on my lips. I felt the heat of his breath against me. Reluctantly, my arms dropped from his neck. His gaze moved up then, meeting mine.

Damn this alcohol, I couldn't figure out what he was thinking while he stared at me. Then, all at once, he startled, blinking as though he were waking from a dream.

He straightened, and the arm that had pressed against my back fell away.

My stomach still felt as though it were made of sunbeams and laughter. A shy grin spread across my face. Was this how mates felt when they found one another? I'd never been kissed, so I wouldn't know.

Asher's eyes returned to my mouth and I saw him swallow. He glanced away, his attention moving above us.

"We should get going—before I start another fight," Asher said.

Another fight on my behalf.

I tried to suppress my smile, but failed. The look he gave me was a bit more troubled.

I should be troubled as well. Falling for the hunter would be bad for so many reasons. It didn't matter, my heart couldn't be reasoned with. Already it was fluttering at the memory of his lips on mine.

I let him take my hand and lead me through the streets; he walked a step ahead of me the whole time. I found it a bit strange—the silence, the distance. I assumed natives talked about these things, but what did I know? Human customs were strange. So I settled instead on drinking in in the sculpted muscles of Asher's back and the tousled hair that I *touched* only minutes ago. My stomach felt like all the cicadas we ran from were now trapped inside it. I let myself smile again, high on the feeling. And I let myself hope for the first time since we met that this might end well.

I glanced at our entwined hands and bit my lower lip.

It might end really, really well.

Asher

BACK IN MY room at Grandmaddox's house, I paced in the tiny space between the bed and the French doors, furious with myself, then spun and kicked the bed frame. The whole house shuddered.

Come on, Asher.

What were you *thinking?*

Kissing her? Are you insane?

I stormed back to the opposite wall, where hideous paintings of ghoulish demons leered down at me . . . judging me.

In that moment, everything had melted away. Me being a human, her being a demon. In that moment, she was just a beautiful girl, and I was a lonely, lonely man.

You idiot.

I'd never felt this way about a demon before. Attraction. Desire. Protectiveness.

How could I justify that when demons had cursed my family? When they fed off us like parasites? When their very existence meant humans must suffer? Demons were a vile pestilence that needed to be eradicated.

Yes, demons.

But not Lana.

In my brain, there was a category for demons like Azazel, Grandmaddox, the portal master. But Lana wasn't in that category. She was in her own category, all by herself. A category for what . . . *innocent demons?* Please. It was an oxymoron. There was no such thing.

If I followed that logic, the portal master should go in that category, too. He wove portals, he didn't kill. In fact, few demons killed willingly now that their civil war was over. It was their blood magic that killed, that cursed, that wreaked misfortune. She might be a healer, but Lana had culled human blood to do it. She had cursed humans unwittingly.

How many wrecked families were her doing? How many widows? How many fatherless children? How many weeping parents?

An innocent demon . . .

Evil wore all kinds of faces, a pretty one the most deadly of all.

But Lana wasn't evil. She couldn't be.

Guilty, but not evil.

But not innocent either.

No, she belonged in her own special category because she was a demon I could forgive.

And there it was. That was the difference. I could forgive her.

Maybe I already had.

The floorboards groaned under my boots. I stopped pacing and dragged my hand back through my hair, glaring down through the rotted gaps where I could see Grandmaddox shuffling about her dark kitchen. My room spun in dizzying circles. The alcohol was turning on me.

I'd been cold to Lana after the kiss. She didn't deserve that.

Kissing her was my fault, my lapse in judgment, and she shouldn't be made to suffer for it. I could at least apologize to her.

I opened the door to the haunted, creaking hallway, hoping to catch her before she went to bed.

Really, I just wanted to see her again.

I LAY SPRAWLED across my bed, my eyes absently trained on the ceiling. I traced my lips with a finger.

Kissed!

I remembered the sensation of being caught up in Asher's arms, his body dwarfing mine. That intense personality of his focused wholly on me.

What would it be like to always get to kiss him? To do more with him?

I felt my already flushed cheeks heat at the thought.

That cold human was not so cold when I was in his arms. The stories had gotten it wrong—Primus Dominus had gotten it wrong.

They are lying, calculating creatures, he'd told me. *Disloyal to their core.*

Asher was loyal to a fault. So loyal that he still avenged his wife and daughter, though their bodies were likely nothing more than bones beneath the earth.

My mind went to his wife and that photo he kept of her. To her lovely, pale hair and her wideset blue eyes.

I got up off the bed and approached an antique mirror propped up in the corner of the room, its silver edges blackened with age.

I frowned at my reflection. I looked nothing like her. Not my violet eyes, not my restless, glowing hair, not the shape of my face.

I closed my eyes, remembering exactly what his wife—what Nicole—looked like. Her face was wider than mine, and her eyes, thinner. She had cleverly arched eyebrows and a small, pert nose. And her smile . . . That alone would have made her beautiful. I pictured it all, and I didn't even think when I drew on just enough of the blood culled from Clades for my face to subtly shift.

When I opened my eyes, my hair had shortened and lightened, my irises now cerulean blue.

I wore Nicole's face, the face of a dead human woman.

And I envied her. I brushed the pads of my fingers over a cheekbone, then over that achingly sweet nose of hers. I smiled, just for the hell of it and felt a pang deep within my chest.

I can't compete with this.

I ran my hands through my hair—her hair—humming a sad melody as I tilted my head from side to side.

I didn't hear the door open, but I did hear the sharp intake of breath.

I swiveled around. And there, standing at the threshold of my room, staring at me like I just fulfilled every one of his deepest desires, was Jame Asher.

CHAPTER 14

Asher

"Nikki?" I whispered.

Staring back at me from the opposite end of the room was Nicole Asher, my wife, her blue eyes lit up in surprise. My stomach plunged into freefall, my heart galloped, I couldn't breathe.

Back from the dead . . . like an angel.

But then I noticed the details. Her blonde hair flowed around her like she was underwater, defying gravity. *Not real . . . she's not real.*

Her blue eyes flickered crimson.

Not human.

My hope died with a sickening crash.

I looked around for Joy, our daughter, who would surely be with her mother.

But my daughter wasn't there.

My daughter was dead, and so was my wife.

There was no one in the room but Lana.

No one but a demon.

Nicole began to change, morphing back into Lana. See-ing it happen, something tugged painfully at my heart.

Deep down, I felt hollow. Emptied of something essen-tial.

"Never . . ." I rasped, my voice shaking, "*never . . .* never do that . . ." My fingers coiled into fists.

She swallowed, her eyes wide. "I didn't do it to hurt you," she whispered, backing up. She banged into the mir-ror behind her, its surface vibrating. "I wanted to see . . . I'm sorry."

I was dying inside at the reminder of what I'd once had—a beautiful wife, a perfect daughter, a blissful fami-ly . . . oh God, I'd had it all—and it was stolen from me. And this demon, she was like rot in the wound, making my grief fester.

"How *dare* you wear her skin," I said, my voice hoarse with anger. With pain.

My wife. My *wife.* Lana wore her face like someone would a coat, and she used her black magic to do it, curs-ing someone else by doing so.

I prowled toward her, my chest rising and falling faster and faster, my breath escaping in furious hisses. I stepped into her space, my body towering over her.

"How *dare* you disgrace her memory, how dare you mock her, how dare you defile her, *demon.*"

Lana's eyes welled with tears.

Letting a demon into your heart . . . it was like swallowing cyanide. I should kill her right here, right now, just as I would any other demon. But even now I couldn't, much to my everlasting shame.

Instead, I spun and punched the wall, putting a hole in the rotting, termite-infested wood. The nearby photo fell, its flimsy frame breaking apart.

I stormed back to my room and slammed the door. All through the house, I heard frames thunk onto the floor.

The last thing I heard, before I roared in agony, was the quiet whimper Lana tried to suppress.

Lana

I COLLAPSED AGAINST the wall, letting my body sink slowly down to the floor. A sad sob slipped out. I covered my mouth, afraid Grandmaddox would hear it.

That *Asher* would hear it.

My tears rolled down my cheeks and onto my hand as my shoulders shook. I bowed my head, my hair lank and listless around me.

What had I been thinking? Wearing her face was torture enough. But then to get caught? And by Asher of all people? If only what I felt right now was simply embarrassment . . . It was so more than that. So much more.

In those first few moments when Asher had caught sight of me, before he realized I was Lana and not his wife—the expression he'd worn was somewhere between hope and rapture.

He'd never looked at me that way. *No one* had ever looked at me that way.

But the way he had looked at me once he realized who and what I was?

Disgust. Horror.

I pinched my eyes shut, two more tears squeezing their way out.

You are an Infernari, one of the last of your people. I comforted myself. *You are strong, and brave, and kind.*

I dropped my hand from my mouth and pressed my forehead to my knees, which I gathered in close to my body.

I wanted to hate Asher for the way he looked at me, the way he made me feel, but I understood. I'd worn the skin of fallen Infernari many, many times, and every once in a while someone recognized my likeness. No one wanted that kind of reminder; it mocked their grief.

It was just that this time my heart had also gotten stepped on.

I didn't know how long I sat there like that. Long enough for my shoulders to stop shaking, my tears to stop falling. Long enough even for the sounds outside to die down just a bit.

I drew in a shaky breath, and pushed myself up to my feet. Heading into the bathroom, I turned on the faucet to wash my face.

The spout gurgled and spat. I almost groaned when I remembered the water here didn't work.

I began to leave, but then my eyes landed on a razor.

It was carelessly lying on the counter amongst dozens of other old knickknacks, the color of its green handle faded with time, a relic from some long forgotten guest.

I was mesmerized by its blade, which was mostly dark orange from age. Without thinking, I reached out and picked the razor up, turning it over and over in my hands.

It wasn't a real weapon, but it could cut all the same. And being in this world, my body depleted of magic for long stretches of time . . . I wanted to cut. To release my blood from my body, savor the sweet pain of it, then cull my magic.

With a swift twist of my wrist, I snapped the handle off. Then I worked my fingers under the edges of the brittle plastic, trying to pry the razorblade out from it. With a pop, the small, flat blade was free.

I stared at it in wonder, then ran my thumb over the rusted edge. It wasn't very sharp, but if I pressed, it could split my skin.

I moved the blade to the crook of my arm just to test the theory. The edge of it pressed into my skin, then I sliced the razorblade across my flesh.

My skin split, and the pain that flared up was instantly overshadowed by the satisfying feel of it burning up into magic. I didn't bother healing the skin, even as I converted the blood. I didn't much care that I was cursing myself.

I pocketed the razor. I would be keeping this. Sometimes—sometimes the urge to blood-let came over me. This little razor, it could control the urge if I turned it on myself when the need got bad. For now I still had a small reservoir of magic, but it wouldn't last forever. Once it was gone, I would need to control the urge to cull because, from my best guess, Asher and I were still a ways from the portal.

The portal . . . through my drunken haze I remembered. The bargain I struck with the hunter, the one that would allow me to fulfill all my oaths, it all rested on Grandmaddox lifting the memory spell.

She would never lift it, she said as much.

But I didn't technically need *her* to lift the spell; I just needed her elixir. And as a potion master, she'd undoubtedly have a bottle of it here in her house.

Those conniving humans had rubbed off on me, I thought as I began moving, heading toward the door to my room. The floorboards beneath me creaked, and I heard wood splinter. It wouldn't surprise me if this house was held together by magic alone.

I stepped into the hall, closing the door softly behind me. At the end of the hall, a narrow staircase continued up the rickety house. I made my way toward it, the ancient wood floors creaking under my boots. Grandmaddox had told me once that she kept her potions up in the attic; now I followed her old words.

I shuddered as I began to ascend the stairs. Back in Abyssos, we never made indoor spaces this narrow. Almost all Infernari needed the elements to be close at hand. The stars above us, the land around us, the earth beneath us. We loved wide open spaces.

The musty smell of decay clung to this place. And that was another thing we were unfamiliar with. Decay. Magic never died, even if bodies did. If an Infernarus's remains were left alone for long enough, the magic trapped beneath their skin would burn through the body, escaping outwards and converting flesh to ash as it did so. I'd seen it happen often enough in the years of the war. I didn't know why Gandmaddox chose to live like this.

I summited the stairs, the attic door in front of me fitted with a half a dozen locks. I knew what I'd find behind it.

I would curse Clades a little more by using my power to break in, and he wouldn't agree with this. Ignoring a pang of guilt, I reached for the door and used a pulse of magic to tumble the locks. The door creaked open, and beyond it . . .

Shelves and shelves of bottled curses and tinctures, hexes and elixirs. Some of them glowed luminous colors, others looked like sludge, and some still moved and pulsed inside their containers.

The rows that weren't taken up by Grandmaddox's concoctions were filled with raw ingredients. Hair, fingers, eyes, teeth, shriveled, desiccated things. The room reeked of death.

Death and power. The hair on my arms rose as I moved deeper inside, my fingers trailing over some of the glass jars, reading the labels. Affection, friendship, lust, infatuation—all spells to evoke feelings in the natives. I remember how scandalized I'd been the first time I heard of them; they were so blatantly deceitful, and Infernari weren't deceitful creatures.

Except when they wore the face of another . . .

I pressed my lips together, my hand dropping away

from the containers.

This room was full of bastardized magic, begotten from Infernari power and human technology. Some of it taboo, which was partly why Grandmaddox lived here rather than Abyssos.

She lives here because she is half human, and the primus hates humans.

I rubbed my temples, my head beginning to pound. That human brew was souring inside me. I was almost tempted to scour the room for something that could nullify the effects of the comedown from the alcohol, just so I wouldn't have to use more magic.

My eyes returned to the racks of potions. Of course, the most important ones Grandmaddox kept locked up in her curio cabinet. It rested at the far end of the room, the bottles within it practically vibrating from the spells they contained.

Retributor. Death curse. Memory suppressor. Forget-Me-Not. *Rememory.*

Gotcha.

I reached inside and grabbed the vial of rememory, the opaque, white liquid sloshing inside. I uncorked the lid and ran it under my nose. I winced as the magic stung my nostrils. Powerful. I would only need a drop or two.

I brought the glass to my lips and tilted it up. Just a sip. That's all I needed.

I didn't mean to swallow a whole mouthful of it, enough to go noticed; I was still blundering from the alcohol.

I almost spat it back out, but that too would go noticed. So I forced myself to swallow the entire mouthful of rememory, cringing against the sickly sweet taste of the tincture.

I could feel the magic slipping down my throat, coating my stomach. Hastily, I corked the vial and put it back into the cabinet, my hands beginning to shake.

A thin sheen of sweat broke out along my skin.

Drank too much.

I backed away from the cabinet, my insides beginning to feel tingly, like the sensation of falling. Out of nowhere, my stomach convulsed. I stifled a gasp at the painful contraction. My stomach convulsed again, this time more powerful than before.

I staggered, then fell to my knees, a hand pressed to my belly, and I moaned softly.

I could feel the magic working, spreading. Slithering into my veins and circulating through my body until the entire thing was abuzz with the spell.

As quickly as it circulated, the magic moved upward, into my head. I moaned again as tendril after tendril snaked up my spinal column. My headache throbbed, each pulse of my heart making the pain flare brighter. I bowed my body until my forehead touched the floor, taking on a prayer's pose.

There was nothing graceful about this magic. Whatever shields blocked my memories of the portals, they'd become embedded in my mind, the same way foliage overtook ruins. And this potion, it ripped away the shields violently.

I forced a fist into my mouth, biting down my own flesh to muffle my screams. My skin split beneath my teeth, and

I tasted the metallic tang of my blood.

One by one the portals presented themselves. One sat at the juncture of two ancient rivers. Another lay in the catacombs beneath a city.

The second to last portal was the one I was looking for.

An enormous mountain rose high above the rest, purple and snowcapped. Near its base it was covered with dense plant life. I could practically feel the thick humidity of the place clinging to my skin. It was so similar to our capital. To home.

At the foot of this mountain were caves. Ancient caves with whispering walls and something that shouldn't belong. A gateway to an entirely different world.

The portal.

This one will take you home.

I opened my eyes, not realizing I'd closed them in the first place. I could sense even from here the tug of the portal, like a lodestone trying to lure me closer. I knew how to get back.

I knew how to get *back*. I let that realization work its way through the pain. Up until this moment a part of me believed I would never make my way home.

My bargain with Asher was back on.

I began to rise, but the grip of the potion hadn't loosened. Another wave of agony washed through me as another shield was ripped away. My mind recalled portals that no longer existed—it recalled and *mourned* for them. Weaving a portal took time. Lots and lots of time. Time and magic. It was almost a living thing itself.

And so many of them had been destroyed.

But it was more than just the portals that resurfaced from my shielded memory. Another lost memory came to me. A horrible memory, one that was both an end and a beginning.

I was falling back, back into it . . .

I ran through the encampment, my battle leathers straining with the movement, my ivory necklaces shivering as the pointed beads rubbed against one another, my hair snapping behind me.

The world around me was on fire. I screamed as the web of lives I held inside me shrank and shrank, soul after soul snuffing out. Death felt worse than I imagined. It felt like I was being unmade piece by piece.

Everywhere bloody, slaughtered bodies lay. Screams and smoke and magic released from the dead—it all filled the air. It was terrible and beautiful, and it was killing me from the inside out.

I sprinted toward where I last saw my mother and father—my blood parents. They'd been in their tent, eating breakfast.

Please don't be in there.

An arrow sliced through my shoulder, and I released an agonized cry.

I ran on, using my magic to force the arrow out of the wound, then using more magic to patch the skin up. There were so many mortally wounded Infernari—there was no need for temperance when it came to spending my powers now.

Then I saw it.

In the distance, through the burning haze, I could

make out the top of my parent's tent. Flames enveloped the faded fabric, letting off great plumes of smoke. Inside I could hear howling shrieks.

Down my web, I felt their life forces pulse, then flicker.

I was young, still unskilled at healing through my connection . . . I needed to see them, touch them for my affinity to work.

I forced my legs faster, even as I took another arrow in the gut. And then I was limping as I shoved magic at the wound, ordering it to purge the weapon and heal the flesh. Then I turned my power on my burning lungs. My hair whipped about me, snapping at the air.

I leaped over fallen bodies. Any other time I would've stopped to heal those that could be saved. But my parents . . .

In the next breath, my mother's life force snuffed out. I shrieked out of anger and pain. Five steps later, my father's joined hers.

Horror—such immense horror. It choked me from the inside out. My lungs heaved but I couldn't catch my breath. I stumbled, falling to one knee.

Far worse than death, this feeling.

I pushed myself up, refusing to listen to the truth inside me. Refusing to accept it.

By the time I reached my parents' tent, a tent I'd so recently moved out of, there was nothing left of them but charred bones.

I collapsed in front of their skeletons, uncaring that the fire burned me. All I wanted was to die with them; I felt like I was dying as the web of souls shrank and shrank.

I crouched in front of their remains, and I could smell my hair smoldering and my flesh cooking.

But my powers wouldn't let me die. Like a parasite, it culled from the fallen soldiers nearest the tent, using the blood magic to continuously regenerate my flesh.

The tent had long since burned away, most of my clothes incinerated along with it, when they found me.

The primus's men.

The rest of the memory was an afterthought. How I was dragged, naked, to the soldiers and the other Infernari. How I was called *slave*. How Clades, when he saw me, cut his pelt in half to fashion it into some sort of covering. His comrades had laughed at him, but he didn't spare them a glance as he roughly covered me.

I didn't even thank him, so lost was I in my grief.

After that, they tested our affinities and sorted us by them. And once they found I shared the primus's, I was handed over to a special unit.

That was the first time I saw Azazael, the flames dancing in his eyes. He burned me on purpose when I was handed over to him. I knew then what a curse it was to love your people even when they didn't deserve it.

And then I was taken to the capitol. There I met the primus. There he spared me when he had no reason to. There I began my life, in earnest, as the primus dominus's healer.

The memory was ten years old.

Someone made me forget it. The details of how the primus and I first met.

Why had that memory been taken from me? What did

it matter how I'd come to be the primus's beloved? War was war.

I opened my eyes, unaware that I'd closed them to begin with. Grandmaddox's rotted floor was stained with my tears.

I could still feel those lost lives in me, the ache so acute. And my parents . . . my parents . . .

They would not wish for me to linger on that memory.

I cleared my throat and wiped the tears away with the back of my hand. The cut I had made on my arm had reopened and started to bleed again. I liked the feeling of the open wound, the way my magic felt raw and exposed.

Enough of this sadness for one night. Enough of the questions that burrowed under my skin the longer I was here.

Rising to my feet, I brushed myself off. The last vestiges of my headache disappeared along with the effects of the spell. I left the potions room quickly, making sure to lock the door behind me.

The stairs creaked as I descended down from the attic. It was only as I stepped off of them and into the hallway that I caught sight of Grandmaddox. She closed the door to Asher's room behind her, her eyes finding mine a moment later.

Her surprised face must've mirrored my own. We each surveyed the other, her milky, sightless eyes moving from me to the staircase at my back. My own gaze bounced between her and the door.

What had she been doing in Asher's room?

I forced my feet to move forward, down the hallway.

We eyed each other warily as I passed her, neither of us sure whether to be suspicious of the other.

I reached my door. "Night," I finally said over my shoulder, brushing off a centipede from the knob. I didn't wait for her to respond before heading inside.

I collapsed on the bed, not bothering to take off my boots before I hastily slipped under the covers. Sleep took me within minutes, and I welcomed it.

I was done with this gods-forsaken day.

Asher

I WOKE UP to a numb tingling on my chest, my bare torso soaked in a cold sweat as my body tried to purge all the alcohol through my pores. The moth-eaten sheets of the twin bed tangled around my limbs. I kicked them off, disgusted with the filth of this house.

And that's when I felt something slimy slither along my rib cage.

I jolted up, breathing faster.

My eyelids blinked against the darkness.

Then I felt it again, as something detached itself from my side and rolled into the sheets. *The hell?*

Panicking, I shuffled backward, propping myself on my elbows.

The city lights fell across my abs and pecs, and I sucked in a sharp breath.

A dozen black worms adhered to my skin.

Leeches.

Oh, *hell* no.

I scrambled out of bed and yanked them off, flinging each one away. I patted down the rest of my body in a panicky flurry, ripping two more off my neck. Then I ran my hands over my skin once more.

Gone. I got them all.

I stared at their wriggling carcasses on the floor, my lungs heaving and my skin crawling.

They wriggled their way from the floor to the base of the wall, inching upward in a single file line, their suckers still dripping with my blood.

Horrified, I watched them vanish one by one into a hole in the wall boards.

Taking my blood to Grandmaddox.

She'd stuck them on me to harvest my blood.

To curse me.

Fuck this house.

I wasn't spending one more second in this nightmare.

Jaw clamped in rage, I swiped my holster off the bureau and dragged on my jeans, tripping in the leg holes. Boots on, I crushed as many leeches as I could, mashing them into a bloody goop. Screw the rest of my stuff. Shirtless and cursing, I raged down the hall and kicked down Lana's door. It exploded in a blast of splinters.

She bolted upright in bed, her hair disheveled.

When she saw me, her eyes widened. "What's going on—?"

By way of answer, I scooped her off the bed and threw her, shrieking, over my shoulder. Securing her by the legs, I kicked out the remaining door shards and strode back into the hall and down the stairs.

"Gods above," she said, "Asher what are you doing?" Her hands pressed into either side of my exposed torso.

"We're leaving," I growled.

"That's obvious enough." Perhaps if I'd been in another mood, a better mood, I would've cracked a smile at a demon saying such a thing.

The halfling took my blood. With leeches, no less. Horror and fury battled for dominance.

I stormed out of that blighted house and burst out onto the cold street, the sky now a ghostly predawn blue.

Lana immediately began to shiver in my arms. But she didn't fight my hold; half of me thought she would after what happened earlier.

Not until we reached my Hummer, parked a block away, did I release my iron grip on her to set her in the passenger seat.

Circling to the driver's side, I hopped in the vehicle and cranked on the engine. Laying on the gas, I peeled out of there.

Back on the road.

Leeches.

I squeezed the steering wheel.

Motherfucking *leeches*.

Next to me, Lana pulled her knees up to her chest and continued shivering. A yawn worked its way through her body, shaking her limbs further.

I ground my teeth together. It would be easy enough to despise her if she acted anything—*anything*—like the bastards I hunted. Even now it was hard to hold onto the fact that she'd worn my wife's face only hours ago.

Working my jaw, I cranked up the heat for her benefit. Reaching behind the seats, I pulled out the wool blanket I kept for emergencies and tossed it at her.

"Th-thank you," she said, her teeth chattering. She wrapped herself up in it. She leaned her head against the window, failing to react to the fact that I dragged her out of her beloved Grandmaddox's house in the middle of the night.

"You smell like blood, Jame Asher," she said, finally breaking the silence. Her eyes had drifted close.

I gripped the wheel with my knees and pulled on a spare T-shirt. Half a dozen bite marks bled into the fabric where the leeches had bitten me.

I tugged at my collar, airing out my inflamed skin. Ooh, it boiled my blood.

What was left of my blood, at least.

Couldn't tell if the dizziness was from a hangover or blood loss. No doubt Grandmaddox had been gathering it to curse me, and she'd gotten more than enough. My middle name might as well be *Fucked*.

"You led me right into the lion's den," I said, barely controlling my rage. "Right into a goddamn witchhouse."

"Which part are you mad about now, Jame?" Lana said, folding her arms tightly over the blanket. "You kissing me, or me wanting to be Nicole, or the beads, or me kissing you back, or dinner, or what? What is it now? Why are you so mad?"

"How about the army of leeches that tried to eat me alive in my sleep? That's a start." I dragged my hand down my face. "You know, she put leeches in the jambalaya, too. It's like she can't figure out who should be eating who. I'm telling you, that woman is sick."

"So you're still mad about the jambalaya?"

"No, I'm mad about the leeches, Lana. The *leeches*." I sighed and slumped in my seat. "Not at you. I'm not mad at you, I'm just . . . *mad*." It took saying it for me to feel the truth of my words.

I wasn't mad at Lana.

God, what was fucking *wrong* with me?

You're losing your edge, Asher.

Lana stared straight ahead. "Huh. So that's what Grandmaddox was doing in your room. I was wondering about that."

"Madwoman," I muttered.

"You didn't have to drag me out," she said. "You could have just asked to leave nicely."

"And what did we get? Did you lift your spell? No. Do we know where the portal is? No. Do we know *anything*? No. We just spent the night in an insect zoo for no reason."

"Actually . . ." Lana rubbed a strand of her faintly glowing hair against her cheek, "we might know something."

"Yeah? What?"

"Well, while you were sleeping, Jame Asher—"

"Getting eaten," I corrected.

She gave me a look like I was being a baby about it.

"—I snuck into Grandmaddox's potion room, and I drank the remem . . . I released myself from the memory block."

My eyebrows drew together, and I peered sideways at her. "Wait, you did what?"

"I got my memory back."

"Of . . . ?"

"The portal . . ."

I swear she was about to add something else.

Whatever it was, she bit the words back and finished, "I know where it is now."

I blinked, taking a moment to process. "Wait, so you . . . ?"

"Stole the potion because she wouldn't give it to me. Now I remember."

I stared at her. "And now you . . . now you . . . ?"

She pulled her blanket around her tighter. "I know where the portal is, alright? It's in a cave on the slope of a tall mountain above dense jungle. I can see it as clearly as if it were right in front of me."

I broke into a grin, all my prior anger forgotten. "Attagirl, Lana!" I leaned over to slap her knee. "Way to step it up. So you know where it is?"

She nodded and sat up straighter, looking proud of herself.

"Okay, so where is it?" I focused on the road again. Thanks to Lana, things were starting to go in our favor.

"I just told you," she said.

"Yeah, but *where?*"

She looked confused. "Uh . . . in a cave on the slope of a tall mountain above dense jungle, what I just said."

I started to sweat. "What . . . what is that? That could be a description of literally anywhere on Earth, that's not a location."

"Well, that's what I remember," she snapped, turning defensive. "Once we find the mountain, I'll know where it is."

I groaned and tilted my head back. "How are you supposed to find the portal with that? That's like saying it's near water, or on land—or on a planet. They didn't give you *anything* else?"

She crossed her arms. "I'm not going to help you anymore."

I quelled my frustration and put on my game face. "No, you're right, you did great . . . you're doing great, Lana. Is there anything else you can remember? Anything *specific?*"

"Only that it's the tallest mountain where we're going . . . but I doubt that'll help you. I doubt anything will help you, you stubborn ox."

"I can work with that." I whipped out my smartphone, which thankfully I'd left charging in the Hummer. "Tallest mountain in Mexico . . . Pico de Orizaba, right here, a dormant volcano. Beautiful." I showed her a picture of the snowcapped peak. "That it?"

Her eyes lit up. "Yeah, it's down in a valley on the other side, just over here—" She touched the screen, and the image vanished, replaced with a series of bloody, half-rotted bodies. She flinched back. "What happened? What did I do?"

"You just changed tabs, chill." I closed out the old search, regarding Azazel—*how to dissolve a body in acid*—and got back to Pico de Orizaba.

So there it was.

The next portal.

Thank you, Lana.

"Watch the road for me." I hopped onto a trip-planning website and booked us a villa in the valley she was talking about, deep in the jungle.

"*Asher* . . ." she whined, her knuckles turning white on the sides of her seats.

I glanced up to see a semitruck bearing down on us. I swerved back into my lane just in time.

I tossed the phone into her lap and resumed driving, a smile on my face. "It's ten hours to the border, and then another fourteen hours to our villa. Just a few more days' driving."

"I kept up my end of the bargain, now you keep up yours," she said. "Give me back your blood. The vial you still have."

"So you can curse me?"

"Only if you misbehave."

Didn't matter anyway. Grandmaddox already had plenty of blood to curse me with. Might as well give Lana some, too.

"You know, you shouldn't trust me to keep my word," I warned her.

Naïve thing. She *was* too trusting. It was going to get her killed, and she might be the only Infernarus who didn't deserve it.

Begrudgingly, I dug the vial out of my pocket and handed it to her. "I'm not an Infernarus. You told me where the portal was, but I didn't have to give you this."

She put it around her neck again, pausing to marvel

at my blood and looking quite pleased with herself. "But you did."

CHAPTER 15

Lana

I SLEPT SEVERAL hours. When I woke, it was to the smell of Asher's sweat, the scent some combination of salt, alcohol, and human man. Not just human man—Asher.

He didn't smell like some of the other natives I came across—like prey, or sickness, or filth. Quite the opposite. I wanted to run my lips over the sweat and taste it even as I mixed my scent with his.

That had me waking up real quick.

He still hates you. And you're not too fond of him at the moment either.

I rubbed my eyes, catching sight of the beads of sweat that collected on his forehead. A droplet had already snaked its way down his cheek. Meanwhile, hot air still poured from the vents. It was warm enough that I'd kicked off the blanket.

He'd left the heat on at his own expense so I could be warm.

I reached over, beginning to press buttons at random as I searched for the one that would turn off the heater.

Asher startled at my movement, waking from whatever reverie he had been in.

"Lana," he said, reaching forward and trying to remove my hand, "we talked about this already. I don't want you touching—"

"You can turn off the heat," I said.

He glanced over at me. Another bead of sweat slid down his cheek. I almost reached out to touch it before I remembered the shaky terms we were still on.

Without responding, he reached over to the dartboard and turned a knob. Immediately, the heat blasting through the vents shut off.

The silence that descended on us felt heavy. My eyes landed on that picture taped so close to the buttons I was pushing.

Finally, I said, "Are we going to talk about it?"

I saw his hands tighten on the steering wheel. "Nope."

"You don't even know what it is I want to talk about."

"My wife is none of your business."

That stung. "Last night, I did it because—"

"I don't want to know," he growled, the muscles of his arms straining, they were so tense.

"She was very beautiful," I said quietly, "and she must have been a saint to deal with you."

His mouth was a tight line, and I could hear his labored breaths coming in and out. He didn't bother telling me to stop talking. I'm not sure at this point he could have. Not without losing control, and a cold human like Asher wouldn't dare lose control.

"You shouldn't have kissed me," I said.

"You don't think I regret it?" he said, finally looking over.

His words were daggers to my gut.

He steeled himself against whatever expression I wore. "Damnit, Lana, you and I are *enemies*. I lost my family to your kind."

"Do you want to know why I like you, even now?" I said.

"You have a bad habit of seeing good in people who don't deserve it," Asher said. He made it sound like that wasn't a compliment.

I wrapped my hand around the vial of his blood. "Because you're loyal." I let out a breath. "I was taught that humans weren't capable of loyalty, not like Infernari. But you are. You defend your family even now. That's admirable."

His expression crumbled, his throat working. "Stop, Lana," he breathed. "For the love of God, please, stop."

This man burned for his mate. *Burned.* Another fallacy I was told. That the cold natives here were unfeeling. This man wasn't unfeeling. Behind his stony façade, he was all fire and heat. His passion burned hot, and his grief smoldered.

We *were* enemies, and yet I feared he and I had it all wrong.

And I feared it would make a difference in the end.

We fell into an uneasy silence, only interrupted when we stopped for lunch. He ordered a kid's dish for me, which I assumed was supposed to be some sort of insult, but the joke was on him. Chicken fingers were delicious and I got four colorful crayons out of it.

"I didn't know chickens even *had* fingers," I said now, hoisting myself into Asher's car.

The vehicle dipped with his weight as he got in. "They don't."

"Oh," I peered down distractedly at the crayons in my hand. "Then why are they called that?"

The engine roared as he turned the car on. "Beats the shit out of me." He raised an eyebrow at the crayons in my hand. "Do you want to make necklaces for each of those?"

My eyes brightened at the idea. "*Yes*. You are brilliant, Jame."

I reached back for his rope.

He gave me chagrined look. "It was a joke, Lana." He snatched the rope out of my hands. "I need that."

"For what? Killing more Infernari?"

"Give the girl a trophy."

I frowned at him. "You know, I was told you were the scariest, most lethal hunter out here. And yet since I've been with you, you're the one getting your ass kicked by my kind."

Asher tossed the rope behind us. "You shouldn't believe everything you hear," he said. "Plus," he eyed me up and down, "I managed to capture you."

"Give the man a trophy," I mimicked.

He cracked a smile at that, and his already gorgeous face was now almost painful to look at. My attention moved to his mouth. The mouth that had kissed me . . .

"We're about to cross the border," he said, his smile vanishing. "We need to get you a passport . . . if I steal one for you, you think you could make yourself look like the photo?"

"A passport? Is that one of those little blue books?"

"Yeah, they mean you're a citizen. Since you don't have one, you're an illegal alien . . ."

He trailed off when he saw me reaching down my suit, my beads from New Orleans shivering as I did so.

I grabbed the little book and the strange, rectangular piece of plastic I was assigned when I began visiting the United States. "Is this what you're talking about?" I asked, handing them both over.

"Where did you store that?" he asked, his expression dumbfounded.

I flashed him a bewildered look. "In my outfit. Where else?"

His eyes skimmed me over from head to foot. He gave a shake of his head and took the two pieces of identification from me. He spent several seconds reading over the plastic card. "How the *hell* did you get a license?"

I opened my mouth to answer, but he put a hand up. "You know what—I don't even want to know." He handed them back to me.

I scratched my arm absently, right where I cut it earlier.

The wound had begun to itch.

"Jame Asher, you worry too much. And you ask too many questions."

Asher gave me an indulgent look. "Oh, to be an Infernarus."

Asher

THANKS TO LANA'S forged passport, which she'd been hiding God knows where this whole time, we made it across the border without much hassle.

Okay, so Infernari were cleverer than I thought.

We got the green light at Mexican customs—a good thing, since a vehicle search would have turned up the small arsenal I was carrying—and then we were back on the road. Maybe Lana was right, maybe I did worry too much.

That night we stayed in the town of Soto la Marina, about three hours south of the border, where I bought her jeans, shirts, a sweater, and a Mexican knockoff of Vans tennis shoes so she could at least look like a tourist rather than a cosplay character.

Then it was back on the road, with Highway 180 taking us along the coast overlooking the Gulf of Mexico.

Lana leaned over me to see the view, her hair spilling into my lap and blocking my sight. I swerved and leaned around her. "Seatbelt, Lana . . . seatbelt!"

With a huff, she collapsed back in her seat, where she shifted and shimmied in vain to get comfortable, tugging at her new denim jeans. "Ugh, these are so *tight*."

I glanced at my phone. We were making good time.

Next to me, Lana tugged at her crotch again. "It keeps *rubbing* me."

I hadn't bothered mentioning the fact that humans had invented a thing called underwear, so she was going commando. Explaining thongs and g-strings to her could have gotten a bit dicey.

"Oh, come on, tell me those aren't more comfortable than that animal hide you were wearing before."

"That was *skin*," she said. "Skin on skin feels good. Skin on this scratchy, stiff, *horrible* fabric feels awful. It's like that time I got sand in my clothes."

"Mmm." I suppressed a smirk at the image. "I told you to go with a skirt, didn't I?"

"And walk around with my private parts exposed? I don't think so, Jame Asher."

I glanced sideways at her. Seeing her dressed like a normal *human* girl messed with my head; she was even more distracting than usual. Now her exoticness was tempered by this new girl-next-door look; when she looked like this, Lana was a lethal package.

She stopped fidgeting and stared at me, her gaze taking in my torso. "Why can't I wear what you're wearing? You look *comfortable*." She said it like an insult.

"Because you'd freeze your ass off."

Though I'd stripped down to a wifebeater, Bermuda shorts, and flip-flops to weather the arid hundred-degree heat, she was still shivering in her sweater. It made me nervous.

"How'd you stay warm until now, anyway?" I asked. "It's hotter here than it was in Virginia."

"I'm fine," she said, fighting another shiver. "I'm not cold." She readjusted her position, holding her left arm gingerly.

Thirty minutes later, her shivering had ratcheted up, enough to make me consider turning on the heater again. I glanced over at her. Her hair had stopped moving, and her usual exuberance was gone. We hadn't stopped once for her to relieve her pea-sized bladder.

"There's another rest stop coming up in ten minutes," I said, now eager to get her to act like herself.

She ignored me, gazing blankly out the window.

"Alright, Lana, what's going on?" I said. "Normally I'm pulling over every five minutes because you need to take a piss. Today you haven't once mentioned it."

All sorts of warning bells had been going off in my head for the last few hours.

"I don't have to go," she muttered, "stop pressuring me."

I chewed my lip, sensing what she wasn't telling me: she was coming down with a fever.

Demons might be incredible athletes, nearly invincible warriors, and lightning-fast healers, but they had one weakness.

Disease.

The reason was simple. Humans had a larger population, and a larger population bred more pathogens—bubonic plague, cholera, Influenza, HIV, malaria, smallpox, Ebola, SARS, West Nile virus, avian flu, swine flu. The list went on.

The human immune system had been honed by eons of killer pandemics.

Demons barely had an immune system.

It was like the Old World colliding with the New World all over again, except the Infernari were the Native Americans.

That was why they never stayed topside for very long.

Only a half demon like Grandmaddox could truly make Earth her home—she had inherited human immunity.

For full demons, blood magic could keep them healthy for a while—a few weeks, a few months.

But when their time was up, they had to go home.

Which, of course, Lana had been trying to do when I captured her.

Instead, I had kept her on Earth, in this breeding ground of pathogens, for five days longer than she should have been. Because I had destroyed her portal.

And I hadn't let her cull enough blood to heal herself.

For five days.

I had kept a girl without an immune system trapped on a diseased planet, and now I was taking her into the heart of the Mexican jungle.

For a demon, that was as close to a death sentence as it came.

Shit.

I reached up and squeezed the back of my neck, mulling it over. She broke into another fit of shivers next to me, and this time, her teeth chattered despite her full-body efforts to suppress it. She curled herself tighter, cradling her left arm against her body, as if it hurt her to move it.

I watched her, something restless stirring just beneath my sternum. Slumped against the window, she was taking too-fast breaths, as if unable to get enough air. Her face had paled and taken on a sickly sheen of sweat, and her hair hung lank around her face.

I pulled off the freeway, unease threading through me.

Once the car was parked, I reached over. "Hold still." I pressed the base of my palm to her forehead.

Fuck, I couldn't tell . . . 104° . . . 110° . . . whatever it was, her skin felt blazing hot—

She flinched and shrank against the window.

She definitely had a fever.

But with what bug?

She touched her arm through her sweater sleeve, and winced.

This time, I noticed.

"What's wrong? You hurt your arm?"

Seeing me watching her, she twisted away to hide the arm and glowered at me like a cornered animal.

"Lana," I warned.

"It's nothing," she said quickly.

Jesus, even Pinocchio lied better than her.

"Listen, I got ibuprofen," I said, "it's a pill, medicine, you take one and it'll knock out your fever—

"I'm not taking any *pills*," she said, like the thought of human medicine was abhorrent to her. "I'm fine."

I raised an eyebrow at her. "Fine? You're not fine."

"Well, pestering me isn't going to make me better." She closed her eyes and readjusted her left arm again, cringing a little. "At least let me die in peace. That's what you want, isn't it?"

Without blood to heal herself, an infection could easily take hold in her body.

Yesterday, she'd been so desperate for blood she'd even cut herself—back in Soto la Marina, I'd seen the evidence when she was only wearing a T-shirt: a long, angry-looking cut on the inside of her arm. Self-inflicted, I was sure.

I chewed on that, not liking the taste in my mouth.

Wait . . .

As it sank in, I felt my eyebrows scrunch together.

She cut herself.

My gaze flicked to the sleeve of her sweater, now hiding the wound. "Lana, raise your sleeve," I said with icy calm.

She angled the arm away from me, looking terrified.

"Raise your sleeve," I ordered.

She shook her head, her eyes pleading.

I leaned toward her and said, "I need to see. Show me your arm."

Finally, with trembling hands, she pulled back her sleeve.

When the cut came into view, my heart sank.

In less than a day, it had grown into a festering infection, the inflamed welt spreading into the skin around it. But most terrifying of all were the red veins snaking up her forearms and into her slender biceps, pulsing underneath her skin as they carried the infection into the rest of her body. Bacteria had gotten into her bloodstream.

She had blood poisoning, and her body was going into septic shock.

If we didn't get her antibiotics soon, she would die.

As if to confirm my diagnosis, she keeled over and just had time to grab a plastic bag before she vomited.

Lana

"HEAL YOURSELF," HE ordered. Something entered his voice, something I was too fatigued to muse over.

I could taste my death on my tongue, could feel it slithering through my lifeblood. I'd used up the last of my magic trying to heal it, but the foreign spirit still slipped through me, *killing* me,

"I can't, I tried. I don't know what this is." I actually felt hot. That was a first on this cold planet. But only moments ago I'd been freezing.

"Blood poisoning, that's what it is."

Blood poisoning. It seemed both fitting and ironic for me to be killed by the very blood that was supposed to save my people.

My people . . .

"It's not of my world," I said weakly. "My magic doesn't work on it."

Asher swallowed as he stared into my eyes. "Lana," he said, and now his voice was as gentle as I had ever heard it, "you're going die if we don't fix you."

I swallowed thickly. "I already tried fixing me. It didn't work."

Asher cursed. He pulled out his phone, his eyes flicking over to me every few seconds, like he couldn't help it.

"Then I'm going to."

A moment later, he announced, "There's a pharmacy close by. We're going to get you antibiotics—medicine that will make you feel better."

He pulled back onto the road.

Human medicine. Asher wanted me to put it in my body. The proud part of me revolted at the thought, but the dominant part of me, the instinctual part that desperately wanted to survive, it was willing to give the medicine a try.

"Why bother saving me?" I mumbled.

My enemy was demanding that I live when he could just let me die. It would be easier. Asher had the information he needed. A wily human like him could track down the portal from here. He didn't need me.

I felt his gaze on me, burning, burning.

"Why?" I said louder, straightening in my seat. Even my eyes ached, but I forced them to focus on the hunter next to me.

The engine of this metal beast screamed as we flew down the highway.

Asher's muscles strained beneath his skin and his jaw was locked, his brows sitting heavily upon his eyes. "Live and I'll tell you."

I stared at him for a moment longer, something soft and delicate unfurling in my stomach even after another wave of chills swept over me.

"I'm holding you to that, Jame," I said softly.

He looked over at me, a lock of hair falling across one of his worried eyes before he nodded and faced the road once more.

I'd been sick a couple times before this. Blood colds as we called them. They were mild, gradually setting in and quietly leaving.

There was nothing gradual or mild about this.

I groaned as we took an exit turn far too fast, my earlier car sickness rising from the momentum of it. My left arm was stiff and painful, and every second that went by, I got hotter and hotter until the car seemed as though it was smothering me.

"Air," I whispered.

Asher's gaze was on me. I could practically feel his icy resolve, forbidding me to die.

A moment later, the windows rolled down, and a cool breeze blew over my feverish skin.

I closed my eyes, savoring it.

Maybe I nodded off, maybe I didn't.

A dense thump sounded as some large object fell onto the roof, and my eyes snapped open. I looked up at the dented metal roof above my head.

"They found us," I breathed.

Asher's upper lip curled, and he yanked his gun from its holster.

"Hiding in the fucking trees, the bastards . . ." he muttered.

He thrust his gun out the window, elbow cocked, and blindly shot at the roof of the car.

Bang–bang-bang-bang!

He gritted his teeth as he steered, one-handed. The car veered back and forth across the road as he tried to shake whomever clung to the roof of the car, but they held on.

He cursed and kept firing, glancing out his side view mirror as he did so.

I scented the air, hoping to catch a whiff of blood, but all I caught was smoke.

"Keep shooting, keep shooting!" I shouted. "You haven't hit them yet—"

It was precisely then that I felt warm arms snake around me. I barely had time to yelp before I was yanked up and out of my seat through the open window.

Right into the waiting arms of an Infernarus.

CHAPTER 16

Asher

When I looked over at the passenger seat, it was empty.

"Lana!" I slammed on the brakes and skidded to a stop on a gravel turnout. In the rearview mirror, a shadow dropped through the cloud of dust kicked up by the tires, and it loped toward the dense brush bordering the road.

A demon.

It had snatched her right through the open passenger window.

Cursing, I leaned over Lana's seat to see better. A palm frond scraped against the side of the car, like nails on metal. The demon could be anywhere, and not knowing where made my skin crawl.

It darted into the trees.

All I glimpsed, before the surfboard-sized leaves of a philodendron swished back over the brief gap in the foliage, was a flash of blue fish scales.

Then nothing.

No sounds but the quiet swish of wind through palm fronds.

Blue fish scales? I had a hunch what demon this was. I only prayed it was wrong.

It had taken Lana. Sick, dying Lana.

My earlier restlessness ratcheted up.

My fault.

I hadn't been paying attention. And now she was gone, because of my own carelessness.

The guilt stung. Beneath it, something else burned. Something that put fire in my veins.

In her current state, Lana wouldn't be able to resist or fight back. She was vulnerable, helpless, defenseless. And now that I knew Lana's magic couldn't heal her . . .

Disease wasn't like other injuries that afflicted demons. Bodily injury they could recover from—broken bones, severed limbs, gunshot wounds—given enough time, or enough magic, a demon could heal from any physical damage. As long as any cell still lived, the demon still lived.

But infection was different.

Infection rotted the body from the inside out, it staged a viral attack on the cellular level, hijacked the body's own resources, devoured all tissue in its path until the organism was more bacteria than animal.

I thought that a healer would have been able to reverse the infection, but in the wake of what Lana told me, I had to face another possibility—that rapid healing accelerated the decay.

And Lana had been pouring her magic into healing.

That's why the onset was so rapid.

A late-stage infection, like what Lana had, would kill a demon every time.

What she needed was penicillin, and she needed it within the hour.

Or she would die.

Every minute that demon had her was a minute less she had to live.

At the thought, a terrible fear took hold low in my gut, sinking in like claws—a fear I hadn't known in two years.

Fear for another's life.

Fear for Lana.

In the five days since White Sulfur Springs, I had gone from her captor to her reluctant ally. At some point in the last twenty-four hours, I had become her protector.

Maybe it was seeing her sick and hurting, the pang of sympathy every human feels for a wounded creature, maybe it was seeing her own kind turn on her, or maybe it was the fact that she'd helped me find the portal.

All I knew was I couldn't let her die.

Not now, not like this, not at the hands of the very demons she had sworn to protect.

That just didn't seem fair.

I reloaded my Glock, then dug under the backseat for my sawed-off shotgun.

Locked and loaded, I muscled my way into the foliage, following the trail of trampled grass.

Low ferns scraped my bare calves and wedged under my flip-flops, while the sun winked through a high canopy of palms and broad-leafed hardwoods. As I pushed into the underbrush, the shadows deepened.

I imagined what would become of Lana. Demons didn't understand antibiotics. Nor did they care. They would let her die, unable and unwilling to help her.

The ground began to rumble.

I paused to listen, knuckles tight on the shotgun's pump-action handgrip.

It built like a slow thunder, vibrating up through my knees. On the ground, pebbles danced and settled into quivering piles. A wet breeze blew in from the side, whipping the broad leaves to and fro and popping my ears.

I spun toward the approaching thunder.

My hunch had been right; I knew exactly which demon I was up against.

Fuck.

A wave of water crashed through the trees, splashing around their trunks and uprooting bushes, rising ten feet over my head. The wall of seawater slammed into me, dragged me backward, tore the gun from my hand and flooded my nostrils.

Then I was tumbling like a rag doll, dragged under by the currents, pummeled by rocks. My head broke the foamy surface, and I gasped for breath. A swirling vortex slammed me into a low tree branch, and I clung to it for dear life as the flood swept past me, finally draining to rivulets and puddles. With a groan, I dropped to the ground, soaking wet and bruised everywhere.

Then, from out of the dripping trees stepped the demon.

Clad in a skintight suit made of blue fish scales, she had long, flowing blonde hair and watermelon-pink eyes. The demon was more mermaid than girl.

Aecora, tamer of oceans.

Major affinity: controlling water.

Minor affinity: conjuring stupid glass structures.

A human would imagine a million uses for that minor affinity, but Aecora used it for one purpose and one purpose only: creating bubbles to drown you in. Back during Brad's and my mercenary days, we'd had a few run-ins with her nasty tricks.

She kicked Lana forward into the clearing she'd made, and my whole body tensed up.

Lana landed in a heap, her hair dripping. Slowly, she raised her wounded eyes to mine, and then her elbows buckled and she slumped over. She was sickening fast.

My jaw clamped, and I drew my Glock, aiming it at Aecora's head.

Before I could squeeze off the shot, a wave rose out of the dirt behind me and broke over my back. I sprawled forward, and the gun tumbled out of my grip and splashed at Lana's feet.

Hold onto your fucking guns, Asher!

"Too slow, Jame," Aecora taunted. "Much, *much* too slow. My, you've lost your touch."

I climbed to my feet, wiping water and silt from my mouth. "Alright, Cora, you got me. Let's make a deal. You let me live, I let you keep Lana. You have my word I won't kill you."

I had no intention of honoring that deal, but Aecora didn't need to know that.

I had to steel myself against the wounded look Lana gave me.

My gaze flicked to the gun, lying a foot from her hand. A yard from mine.

"Now why would I trust your *word*," Aecora said, "when you've never kept your word before in your life? And why would I even make that deal, when I can just kill both of you right now? Which option sounds smarter to you, Jame?"

She had a point. I focused back on the demon. "How about you spare an old friend, huh?"

"An old friend," she scoffed. "How about you die with some dignity? Or is that asking too much from you?"

I raised my palms. "Cora, come on, I'm unarmed . . . you know you won't get glory from killing me like this." Unable to help it, I peeked at Lana again, who looked sicker by the second.

I needed to get her to a pharmacy *now*.

"My gods, did you come to rescue her, Jame?" Aecora cocked her head. "I'm not sure which one of you is the bigger traitor. It's too bad I don't trust your word. There are others who would allow you to surrender and keep your life, and for Lana to keep hers . . . *no one* would have to die.

"The trouble is," she continued, "I am not one of them. You have no honor. You're an animal, no better than a mangy cur . . . and what you do with a cur that keeps trying to bite your hand? You put it down. You kill it. You don't try to *reason* with it."

"Lana's infected," I said, trying a different tack. "You touched her, Cora, which means you're infected too. Only way you live is if I get you the antibiotics. Your choice."

Aecora drew back from Lana, her lip curled.

That was the best opening I was going to get.

I dove for the gun.

"Nuh-uh-uh—" Aecora raised her hands, and out of thin air, a glass bubble materialized around Lana and the gun.

I thunked into it.

Behind the thick glass, the gun was unreachable. Inches away . . . yet so far.

Trapped inside the bubble, Lana scrambled backward, hit the other side, and frantically slapped the walls with her palms, her eyes wide.

Then, it began filling with water.

My breath left me in a rush. *No . . .*

I skidded to my knees in front of the glass encapsulating Lana, raised my fist, and punched the surface. My knuckles split open, leaving a smear of blood. Too thick.

I hit it again, elbowed it, kicked it, but to no avail. I'd seen Aecora kill before; you couldn't punch your way through her creations. My pulse pounded in my temples, rang in my ears.

No use. It was no use.

I laid my hand on the fishbowl. I could do nothing but watch as Lana's wet fists thumped the inside of the dome. The water moved up to her chest, and then it lifted her feet off the ground, filling the container far too quickly.

She gave up trying to shatter the glass as her beautiful face pressed against the top of the dome and she took her final breaths of air.

I was going to have to watch her drown.

She opened her sad, solemn eyes underwater, and they found mine immediately. I swear forgiveness flashed through them.

Forgiveness. For all the killing. For the violence. For taking her. For everything. Because demon or not, her heart was pure.

Lane stopped battling the water. From the other side of the glass she pressed her palm up against mine. And then she simply watched me. I knew that moment; I'd seen it often enough. When someone accepts their death.

Lana had the audacity to give up.

I could feel my face contorting. Good people always died while evil fuckers like me and Aecora got to keep our insufferable lives.

It was the laugh that made me snap.

Aecora let out a shrill giggle, and that, that laugh that mocked my pain and Lana's life, that made me see red.

I charged the water demon.

She waved her hands again, and I slammed into another glass wall, this one encircling me. It, too, began filling with water. I backed away, my anger now mixing with panic. Lana and I were now both trapped, we would both drown.

Fucked three ways to Wednesday.

Smirking, Aecora knelt to watch, like death was entertaining.

This was why I hunted these assholes.

I splashed back toward the side closest to Lana's bubble.

As she moved underwater, her heel struck the gun, which settled to rest against the glass.

The gun.

It was our only hope.

I'd shown her how to fire it. The safety was off.

All she had to do was pull the trigger.

"Lana!" I screamed, slapping the glass. Water sloshed over my knees. "Lana, the gun . . . grab the gun!"

Her brows drew together. She had to almost be out of air. Her hair swirled around her like the plume of an exotic fish, glimmering blue and violet and purple. Under stress, her inhuman side came to the surface.

"Shoot the gun at the glass!"

I made a gun with my hand and shoved it against the glass, then pantomimed pulling the trigger.

She got it. Her eyes lit up with the realization. She swam down to the bottom of her cage and felt around for the gun.

Water bubbled up to my chest.

She found it, and fumbled it around in her hands until it was pointed away from her.

"Good, good . . . now pull the trigger—"

The gun flashed and made a burst of bubbles.

She flinched and dropped the gun to clutch her ears. Underwater, the explosion would have been deafening.

The glass cracked, but didn't break. Lana stared hopelessly, her chest convulsing as she fought her instinct to breathe.

Aecora frowned and stood up.

"Shoot it again," I whispered. "Shoot it again, Lana. You can do it." Water rose to my neck.

Lana went back down for the gun, aimed it at the same spot—*good girl*—and pulled the trigger again.

Her bubble shattered.

The waterfall dumped her, coughing and gasping for breath, on the muddy ground.

Still holding the gun, she took aim at my bubble, her eyes burning with fierce determination, and managed two shots before she collapsed from exhaustion.

My bubble splintered, then cracked, then burst open, and I was dragged out with the escaping gush of water.

This time, I was ready.

I hit the ground and ducked into a roll, swiped the Glock out of the mud, and darted into the trees, already swinging my arm back toward Aecora to fire. She flinched and conjured another bubble around herself, which absorbed half a dozen bullets before shattering.

She whipped her hands out, palms raised. I threw myself sideways as a glass cage clamped around the space where I had been, just missing me. I scrambled into the underbrush. Having lost sight of me, she screamed and spun around in circles, conjuring bubbles haphazardly around the clearing, then she brought another wave smashing through the trees.

This time, I was ready. I anchored myself to a thick tree root and weathered the flood. When it passed, I military crawled through the bushes.

She was moving too fast, whipping around in circles, wrapping every twig that moved in a shiny glass bubble. I couldn't get a clean shot, and I needed a clean shot.

A headshot.

Only thing that would incapacitate a demon.

It wouldn't kill her, no, but it would scramble her brain long enough for me to burn her.

But if I missed, I'd find myself right back in a bubble again, likely with my gun and severed hand in a different one.

Across the clearing, the bushes rustled.

Aecora swiveled toward the sound, hands raised to attack.

To both our surprise, a stark naked man stepped into the clearing, arms raised in surrender.

The man I recognized as myself.

"I give up, Cora," he called in a gravelly voice. "I'm unarmed, I'm no threat."

"Attagirl, Lana," I whispered.

Well, now she'd seen me naked.

Technically, more than that. She'd *been* me naked.

Aecora imprisoned her in a bubble anyway, then sauntered up the glass, giggling. "Are you trying to seduce me, Jame? My, *my*, you've lost your touch. But not your body, I see. Maybe I'll take you home and put you on display, *just . . . like . . . this*." The words slithered off her tongue.

Sick bitch.

I tiptoed up behind her, raised the gun.

Lana, impersonating me, merely stared at Aecora with slitted eyes, giving nothing away.

A stick cracked under my heel.

Aecora whipped around, and I fired. The bullet lodged itself right between her eyes. The demon remained standing for a second longer, then her body tipped forward, comatose for the moment.

Crouching to catch my breath, I shot Lana out of the bubble. The glass splintered and rained down around her feet.

Lana took a step forward, then went down on a knee, her body—my body—swaying with fatigue.

I went to her then, wrapping her arm around my shoulders and hoisting her back up.

"Where are your clothes?"

She nodded weakly to the bushes.

"Can you put them on yourself?"

Her lower lip quivered as she took in her comrade; she looked to be about to cry, which was pretty fucking unsettling to see on my face.

Lana ripped her gaze away to give me a small nod.

I left her at the pile of her clothes, turning my back while she changed.

"You got us out of a pinch, there," I said over my shoulder. "You did well."

She stepped out from behind the bushes, clothed. She smoothed down her hair, her body shaking.

Still feverish.

Her gaze returned to Aecora's fallen body, the smoking hole between her eyes.

"I lied," she whispered. "I lied to protect you . . . and I betrayed her."

"She was going to kill you. Seems like a smart move to me."

"But I *lied*." She cradled her head in her hands and peeked out in horror through her fingers. "An Infernarus *never* lies."

My eyes flicked to Aecora. To me, this was no moral quandary.

"Lana, listen to me." I stalked over to her and lifted her chin with my finger. "You said nine words. You said, 'I give up, Cora. I'm unarmed, I'm no threat.' Everything you said was true. If she thought it was me talking, then that's her problem. But you didn't lie."

Hope flashed in her eyes. She searched my face, as if pleading for it to be true.

"You're still an Infernarus," I said. "You've been nothing but honorable."

I saw her body relax with my words.

"Now," I said, turning my attention to Aecora, "let's grab some gasoline so we can burn this bitch and get out of here."

I wanted to finish the demon while she was prone. She would be up and lethal within the hour.

"No," Lana put her arms on her hips, "we're going to leave her so she can heal."

I frowned. "Lana, she just tried to kill us, she just tried to kill *you*. She tried to drown you in a glass bubble."

Her arms were wrapped tightly around her body, her entire frame racked with shivers. "I don't care," she said stubbornly. "She's an Infernarus; she's my sister."

My nostrils flared. "You want me to just walk away?

That's now *three demons* I've walked away from that I could have killed. What kind of lousy demon hunter do you take me for?"

She reached up and touched my cheek, and I felt just how hot her skin was. "You're not a demon hunter, Jame Asher. You're a faithful mate and a loyal father who's lost the ones he loves . . . and I forgive you, too."

At her words, my heart stilled. I'd seen as much in her eyes earlier, but hearing it voiced . . .

The person she took me for clashed with what I'd done, the violence I'd committed . . . the monster I'd become. I barely remembered who I was before demons had taken my family. But for a moment, lost in Lana's deep, soulful eyes, I remembered.

She swayed forward, her eyelids fluttering, and for an instant I thought she was going to kiss me. And God help me, even sober I was okay with that.

Instead Lana collapsed into my arms, shaking uncontrollably.

Fuck, fuck, *fuck*.

She was still dying.

I scooped her up and carried her back to my Hummer, leaving Aecora forgotten behind us.

Lana shivered in my arms. She pressed her cheek against my chest, her teeth chattering. Like strands of fiber optics, her hair swirled around her in a protective cocoon, weeping blues and greens in a vivid rainbow. But that wasn't what got me.

What got me was her dainty fist clinging to my shirt.

A lump formed in my throat.

I couldn't save my wife. Couldn't save my daughter.

But maybe I could save Lana.

"Come on," I murmured, brushing the kiss I couldn't claim earlier against the crown of her head, "let's get you to a pharmacy."

Lana

THIS HUMAN HOUSE of medicine smelled like evil spirits. Spirits like the one that still slunk through my veins.

I was cradled in Asher's arms, content to just stay here till the end.

A day ago I was a powerful Infernarus. Now I was little more than a defenseless child.

I leaned into Asher, breathing in his scent as he stalked through the pharmacy.

Perhaps it was wearing his body or perhaps it was being sick and vulnerable, but I felt comfortable with him.

No, more than that.

In my delirium, I trusted him, completely. I didn't fear death right here in his arms. And how death sang dirges in my ears.

Distantly, I heard Asher speaking, his words controlled. "Infection . . . antibiotics . . . dying."

My eyes had drifted closed, and I listened to the *thump-thump-thump* of Asher's heart. It was beating fast for a human, and especially fast for the unshakeable Asher.

An icy hand pressed against my forehead. I flinched at the touch, trying to turn my head away.

Not Asher's. This one smelled like chemicals.

"It's okay, Lana," Asher soothed, "he just wants to help."

The human medicine man spoke then, his voice alarmed, and the language . . . I didn't understand this one.

I found I didn't much care.

Asher began to move again, only stopping to set me down into a chair. He had to pry my hands off of him. As soon as he did so, I began shivering violently.

He sighed, murmuring once more with the medicine man.

Then Asher's arms were around me again. He lifted me and resettled the both of us in the seat.

"Lana, look at me," Asher said.

I forced my eyelids back, my eyes burning, and gazed up at the hunter.

A concerned crease had formed between Asher's brows. "The pharmacist has to give you a shot."

I blinked slowly, as if surfacing from a dream. I had made a pillow out of Asher's shoulder; now I pulled away from it to look around. I was surrounded by rows upon rows of human medicine; the place smelled of chemicals and human malaise.

Then I caught sight of the pharmacist. He held a tube with a needle attached at the end—a syringe.

At the sight of it, I cringed back against Asher, shaking my head frantically. I held my injured arm tight to my body.

The hunter nodded to the medicine man, and I tensed,

286

preparing to use up the last of my reserves to fight this.

Before I had the chance, Asher tilted my chin to face him. I stilled at the touch, still transfixed by it. By him.

"You're an Infernarus, a fighter," he said, his voice hypnotic. "You will do whatever it takes to save your people, including this."

I stared at him, mesmerized by his words. A sheen of sweat coated his face, and I realize the heat of my feverish body was too hot for him. Still he held me.

He was right. The human was right.

I gave him a small nod. His eyes left me only long enough to give the medicine man a signal.

I let out a cry when the pharmacist touched my swollen arm.

"Not that one," Asher barked, and he sounded legitimately angry on my behalf.

I stretched out my other arm, gritting my teeth when I felt the other human's cold hands on my skin. My gaze drifted to the syringe once more. The moment I saw that long needle, I squeezed my eyes shut.

"Hey, hey, look at me," Asher said, again turning my head to face him.

Maybe it was his touch, maybe it was the unexpected gentleness in his voice, but I did force myself to look at him.

My breath caught at the expression in his dark eyes.

He *wanted* me to live. Demanded that I do so.

"You've seen worse, Lana Malesuis," he said. "I know you have."

My eyes widened. "You remember my full name."

"One of them," Asher clarified. "Lana of the Badlands. Are you going to take me there when we cross over—?"

I winced as I felt the prick of the needle slipping beneath my skin.

I swallowed, then nodded, then shook my head. "I don't know. There's nothing out there."

The needle slipped out and I relaxed.

"I want to see it," Asher said. "I want to see it all."

I WAS STILL in a delirium when we left the pharmacy. I don't remember much, mostly tactile things. The feel of Asher's sweat-drenched shirt, the chill he left in his wake when he deposited me in the passenger seat. The jostle of the car as he got us back on the road.

I don't remember several hours after that. I fell into a feverish sleep, waking only to be sucked right back under. Minutes or hours or days could have passed like that for all I knew. It seemed endless.

At some point we stopped at a hotel, and the smell and feel of Asher enveloped me once more as he carried me to a bed. He tucked me in the same way my mother and father used to do when I was little.

"I'll be right back," he whispered. Or maybe he didn't and I dreamed the whole thing.

"*Lana . . . Lana . . .*"

I squinted my eyes open.

Asher crouched at my bedside, a bowl of soup in his hands. "You should eat," he said gruffly.

I lifted a shoulder and let it fall. Not hungry.

He set the soup on the table next to the bed, next to several bottles of water.

He's taking care of me.

I would have found it absurd if I wasn't so sick.

"Thank you," I said weakly.

He frowned. "Don't thank me." He nodded to the soup. "Eat."

How to tell him that I was too weak to do much more than shiver? I gazed at him sadly.

He must have understood because he cursed quietly, then stood. Much more gently than I would have imagined, he helped me sit up, making sure not to jostle my bad arm.

I reached for the spoon and dipped it into the broth. I wasn't incredibly hungry, but it smelled decent enough, and it was hot. But as I brought it to my mouth, my shivering body shook my hand, and the liquid dripped off the spoon and onto the blankets.

Asher's frown deepened. He took the spoon from me and grabbed the soup, sitting down on the edge of the bed. "We're not going to bring this up ever again," he said, dipping the utensil into the broth.

I didn't know what he was talking about—feeding me, saving me, or caring about me. Probably all of them.

He shook his head to himself, then passed the spoon to my lips. All the while he looked angry.

"You don't have to do this," I said.

"*Eat.*"

My mouth parted, and I had my first bite of native soup. It was mild and savory and warm, the combo everything my sick body craved.

Asher fed me most of it before I insisted I was full. Then he gave me a pill—antibiotics given to him by the pharmacist, which apparently I would have to take three times a day for the next two weeks. I swallowed it, having no strength left to resist. The entire time his features were hard, unyielding. But he didn't once complain, and after I finished, he helped me lay back down.

He stood, the mattress squeaking as he did so. "I need to check the perimeter."

For my kind.

They were after us, and he was protecting me from them. He could have left me here; he knew enough about the portal to finish the journey alone. Staying with me, saving me, put him in danger.

He hadn't once looked torn about his decision.

Asher headed for the door.

"Jame," I called to him.

He paused at the door, that impressively muscled back of his to me.

"What, Lana?" he said over his shoulder.

"I owe you another debt." He'd saved my life. *Again.*

"You owe me *nothing.*"

But I did. That's how my kind worked. We repaid kindness with kindness, mercy with mercy. Only mates weren't required to repay debts, but that was only because they were bound by a bond far stronger than a blood debt.

I doubted *that* was what Asher was suggesting. He was just being . . . selfless.

"You are the best kind of human," I said.

290

He bowed his head, like my words weighed him down. "Get some sleep. I'll be back soon." With that, he left.

IT TOOK A full day for the antibiotics to really begin to work. By the time we were back in Asher's car, I felt weak but better. My arm was still swollen and tender, but I could move it a little without hurting.

But most importantly, it was sunny out, the sky was bright blue, the ocean gleamed like a jewel, and for once I didn't even mind being in the car.

Because I was *alive*.

Alive, thanks to the killer next to me.

I wiggled my toes, practically bouncing in my seat. "How much longer?" I asked.

"You are such a kid," Asher grumbled.

"It's called *enthusiasm*. It's a human word, so I know you know of it."

His hard look only deepened. "We'll get there tonight . . . stay in the villa . . . we'll destroy the portal tomorrow."

"You mean go *through* it?" I threw my head back against the seat rest. "The one time I would've appreciated a human lie you tell me the truth."

Even that couldn't bring down my mood for long. I tucked my feet under my thighs and began rolling the beads of my various necklaces together. They were especially beautiful in the sunlight. Everything was beautiful in this earthly light.

"Thank you for saving my life," I said. It was unprecedented for one of our kind to survive the sickness of this world.

"Lana, you don't need to keep saying that," Asher said, rubbing his jaw.

He glanced over at me, and butterflies blossomed in my stomach. I remembered being cradled in those arms, cared for by those hands.

"My life is yours," I said.

"Stop it. Stop saying shit like that." He scrubbed that hand over his face. "I don't want you to give up your life. Not for me or anyone else."

"But my life *is* yours. You healed me." I reached for the vial of Asher's blood, my hand groping through the many ropes of necklaces for it.

"Just please don't cut yourself again."

I dropped my hand when I didn't feel the vial.

Having come this close to death, I doubted I'd be cutting myself again anytime soon. The urge was gone, in fact, which I suspected had everything to do with Asher taking care of me . . . with me *trusting* him. Those first few days around him, I'd been a complete wreck. He'd brought out all my nervous habits.

But now he . . . didn't.

Now I felt safe around him, cared for. Somehow, he made me less neurotic.

I peeked at him before looking down at my lap, suddenly feeling shy. "I won't," I said softly.

"What'd you do it with?" he asked.

"A razor."

"Do you still have it?"

Reluctantly I removed it from my pocket and handed it over.

When Asher saw it, he whistled. "No wonder it got infected," he said, holding it up to the light. He shook his head, then pocketed it.

"You're keeping it?" I asked.

"No," he said, "I'm just not giving it back to you."

My hands twisted together at that. But I would be okay.

"Why did you do it?" he asked a minute later.

I pressed my lips together. I didn't want to answer this. Not when he was starting to look at me like he actually cared.

But if he wouldn't let me pledge him my life, I could at least answer his questions.

"I was testing out the sharpness of the blade," I answered honestly.

"And you were doing that because . . . ?"

"When it's been awhile since I've culled . . . I get urges." I glanced down at my hands, afraid to meet his eyes. "I need blood—if I don't want to hurt someone else, then I have to hurt myself." I furrowed my brows. "But it's better now . . . around you."

When I finally did look at him, I saw such conflict in his eyes.

I reached for Asher's vial again, like it was a talisman. And again, my fingers didn't close over the glass. I glanced down at my chest, peeling necklaces apart one by one as I looked for Asher's blood.

I sucked in a breath when I didn't find it. "The *vial*," I said.

"What about it?"

"It's gone."

CHAPTER 17

Lana

"Gone?" Asher took his eyes off the road to stare at me. "What do you mean *gone?*"

"I mean it's not here."

"You mean you *lost* it?"

Golden skinned Asher went pale at that, and the look in his eye . . . moon-touched. A muscle in his cheek feathered. I could see the anger building up, his muscles taut with it.

My fault. "Asher, I—"

"*Don't.*"

"But—"

"Just . . . *don't.*" He looked like he was barely keeping it together.

I chewed on my lower lip. "It could've just fallen some-where."

"It *didn't*," he all but growled. "You and I both know exactly where it went."

Into Aecora's possession. I unwittingly managed to screw over the very person I owed my life to.

I decided then that silence was probably the best.

Next to me Asher seethed. I could sense his fury, feel it building up beneath his skin. Like an Infernarus who's taken in too much magic, he needed to release it.

He wasn't releasing it. And I was trapped in the car with him.

I waited for it. For him to curse, to yell, to rage.

Instead, Asher began to laugh.

Laugh.

Definitely moon-touched.

"Wh—why are you laughing?" I was almost afraid to ask.

He shook his head. "Now that Aecora has my blood, you might just get the opportunity to repay your debt after all."

THE NEXT SEVERAL hours were tense. The thing about mis-fortunate magic is that you can't always tell when it is responsible for bad luck. Sometimes unfortunate events happen without the aid of curses. And then sometimes you endure the aftereffects of dark magic and never fully realize that the skirmish you lost or the food poisoning you acquired were not chance events at all.

But if Aecora did indeed have Asher's blood, she would

use it, and the curse would be strong enough for us to know.

"I'm really sorry," I said quietly, staring out the window.

"Stop apologizing," Asher said, aggravated.

"You don't want me to apologize, you don't want me to save your life—what *do* you want from me?" I asked.

"*Nothing*," Asher said. "I want nothing from you."

I flashed him a strange look.

He tore his gaze away from the road to search my face. "Has anyone ever *not* wanted anything from you?"

"All Infernari are indebted to one another from birth. We owe each other allegiance. The only ones not indebted to each other are mates—"

Before I could finish the thought, a dark creature flashed in my peripheries, darting across the road. I swiveled my head in time to see a furry animal cross in front of the car.

"Asher!" I cried, my eyes widening.

His head snapped back to the road.

He didn't even have time to curse before he jerked the wheel. The car swerved violently off the highway. It bounced as it left the paved road, driving over rock and underbrush.

My eyes were peeled to the sight in front of us. We careened toward a small guardrail mere feet away. Beyond it . . . the land dropped off, and I couldn't tell how deep the gully beyond it was.

We were far too close to stop our momentum.

Asher laid on the brakes, our tires squealing. It wasn't enough. Not nearly. Our vehicle smashed into the guardrail, which groaned and bent, and then we were moving over it. I didn't have time to scream before the vehicle careened over the edge. There was nothing beneath us but empty air.

I gripped the door handle and the center console as I stared at the ground far below. Far, far below.

The edge of the car connected with the walls of the gully. Metal groaned as it met resistance, and then the world was flipping.

Mother above, save us.

Asher's side of the car slammed into the sloping side of the gully again, the frame of the car making a shrieking noise as it crunched together. My body whipped about at the impact, my hair scattering. Next to me, I heard Asher grunt, and then the vehicle was rolling again, the metal banging into the sides of the mountain, and all that wondrous human technology we sat inside was now nothing more than a cheap parlor trick to the force of nature.

The window in front of us cracked, then shattered completely, hundreds of little bits of glass raining all over me.

I screamed as my side of the vehicle smashed into the mountainside, the window splintering into a web of cracks, the door denting inwards. The force of it threw my neck back.

The vehicle tipped over once more before landing awkwardly on its tires and coming to rest.

For several moments, I sat there, catching my breath.

"You . . . okay?" Asher wheezed next to me.

My eyes closed. He was alive. I was alive. We'd survived.

I swallowed and nodded. My stomach churned violently. I yanked on the door handle. When the door didn't budge, I gave it up and scrambled out the shattered front window and slid off the hood of the car.

I barely made it to the ground before I vomited.

Just when I thought I might be over my car sickness.

I leaned over my legs, swallowing deep gulps of dusty air.

Aside from a bit of lingering nausea and sore muscles, I had escaped the crash unscathed.

Straightening, I headed over to the driver side door.

Asher watched me, a sheen of sweat on his forehead as he leaned back in his seat.

He hadn't left the car. Unease pooled low in my belly. Why hadn't he left the car?

Now it was my turn to ask, "Are . . . are you okay?" My heart beat madly.

"Fine . . ." A thread of pain slipped into his voice. Between that and his pinched expression, I didn't believe him.

"You're *not*, are you?" I was getting better at seeing through his lies.

"It's just a cut," he said, grimacing. He adjusted himself in his seat, but he wasn't moving much.

Considering what my cut had done to me, this was not reassuring.

I was beginning to panic.

I yanked on the door handle. Metal groaned, and it gave a little, but it wouldn't open. I tried again. This time it shifted even less.

I let go. "Can you move?" I asked him.

"My leg's pinned," he admitted.

The thought of him stuck and injured left me anxious. Desperate.

My hair snapped about my face.

Resolve settled over my shoulders. I *would* be getting Asher out.

Tucking my still tender arm close to my side, I scrambled back up the hood of the car and inside once more. The space was cramped, all sides of the vehicle had collapsed inward, especially toward the back of the car. There the frame had almost completely collapsed in on itself. Praise the Mother that it was the back end of the car that sustained the most damage. Stashed back there, Asher's precious supplies were beyond retrieving—his weapons, his ammunition, his machines—all crushed. Everything except the gun on his hip.

I squeezed myself onto the center console, so close to Asher that my side brushed up against his.

I ignored the frantic tap of my heart, and I ignored my own fatigue. All I focused on was the way Asher's thigh was trapped beneath the door. That part of the car had crushed inwards into the hunter, and I could smell his blood.

Bad injury.

It was an effort not to convert his blood to magic so that I could shift into something bigger, stronger. I could get him out of here if I was a giant.

But dark magic had undoubtedly been behind the crash. Best not tempt misfortune twice.

Instead I reached across him and slid my hands over his

pinned thigh, shifting into my role as healer.

I felt the muscles of his leg go rigid at my touch.

"I'm feeling for your injury," I explained.

He made an affirming noise. Or maybe it was just a grunt of pain.

I probed around the injury, hearing hisses every now and then from Asher. My fingers traced the shape of the metal that dug into his thigh, metal that appeared to be attached to the door.

Heal him. Heal him. Heal him.

The urge rode me even though I had no magic and no way of connecting with him.

I removed my hands, my eyes moving to the door.

It needed to open.

I grabbed the driver-side door handle, my body stretched across Asher's. His hands came up, loosely bracing me by the waist. It was embarrassingly distracting, and a stab of guilt sliced through me. The man was injured and my mind drifted there.

Metal groaned as the door gave a little. It came to a halt. I pushed again. It gave just a smidgen more.

Leaning my shoulder into door, I shoved against it. Now it hung open the span of a knuckle.

All I needed was a little more leverage.

"I have an idea."

"Lord save us," Asher mumbled. I swear I felt his hands squeeze my sides a little tighter though, silent encourage-ment.

I repositioned myself on Asher's lap, trying to jostle him as little as possible. I saw him grit his teeth anyway.

"Didn't realize you were any good at lap dances," he commented.

"I don't know what a lap dance is, Asher," I said, distracted, "but if this is it—" I swiveled my body so that my feet pressed against the door, and my arms were braced against the center console, "then I maintain that you humans are strange."

I pulled my foot back. "Oh, and this might hurt." I slammed the heel of my shoe into the door.

Asher groaned along with the car as the door opened the span of another knuckle, the metal digging into his skin as it slowly withdrew its hold. I kicked the door again, and again, and again, each blow opening it a bit further. All the while, I avoided looking at Asher, who was panting through his clenched teeth.

My arm throbbed in protest, but icy determination overrode the pain.

On the seventh kick, I heard Asher's breath leave him.

"It's off me," he said. "I can move."

"Can you climb through the window?"

"I'll be fine."

I'd heard that line so many times. Famous Infernarus pride. It took me a moment to realize Jame wasn't an Infernarus.

Just one more way we're not nearly so different as we'd imagined.

He refused to let me help him exit the vehicle—again, a trait I was familiar with—his leg bleeding all over the car as he dragged himself out.

After several agonizing minutes, Asher dropped to the

ground outside the vehicle. He slung his arms over his knees as he panted.

I crouched down next to him, his cool breath tickling the side of my cheek as I probed his wound.

It ran the span of a palm, and it looked deep and angry. My hands shook with the need to lay them on the gash and heal it.

Won't work, I reminded myself. That restless energy wouldn't leave me. And now I felt as helpless as Asher had been only minutes ago. I had no ability to heal him.

I sat on my haunches and looked on hopelessly.

"I'm fine, Lana," he said.

That didn't reassure me.

He huffed out a pained laugh and shook his head. "Well, now we know one thing for sure."

I waited for him to continue.

"Someone made good use of my fucking blood."

Asher

SEVERAL HOURS AND a shit ton of disappointments later, we continued in a rusted, beat-up rented Kia Picanto. Driving over potholes, my head thumped against the low ceiling, forcing me to scrunch forward. On any incline whatsoever—or even in a gentle breeze—the gutless three-cylinder, sixty-horsepower engine revved up like an angry fruit fly pissing around your ear.

The gash in my leg throbbed like a bitch, so I drove with teeth gritted, hunched over like Cruella Deville.

A weaponless Jame Asher with a bad leg driving up in a golf cart, just the thing to strike fear into every demon's heart.

This day could suck it.

"You just had to wear it around your neck," I muttered darkly. "Couldn't have hidden it in your pocket, or in a purse, or in your shoe . . . no, you had to flaunt it around so every bloodthirsty demon could be like, 'Oh, look, there's Jame Asher's blood . . . let's get some of that and *curse him.*'"

"That was wretched of Aecora to steal it," Lana said sadly, touching the empty spot around her neck. "But at least it wasn't enough to kill you."

"No, but there's still the blood Grandmaddox stole, which she's clearly saving—and I have a feeling whatever she curses me with will be worse than death." I shifted my leg, cringing as the scab reopened. I needed stitches.

I sensed Lana watching my pathetic movements out of the corner of my eye.

"I want to try to heal you," she blurted out.

"You can't. I'm not in your network," I said, then added, "although I'm touched."

"I know, but I want to try. I think I know a way." She sat crosslegged on her seat and faced me. "I could tap into my healing power, as if I was going to heal Infernari, but then we could both cut ourselves and push our wounds together, so we have our own blood connection . . . and then I could direct my healing power into you." She described this scenario as if she would enjoy it very much.

"Like a blood mixing, blood brother kind of thing, I get

it." I shook my head. "Thanks, but I'll heal on my own. I'm not cursing anybody. And put on your seatbelt."

I'd buckled her into my Hummer this morning while she was mostly out of it, and that had probably saved her life.

"You'll heal much faster if I do it," she said. "Right now you're healing as fast as a stone."

"Adding insult to injury—nice," I said dryly. "*Seatbelt*, now." I snapped my fingers, then flipped on the radio. It blared staticky music.

She continued to study me, biting her lip. *Wondering just how mad I would be if she did it anyway.*

I tried another station. More static.

The seatbelt buckle clinked uselessly behind her head.

Exhaling loudly, I reached across her and dragged the strap across her chest down to the buckle, clicking it in place. "There, so when I crash again because you're acting like a five-year-old, you don't go skidding two hundred feet on your face."

After the Primaxin antibiotic injection, she had perked right up. The infected cut on her arm had already tamed, and she was even managing to keep warm in a normal T-shirt. Thank God for modern medicine.

For the next two weeks, she would be on a course of oral antibiotics, and I intended her to follow through. I wasn't going to risk Lana relapsing.

I gave up on the radio and straightened, bumping my head again. "So you share blood with other demons . . . *literally?*" I asked. "Like, their blood is your blood, and your blood is their blood, right? So how does that work when you have sepsis?"

"Sepsis?" she repeated quizzically.

"An infection in your blood," I explained. "What you just had. Doesn't that bacteria get spread around to other demons?"

Lana pursed her lips, considering it. "Well, it feels like decay lingers in my blood when I'm sick, and if I healed others while I felt that way, the bad spirits would slip from my veins to theirs. So I don't try healing them. I guess that if I did, I could get other Infernari sick, too."

"So you can turn it off? The blood connection?"

"Yeah, it's like a gate. I have to open it to pass my magic onto others."

"Huh." I chewed my lip, my heart rate picking up at this news.

I didn't like where my brain took it.

Lana had a blood connection to other demons. To *all* other demons. She could access this connection at will, and when she did, her blood would literally be flowing in their veins . . . along with whatever else was put in her blood.

And here, I'd thought she was only valuable as a hostage.

If what she said was true, then Lana could very well be the Infernari's Achilles' heel.

God knew they already had a weakness to disease . . .

No.

To do such a thing would be unthinkable, too cruel to imagine. I couldn't do that to Lana.

I couldn't betray her like that. If ever there was an Infernarus deserving of redemption, it would be her.

I sighed and rubbed the back of my neck, wondering when I had grown a conscience . . . and when I had stopped hating the demon in Lana and started liking it instead.

She was turning me, just like she'd said.

But it didn't matter; I would still follow through on my original plan. I wasn't doing this out of hate, I was doing it out of duty. And the plan was still the same: destroy demons' portals, cut them off from Earth, make them fend for themselves on their dying planet rather than leech off ours.

That was the only justice.

Lana could stay.

Suddenly, she gasped, unbuckled her seatbelt, and leapt out of her seat, pressing her face and palms to her window.

"*Seatbelt,* Lana." Jesus.

"Can we stop here?" she asked.

The last few hours, we'd been chugging up the rim of a volcanic caldera, and we'd just reached the top. I followed her gaze out across the hellish landscape at the bottom of the crater. Stretching as far as the eye could see, miles and miles of blackened, charred rock were pockmarked with steaming, bubbling pools of milky acid, the edges crusted with yellow rings of sulfur. The smell of rotten eggs invaded the car.

"Augh—" I dragged my tank top over my nose. "You want to stop *here?*"

Lana nodded, gazing wistfully out at the crater.

"Oh-*kay*." The road took us down into the crater, and I pulled over near a particularly nasty pool of bubbling goop. "Just don't, like, swim in it."

"It's just like Abyssos," she marveled.

Me, I wasn't that impressed. But hey, she seemed to like it.

The moment the car stopped, she was out the door and prancing out across the barren, alien landscape.

I stepped out and cracked my back, grateful to straighten my spine for once. Then I leaned against the car and pushed up my sunglasses to watch her, one eyebrow cocked as she twirled around like a kid trying to catch snowflakes.

I couldn't help but smile.

I'd heard about Abyssos, about the vast plains of charred lava rock, the bloodred sun setting behind purple clouds, the weathered castle spires that looked like they'd been there since the dawn of time. It all sounded terrifying and eerily beautiful. I could see how this reminded her of it.

I guess you just loved the place you grew up in.

You know what, I did want her to take me through the portal and show me her world—not to fulfill some oath, but just because.

I wanted to watch her carve a bone shiv, and train a gargoyle, and whisper prayers to her gods. I wanted her to show me everything. To teach me. I wanted to see it through her eyes, marvel at the strangeness of it, blunder through her people's customs like she had through ours. And I wanted to watch her hair snap about when I irritated her, sink when I made her sad, and purr when I made her happy.

I wanted to make her happy.

Right then, I did something very strange.

I pulled out my cell phone, centered her in the screen, and took a video of Lana dancing around the craters . . . because I wanted to keep this forever.

This moment, this feeling, this magic.

I wanted to keep *her*.

CHAPTER 18

Lana

TODAY WAS OUR final day on the road.

Our. Last. *Day.*

My necklaces jingled from the jittery excitement that buzzed through me. Tomorrow, we'd truly begin the hunt for the portal. And once we found it, we'd cross over, and I'd show Asher my world.

I tucked a strand of hair behind my ear, suddenly nervous. He hadn't seemed too impressed with the sulfur springs. What would he think of the rest of my world?

Outside my window, dense, bright green foliage covered the land. The thick heat of the place seemed to cling to me.

This was surprisingly similar to Abyssos's capitol. Well,

similar enough.

The road curved, and a copse of trees that lined the street fell away. The land spread out before us; at the sight of it I gasped.

"Asher . . ."

Rising far above the horizon was the mountain from my memory. Snow-capped and purple, it dwarfed the landscape around it.

Goosebumps broke out at the sight of it. Old magic lingered here. Old magic and old gods. I could feel them. Restless, ancient spirits. Things even humans gave respect to.

Next to me, Asher peered up at it. I saw excitement spark in his eyes; his expression was utterly devoid of the trepidation I felt. This land was sowed with centuries of human blood. The earth hungered for it, and Asher was oblivious to it.

And why would he notice it? Humans hadn't gotten to where they were by listening to quiet things.

We passed a collapsing structure, the faded paint peeling off its walls, half of the tiled roof missing. Derelict, *rotting* structures dotted the land. But then there were dozens more that weren't abandoned. Even out here, people lived.

Is there any corner of this world that is free from humans?

A single one of these cities held more inhabitants than my entire homeland. And the lush fauna I should've seen co-existing with the natives was noticeably absent, save for a few herds of domesticated beasts, corralled together behind fences.

How could Asher not see that humans had grossly over-extended themselves? All other creatures were suffering for it, not just my own people.

He loves them, just as you love your kind.

I couldn't fault Asher for caring too much.

I spared him another glance. Grim, as usual. I suppressed a smile when I took in that body of his hunched over the steering wheel, his head dipped to avoid bumping the ceiling. The small car made him look comically large.

He caught sight of my smile. "What?"

I shook my head and played with a strand of my hair. "Nothing."

"Whenever you smile, I worry."

Asher wasn't looking at my smile like it worried him. He was looking at it as though vividly remembering the last time his lips were on mine.

My grin dropped away as my thoughts moved in the same direction. His large stature hadn't been comical then. No, I'd distinctly enjoyed the way he enveloped me when we kissed.

"So . . . have you ever been serious with anyone?" he asked out of nowhere, clearing his throat a little.

I tilted my head at him.

"Ever had a boyfriend?" he clarified.

"Of course—many." Was this some sort of wily human question?

"Many?" he raised his eyebrows.

"What is that look?" I said.

He tore his gaze away from me to watch the road. "I'm just surprised is all."

Asher was acting weird. This whole conversation was weird.

I continued to stare after him. "Doesn't everybody have boy friends?" I said.

Now it was his turn to look quizzical. His eyes widened and his mouth parted as a thought hit him. He huffed out a laugh, rubbing his jaw with his hand as he shook his head. I pretended the gesture didn't make my pulse race.

"No, not like that, Lana," he said, his voice gravelly.

My brows pulled together. "Then like what?"

"A boyfriend is someone you're romantic with . . . a lover."

He had my full attention. "A lover?" I felt my face heat.

Now I remembered the terms. *Girlfriend* and *boyfriend.* The words always confused me because Infernari didn't really have an equivalent. We had betrotheds and courtships and mates. The human equivalents never quite worked out right in my mind.

"What do you mean, romantic?"

"Dates, kisses, sex."

I swallowed, my cheeks flaming. Asher knew all about those things, and I knew nothing, save for what he showed me. For the first time in my life I felt . . . *inexperienced.*

I couldn't look at him when I answered, "We don't— no, I've never been courted."

I saw concern—and curiosity—pass across his expression. "Why not?"

I lifted a shoulder. "Dating is something humans do. Infernari don't think of romantic relationships the same way."

"But no one's ever tried to . . . *court* you?" Asher seem to be grappling with this idea.

There had been a soldier, Figulus, who had given me a starflower the day before he went into battle. I threw his flower away in a fit of grief when I felt his death. That was the closest I'd ever come to a mate, though I'd felt the weighty, wanton gazes of many Infernari over the years. Nothing ever came of those looks. Once I was under the tutelage and protection of the primus dominus, no one wanted to pursue me, not when that would bring them under the close scrutiny of the primus.

"Some have tried," I said. "None have gotten very far. Why do you care?"

Asher shook his head. "I just find it hard to believe that you've gone this long without being snatched up."

"If things were different, would you snatch me up, Jame Asher?"

His gaze focused on the road, no longer playful, but brooding. "If things were different, someone better than me would snatch you up," he admitted.

That made me sad. "I don't know why you think you're a bad person."

"There's no thinking about it—I *know* I'm a bad person. But I'm a bad person that hunts worse people, so I've made peace with what I am."

"Almost every Infernarus kills," I say. "Most well before the age of twenty."

Asher flashed me a disbelieving look. "Is that supposed to make me feel better?"

"Yes," I said simply. Just because one killed didn't mean

314

they enjoyed it. Often it was duty, loyalty, love that drove my kind to end a life.

"You're comparing me to demons," Asher said. "Of course I don't seem bad—the last one we came across tried to drown us both in glass jugs. And the one before that snuck into my room and put leeches on my chest. Your kind is all sorts of fucked up. Now, compare me to an average human—"

"Your kind refrains from killing because there's no need to. But the moment humans start to get a bit desperate . . . we have records detailing the carnage they've wrought. Carnage that we played no part in. Don't act like your kind is any better or worse than mine."

"You're right, we're a bunch of douchebags . . . but at least we don't feed off others' misfortune."

"Every creature alive feeds on anoth—" My spine stiffened as a thick, cloying sensation washed over me.

I sat up straighter, glancing at the land around us. The thick, green landscape was giving way to buildings as we entered a crumbling town.

I felt Asher's eyes on me. "What is it?" His tone had completely changed.

I shook my head, the tips of my hair flaring red. "Something is amiss."

Our car slowed as we entered the town.

Alpatlahuác, a sign read.

Nothing stirred, nothing but that feeling, which mounted the deeper in we drove into the city.

Black birds—*crows*—perched on the edges of buildings, cawing as we passed. Lines of them watched us, but others . . . they seemed to fight each other, clawing at one another with their talons.

The grisly sensation closed up my windpipe. Sometimes I felt this way, but only after . . . only after . . .

"Asher," I whispered. "Pull over."

Whatever he saw when he looked at me, he didn't question my request or my motives. Our car pulled to the side of the road.

Dread filled me.

"We need to check on the townspeople." I said, my voice hushed.

His brows knitted as he took me in. "What's out there?"

I swallowed. "I don't know."

But we'd find out soon enough.

THE STREET WAS devoid of human life. Not even the sound of distant engines filled the air. Now I had to reconsider my belief that humans couldn't sense this *wrongness* in the air; no other outsiders but us entered the city.

More crows gathered along storefronts and power cables of the main street. *Scavengers.* Asher and I exchanged a look as we began heading into the town on foot.

Alpatlahuác was a small but pretty city, with its red tiled roofs and brightly painted buildings, and it was its beauty that made the unnatural stillness of the place all the more ominous.

We turned down a side street, and at the other end of it I heard an echoing Spanish melody coming from what looked like a small market, its door propped open.

I pointed to it and Asher nodded, his gun now in hand.

As we got closer, the music got louder, blending with the caws of crows.

My heart beat faster and faster and faster as I choked on the macabre sensation.

Magic gone wrong.

Everything grew—the cawing, the music, the pulse pounding between my ears. Once we reached the door, Asher stepped in front of me, his gun pointed inside. My boots crunched against something, and I glanced down. The glass of the door had shattered.

I was beginning to feel faint. Hadn't I seen this a dozen times before?

"*Jesus Christ.*"

My head snapped up.

Asher stood just a few steps ahead of me, his hand dragging down his mouth and chin, his gaze sweeping over the store.

Several bodies littered the area.

I staggered back, my body bumping into the doorway. I choked on shock, on the bastardized magic, on the smell of meat, of rot, of *death.* The kind of death that left a body to fester and decompose.

It surrounded me. These had been people—beings that once had vivid, beautiful existences. They'd loved, and laughed, and *lived.*

But no more.

One tear dripped down my cheek, then another. So much death.

That's what I felt here. Senseless death and dark magic

taken by force.

I'd seen this years ago. Entire villages massacred in an instant so that an army could cull their power. Only, I'd seen this in another world, *my* world. Then it had been Infernari who were victims of such wholesale slaughter.

The practice had been outlawed.

Against my will, I began to move forward. I approached the nearest woman, her hair gray with age, her body pale and shriveled—sucked dry of every last drop of blood. She lay on her back, her glassy eyes staring up at nothing, her mouth open in a silent scream.

She had not died cleanly, that was plain from her expression.

I fell to my knees next to her, my hands hovering over her still form. Cuts lined her body, the deepest gash slashed across her neck. The skin around it was burned, as though the Infernarus that culled her blood couldn't wait until it spilled from her body.

"It's just like Abyssos," I whispered, another tear dripping out.

Even though I didn't carry the souls of humans inside of me, a phantom ache took root.

Asher stepped up behind me, his presence ominous.

"What is this, Lana?" he said, his voice low and angry.

"They came," I said softly, half looking over my shoulder. "The primus's soldiers. This is their work."

Savage, cruel work.

Asher's hand wrapped around my upper arm and he jerked me up. "They *slaughtered* these people."

"It's forbidden," I said. "They used to do this in the

war. But the magic, it's bastardized, it's unclean. And culling it like this—the method is excessively cruel. It kills its victims from the inside out."

His eyes searched mine, his lips curling back in anger and anguish. "And they did this to these people?"

I swallowed down bile. Another tear slipped out. "I think so," I breathed.

Asher released my arm roughly, running both his hands—gun and all—through his hair.

Out of nowhere he let out an animalistic cry, kicking over a stand of religious votives.

"This is *forbidden*," I reiterated. We weren't all like this.

And this . . . I couldn't even contemplate this kind of cold-blooded killing. All for power. Right after I had defended my people to Asher.

"You think your beloved primus gives a shit about what's forbidden? Because it looks to me like he doesn't fucking care."

Bereft. Betrayed. The ache grew in me. "I don't understand this." My eyes moved over the other victims, their skin flayed and burned where they were cut open and culled of their blood.

For the primus, a lifebreather, to do something so cruel, something he himself had forbid . . .

It was one of the worst taboos to commit. A man without honor.

That thought was followed by another, one that had me hugging my arms close.

The same affinity that ran through the primus's veins ran through mine.

It made me feel dirty by association.

"How many?" Asher asked, his back to me.

"How many what?" I asked.

"In the past, when they did this, how many did they kill?"

I swallowed, my throat dry. "Everyone."

Asher

I GRIPPED THE steering wheel with renewed fury, navigating us higher into the mountains, up twisting, barely paved roads that skirted precipitous cliffs.

They'd drained an entire village. Killed everybody. We'd walked into building after building only to find more dead bodies.

No one was spared. Not the elderly. Not the children. *No one.*

The images of all those people were burned into my retinas. My own personal tragedies replayed in my mind alongside these new victims. This was what demons did, Lana excepted.

No doubt, they were fueling up. Arming themselves. Preparing for war.

Culling enough blood magic to wipe Jame Asher off the face of the Earth.

They knew my plan, and they were taking no chances. They would hold the portal at Pico de Orizaba.

With that much blood, the misfortune would spread beyond the victims, it would seep down their bloodlines, curse their families for generations. The blight would hang over the land like a shadow for a thousand years.

Lana had said as much earlier. She could still sense the curses that draped over the land from millennia ago, when the people here worshipped her kind and bled for them. Died for them.

That was the legacy of demons.

Death and curses and misfortune.

Lana sat in stunned silence, staring straight ahead and knotting her fingers in her lap. She was an innocent amongst monsters. Monsters with no moral compass.

I pitied her. But that wasn't what was carving up my insides.

I had let her into my heart somewhere along the way, and I knew she'd let me into hers. I could see it in her eyes every time she looked at me.

I lusted after her, too. It didn't hurt to admit these things. Not anymore. But this was bigger than that, bigger than me, bigger than her.

And I was no less a monster than the demons that had massacred the town we just left.

She was an innocent pawn in this game.

And sometimes, pawns had to be sacrificed for the bigger game plan.

I chewed the inside of my cheek, wishing I could forgive her people's sins like Lana could forgive mine. But I couldn't. They had killed a part of me when they killed my family. A part of my soul.

And that village . . .

The need for revenge burned through my blood like

acid.

I looked over at Lana, pressure stinging my sinuses. I wanted so badly to let her save me, to let her change my mind, to let her replace my broken heart with hers.

But it was too late.

The idea had already sunk its claws into my brain.

It was simple.

Genocidal, but simple.

She would have to be induced to open her blood connection, either through coercion or trickery. A lethal toxin, injected into her heart, would then spread from her, down her connection, into the blood of the thousand remaining Infernari.

Every last demon would fall.

Paralyzed, unable to wield magic, their bodies would rot from the inside out.

All would die.

This was no longer about the portal. I could no longer hope to pull off a full-frontal attack against one this heavily defended, not without an arsenal, not without the element of surprise.

Nor would I try.

Attacking the portal would be the decoy, the feint, the misdirection.

An all-or-nothing crapshoot.

If I succeeded, the Infernari would go extinct.

Including Lana.

The nausea I'd felt at the sight of so many dead bodies resurfaced at the thought of innocent Lana dead.

Killed by my own hand.

"What are you thinking about?" Lana whispered.

I shook my head, jaw clenched.

"Infernari don't normally cull that aggressively," she said. "It's because they feel threatened . . . by *us*. If we turned around right now, this would all stop. We could run away together," she suggested quietly. "We could disappear, become someone else."

She had forsaken her people to uphold her oath to me, and in so doing had become fiercely loyal. She had to know Earth would kill her. She'd sicken again or waste away without the necessary blood she needed. And without her, her people might very well die.

Surely she knew this. And still she offered.

In another life I'd have given a kingdom for a woman like this.

Star-crossed. That's what poets would call us.

Because in return for her loyalty and sacrifice, I would betray her. And it would kill every last good thing in me to do it.

I swallowed the dry knot in my throat. "Together?" I had to breathe through my nose to control the terrible emotions taking hold. The self-loathing. The guilt. The premature remorse.

"I'll never be welcomed by Infernari again. You're the closest thing I have to family now."

I couldn't look at her. I squeezed my jaw. "I thought you wanted to show me Abyssos?"

"I wanted you to see my home," she said, looking down, frowning. "But you've taken my home from me, and now you're all I have left to protect. I can't lose you, too."

As she spoke, my heart felt like it was being slowly crushed.

To betray her when she felt this way about me . . . the very thought had my stomach kinking up.

I couldn't.

I couldn't do it.

She was too precious. She had bared all of herself to me—her good side, her brave side, her wicked side, her dark side—and instead of loathing her, I had fallen for her. All of her.

I had fallen for the sinful, exotic creature she was.

I couldn't do it. And I didn't know if that made me a worse person or a better one.

Just utterly fucked.

I would have to find another way to destroy demonkind without killing Lana . . . or run, like she said. Run away.

Put this all behind me and start fresh. She might get sick again, but modern medicine could combat most illnesses. And that blood magic of hers . . . we'd deal with that when it came.

Maybe, just maybe, it wasn't too late.

Maybe she could still save me.

I felt something right then I hadn't felt in years . . . hope.

Lana

When our car finally came to a stop in front of our villa, I took in the large building.

"Are you sure this is it?"

"It's it," Asher said as he stepped out of the car, grabbing a bag of groceries in the backseat that we'd picked up on our way.

I stared at the white stucco house, a row of columns holding up the second story. Some sort of flowering vine grew up the sides of it, the deep pink petals bright against its lush green leaves.

It was . . . beautiful. Exceedingly so.

I followed Asher out of the car, my eyes drinking in our surroundings. Everywhere grew green plants with waxy leaves, some with strange, brightly colored flowers. The air was thick with moisture and the sounds of birds and other creatures.

Another pang of homesickness hit me. Many aspects of this place reminded me of Abyssos.

This entire time I'd been counting on going through the portal, talking with the primus, and figuring out a way for me to fulfill all my oaths.

That no longer appeared to be a possibility. Not now that my people had slaughtered an entire village, a village that likely contained more people than our entire population. Not now that they were taking the threat of Asher— and me—this seriously.

I'd hoped that the primus would understand, but those lifted memories of mine and his most recent orders left me angry, confused. I had admired the man; I didn't know what to think of him now.

Ahead of me I heard Asher whistle from inside the house.

And then there was Jame Asher. An enemy-turned-ally. But Grandmaddox had been right. He was more than that to me.

A lot more.

He might have regretted the kiss, but I didn't.

I followed him into the house, my eyes going wide as I took in the high ceiling and the carved wooden beams that held it up. A wrought iron chandelier hung in the spacious living room, and a staircase wrapped around the side of the room.

Asher was watching me avidly. The intensity of his stare made my cheeks flush.

He prowled toward me slowly, and Mother above, I couldn't figure out whether that was anger or longing that sharpened his features. I backed up against a side table, jostling a lamp that sat on it.

Asher didn't stop until he was nearly touching me. He braced a hand on either side of the table, caging me in. I looked up and up at him. His shoulders were impossibly broad, thick bans of muscle curving around them.

This close I could see the golden tan of his skin and a couple faint freckles that dotted his straight nose. That strong jaw, those serious eyes. I felt like prey beneath his stare.

He dipped his head, a lock of his hair sliding in front of his brow.

"We need a drink, and then we need to talk."

Asher pulled the cork out of the wine bottle, his arm

muscles bunching as he did so, his hair sliding in front of his face.

My mouth went dry.

He glanced up from his work, catching me staring at him like he was my next meal. Very un-Infernari of me.

My cheeks heated again. Even my hair swayed around my shoulders as though it were flustered.

Asher took it all in, his face giving away nothing. He turned his back to me to pour the wine, and I sagged against the counter I'd been leaning on.

You would've thought I'd learned, but my damn eyes now moved to his broad, muscular back and the T-shirt that stretched over it.

Infernari *didn't* do this—lust after people. Or, rather, they only did this when they wanted to mate with the person in question.

I felt myself pale.

Gods above . . .

No.

Please, no.

The Book of the Lovers, one of our holiest tomes, said that the heart finds its mate first. The body follows its lead, then, lastly, the mind.

I pinched my eyes shut. Mother of gods, that was what was happening.

I didn't want this. I *couldn't* want this. To yearn for a human . . . for my heart to choose him—

I breathed deeply through my nose.

But I did want him, didn't I? I had wanted him for a while, and now my life was inexorably tied to his through the oaths I'd made.

"You alright?"

I blinked several times. Asher stood in front of me, extending a wine glass.

I nodded far too quickly, taking the drink from him and swallowing a huge gulp of it.

"Cheers," he said belatedly, clinking his glass against mine.

My heart has chosen him. He doesn't even like me. And we're likely a day away from dying in some grisly death.

The gods had made a tragedy of my life.

Infernari mated for life. If I denied the pull, would my heart choose another? Ever?

I clutched my drink tightly to me, my hands trembling.

"So, about the portal," Asher said, moving away from me to look out the window.

I released a long breath. The portal. Right.

"They're going to be there tomorrow, aren't they?" He glanced over his shoulder. "All the demons that culled that town."

"Yes." I took another gulp of my wine. It tasted like water on my tongue.

"So they know that we're here. And now they're waiting for us."

My eyes lost focus. Distantly, I noticed Asher swivel around.

I nodded.

He pressed a thumb into his lower lip, mulling over our situation. "So what do we do?" he asked aloud.

I squared my jaw. My entire life I had fought to save my

kind. *All* of my kind. Perhaps I had been topside for too long, but I was beginning to see the unfairness of my fate when I had given so much.

"We meet them."

"Lana, they have an entire city's worth of power amongst them. We have a single gun and a half-empty clip." He said this all gently, like I was naïve.

I gave him a deep look. "I'm not planning on fighting them."

He raised an eyebrow.

"Death isn't our only option," I continued. "If we can convince them you're no longer a threat, they'll stop hunting us, and they'll stop culling so aggressively, and we can all stay alive."

Asher rubbed his forehead. "But I am still a threat. As long as I live, I'm still a threat. They know that."

"Not if you formally surrender to them. When Clades attacked us with the swarm, he told me the only way for us both to live was if you surrendered, but he didn't think you would at the time, ever. Prove him wrong. Tomorrow in the cave, lay down your guns."

"My *gun*," he corrected. "I'm down to just my Glock and . . ." He unholstered the gun and ejected the magazine. "*Eleven* bullets. It's a wonder they're still scared of me." He snapped it back into place, the corner of his lip twitching.

"In exchange for your *sworn* surrender," I said, "we make them swear an oath that they won't hurt us."

"Please. They'll blow me out of the water before I even get close."

"I can reach out to them through my affinity," I said, "I can ask them to hear us out, like I did with Clades."

"Who I then shot. They learned their lesson, Lana. They don't trust me anymore to swear oaths."

I hesitated, then continued. "There is one way. One way to bind a human to an oath . . . which you won't like."

His eyebrows pinched together. "How?"

"We've done it before, sort of. You give them your blood, enough for them to curse you with. So you can't renege."

He stared at me incredulously. "Should I cut off my own head while I'm at it?"

"Have I not proven that you can trust Infernari to keep an oath, *no matter what?* Alive, dead, it doesn't matter to them. They just want you to stop killing our kind. *I* want you to stop killing our kind . . . and I want you to live past tomorrow."

"And rot in a dungeon for the rest of my life?"

"I'm a lifebreather, I'm the princeps of Abyssos, I'm the primus's daughter. Even deathmarked, I still have some sway."

He studied my expression, and I waited, and waited.

Finally, he seemed to deflate, and he said, "Maybe."

I felt my entire body relax, too.

Maybe was good enough for me.

HUMAN AROMAS FILLED the kitchen as several of the pots and pans in front of me bubbled and simmered. Next to me sat my mostly empty glass of wine.

"I can't believe I'm making Italian food in Mexico," Asher muttered from where he cut vegetables.

"I can't believe I'm making *human* food!" I was practically bouncing on the balls my feet.

I might've drunk my wine a little too fast.

"You're watching noodles boil," Asher said over his shoulder. "Let's not get ahead of ourselves."

He stopped chopping. "And—" He came over, stepping up behind me, so close that his chest pressed into my back.

I didn't breathe for a moment.

"—you're supposed to be stirring."

"Hmmm?" I said, distracted by the way I fit against him. The crown of my head came up to his sternum, and my torso was engulfed by his broad chest.

He was big, even by Infernarus standards.

Asher picked up a large wooden spoon and put it in my hand. Then he wrapped his fingers around mine, our arms brushing together. He directed our hands round and round the pot in front of us, stirring the long flat noodles.

If this was how humans always cooked, I'd found myself a new hobby.

A lock of my hair draped itself over Asher's arm. He paused, and I bit the inside of my cheek. Human hair didn't do that—lay claim to things it liked. And Asher was pretty skeptical of anything not human.

I could practically feel his eyes on the dark strands that lay against his skin. After a moment, he resumed stirring as though nothing were amiss.

We stood together like that for a while. I wondered if he was as tense as I was; I couldn't tell. He seemed like a natural when it came to physical closeness, despite his cold and aloof attitude. And he seemed content to stay pressed against me.

"Are you sure this is going to taste good?" I asked, dragging my attention back to the boiling pot. The noodles were interesting enough to look at, but earlier, when I tried to bite into one, it was hard and bland. Even softened, I couldn't imagine these tasting all that appetizing.

"I'm sure," Asher said, his breath tickling my ear. "In fact, now's a good time to check if the noodles are ready."

"How do you check?" I asked, only slightly interested in what he was saying. I was more enraptured by this strange intimacy between us.

"You taste one. If they're soft, they're ready."

Sounded easy enough.

With my free hand, I reached into the boiling pot of water.

"*Lana—*" Asher said, alarmed.

"What?" I asked, pulling a long noodle out. It flopped around my hand.

Asher grabbed my fisted hand, his brows pinched together with concern.

Thinking he wanted the ribbon of pasta, I handed it over. It draped itself into a pile in his palm. He stared at it bewildered.

I missed something.

Finally, Asher said, "Your hand. You stuck it into boiling water. Didn't that hurt?"

Oh.

I held the hand up and wiggled my fingers. "It's fine."

Dumping the noodle onto the counter, he took my hand and turned it over.

I froze as his hand encased mine, his thumb brushing over my knuckles. He gaze scoured my skin, looking for some injury that wasn't there.

He was concerned that I was hurt.

And now, watching him, I had the oddest sense that he was fighting the urge to do more. To reel me in, to move his hands up my arms.

My mate my mate my mate.

Now that my mind had acknowledged it, my blood seemed to sing it.

I swayed a little on my feet. All those pretty delineations between Asher and me boiled away. Human. Infernari. Victim. Villain.

My hand began to tremble. He had to notice.

"Jame Asher, I don't want to be your enemy," I whispered.

He shook his head slowly, his cheeks sucking in. "You're not."

I could feel it searing through me—*hope*. Hope that even though he didn't think and feel like an Infernarus, he might care for me the way I did him.

The alcohol made me bold. No, my heritage made me bold.

I dared to look Asher in the eye. "What am I—to you?"

His jaw clenched as he stared at me. I thought he would answer, I really did. But then he blinked slowly, and his gaze shifted. He reached around me and turned off the burner, grabbing the pot and moving to another area of the kitchen.

"Asher, what am I to you?" I repeated. Because now, on the eve of battle, I needed to know.

I could hear water splashing as he poured the noodles into a metal bowl with holes.

He brought the bowl over and dropped it on the countertop next to me. "What do you want to know? Whether I like you? What do you think, Lana?" He jutted his chin as he asked. "I was supposed to kill you just like every other demon. I couldn't. You were supposed to be my prisoner, and now we're making dinner together. I saw you dying, I saw you giving up, and it broke something inside me, and I couldn't let you. I've been alone for years, and now I don't want to be."

Gods, he looked so angry. All I could hear was the pounding of my pulse.

"So yes, I like you. I feel a helluva lot more than that for you. And that's got me all kinds of conflicted right now . . . because I *shouldn't*. But I do."

So he felt it too.

I didn't think humans could, but from the very beginning, something had come between him and that vendetta he carried. At least, when it came to me.

I laid a hand on his cheek. "I like you too."

He held my gaze for another second, his nostrils flaring with each deep breath he took.

I could tell he was still uncomfortable, so very deliberately I turned my attention from him to the food. "So what happens next?"

And then we moved on with dinner.

"What's the primus like?" Asher asked.

We sat outside on the back patio, our food long since finished. The pasta might've been good; I didn't taste much of it sitting across from Asher, every fiber of my awareness focused on him and the space between us. The sun was setting, turning the hunter's hair into a corona of fire. The dying light of the day also burned in his eyes. He was almost painful to look at.

Beautiful, cold man.

"The primus is a . . . complicated man."

Asher gave a little huff at that.

"To be honest, he's one of the only Infernari I don't know," I admitted. "He and I have chatted plenty about our affinity, the war—little things. He shares what he wants to, but there is a lot of him that no one will ever know."

"Can't you feel him through your affinity?" Asher asked, leaning forward a little bit.

"I can and I can't." I had to pick my words precisely. "When I reach down my connection, the primus feels like—like life itself. He feels inherently good. But he can sense my presence down the line—as I can his—and he's made me swear an oath not to peer into him through our connection. It's been a long time since I studied his essence, but I feel it there, along with every other Infernari's."

Asher's eyes narrowed. "He made you swear an oath?"

I lifted a shoulder. "He wanted his privacy. How can I not be okay with that?"

"But he didn't swear an oath to do the same when it came to you, did he?" Asher's voice dripped with so much disdain.

I bristled. "He is the *primus*. The king. I don't get to make demands of him."

He leaned back in his seat, somewhat appeased by that. "And he loves you?"

"Not in any romantic sense." It seemed important to clarify this to the human, even though an Infernarus would understand the distinction immediately. "He used to have a mate and a child, but they died a long time ago from what I understand."

Asher frowned.

"His birth family was long gone by the time I was dumped in front of his throne. I think he got lonely, and healers like us . . . There is the urge to heal and nurture. He wanted to find the last of his close kin, those that share his affinity. He'd looked for me a long time, from what I hear."

It was my turn to frown as those resurfaced memories flashed through my mind. Of burning tents and burning flesh, of my parents dying.

"I thought for healers like you, all Infernari are close kin."

Asher had me there. I shrugged again. "Like I said, the primus is complicated."

Across from me, the hunter leaned his forearms on the table. "So what's it like being related to the primus?"

All those scared looks from the servants and foot soldiers. All the posturing from the primus's inner circle. All those long, lonely days spent wandering through the ruins of the old city. Coming topside, as uncomfortable as that process was, was far more enjoyable than the sad monotony of my existence in the capitol.

I looked at my nails. "It's fine. What's with all the questions?"

Humans could weaponize questions the way Infernari did magic. Wasn't that one of the first rules I learned?

Your mate would never harm you, my mind whispered.

"This is what humans do when they want to get to know someone better," Asher said. "They ask them questions."

And now my heart was back to pattering along in my chest because he wanted to learn more about me. He *liked* me—he *helluva lot more than* liked me.

"If you want to get to know me," I breathed, "maybe we should stop talking about the primus."

The corner of Asher's mouth curled upwards. "Fair enough. What do you do for fun?"

It was such a benign question, it had me smiling. "I make dinner with strange human men. Next question."

That caused his eyes to crinkle. "What is your favorite flavor of ice cream?" Now he wore a wry grin, something I'd only seen once or twice.

A laugh escaped me. "Asher, these are terrible questions."

Please keep asking me them.

"Favorite flavor," he pressed.

I popped one of the Mardi Gras necklaces in my mouth, running the beads between my teeth. "I haven't tried enough ice cream to know," I said, letting the necklace fall back down. "Maybe the white one? Vanilla?"

He was shaking his head. "Rainbow sherbet. I'm positive that one would be your favorite."

I laughed again. "Then you shouldn't be asking me the question."

Asher's eyes twinkled, and Mother above, there might not be anything more breathtaking than him happy.

"If you were stranded on a desert island and you could only bring one thing with you, what would it be?" he asked.

"I've already been stranded, and so far, you've managed to keep me alive. I'd say bringing you with me would be a good idea."

The twinkle in his eyes deepened, becoming something else, something that made my skin flush. "Would you like to go up to the balcony to see the sunset with me, Lana?"

I couldn't tell if there was more to the question than that, but I didn't care. I wanted more. I welcomed it. The gods couldn't keep me away.

"I would love to."

CHAPTER 19

Asher

THE VILLA'S BALCONY overlooked a densely jungled river valley. Beyond it, Pico de Orizaba rose into the heavens, high above the clouds that were still smoldering purple and violet from sunset.

They were the color of Lana's eyes.

Next to me, she shivered, the night air too cool for her.

I pulled her into me, letting my body heat keep her warm. I was done fighting this attraction to her.

Her back pressed against my chest, and I wrapped my arms around her midsection.

Tentatively she laid her hands over mine. "Is this something else humans do?" she asked.

I breathed in her ashy scent. "It is."

She leaned into me more, and I could tell she was trying to relax. Feeling this small, delicate body stiff with nervousness had me tightening my grip.

I thought I'd be rusty at this . . . I thought the guilt, the betrayal, of doing this with someone other than my wife would be impossible. But Lana was poles apart from anyone else I'd ever met. She knew loneliness like I did, and she had a past with just as much baggage as mine.

"You're different from when you captured me," she said. "Do you feel different?"

"Toward you, yes." Toward the rest of her kind . . . I wouldn't ruin the moment by mentioning what I thought of them.

In the silence that followed, her hair pulsed with color. "What I feel for you," she said, "wasn't supposed to happen, either. And now we're here, standing at the edge of your world and at the beginning of mine. What do we do now, Jame?"

Gazing out, I followed the volcano's slope to its snow-capped summit. Somewhere on that mountain was a cave that led to a portal that led to Abyssos, the homeland of the Infernari. A cave guarded by some number of Infernari. They were waiting for us, waiting to take down the infamous Jame Asher and the traitorous woman in his arms.

Reflexively, I squeezed her closer to me.

We could still run from this fate we were hurtling toward.

The Infernari would continue to cull, but why did it have to be my problem? We had seven billion people, they

340

had a thousand. Was it that hard to believe that their race deserved to live as much as ours? Wouldn't it only be *fair* to let them cull from us?

For two years, I had buried those questions.

Now they clawed back to the surface. Why *was* I so angry?

I tried thinking about it the way I was used to, putting myself in my demon hunter shoes.

Every day that portal was open, more demons arrived on Earth . . . and they were after my blood, they were after Lana's, and they were going to kill and cull and curse everything that breathed until we were all dead. We couldn't just run; it would be suicide. Our only hope was to head them off at the portal.

Which might also be suicide.

Damned if you do, damned if you don't.

I never imagined I'd get myself into one of these conundrums the Infernari so often found themselves in.

I nuzzled Lana's hair.

Nor had I ever imagined wanting to know anything about an Infernarus aside from the best way to kill it. But holding this proud, strange creature in my arms, I was curious about her the way any man would be curious about a beautiful woman. No, I was more than just curious, I was fascinated . . . I was obsessed. I wanted to know her fears, her desires, what made her laugh. Why her hair lit up, what each color meant.

I wanted to learn everything about her, absorb her into my pores, memorize her.

And I hadn't felt that since Nikki. And even then . . .

Lord forgive me, the pull had never been like this. Nikki hadn't had to overcome my hate; back then I hadn't harbored hatred.

Goddamn, but none of it was fair.

Lana's fingers trailed over my forearms. "I think sunsets are tragic," she mused.

And then she said shit like that. My heart squeezed. I wanted to see the world the way she saw it. Like the world was beautiful. Like it was good. Like the saddest thing out there was a sunset.

All my jaded layers were dissolving away around her.

I was so fucking doomed.

Lana

BY THE TIME the sky was a deep blue, the two of us were sitting on the balcony, Asher with his back pressed to the now closed doors that led back inside, and me between his legs.

Just this contact was almost too much. And it might be casual for him, a human, but nothing about this was casual for me.

"Do you fear death?" I asked, softly, like raising my voice might catch the attention of the gods.

I felt him shake his head behind me, trailing his thumb over one of my arms as he did so, the gesture almost absent. "For a very long time I wished for it. Death is easy. It's life that's hard."

"That makes me sad, Asher."

He peered down at me, a wry grin lifting the corner of his mouth. "Lana sad? Is that even possible?"

When it came to him, a great deal made me sad.

"What about you?" he asked, his tone turning serious. "Do you fear death?"

My eyes roved over the dark landscape. "It petrifies me," I admitted.

I'd seen enough of it, I knew that the dead found peace with the Mother, but it didn't matter. Death went against my very nature. To heal. To live. To thrive.

"You are not going to die tomorrow, Lana."

"I would believe you if you didn't have a penchant for lying," I said, my mouth twisting in a reluctant grin.

The arm that wrapped around my waist tightened. "Lana," Asher said hesitantly, "tomorrow, if there's a fight, don't waste your life attempting to save mine. I'm ready for death if it comes."

I shivered at what he was asking. He didn't realize that even now that was impossible.

"I am oathbound to protect you," I said.

"Then I release you from it."

I sighed. "It doesn't work like that."

He growled, "I don't give a shit about your oaths. I care about your *life*."

I swiveled to face him. "You know, you're so very human, Asher. So very human, and so very inhuman."

"If that's supposed to be a compliment . . ."

I smiled. "It is."

I faced forward again, leaning back into him. I closed my eyes, feeling that horrible ache that came with losing someone beginning to set in.

Strange sounds filtered in from the jungle around us, each bird and insect and mammal filling the night air with strange music. It was getting too cold out here, but I didn't want to leave. I didn't know what tomorrow would bring, but tonight, it felt like the end of something. The end of this journey across the human world, the end of this tiny two person cosmos that had developed between me and Asher. The end of living without consequences.

But it also felt like a beginning of sorts.

"What do you want out of life?" I asked.

He was quiet for a long time. Finally, he spoke. "A week ago I would've told you justice."

"And now?"

He stood abruptly, pulling me up along with him. "Redemption," he said, his gaze pinned beyond me to some far off point on the horizon. And I sensed . . . I sensed Asher was holding back. Even the way he stood was poised like he was readying himself for attack, his shoulders tense.

"What changed your mind?"

In the fading light, Asher's eyes met mine. And they held everything. His world, mine.

And in that look, he *saw* me. We have a word in the old language for that. *Hauza*. Soul-sight. To see everything that makes someone a unique entity.

He leaned forward, his breath brushing over me. "You already know."

I could feel my connection hurtling me toward him.

My *mate*. I'd been sucked into this cyclone we created and it was too late to escape. And far too late to want to.

Asher's hand cradled the back of my neck, and his head dipped toward mine. This time I knew, I *knew*, what was coming.

When he kissed me, my lips were hesitant as I breathed in his essence. I remembered what happened last time, and I felt the weight of all I had to lose.

Asher paused, his breath fanned against my cheek and chin. Then his mouth was back on mine, moving slowly, coaxing a reaction out of me. Life boiled down to this one moment, this one connection.

Asher's teeth nipped my lower lip, and without meaning to I moaned into his mouth. Suddenly I didn't mind the cold so much. It felt like just one more sensation, and now that Asher was so close to me, his front nearly pressed to mine, I didn't feel a chill, but a burn.

My hands fell to his lower back, the muscles taut beneath my fingertips. All that bottled up longing, and finally I was touching him again like he was mine. My fingernails dug in.

He backed us up until my shoulders banged into the door. With his free hand he reached up and braced himself against it, his other hand still buried in my hair.

He broke away long enough to whisper, "Lana, I—"

I leaned forward and silenced him with my mouth, dragging him back under.

And then he was fumbling for the door, dragging us both inside. Absently he kicked the door shut behind him, the glass panes rattling as it slammed shut.

This man was a force of nature, a human who bent the world to his will, and I was bending with it. His hands moved through my hair, down my back, pulling me closer, closer.

Not close enough.

My breaths were coming quicker as we gasped into each other's mouths. All this talk of death, all the awful memories we carried with us, this was the kind of magic that banished them.

We might not survive tomorrow. Not when my comrades had broken our most sacred law and amassed so much power.

Not unless . . .

There might be one way. A possibility I hadn't considered until now.

The bond between mates was sacred. If the Infernari didn't outright kill us both, then they had to respect the bond. They wouldn't kill Asher so long as he was bound to me. Not if they wanted me alive. And they would want me alive; I was their last healer, aside from the primus, but he hadn't used his affinity in a long time.

The Infernari would take me and Asher back to Abyssos, back to the primus, and once there, he and I would talk. I would make him understand.

All I needed to do was convince the Infernari that waited for us at the portal to let us live. That, and complete the bond.

Already I felt Asher's thumbs rubbing the skin of my belly, causing it to tighten.

I reached for the edge of his shirt, my hands suddenly fumbling. I couldn't catch my breath as a new type of excitement and nervousness rushed through me.

Completing the bond. My throat was suddenly dry.

Asher helped me out with his shirt, barely breaking away from me to toss it to the side of the room before his lips and arms returned to mine.

This no longer felt like a sweet, slow burning kiss. This was world-devouring, like fire burning through a field.

And now my hands smoothed over his torso, over the ridges of his abdominal muscles, then his pectorals.

I was beginning to shake, and my hair was flaring all sorts of colors.

Almost shyly, I reached between us, undoing the top button of his shorts.

Asher froze beneath my hands, breaking off the kiss. The only sound between us was our heavy breathing.

He caught my hands and leaned his forehead against mine. "Lana . . ." he breathed. Wrapped up into a single word was desire and uncertainty. "You've never . . ."

My hand slipped out from beneath his and I began to kiss him again. And this time I was the force of nature, sweeping him along. His mouth moved reluctantly beneath mine. Slowly, he caved into it, and the burn ratcheted back up. I sensed more than saw him step out of his shorts.

He palmed my breast, and I hissed against his mouth as he began to massage it. He pushed the edge of my top aside, pulling it down until my breast was exposed between us. His head dipped, his breath fanning against my skin, and then I knew what it was like when Asher kissed other parts of me.

Like life itself.

I arched into him, my body feeling foreign, every fiber snapping with awareness. My knees went weak, and if one of his hands hadn't cradled the small of my back, I would've fallen.

Fire spread low in my belly, and he kindled it with every movement of his mouth. His teeth grazed my nipple, his tongue skimming over it.

Too much sensation. I almost doubled over with it, settling instead on gripping his hair tightly.

His lips left my breast, and he straightened, pulling my top off as he did so.

My face heated with embarrassment as my upper torso was exposed to him. I shouldn't have been, the moment his eyes fixated on my chest, all I saw was wanton need.

As he drank me in, I got a good look at him. My blush deepened. Only one bit of clothing remained on him, one that covered the area between his hips and thighs.

He stalked forward, forcing me to back up until my shins hit the bed. We went down together, our bodies a tangle of limbs.

Splaying a hand of his on my chest, he dragged his eyes down, down.

I couldn't pull air in fast enough, especially when I felt those deft fingers of his peeling back my pants, exposing the rest of me.

This was all so foreign, so foreign and arousing. I'm sure Infernari did things like this, I'm sure sex wasn't so very different between our kind, but this seemed very human.

My breasts rose and fell, rose and fell, as I pushed myself up to my forearms and peered down my body at Asher. His touch slid down my thighs, over my knees and calves, burning, branding. My pants slipped off, and with them, the last of my clothing.

From the foot of the bed, Asher met my gaze, the dim lights of the room reflecting in his own, and he looked like some strange, dangerous specter.

He bent over, removing the last bit of his own clothing. And when he straightened . . .

I barely had time to swallow back my anxieties before he draped himself over me.

I sucked in a breath at the exquisite feel of all that cool skin meeting mine.

He didn't stop lowering himself until his chest touched mine and his head hovered near my face. I reached up and cupped his cheeks, my thumbs rubbing over his beautiful, unforgiving features. This close to him, I could see the flecks of gold in his eyes.

I could feel him hard and thick against my thigh. He shifted, and then I felt him settle right at my entrance.

I still had time to save myself, to save my heart and soul from what I was about to do. But the longer we held each other's gazes, the more right this felt.

He hooked a hand around the back of one of my knees, spreading me. It seemed so inappropriate, to be splayed wide open like this—inappropriate and absolutely natural. And the way he looked at me! Nothing seemed wrong or inappropriate about that.

I didn't know whether Asher moved or whether I did, but—*oh gods oh gods oh gods*—he began sinking into me.

I made a small noise.

The size of him!

"*Asher*," I gasped. I hadn't planned on *this*, on our anatomy being at odds.

He stopped moving altogether. Above me, I could feel him shaking as he held back, his body quickly slickening with sweat. "Give it . . . a moment."

I nodded, biting my lower lip, trying to hold back the franticness I felt.

His hand slid between us, touching me right between—

"*Asher*." This time I said his name with shock as his fingers rubbed against me.

Mother above. I was going up in flames, my body bending, opening, *yielding* to him.

He took my lower lip into his mouth and bit it softly, only further drawing out my growing ecstasy.

It took more than a moment, but I felt myself accommodate him.

His hips began to stir as he sensed my response. "Better?" he asked.

I nodded again.

He was inside me!

Air hissed between my teeth as he sunk deeper, eliciting a moan from me.

My vision clouded as I felt it—our connection. I'd assumed the mating bond was something instantaneous, something that snapped into place the moment it was consummated, but now that I was experiencing it, I could tell it worked another way entirely.

Or perhaps it was just different with a human.

I could feel it growing, strengthening, reaching out for Asher . . . who didn't have a connection for it to grasp.

My vision cleared as Asher pulled away only to thrust into me.

I gasped out something incoherent, something that made him let out a husky laugh before he repeated the act. Again, and again, and *again.*

My nails dug into his back as he pumped in and out, in and out, our bodies rocking together, our sweat mixing, our scents mingling.

He watched me the entire time, those eyes of his unguarded for once. He looked at me like I would save him, like I was saving him.

"So goddamn beautiful," he murmured as he stared.

But he was wrong. He was the one who was beautiful, his face, his heart, his soul. I could still feel all that anger in him, caged and locked away at the moment, anger that he had let fester for years. I was sure that if we were together long enough, that if tomorrow didn't kill us, I would see that anger dissolve away. I would help it dissolve away.

Asher's hips stirred, and I ceased thinking about anything beyond where our two bodies met. I became almost mindless with ecstasy.

His thrusts quickened, the force of each one bringing me closer and closer to the edge. Our hips met again and again, each one, wondrous.

This was really happening. Us.

Asher knew what sex meant. He knew that a bond came with it. He knew that long before tonight, and still he lay with me.

This was no drunken mistake. He chose me every bit as much as I chose him.

Asher kissed me roughly, passionately, and that was enough.

Pure sensation ripped through me, pulsing again and again.

I cried out, my nails dragging down Asher's back as I pulled him closer, drawing out my orgasm. I felt him thicken inside me, his swift breaths sounding against my ear. And then he was coming on the heels of my own climax, his body a machine as he drove into me with each wave of his release.

His hips slowed, gentling before I felt him leave me.

My mate.

My *mate.*

This was everything I imagined joining to be. Intimate, forbidden, wonderful.

My connection to Asher, though incomplete, had formed, and it felt like a small flame that would grow the longer it lasted. And wrapped up in that bond was the very essence of all things pure and good.

I couldn't stop my smile from blooming, even as my arms, my body, felt empty. It only lasted a moment. Asher gathered me to him, my body pressed against his.

Almost uncertainly, I placed a hand just below his sternum.

My chest, my man, my mate. A heady combo of happiness and satisfaction unfurled within me.

For better or worse, it was now him and me against worlds.

CHAPTER 20

Asher

AFTER LANA FELL asleep in my arms, I untangled myself from her and swung my legs off the bed to stare at the floor, fingers knotted in my hair. It hurt to breathe, to lay, to think.

Even as my insides seemed to go weightless and do somersaults, I felt a crushing weight of gravity pull me back down. Back to reality. A nervous, jittery adrenaline vibrated in my nerves. Overstimulation.

The aftershocks of pleasure mutinied under my skin and turned sour, leaving a washed-out burn wherever we'd touched, wherever my body had lain against hers. Like smoldering bruises.

What are you doing, Asher?

I just had sex with a demon. I wanted her so badly. Like she could save me from my life.

Too far. I'd taken this too far.

With shaking hands, I reached for my wallet on the bedside table and slid out the photo of Nikki. The photo trembled out of my fingers and fluttered to the floor, along with a burning hot tear. I didn't pick it up. I refused to face that guilt right now.

That, on top of everything. I couldn't.

I had just given the last of my heart to the girl who would doom my race.

A demon was a demon. For too long, I'd forgotten. Now I was twisting the knife. In myself. In her. Through that one forbidden act, we had *both* betrayed our kind.

The mixed emotions raged in my soul.

The shame, the heartache, the white-hot lust for her that had not been sated, but fueled. Like that first shot of heroin, Lana was an addiction after a single hit. Already, I craved her again. Craved her in a way that went beyond sex. I craved her thoughts, her affection, her soft smiles. Craved it all down to my bones. One taste, and I was hooked—hooked and already frantic for my next fix.

An old Leonardo da Vinci quote rang in my ears.

When once you have tasted flight, you will forever walk the Earth with your eyes turned skyward, for there you have been, and there you will always long to return.

That was Lana.

Do you love her, Asher?

Because she loves you.

She hadn't said it yet, but she did. She had chosen me

to mate with; love went hand-in-hand with that. We were bonded for life.

I had chosen her to betray.

Cupping my hand over my mouth, I looked back at her—her naked body contoured under the sheets, her flushed, glistening cheeks, her long hair spilling across the bed, gently stirring like it was its own living thing.

Such a magnificent, lovely creature.

Such a seductive, wicked creature.

Yes, I might have loved her in that moment when our bodies arched together, when I thrust myself deep inside her and drew her in close, our broken spirits longing to touch each other . . . if just for a blissful instant.

The memory alone brought a dull ache to my abdomen.

But she was a demon.

And I was not allowed to love a demon.

I was not allowed to fuck a demon.

I was supposed to kill demons, burn them, eradicate them.

But tonight, I had done the cruelest thing of all: I had let myself have a whisper of hope.

For happiness, for an end to the violence, for a future . . . for *her*.

She had almost convinced me, too.

Almost.

But not quite.

In the terrifying silence that followed the lovemaking, the anguish sank its claws in anew.

I had already come too far to back down.

A man got an opportunity like this only once. *Only once.*

I intended to seize it.

Even if it crushed me, even if it destroyed me.

Because I was Jame Asher, I was a human . . . and I had a job to do.

Lana

I BLINKED MY eyes open as a shaft of morning light shone into the room. Outside I could hear all those odd sounds that came from the jungle surrounding the villa.

Beautiful earthly place. I would miss it when I was gone.

I stretched, my body pleasantly sore in strange places.

Last night came rushing back, and my heart galloped all over again. I lay there for several seconds just remembering. I could practically feel those hands, those lips, that body even now, moving over me, drawing me in.

I was queasy with excitement, with giddiness and nerves. It all happened.

Mated.

A smile spread across my face, so big it hurt my cheeks. I should be somber, considering what lay ahead of me, but nothing could shake this elation I felt.

My hand glided down my skin. I could still smell Asher on me—his sweat, and . . . other fluids.

His scent lingered on me and the sheets, but he was gone, the bed empty.

I sat up and cocked my head, listening for him. All I heard was a songbird's melody.

Reluctantly I slid out of bed, picking up the scattered

pieces of clothing I'd shucked off last night. I headed to the bathroom and began to wash them in the sink.

I hadn't sang in a long time, but when I was young I used to do so with my mother. Now hearing those birds, and waking up feeling like the world was new—like *I* was new—I began singing a song from my childhood, my voice rising and falling as I first scrubbed, then dried my clothes. By the time I clicked off the blow dryer, I still hadn't heard or seen Asher.

The first tendrils of unease crept through me.

It's fine, I told myself, even as a dozen different worries rose to the surface.

It didn't seem fine.

Slipping my clothes on, I left the room—*our* room.

"Asher?" I called out.

Only the quiet chirping of birds and bugs responded. I moved through the rest of the house, searching for him, calling out to him. When I didn't find him, I exited the front door, only to stop in my tracks.

The car was gone.

He WENT OUT to get us *breakfast*, I reassured myself as I stood under the spray of the shower. Or he went out to purchase more clothes, or a map, or gas.

There were a hundred different logical reasons for him being gone. None of them drove away the horrible feeling taking root.

Something's wrong.

Had Infernari found him? It was possible, but then

again, I would've known, right? They would've come for me too. And they would have left the car.

Asher abandoned you.

I had to lean against the wall of the shower as the most terrifying possibility of all slipped its way in.

I wouldn't believe it. Couldn't. He knew what he was doing last night. We both did. Most of all, he was *loyal.* Loyal to his core. He wouldn't leave me like a coward.

And then, amidst all my worrying, I heard the front door slam shut. I turned off the water and hurriedly dried. If it wasn't Asher, I didn't want to be caught naked in the shower. And if it was him, then . . .

Then what?

I didn't have a good answer.

I drew in a shaky breath and left the bathroom, heading downstairs.

I found him in the dining room, unholstering his gun, his back to me.

I paused on the railing. More than ever, he took my breath away.

"Asher?" I breathed.

He paused in his work, his head half turning toward me. "Hey . . . I didn't want to wake you," he said. Then he returned his attention back to his weapon.

I don't know what I expected, but it wasn't *this.*

"Where'd you go?" I asked as Asher picked up his gun.

His body twitched at the question, as if I'd cursed at him.

"Nothing, just . . . had to grab some things," he said, unloading the ammunition from his gun.

I forced myself to take a step down, my hand lightly resting on the railing. My legs felt like lead.

He wouldn't look at me.

Gods, *why* wouldn't he look at me?

With grim determination, Asher laid the bullets along the table, his fingers passing over them, taking stock.

"Why are you counting your bullets?" I asked.

"In case things go south," he said, his head bowed over his work.

It took sheer willpower to keep moving down the stairs. Something felt so *wrong* about this moment.

Humans deal with relationships differently, I reassured myself.

But as an Infernarus, there were things I needed.

I came up to Asher, his back still to me. I reached out to him, but then I hesitated.

He set his weapon down, and then he did turn to face me.

His expression was soft. And now he did the reaching out, pulling me into him. I almost sighed my relief as his arms encircled me and my body was pressed up against his. His lips brushed the crown of my head.

"I was worried when you were gone," I admitted.

At my words, his embrace tightened.

Asher began to speak, but then his voice broke. He cleared his throat and tried again. "I'm all right, Lana."

Of their own accord, my hands began to run gently over Asher's back. Now that I knew he was all right, my relief morphed into a sort of restlessness. I rubbed my cheek against his chest.

His hands reached around and covered mine. With care, he pried them away and maneuvered them between us.

"Later," he promised. How agonized he looked as he spoke.

I reached up and touched his temple. "Your eyes are sad."

He took my hand and squeezed it. "How could I be sad?"

I almost believed him. I wanted to, desperately. But I couldn't shake the worry that something was off. Maybe it was just the incomplete bond . . .

"You don't regret it?" I asked, my voice nothing more than a whisper. I felt my heart laid bare.

Asher tilted my head and claimed my mouth. His lips were so much softer than any other part of him, and the sweetness of the kiss alone reassured me. All over again I felt wrapped up in Asher's very essence.

I responded to the kiss, parting my lips as it deepened, turning hungry. This is what I wanted. Physical reassurance. To know that he was as pleased to be with me as I was him.

Last night came back in all its burning glory, and I felt my nails dig in. But before the kiss could escalate into anything more, Asher broke it off.

Our foreheads pressed together. "Lana, only a fool would regret being with you," he said, answering my question.

I smiled a little at that.

"Let's get today over with. Then I'll show you exactly

how much I don't regret it. I promise."

I COULD FEEL our time slipping away as our rental car drew ever closer to the portal.

"Turn right here," I said. This close to the gateway, I could sense it and, in the roughest of terms, I could navigate us toward it.

Asher slowed the car and flipped on the blinker, brooding as he did so. My earlier unease had returned. I didn't know if it stemmed from something personal between me and Asher, or greater worry that today wouldn't end well. That last night was all I got with the hunter.

My eyes drifted to Asher's gun. "You're still planning on giving a blood oath, right?" I asked, daring to look over at him.

Blood in exchange for surrender.

He nodded, his eyes riveted to the road.

Somewhere out there, dozens of Infernari waited for us. They would kill us on sight unless I told them we were coming to surrender. They still might.

I drew in a deep breath. "I'm going to try to contact the Infernari through my connection. If I give them my word we're not here to do violence, they should at least hear us out."

Again, he nodded, his face stoic.

I closed my eyes, pushing away the jumble of my emotions, and focused on the web inside of me. I didn't know who all waited for us, but I assumed Azazel, Clades, and Aecora were among them. I slipped into the web, seeking out their essences. I could feel the breath of hot winds, the pull of a riptide, the smell of oiled leather—all of it and more as I touched each essence.

Comrades, I spoke through our connection, *I know you are out there. I have the hunter. We want to end the violence; we want to surrender. Asher seeks to make a blood oath as proof of his word. All I ask is that you let us speak to you . . . please.*

I repeated the request over and over, hoping the message got through.

"Did it work?" Asher's voice cut through my focus.

My eyes fluttered open as I released the connections.

"I don't know." I frowned. "Hopefully." Placing an idea in someone's mind wasn't exactly my affinity, and I didn't have any magic left in me. The connection, however, didn't require magic. It was always there, always accessible. "I can't tell how many are waiting for us." But it was probably more than the three I'd reached out to. My plan suddenly felt paltry, insufficient.

I saw Asher's hands tighten on the steering wheel. "I guess we'll find out soon enough."

Asher

WE HAD ARRIVED.

The first stirrings of adrenaline spread through my veins at the thought of the portal and the creatures that waited for us.

I parked the Kia Picanto out of view behind a rocky outcrop and sat for a moment, lungs heaving painfully. My heart pounded like a jackhammer, reminding me what I was about to do.

I'd never hated myself more than I did right now.

Next to me, Lana had been oddly quiet. Fidgety.

She knew.

She had to know.

I glanced at her—all doe-eyed innocence—and guilt stabbed my chest like a hot spike. My coldness was torturing her.

I could see it in her eyes, the way they darted between mine, searching desperately for something that wasn't there.

Something I'd locked away.

I could sense her fear, her mortification, her shame . . . as it slowly dawned on her.

That she had given herself to a monster.

That she had chosen a mate who was neither demon nor man, but something else.

A remorseless killing machine.

A betrayer.

That was what I had become.

"There's an island on Abyssos we can go to," she said softly. "It's like Earth, it's cool and green and there's a spring of clean water. It's to be my inheritance, and I think . . . I think you would like it there . . ." She trailed off and tucked her hair behind her ear, looking unsure of herself. "You will come to Abyssos, right? Even though I don't have your blood to bind you, anymore?"

I swallowed the lump in my throat and nodded.

"I will," I lied.

Outside, the wind whistled up the barren volcanic slope. It blew right through me, chilling me to the bone. We were nowhere near the snow-capped peak of the mountain, but even this far up the air was icy.

I stepped to the edge of the crevice Lana had led us to and peered down. Jagged rock twisted down into inky blackness. The portal lay somewhere deep inside there. Warm, sulfuric fumes vented up from its depths. My nose scrunched at the smell.

I wedged my fingers into cracks and began to ease myself down, wincing on my bad leg, which hadn't recovered much since the car accident.

Much more nimble, Lana hopped down to the bottom and waited patiently, and when I reached her, she ducked into the mouth of the cave, shimmying sideways until she vanished. I crawled after her, jaw locked against the sickening claustrophobia setting in.

To my relief, the cave opened up the other side. I stood up, marveling at the sight beyond.

Lined with flickering torches, a broad staircase spiraled down into the earth, carved right into the rock.

The entrance to the underworld.

Unlike the portal at White Sulfur Springs, this one looked like it was meant for kings, the walls and floor intricately carved.

As we started down the stairs, Lana reached for my hand, her grasp timid at first. I squeezed her palm before I remembered and my stomach knotted up.

Still, I didn't let go.

"You're awfully quiet," she said, trying to sound teasing.

"I'm nervous." That wasn't entirely a lie.

"You don't have to be," she said. "I'll protect you."

I winced, my sorrow bordering on nausea. How could I do this to someone so pure, someone so brave, someone so precious as Lana?

It was unthinkable.

"I don't know what's bothering you," she whispered, "but it's going to be okay . . . I promise."

When I didn't answer, she stopped me and stood on tiptoe to kiss me, her lips urgent against my own. "I *promise.*" When she pulled back, her luminous eyes mesmerized me, moved me . . . and in that moment I came closer to changing my mind than I ever had.

It would be so easy to surrender to my feelings for her.

So easy to give in.

So easy to lay down my gun and give them my blood in exchange for an oath.

A chance to walk away with my life, my conscience, my future.

My girl.

I could whisk Lana away to paradise, lay with her on sunny beaches, swim naked in tropical coves, make mind-blowing love to her under the stars until we collapsed, utterly exhausted, at dawn.

It would be so easy to fall in love with her.

So easy to be happy.

The Infernari were an honorable, proud species. If they agreed to let me surrender, they would be true to their word. I knew they would.

It was humans who connived and backstabbed and

cheated to eke out every advantage they possibly could. It was humans who hungered and raped and lusted, it was humans who plagued the Earth. It was humans who deserved retribution.

It would be so easy.

But then the moment passed, leaving me with a cold ache in my heart.

"Come on, let's not keep them waiting." I pushed past her, my insides twisting ever tighter.

What I did today would doom me to a lifetime of guilt and regret.

But I'd given up on happiness a long time ago.

The stairs deposited us in a large, dimly lit cavern. At the opposite end, five rock columns formed the pentagram of the portal. The air around them shimmered, as if giving off heat waves. The hairs on my forearms instantly rose, pulled toward its rippling core.

A gateway to hell.

While I stiffened at the sight, Lana breathed out her relief. The last portal she'd sought in a cave, she had found in ruin, thanks to me.

My ever-scheming brain kicked into gear. A masonry drill bit ought to do it. Punch a hole in each of those columns, slide in five sticks of dynamite, run the cables to the surface, and then . . . BOOM.

But I wasn't here to blow up the portal, and now, of all times, my conniving thoughts disgusted me.

I stepped forward, and the crunch under my boot echoed around the chamber.

Bone fragments.

They littered the ground. I lifted my toe off a jaw bone, missing half its teeth. I could only imagine what they signified—the millennia of human sacrifices brought here to bleed.

I didn't get the chance to muse on it.

Out of the darkness loomed a pair of red eyes. A moment later the demon Azazel strolled out, his mouth curved up in a sadistic smirk.

Instinctively, my hand went to my holster. A useless reflex, considering how well he fared last time I shot him.

More eyes glimmered from the shadows, and more demons converged around us. Dozens of them. The entire demon population of the Americas, it looked like . . . and some. Enough to drain an entire town's worth of humans.

All here to bring Jame Asher to his knees.

Some I recognized—Azazel, Clades, Aecora, Fidel.

Some I didn't.

Any one of these creatures could single-handedly wreck me—they had that look in their eyes, too, like when a hungry Bengal tiger catches sight of its prey through the brush—and here I was with a bad leg, eleven bullets, and what was starting to seem like a very, very stupid plan.

As they formed a circle of smoldering eyes, my breath quickened. How many had Lana contacted? Two? Three? The rest of them might not even know we came to make peace.

Finally, Clades stepped forward, one of his hooves kicking up a plume of bone dust.

Lana dropped to her knees next to me and bowed her head.

"*Kneel,*" she hissed at me.

I sort of did a half crouch, unwilling to give up my fighting stance.

"Jame Asher, our sworn enemy," Clades said, his eyes and voice hard. His gaze flicked to Lana, and everything about him softened. "Lana Malesuis, oathbound to protect him . . . We will hear you speak, because you were once dear to us. You say the hunter wishes to surrender by blood oath. Before you speak, know that we do not take lightly his crimes against our people, and that we will very likely choose to kill you both where you stand."

From the corner of my eye I saw her dip her head.

Behind him, some of the other demons shifted restlessly; one growled softly.

"If you are honorable, Jame Asher," Clades called, "let us see you lay down your arms."

"I am honorable," I said.

I unclipped my holster and held it in front of me, but hesitated.

Eleven bullets . . .

I could shoot one demon before the others ripped into me . . . one demon who wouldn't even die.

I dropped the gun and raised my hands, remembering a second too late that Infernari believed the seat of all power resided in the hands.

The demons hissed and assumed battle stances.

"Easy, *eeeasy* . . ." I lowered my hands, my heart pounding. "When humans raise their hands, it's to show they have no weapons . . . it's a sign of surrender to my people."

Since when did these fuckers get so scared of me?

"Be that as it may," said Clades, "we cannot trust your word, as you have demonstrated countless, *countless* times."

He nodded to Aecora, who swooped in and patted down my jeans and slid her hands up my thighs . . . with a little too much vigor. Groping my butt, she slid my pen light out of my back pocket and held it up for all to see. "A weapon. See, he lies already."

"It's a flashlight," I growled.

"That also fires a bullet, perhaps? We know your tricks, Asher." She cracked it in half and dumped out the batteries, then dusted the plastic bits off her hands.

"He's telling the truth," Lana blurted out. "He had one of those when I first met him . . . and without it, he was as blind as a bat."

"I'm not going to kill you guys with the flashlight," I added.

"Blind as a bat . . . hmm, I like that," Azazel said, picking at his fingernail. "Why don't we gouge out his eyes? Then we'll accept his surrender."

I twitched.

"No," Clades said. "He offered blood with his surrender, we will take the blood—*if* we decide to let him live." He turned back to me. "Why should we accept this exchange, Jame Asher?"

Clades' calm impressed me, considering I'd shot him in cold blood.

Of all the demons I'd met, him I respected the most.

That would make this harder.

"Why should we spare your life," he continued, "when you have shown such contempt for ours? When you have killed so many of our brothers and sisters? Why should we not execute you on the spot?"

You should . . .

I opened my mouth, but Lana silenced me with a shake of her head. She rose to her feet and spoke for me.

"I *hated* him," she began softly, "I hated him just as much as you did, as all of you did. Jame Asher was once our enemy, but he isn't anymore. He hunted us because our magic killed his wife and daughter. Would you not be angry if a human killed your family? Your mate? Your daughter? Would you not seek vengeance? He fought us, because he was *loyal* to his family, because he was a good father, a good mate . . ."

I closed my eyes while she was talking, each word a successive blow to my heart

My eyes stung behind my eyelids, and I shook my head as she spoke, trying to negate every word. I wasn't good, I wasn't loyal, I wasn't honorable. I was wretched and deceitful and treacherous.

I didn't deserve to have her defending me.

I didn't deserve her. Period.

". . . but he's changed," she went on. "He's a different man now. He saved my life. Clades, brother, he spared your life when you could have killed you, and Aecora, sister, yours too. Today, he came to offer peace, not to fight. I know you want vengeance, we all do, but hasn't there been enough killing? Enough oathbound deaths? Wasn't it our need for vengeance that caused the war in the first place? We will never stop dying unless we stop killing, unless we break the cycle, unless we *forgive* . . . if we are to survive, we must learn to forgive."

She paused, and a cave full of demons that wanted us dead now hesitated. They looked halfway swayed by her words.

She continued in a softer voice, "Please honor this man as he has honored me, as he has protected me, as he has cared for me, and please forgive him, for I know he is good, I *know* he is good . . ." She lowered her head and in a whisper, said, "And he is my mate."

Demons gasped and hissed around the cavern.

It was too much.

I fell to my knees, shaking my head and staring at her in desperation, once again feeling like a drowning, dying man who's seen his salvation. As I beheld her, a girl not of my species who had risked everything—*everything*—to save my life, my chest felt too small to hold my heart.

I couldn't go through with it.

I couldn't betray her.

Not after that.

Her words had crushed me more effectively than any weapon.

She smiled weakly at me, and I knew then.

I would not betray Lana Malesuis.

I would love her, and cherish her, and somehow let go of my hatred of Infernari. I would do it all and more . . .

For she was my mate.

I couldn't breathe as I felt the beginnings of something, something—

Clades turned from us to look over the gathered Infernari. When he swiveled back to us, he gave a curt nod.

"Very well," he said, pulling out a blade. "Jame Asher, you are hereby sworn—as it is writ in your blood, which you give to us willingly—to be guardians to the Infernari and never bring us harm . . ."

Aecora lifted her palms and formed a glass sphere the size of a grapefruit—the quantity of blood needed to curse me to death, should I break my oath—leaving a quarter-sized hole in the top. She handed the container to Clades.

I offered my arm, and this didn't feel like defeat. It felt like hope. Hope that I might be freed from the vendetta that had ridden me for two years, the hate that had shackled my mind and my heart.

Holding the sphere, Clades touched the cold blade to a vein in my forearm, still chanting, ". . . and in return, we are sworn to you, Jame Asher, as is witnessed here at the ninth portal, to never bring you harm, and so henceforth shall we be allies, bound by your blood and our oaths, for the rest of our days—"

"I will not make that oath," spat a voice from the far side of the cavern.

Clades backed off the blade, looking up to see who had spoken.

A demon rushed out of the crowd with superhuman speed, bloodred eyes blazing like embers.

The creature moved so swiftly I never even had time to react. I only had a split-second to make out his face—the portal master, Fidel—before he plunged a dagger into my abdomen.

I felt the blade part skin, heard the wet, slick sound of

it meeting flesh.

And then came the pain.

I grunted and doubled over around the burning agony.

The demon held me close, his hand still wrapped around the hilt of his weapon as he hissed in my ear, "I will *never* make that oath."

Payback for cutting off his hands and head, torturing him, and vaporizing him with bullets.

I heard screaming. The most beautiful voice in the world *screaming*. It sounded as though she were the one dying.

Fidel yanked the dagger from the wound. Immediately, blood began to flow from it, oozing between my fingers. He drove it again into my neck.

I choked on my own blood, my eyes sightless for a second.

Lana's screams turned into a war cry and she tackled Fidel to the ground. They landed in a heap, grappling and spraying up bone fragments.

"Lana . . ." I toppled sideways, wincing and stemming the blood flow with my palm.

We'd almost had peace. Almost. And then the demons had to go and do that.

For two years, I'd been hunting Infernari. Creatures that when fueled by their lethal magic, were strong as tanks and nearly unkillable. For two years, I'd outsmarted them off sheer wit alone.

I'd almost started to think I was invincible.

But in the end, all it took was a nick to the carotid artery. In the end, when you stripped away our machines, our will to fight, our cunning, our insatiable hunger, we humans were fragile, fragile things.

I would bleed out in two minutes.

Hell, I deserved it.

Other demons joined the fray and wrestled Fidel away from me. The brawl quickly turned violent, as some defended the portal master and others defended Lana, and then others defended those defending the first ones.

Lana crawled free and knelt over me, tears streaming down her cheeks. "No, no, no," she moaned, cupping my face. One of her tears hit my cheek. "Wait, let me try to heal you . . . *I can heal you.*"

"Lana, no—" Blood bubbled into my throat, and I coughed it up, felt it slip down my chin. More of it pumped out of my neck with each beat of my heart.

Messy way to go.

As I watched, I saw her lock her panic away until she was nothing more than a war medic.

"Stop moving," she ordered.

"Don't," I sputtered, trying to push her away.

Don't give me that chance. Don't tempt me.

"Shh." She closed her eyes and took a deep breath. Her hair shimmered a deep blue and floated up around her. Watching her brought calm to my own body. When she opened her eyes, they flickered crimson.

She had just accessed her healing power, which meant she'd culled blood. She would always cull blood. That's what demons did.

And now, as her eyes glowed red and she looked so beautiful and wicked, I knew she'd opened her blood connection to the Infernari. All thousand of them.

I stilled, and time seemed to slow to a halt.

The moment was upon me.

With Fidel's dagger, she cut a slash in her palm and pressed it over my neck, mixing our blood. A buzzing, golden warmth poured into me. Her spirit.

Under her palm, the skin tightened and stopped throbbing, the blood tapered off, the wound healed. Our temporary blood connection ebbed away, leaving my flesh feeling strangely lonely.

I saw her sag with relief. "It worked," she whispered, breathless, and now another tear of hers leaked out. She cupped my face, and while demons wrestled and rolled past us, she leaned down to kiss me, her hair falling around us in an aqua-colored tent.

But it was too late. For us. For peace. For escape—for any type of happy ending.

Redemption had been robbed from me.

"I'm sorry, Lana," I whispered into her mouth, savoring the taste of her lips one last time. "I'm so, so sorry . . ."

She pulled away a little. "For what?" she breathed, her brows pinching together.

"For this." In one swift motion, I clamped onto her like a vice, whipped her onto her back, and pinned her to the ground. Her eyes widened, no longer a pretty shade of blue-violet, but lava red. Staring into those eyes, I no longer saw my Lana. I saw the blood of all demons, to which she was now connected. My nostrils flared.

Panting, I dug into my boot and pulled out the syringe.

It was filled with venom from the Inland Taipan,

the most poisonous snake in the world. A dose potent enough to kill two thousand humans. The toxin so deadly it paralyzed the victim instantly and, if left untreated, led to death within forty-five minutes. Against the demons' weaker immune systems, it would be more than enough to kill every last one of them.

This was what I'd spent the morning acquiring while Lana slept in.

I stabbed the syringe into her heart and emptied the barrel.

The look in her crimson eyes . . . it shamed me. It *broke* me.

Nothing, *nothing*, could have prepared me for the absolute devastation, the betrayal, in Lana's eyes, in the eyes of the woman I'd fallen for.

Her body jerked, and she sucked in a sharp breath, her back arching. A tear slipped out.

At this very moment, her heart would be pumping the venom through her veins, and with her connection wide open, it would pass down her connection and into the veins of the last thousand Infernari.

Around the cavern, the warring demons faltered, sensing something wrong. They glanced around, they helped up their fallen brothers, they apologized and hugged.

Then, one by one, they fell to the ground, convulsing.

"Why?" was all Lana could mouth, her body twitching now.

"Because you," I said, pulling out the syringe, "are a demon." I had to drag the words out between ragged breaths. "And I . . . am a human."

I didn't mean to shed a tear of my own. Now wasn't the time for remorse. But I felt it. God, how I felt it.

"Asher . . ." Whatever she intended to say, it died on her parted lips.

My name was the last thing she said. Her eyes glazed over and her body went still. She stopped breathing. Still conscious, she was now trapped inside her paralyzed body, suffocating in agonized silence.

All across Abyssos, demons would be dropping like flies.

I wrenched my gaze from Lana's glassy, doll-like face—Christ, it hurt to look at her—and my own lungs heaved under the weight of what I'd just done. Without a single bullet fired, I had just eradicated a thousand demons.

I had exterminated a race.

I squeezed my eyes shut, and another tear slashed on my cheek. It was wrong.

But it was done.

The demon scourge had been eliminated from the Earth.

Someone had to do it.

This was why they feared me.

CHAPTER 21

Lana

My heart was a dying thing. Crushing, shattering, obliterating into a thousand pieces.

I stared up at Asher as my limbs froze. He'd wanted me dead this whole time. He had done the deed himself, all while staring me in the eye, holding me close, and now I had to endure this slow death.

Everything was a lie. Asher's touch, his kisses—the man had been *inside* me. He'd made me believe he cared for me, and now he was imprinted on my bones. I made him my mate.

If I could cry, I would.

I'd fallen for a human. I hadn't known what I was doing, and I'd fallen for him.

All that time . . . a lie.

I could feel it—my world falling apart. How huge my hubris had become, to think I could tame this man's anger.

To think he could love me.

And how terrible to *feel* love for him—not the fickle human love that grew and then decayed with time, but an Infernarus's love. Something that was woven into my very spirit, something without meaning, without beginning or end. Something that grew with every passing second—even now. Something that was loyal, everlasting.

While I had been plotting how to save Asher, he been plotting my murder. No, he been plotting my species' *extinction*.

It wasn't enough to be betrayed by a mate—something that no other Infernari had ever experienced. No, the horror didn't end there. Because I could feel a thousand different lives inside me all dying, their flames dimming and dimming. All those wondrous essences that I cherished my entire life. Eventually they'd all snuff out, and I would feel each and every death alongside mine.

All that would be left of any of us would be smoke and ash.

Asher had betrayed me, but I'd committed the ultimate betrayal

I wanted to sob. I wanted to scream and lash out at the man above me. But I couldn't move—not even my eyes. They stayed fixed on the cavern ceiling. My lungs had seized up, and I could feel my organs slowing down—*dying*.

Asher leaned over me, brushing a kiss against my forehead, his hair tickling my skin.

How dare he touch me! Kiss me!

I wanted to shriek at him, I wanted to shred his skin from his bones.

There was no justice to this. This was what happened when hate won out. And the irony of it all! Because even now I felt my connection to him growing. Could the sadist above me feel it? Could he feel *anything?*

"Lana," he said softly, "if anyone could've changed me, it would've been you." He began to rise, but then he paused. "It was real, what I felt for you. It just . . . it was too late."

Can't breathe. Can't breathe can't breathe can't breathe.

He stood and moved away from my body, his footsteps fading.

And now my anger and soul-destroying betrayal meant nothing because he was leaving—he was *leaving.*

He killed me, and then he walked away, that's how little he valued this. Us. Me.

And I had given him everything.

My vision was fading, fading . . .

For the best. The pain would all be over soon. Perhaps then my broken soul and shattered heart would be at peace.

But a new, strange feeling blossomed inside me.

I hunger for vengeance.

Foreign, this desire to hurt another. Unnatural this wish to harm a mate. But Mother above, I clutched the emotion close to me, *savored* it. I swear I felt the brush of the primus's dying essence, heard an echo of his laughter.

And then the darkness swallowed me up, and I felt

nothing at all.

Asher

I WOVE THROUGH the demons' fallen bodies, the cave now eerily silent, and climbed the stairs back to the surface. My soul stayed down there with Lana. My heart. My conscience. I was too numb to feel anymore, too hollow.

Back at the car, I wadded up a sock and ducttaped it across the stab wounds along my abs, my hands shaking violently. More than once I had to grip the car frame to steady myself, more than once my face contorted in a silent sob . . . but no more tears came.

It was too monstrous to shed tears. Too soulless.

The stomach wounds weren't lethal. I wished they were.

To die, that would be merciful.

Rather than live with what I'd done.

The job wasn't finished. From the trunk, I pocketed the Bic lighter I'd bought and hauled out the gasoline container I'd filled at the gas station this morning. Breathing heavily, I heaved it back down to the cave.

The venom alone should kill them, but I'd learned not to take chances.

I only trusted a demon to stay dead once it was a pile of ash.

I descended the cavern steps, the smell of sulfur thick in my nostrils. Once more I passed over bodies, not giving any of them a second look—none of them but one.

I dropped the container down on the bone-littered

floor next to Lana, then paused to catch my breath. Of their own will, my eyes found her face.

I thought I'd feel some sort of bitter satisfaction at the end of it all, but even that had been robbed from me somewhere along the way.

Her body lay at my feet, all but discarded. As though her life wasn't important, wasn't cherished . . . wasn't beloved. Her sightless eyes were still open, her body contorted. That beautiful face of hers didn't look like it conceded to death without a fight.

I'd held this woman last night, and she'd felt so *right* beneath me. How badly I'd wanted more nights like that with her.

Instead it had all come to this.

I fell to my knees at her side. An ominous buzzing rang in my ears, the sound of time stretching out like a taut cord. My body gave a violent shudder, as if resisting every second that took me further away from her, from my Lana, from my fateful decision, from that brief, blissful time when she had been mine. I gathered her in my arms and, head bowed over her body, I wept.

Oh God, what have I done?

I had just murdered the girl I loved.

My sobs began to echo around the cave.

"My, my, I cursed you good," cackled a voice behind me.

The skin all down my back broke out in prickles. I set Lana down and swiveled around.

I FOUND MYSELF face to face with the two cloudy glass eyes of Grandmaddox.

"Oops—" She pricked my shoulder with a needle, emptying the contents of the syringe in an instant. "A little dose of your own medicine, Mr. Asher."

I slapped my shoulder and scrambled backward, my heart's thunderous beats already slowing under the influence of the venom she'd injected. "No, you're . . . you're *dead*," I croaked.

Then I realized.

Because she was half human, she wasn't connected to Lana's blood network. The venom hadn't spread to her.

I hadn't even considered.

I reached for my holster, but my holster was lying in the bones ten feet away. Might as well have been a mile. My limbs grew heavy within seconds, my eyes drooped. My elbows buckled and I slumped against the wall.

"Didn't think of that, did you?" she said, answering my thoughts.

Stooping over Lana, Grandmaddox produced another syringe, which she pierced through Lana's unmoving breastplate. A moment later, Lana gasped for breath and rolled over to vomit. Seeing her alive made my heart flutter with relief, like it could breathe again. All around the cave, the rest of the demons groaned and staggered to their feet.

The antivenom.

Grandmaddox had brought the antivenom.

I knew there was one, but I hadn't thought to worry about it.

At the sight of them waking, I rejoiced inside, even as my plan fell to pieces. It had all been undone, my treachery erased, like it was no more than a bad dream. Lana would live. The woman I'd fallen for. My . . . mate.

She blinked at the ground, coughing, her chest rising and falling frantically even as my own breath began to still.

She faced me slowly, her hair hanging in limp cords down her sweaty face. In her feral eyes, I saw something harsh, something that blended with the pain already in them. Something I'd seen in my own eyes every time I looked in the mirror these last two years.

Hatred.

I couldn't react, I couldn't even move my facial muscles. But oh God, I felt that look like a kick to the gut.

A blurry face loomed in front of me, blocking her from view, and it took all my willpower to focus. When I did, I wanted to scream. But I couldn't.

Azazel crouched over me, a slow smirk creeping across his slickly handsome features. "A trickster to his last, dying breath," he mused, waving his hand in front of my eyes. "A pity to see him finally fall."

Up close, his suit pulsated like a living thing, and his ashy, rippling scent rolled over me like poison.

"He's your mate, Lana," he said. "You say the word and I'll torch him."

"I don't care what you do," she said weakly. "Just get him out of my sight."

Azazel cocked his head, his gaze thinning. "No," he said, recanting his earlier words, "death is a mercy he doesn't deserve," he said. "I'm going to take him back to Abyssos and cut out his tongue and then impale him on a spit and roast him slowly, so he screams in agony for all the days of his life. That is how we will honor you, Jame Asher . . . as you have honored us." His smirk widened.

If Lana disagreed, she didn't voice it.

Azazel lifted me off the ground and carried me into the portal, where the air opened up and swallowed us.

Then, in the arms of a demon, I plummeted into the deep, dark abyss of hell . . . where I belonged.

Lana

I WAS NO longer dying, and yet I was. I was drowning in pain, suffocating on my emotions. I forced myself not to call out to Azazel and stop him from literally carrying out the justice my people deserved.

Jame Asher was a monster. My heart burned for retribution.

But it was also dying.

Ah, gods, but everything hurt. I pressed my palms to my forehead and rocked where I sat. This must be a nightmare, a terrible reverie that I would wake from soon.

I didn't almost die, I wasn't nearly killed by my lover.

Grandmaddox's withered hand touched my shoulder. She gave it a squeeze. "He almost got you, child, didn't he?"

He *did* get me. That was a terrible truth I had to live with.

"He will be dealt with. You both will," she said ominously.

At this point, I didn't care what my fate was. Death had to be better than *this*.

Around me, the last of the affected Infernari began to stand. Several of them glared at me. A few wore spooked expressions. Never had something like this happened to us, never had we all been incapacitated so thoroughly and completely.

Of course a clever human would stumble upon this secret: that through my connection I had the power to kill every last Infernari.

I was shaken to my core. I had never imagined anyone would do anything quite this cruel, and by my mate, no less.

And even now, in spite of my terrible, terrible anger, my body trembled as I fought the urge to protect Asher, the very man who'd tried to kill me minutes ago.

I moaned as I rocked. I would go mad with grief, I was sure of it.

The worst agony, though, came from the few Infernari who stared down at me with pity. It shamed me. I'd nearly killed them all, and they felt *pity* for me.

Yes, death would be kinder than this.

As my kin helped each other to their feet, someone crouched at my side. I saw his hooves and heard the jangle of his bone necklace right before his deep, resonating voice spoke. "Don't hide your face from me, Lana Malesuis. You are an Infernarus, the very magic of the world runs through your veins."

My body trembled all over as my connection with Asher burned deep beneath my chest. I swear it was growing still, despite everything.

Slowly, I dropped my hands, my shoulders slumping forward. I could barely look at Clades; I'd almost killed him because I'd been too naïve, too gullible.

"Don't let them see you weak," he said. "You are the princeps of Abyssos. This doesn't change that."

Seeing pity in my comrades' eyes had cut like a knife, but Clades' words . . . they broke me altogether.

I let out a choked sob and, on instinct, I reached for the Infernarus, embracing him as I'd so often seen the natives here do. I buried my face in his chest and I sobbed. And I didn't care that this sort of closeness was far too intimate for our kind, especially under these circumstances. Somewhere along the way I'd become a bit selfish, a bit fickle, a bit clever.

A bit human.

Clades' arms hung at his sides until he realized that I wasn't letting go. And then, reluctantly, I felt him loosely clasp me back. I heard him chuff through his nose, his hot breath stirring my hair.

"We need to leave, Lana. The primus will want to see you. There will be a formal inquisition. You will take responsibility for all that has happened."

I stiffened in his arms. He was right, of course. I would have to answer for everything I had so carelessly let happen.

I began to nod, pulling away from Clades.

"I will do all that I can for you," he said, his voice echoing off the walls.

I dusted myself off and stood, wiping away my tears as I pulled myself together. I straightened my back. "You have always been kind to me, my friend," I said to him. "But I won't involve you in this." I would just bring him down with me. "I am not afraid of the primus's justice."

By the look on Clades' face, he was. He rose, his giant frame towering over me, and one of his hands fell heavy on my shoulder. I glanced from him to it.

His eyes looked apologetic. "I will have to escort you."

I swallowed. "I understand," I said hoarsely.

Prisoner. I might be the closest thing to royalty where we came from, but even I wasn't absolved from justice.

Clades didn't try to bind my wrists, and I appreciated that.

We began to walk, following the others toward the portal. I lifted my chin as Infernari stared. Clades was right—even if I didn't feel strong, I needed to act like I did. My comrades could sense weakness, and the weak never lasted long in Abyssos.

My boots crushed old skeletons as I strode across the cavern, pulverizing the bone to dust. It had never bothered me before, the sacrifices humans made for my kind, but now—but now . . .

Out of nowhere, a sound like the crack of thunder deafened my ears, rolling through my body. My knees buckled. The sound came from *within* me.

I gasped, doubling over, my hand going to my chest.
No no no no no.

"*Lana?*" Clades' voice filtered in from somewhere far away.

Distantly I realized he was all that was holding me up, that my hair shielded me from the prying gazes of every other Infernari in the room. But my eyes had turned inward, inward toward my web of connections, where a new essence had formed.

One that tasted like honeyed liquor, that sounded like stone striking steel, like *innovation.* An essence that looked like the ancient castles of my homeland come to life. In my mind's eye, I reached out and touched that essence, and it brushed back against me like a cool breeze.

I recoiled because I felt it—*him*—on the other end.

A new bond had been forged, a connection that had no business existing.

And as it finished snapping into place, a cold sweat broke out along my skin.

I was now fully mated to the betrayer of my species.

Jame Asher.

To be continued...

If you enjoyed this book and would like to be notified when *The Infernari #2* comes out, please sign up for Laura's and Dan's newsletters at **www.laurathalassa.com** and **www.danrixauthor.com**.

Turn the page for more series by these authors.

Translucent

What if you had the power to become invisible for a price?

I did, . . . and I paid. Dearly.

Translucent, the breathtaking new young adult series by Dan Rix, is now available on Amazon!

The Unearthly

The first time I was declared dead, I lost my past. The second time, I lost my humanity. Now I'm being hunted, and if I die again, my soul is up for forfeit.

The Unearthly, the enchanting YA paranormal romance series by Laura Thalassa, is now available on Amazon!

A Strange Machine

She's dead.

Samantha, her wavy caramel-colored hair, her little Bambi eyes, her angel face...dead.

Killed in a car crash at 1:45 a.m. last night.

But what if there was a way to save her? What if there was a way to send back a warning? What if there was a way to undo it all? The crash. Us. Falling in love. All the way back to the beginning.

What if there was a machine?

Visit Amazon.com to learn more about *A Strange Machine*, book one in Dan Rix's brand-new contemporary YA time travel series.

The Queen of All that Dies

In the future, the world is at war.

Two empires, two bitter enemies, only one solution: surrender.

But when the King of the East and the emissary of the West meet, something happens. Cruelty finds redemption. Only in war, everything comes with a price.

Especially love.

Visit Amazon.com to learn more about *The Queen of All that Dies*, book one of *The Fallen World* series, the NA post-apocalyptic sensation by Laura Thalassa.